Brian Stableford

SPIRITS OF THE VASTY DEEP

Brian Stableford has been writing for fifty years. His fiction includes include eleven novels and seven short story collections in a series of "tales of the biotech revolution"; a series of metaphysical fantasies set in Paris in the 1840s, featuring Edgar Poe's Auguste Dupin, most recently *Yesterday Never Dies* (2012); and a series of supernatural mysteries set in an artist's colony, most recently *The Pool of Mnemosyne* (2018). Recent novels independent of any series include *Vampires of Atlantis* (2016) and *The Tangled Web of Time* (2016). He also translates antique works from the French, with particular interests in the Symbolist and Decadent Movements, *roman scientifique* and the *fantastique*.

Indian River County Main Library
1600 21st Street
Vero Beach, FL 32960

SNUGGLY BOOKS

BRIAN STABLEFORD

SPIRITS OF THE VASTY DEEP

THIS IS A SNUGGLY BOOK

ISBN: 978-1-943813-54-4

for Daisy and Chloe

SPIRITS OF THE VASTY DEEP

Glendower: I can call spirits from the vasty deep.
Hotspur: Why, so can I, or so can any man;
But will they come when you do call for them?

Shakespeare, *Henry IV Part 1*

I
The Mermaid

When Simon had finished the unpacking, so far as he was able to do it, it was after six o'clock. He had checked the fridge and microwave earlier, so he knew that there would be no nasty surprises lurking in the kitchen, and he improvised a meal with the aid of his carefully selected emergency groceries.

He knew, too, that there would be no problem restocking, even though the nearest shop was nearly a mile away in Morpen. Like broadband, the supermarket delivery network had now reached the remotest parts of the Welsh coasts, although it seemed that the truck only came out once a week, so the entire population of St. Madoc had to co-ordinate their orders.

After he had eaten and washed up, he was somewhat at a loss. Normally, he worked until eight or nine and then watched TV for an hour or two or listened to music before going to bed, but his mind was noticeably less sharp in the evenings, so he usually limited himself to proofreading and other peripheral labor, spinoff from more productive composition done during the day. Today, he had been moving house, and his routine had been disturbed for days with the various preparations, so he had no work of that kind in store. In any case, he felt a vague unease, natural in the circumstances, and a sensation that there were other things that he ought to do by way of exploration and adaptation to his new home.

Unfortunately, because it was the end of February, it was now dark outside—and because he was in St. Madoc, and not in Bristol any more, it really was dark. The hamlet's only street had half a dozen lamps in total, which were noticeably less bright than those in the city. A diagonal glance out of the window, however, told him that the public house was illuminated within—perhaps surprisingly, given that it had seemed as dead as the rest of the locale when the removal van had pulled away again before sunset, the porters having deposited numerous boxes of books, the carefully padded trunks containing his computer equipment and the few other personal possessions that he had transported in the two ground-floor rooms of the cottage. He had thought then that the pub might not open outside the holiday season, given that the vast majority of the cottages in St. Madoc seemed to be holiday homes, unoccupied for at least six months of the year.

The same glance out of the window told him that the cottage next door was dark, although he had observed someone peering at him from the window while the van was being unloaded. From his present standpoint, however, he could see that there were lights on in two of the more distant cottages on the far side of the pub—only two, although the total number was well over a dozen, and probably as many as twenty.

The street was not entirely deserted or still, though. A stooped figure was making its unhurried way along the pavement on the far side, beyond the pub, heading inland. Although the person was not tall, Simon assumed that it was a man—because, rather than in spite of the fact that the head was covered and concealed by a black hood. He immediately concluded that it was a monk, and he experienced a strange sense of déjà vu, as if he had seen a similar figure before, on the streets of Bristol—presumably not the same individual, but a monk of the same order. Perhaps, he thought, St. Madoc was still a place of pilgrimage, the site of a tomb or monument. He made a resolution to look it up on the internet, when he had an idle moment to spare.

In the other direction, he could see that several windows in the big house beyond the bridge, on the metaphorical "Central Tine" of the formation apparently known as Morgan's Fork, were also illuminated.

Not quite as isolated as I suspected, then, Simon thought, not knowing whether to be glad or sorry about that. The fact that the pub seemed to be open offered him an option, which required a decision. He had had to make a lot of decisions recently, and really ought to have become accustomed to it, and this one was surely far less important than many of those forced on him by circumstance, but that didn't make it any easier.

He hesitated for a good ten minutes as to whether it might be a good idea to "drop in" to the pub, if only to check out the lie of the land, and perhaps to "introduce himself" to the landlord and any regulars who might be propping up the bar. He had a vague suspicion that that was the sort of thing that people in his situation might do, and might even be expected to do, but he really had little or no idea. The mores of remote Welsh villages were a complete mystery to him. If, however, he were doomed to live here until he died, as now seemed inevitable, it would be necessary for him to find some sort of *modus vivendi*.

He usually avoided pubs like the plague, and he certainly had no intention of becoming a regular at the Mermaid himself, but he was so disoriented by the move that none of his usual habits seemed to have any relevance any longer, and after all the unpacking, which had involved stirring up and inhaling a considerable amount of dust, which the instant coffee with which he had rounded out his improvised meal did not seem to have dissolved entirely—although that was surely an illusion—he actually felt, slightly unusual as the sensation was, that he could do with a drink.

In the end, his general sense of disorientation and having nothing else to do tipped the balance, along with a sense that he would be getting a kind of duty out of the way by putting himself on exhibition, so that any permanent residents of the hamlet and the surrounding farms who were currently taking advantage of its only social facility could study their new neighbor.

It was not unduly cold out, and although there would probably be a frost before dawn, there was no threat to his footing as he walked along the tarmac to the door of the Mermaid.

The only external lantern was placed in such a way as to illuminate the sign, an imitation of an ancient inn sign depicting, obviously, a mermaid—but not what Simon thought of as a "Hans Christian Anderson mermaid" with a scaly tail. This one had a mammalian tail, perhaps supposed to resemble that of a porpoise, or even a seal. His cursory internet search, which had turned up little information on Morgan's Fork, had suggested that Saint David's Head and Strumble Head, some way to the south-west, were both ideal locations for watching porpoises and gray seals, as well as "contemplating druidical mysteries," according to Richard Hoare's 1793 *Journal of a Tour of South Wales*, and the external Tines of Morgan's Fork could not be so very different.

At any rate, Simon approved of the image, on cryptozoological grounds, and of the fact that the mermaid's human face was also no Hans Christian Andersen image. The Mermaid's mermaid looked to be fifty if she was a day, more hagwife than maiden, and the stare of her green eyes, in the yellow lamplight, seemed intimidating rather than seductive.

He decided, after fifteen seconds of contemplation, that that was as long as a man could decently spend staring at an imitation inn sign, so he steeled himself, and went inside

He was already anticipating the sudden cessation of conversations and the suspicious stares that welcome strangers to remoter seaside pubs in clichéd movies when he pushed the door open, but the four young men seated at a table to the left of the door barely spared him a glance, and did not interrupt the flow of their chatter at all. He was slightly dismayed, however, to catch a few syllables in passing, which told him that they appeared to be conversing in Welsh.

The only other customer was a woman sitting on her own at the bar on the opposite side of the room, with an empty glass in front of her. There was no one behind the bar for the moment. The woman in question, Simon realized immediately, was the person he had seen watching him from her window as he moved in: his new next-door neighbor.

She was approximately the same age as himself, he

guessed, somewhere between sixty-five and seventy, gray-haired but not conspicuously wrinkled, and still quite slim—and, he was slightly surprised to observe, well dressed, not ostentatiously, but certainly not cheaply.

She did look round when he came in, and studied him with as much attention as he was studying her, evidently equally curious, and not nearly as anxious about the possibility of seeming indiscreet.

Again, he hesitated, but this time only momentarily; he had already made his decision as to how he ought to conduct himself, and it was merely a matter of summoning up the determination to put the plan into action.

He walked over to the woman, extended his hand as steadily as he could, and said: "I'm Simon Cannick—I believe I'm your new next-door neighbor."

"I believe you are," she replied, in a voice whose lilt came from its strong Welsh accent, but which seemed genuinely warm, as she accepted the hand and the cursory grip that he contrived, while cursing himself for its hastiness. "Megan Harwyn."

"Can I buy you a drink?" he asked, as a wizened barman suddenly materialized, emerging like a shadow from a back room.

"Thanks—gin and tonic," Megan Harwyn replied. "This is Dai, by the way—the landlord. This is Simon, Dai, who moved into Raven today."

Dai contented himself with a nod as he waited for Simon to complete his order. The bar only had two pumps, but there was an impressive line-up of bottled beers and ciders on the shelves. Simon asked for a bottle of dry cider.

Having poured the drinks, collected the money and handed over the change, with an agility that seemed almost balletic, Dai returned without having said a word to the back room again, where the muffled sound of dialogue could be heard coming from a TV set.

"Shall we sit at one of the tables?" Simon asked, adding, with a hint of irony: "There seem to be plenty free."

"Sure," said Megan. "Don't mind Dai—he's not one for chatting to the customers, although he only leaves me sitting on my own when he's feeding his addiction—to soaps, that is, nothing illegal. This time of year, he'd probably rather be shut, but there's some sort of old estate regulation says that he has to stay open, and he's got a guest upstairs anyway—a Reverend, no less—so you're not alone in picking a funny time of year for a holiday. How long will you be staying?"

"Permanently," said Simon, as they took seats facing one another at a heavy wooden table that was clean enough, although the surface had evidently not been polished for some time.

Megan's eyebrows were raised slightly, although it seemed to Simon that she was trying to contain her surprise, desirous of not seeming impolite. Even so, there was naked curiosity in her tone as she said: "Permanently? I thought your van men were carrying an awful lot of boxes—couldn't help noticing, like."

"Natural curiosity," said Simon, dismissively. "I wondered whether I ought to pop round and introduce myself when I caught a glimpse of you this afternoon, but there were a lot of boxes, as you say, and I wanted to get my computer set up as soon as possible, to put some of the books on the shelves, etcetera, etcetera—by the time I looked up it was six o'clock and pitch dark."

"I wondered whether I ought to come and introduce myself, and offer you a neighborly cup of tea—but you seemed to be busy, and I couldn't pluck up the courage. All the old customs seem outdated now that we do everything on the internet, don't you think?"

"Absolutely," Simon agreed. "It's not the world that you and I grew up in any more, is it? I feel more like an alien every day, even living in the city, let alone . . ." He stopped, embarrassed.

"The arse end of nowhere?" she supplied, helpfully. "No need to be shy about saying so."

14

"That wasn't the way I was going to put it," Simon said, defensively. "It's a beautiful part of the world, and I'm sure I'll find living here rewarding . . . it's just not what I'm used to, and for a little while I'm bound to feel a little like a fish out of water."

"Well, you are English," she observed, smiling to emphasize that she didn't mean it as an insult. "This isn't exactly a popular retirement spot, though . . . I presume, that's what you mean when you say permanent?"

"I am a pensioner," Simon admitted, carefully refraining from making the suggestion that she seemed to have retired here herself, "but it's pure chance rather than considered choice that has landed me rather abruptly in St. Madoc. I think I've been fortunate though—extremely lucky, in fact. The sea, the national park, the coastal path . . ."

"The good company," Megan added, still smiling.

Simon could tell that the smile was artificial and ironic, and it didn't seem to him that she was simply being modest about her own company. "That too, hopefully," he said.

"There's not much of it, I fear," she said. "At present, the only permanent residents between the bridge to the Tine and Morpen are me, Dai . . . and you, apparently."

Simon glanced at the four men on the other side of the room. Megan must have seen the glance, but she didn't hasten to explain their presence. Instead, she went on: "Things are changing, obviously, what with the housing crisis, and the absentees dipping their toes in fresh water making deals with Cardigan DHSS, but the owners haven't let any of the cottages out on a long lease before. They've usually been able to make more money in six months letting by the week than by taking permanent tenants—those who don't just regard the cottages as status symbols, because *one simply has to have a second home by the sea*." The mock-aristocratic accent she put on in order to pronounce the final phase seemed even more false than her smile.

"I'm not renting," Simon told her, almost absent-mindedly. "I own the cottage."

This time, it seemed, his new neighbor could not control the effect of her surprise. Her eyebrows twitched.

"You *own* it?" Megan Harwyn repeated, as if he had just announced a genuine marvel. "But I thought . . ." There was a noticeable pause before she changed her mind about revealing what she had thought. Instead, she said: "Well, then, I guess we have even more common than I thought. I own Sanderling, which makes us the only two owner-occupiers in the parish, including Morpen and the old fishermen's cottages as well as St. Madoc. But . . ." Again she stopped.

"Morpen's the hamlet three-quarters of a mile to the east, on the far side of the fields?" Simon queried, sensing that it might be diplomatic to make an utterly neutral remark.

She nodded. "Hasn't got a pub of its own," she remarked, obviously feeling the same way. "That's why . . ." She nodded in the direction of the four men sitting on the opposite side of the room, who appeared to be paying so little attention to the two of them that Simon was beginning to wonder if they were deliberately pretending that he did not exist.

"Are they farm laborers?" he asked.

"No. The old lady doesn't like it, but as I said, James and the absentees are letting the DHSS in Cardigan use some of the cottages in Morpen as emergency accommodation for people they'd otherwise have to put up in B&Bs—only short lets, strictly in the off-season but . . . well Blackbird and Tern in St. Madoc are now occupied as well, by Syrian refugees, no less. James undoubtedly thinks that it's the thin end of a nasty wedge, but there might not be anything he can do about it." She paused, studying his face. "You know who I'm taking about, I presume?" she added tentatively

"Haven't the faintest idea," Simon admitted.

"James Murden, over at the Abbey. Thinks he's the master of all he surveys—not that you can survey much from the Tine, but you get my meaning. The old lady thinks otherwise, obviously . . ."

"The old lady?" Simon queried.

"He calls her his grandmother but as he's as old as Methuselah himself it must be an honorary title, and she's more probably his sister, or a cousin. Complicated family. Anyway, rumor has it that she rules the roost, not him. You really don't know about the Murdens?"

"Not a thing," Simon confirmed. "I googled St. Madoc, obviously, when I found out that I'd inherited the cottage, so I know that there was once an abbey here, maybe dating back as far as the fourth century, but there doesn't seem to be much information about the place on the web. I guess nobody's yet got around to writing a Wikipedia entry on the place, in spite of wanting to promote it as a holiday resort . . ." He stopped, realizing that his interlocutor was no longer listening, her attention having been caught and arrested somewhere along the way.

"Inherited?" she echoed, incredulously. "You *inherited* Raven? Who the hell from?" She immediately went red in the face, and said: "Sorry—none of my business, obviously."

"It's all right," Simon hastened to say.

"I didn't mean to be rude. It's just . . . well, it's just surprising. I didn't think any of the cottages were owned by anyone outside the family, although I suppose it has been a long time since the ownership was divided up—before my time, which is now, I have to admit, quite a long time ago—and I suppose some of them might have changed hands two or three times since. It's not really that odd, I guess . . . it just seems so. I thought I was the only cuckoo in the nest . . . or fly in the ointment."

Puzzled, all Simon could think of to say was: "Have you lived here long?"

"More than thirty years, now," she replied, giving the distinct impression that her thoughts were still elsewhere. "Continuously, that is. I was born here, God help me—in the Abbey, no less, where my mother was in service. I inherited Sanderling back in the eighties. Thereby hangs a tale, as they say . . . but it wasn't a tale I thought capable of repetition, and given that we must be much the same age, if there were any similarity about our stories, I'd surely . . ." Her gaze had become intense, as if she were searching her early memories, trying to figure out whether she had ever seen Simon before, back in the olden days of the 1950s, when they had both been children.

More to settle her mind on that point than anything else, Simon said: "I certainly wasn't born here, unless my mother traveled a hell of a long way before she dumped me."

That, at last, broke in to Megan Harwyn's strange preoccupations—or perhaps intensified them

"Dumped?" she echoed.

"I was a foundling," Simon explained. "Birmingham city center. My birth mother was never identified—but the overwhelming probability is that she was some local teenager. I was less than a day old when I was found, so she certainly hadn't traveled from the wilds of West Wales."

Megan had to make a visible effort to stop staring at him. After a pause, she said: "I'm sorry. You must think I'm mad. I'm doing an even worse job than Dai and the riff-raff from Cardi at putting on a show of good company, aren't I? I really don't mean to—but your arrival here qualifies as a major event in a place where nothing ever happens. I'm not the only one who'll be curious, either. When they hear over at the Abbey that you not only own Raven but inherited it . . . well, James hardly ever crosses the bridge any more, so he probably won't come knocking on your door personally, but I'll lay odds that he'll send Cerys to winkle the whole story out of you. You could tell her to mind her own business too, I suppose, but you won't. She's too pretty. She'll flutter her eyelashes and give you a big smile, and you'll melt, and tell her everything."

"I'll look forward to that, then," Simon said. "Fortunately, I don't have any secrets, and there really isn't much to tell. I confess, though, that I have no idea why this James person would be so interested in me, simply because I've inherited Raven Cottage and come to live in it."

Megan Harwyn drew in her breath. "I'll do my best to explain, then," she said, "but it's a long story, and I don't really know where to start. I seem to have lost the knack of conversation. Too much time at the computer, I guess, or too long having no one to talk to in the flesh but Dai . . . or maybe just living in the arse end of nowhere. Sorry if I'm coming across as some batty old woman—not my intention, I assure you."

"No need to apologize," said Simon. "I know the problem . . . not that it's a problem. I'm the alien, remember. Pubs aren't my natural environment, but I thought . . . well, I suppose I thought that if I didn't show myself, people might think I was hiding myself away. Not that I should care about that, obviously, given that there doesn't seem to be much else to do in St. Madoc in February."

She laughed at that, but humorlessly. "You could say that," she agreed. She was still looking at Simon quizzically, as if he really were some kind of alien.

"Evelyne Augerrand," he said, mildly curious to see whether she might recognize the name.

Plainly, she didn't. "What?"

"Evelyne Augerrand. That's the name of the person from whom I inherited Raven Cottage. The name doesn't mean anything to you?"

"Never heard of her. Sounds French to me."

"Possibly, although she certainly wasn't. I think the solicitor said Mrs., so it was probably her husband's name in the dim and distant past. I don't know of any other name she might have had, though. I only heard that one for the first time from the solicitor. To me she was always just Eve."

"Eve? Never heard of an Eve in the Murden family . . . but I've never been party to its secrets. Anyway, as I said, the cottages have had time to change hands three or four times since the ownership was broken up in the Great Murden Schism. That was in the twenties, I think. Nearly a hundred years ago! James probably remembers it as if it were yesterday, though, and certainly wouldn't let on if he didn't. Not that he and I are on speaking terms, mind . . . and he's the only person around the Fork who'd cross the road to avoid me . . . Still . . ."

Apparently becoming uncomfortably aware that she was rambling, she fell silent momentarily, and then said: "It really is a long story, but I'll try to explain. The Murdens have always regarded the local area as their private estate, even though they had to sell off the farmland before I was even born. There was a big family row in the twenties, and ownership of the cottages was divided between three or four members, with various conditions attached that were supposed to keep them all within the family, but over time . . . "

She stopped—not, this time, because she had lost the thread of what she was saying, but because someone else had just come into the bar, not from outside, but from an interior door that presumably gave access to the stairs leading up to the first floor. Simon deduced that the newcomer must be the guest that Megan had referred to as "a Reverend, no less."

II
The Reverend

"The Reverend" was a tall man, at least six feet in height, with short-cropped gray hair and a neatly trimmed gray beard, although he looked to be at least ten years younger than Simon, perhaps still in his early fifties. He had grave features that seemed entirely appropriate to a clergyman, as did his black clothing, although he was not wearing a clerical collar.

His eyes immediately settled on Simon, after the briefest of glances at Megan, and when he strode over to their table, he somehow contrived to make it very obvious that it was Simon to whom he intended to address himself.

He did not offer his hand, but made a curious double bow instead. "Good evening, Miss Harwyn," he said, before immediately returning his attention to Simon. He did not wait to be introduced, but said: "I'm Alexander Usher. May I join you?"

"Of course," said Simon. Observing from the corner of his eye that Dai had appeared behind the bar once again, he said: "May I buy you a drink, Mr. Usher? I'm Simon Cannick, by the way." He turned to Megan to say: "Another?"

She hesitated, but then said: "Yes, please."

Simon looked back at Alexander Usher just in time to notice an eyebrow slightly raised in querulous fashion.

"Bitter lemon, please," the tall man said.

Simon went to the bar. This time, Dai contrived a smile. "Not just here for the week, then?" he said, evidently having hearing keen enough to catch fragments of conversation from the bar as well as following his soap opera, and evidently having changed his attitude somewhat since realizing that Simon was not just passing through.

"That's right," said Simon. "I'll try not to disturb the peace too much."

"Don't say that, sir," said the landlord, broadening his smile slightly. "The more disturbance the better, in my opinion. Do us a world of good, see."

Simon would not have been averse to following up that line of thought, but Alexander Usher seemed to be waiting for him impatiently, having not addressed any further remark to Megan Harwyn, so Simon picked up the three drinks, handling them very carefully, and returned to the table.

The tall man thanked him, and then observed: "There's a writer named Simon Cannick."

Usually, Simon was delighted when someone recognized his name, given the rarity with which such recognition happened nowadays, but there was something about Alexander Usher's tone prompting the suspicion that there might not be much occasion for delight this time—which might be expectable, given that he was a clergyman.

"That's me," Simon admitted, a trifle warily.

"I'm afraid that I've only heard the name—I've never read any of your books."

"But you've heard enough to disapprove of me anyway?" Simon suggested.

Alexander Usher seemed surprised by the remark, and perhaps a trifle offended. "I wouldn't dream of disapproving of a writer whose books I had never read," he said. "I'm C-of-E, not an Iranian Ayatollah."

Simon assumed that was supposed to be a joke, but he didn't laugh. "Very Christian of you," he said.

"You say that as if it were a bad thing," the tall man countered, but not aggressively, and was quick to add: "I assume that you're here for the same reason I am?"

Caught on the hop, Simon could only say: "I doubt it—although I have no idea what that reason might be."

Alexander Usher glanced at Megan Harwyn, as if surprised and perhaps disappointed, that she had not given Simon a complete account of the reasons for his presence in St. Madoc.

"Mr. Cannick isn't visiting, Reverend," she said, mildly. "He's our new permanent resident. Apparently, he's inherited Raven."

Usher did not react to that information with as much astonishment as Megan had, but he certainly seemed surprised. "Oh," he said. "I seem to have jumped to the wrong conclusion, on the basis of having heard your name. As a writer of . . . the sort of thing you write, I'd assumed that you'd come here for research purposes. I'm here doing research myself, albeit of a somewhat different kind. I'm a historian—I combine my pastoral duties as a chaplain with research into the early history of the church in England, and I'm extremely interested in the Abbey. I hoped to get access to it myself, but I'm afraid I haven't been allowed on to the Tine. Cerys and her mobile phone have been a godsend, though. She's taken photographs inside and outside the house for me, and she's been kind enough to come to the hotel to pore over the floor plans I'd already obtained from other members of the family, correcting their detail. I didn't mean, of course, that I assumed that you'd be interested in architectural matters, but early church history overlaps to such a great extent with legend and folklore that . . . I'm not wrong, am I, in thinking that you're something of a folklorist?"

"I'd like to think that I'm a serious historian," Simon said, "although some might dispute my seriousness—but yes, I'm very interested in the history of mythology and its employment in English and French literature. That had nothing to do with my moving here, though, and I have to admit that I'm completely ignorant of any legendry or folklore associated with St. Madoc or its abbey. I'm delighted to hear that it might be relevant to my work, though. Perhaps you can fill me in, if you don't mind."

Simon did not think that he was taking any risk in making the suggestion. He had never met an antiquarian who was not eager to hold forth at length on his pet subject. To judge by his expression, Alexander Usher was no exception—but there was also an element of incredulity in his reaction, as if he found it impossible to believe that Simon was telling the truth.

"Of course," the clergyman said. "Only too glad." But he showed no sign of making an immediate start.

Simon got the distinct impression that he might be able to kill two birds with one stone if he gave his two interlocutors an explanation of how he came to be in St. Madoc without knowing anything about the place, and he had no reason to hide it, so he said: "Perhaps I should explain my presence more fully. As I was telling Megan before you came down, Reverend Usher, I inherited Raven Cottage from a lady by the name of Evelyne Augerrand. For the last seven years, I've been living in a furnished flat comprised by the first floor of a three-story Victorian house in a suburb of Bristol. The flats above and below were both occupied by old ladies living alone. I met Eve, the one who lived in the apartment above, on the stairs, and volunteered to help her with her shopping, which she was having some difficulty carrying upstairs. She accepted, reluctantly at first, because, although old age was catching up with her—she must have been over ninety even then—she was determined to maintain as much independence as possible.

"Over time, as her mobility problems got worse, she allowed me to do her shopping as well as carrying it upstairs for her. It was no trouble—I work to a very strict routine and I walked for two miles every day, before lunch, doing my own shopping on the way back in Bristol, when I went past the local supermarket. It was just a trivial favor—I wouldn't even say that we became friends. As her health deteriorated, though, her situation became more problematic. We hear on the news every day what a terrible situation the health service and social care are in, but I have to say that they seemed to function perfectly with regard to Eve. She was determined not to go into hospital if she could possibly avoid it, and the people who came in with increasing frequency to help her complied with that. Although I continued to do her shopping for her—that was tacitly built into the care plan—health visitors did all the hard work of tending to her needs, in cooperation with the district nurse and her doctor.

"Once she was permanently bed-ridden though—about four years ago—I began going up in the evening, when I had finished work and was pretty much at a loose end, to see whether she needed anything. I made her cups of tea, and just sat with her for a while—occasionally, at first, but eventually building it into my daily routine. She could still make herself understood perfectly when necessary, but she had difficulty speaking at length, so I fell into the habit of doing most of the talking. I rambled on about what was in the news, what I was writing, and filled her in by degrees on my life story—but as I say, we weren't actually friends, as such. She never told me anything about her own history. Toward the end, though, before she was finally moved to a hospice, I held her hand while I talked, just because I thought she might appreciate the contact. Evidently, she did.

"I didn't visit her in the hospice, and I only found out she'd died when her solicitor came to see me. I'd met him before because she'd asked me to phone him to ask him to come to see her, and I'd had to let him into her flat. Anyway, it turned out that she actually owned the house, including my flat, and had always been my landlady, although I'd only ever dealt with the letting agency. The solicitor said that she'd wanted to leave my flat to me, but that she needed to keep ownership of the whole house intact, and was under some kind of obligation, moral if not legal, to leave it to a family member. However, she owned another property—Raven Cottage—which she'd inherited a long time ago, from her mother, and from which she derived an income as a holiday let. As I was a writer, she had figured that I could do what I did anywhere, and she thought that I might actually find living on the coast, in peace and quiet, more conducive to my work than living in Bristol, so she had left me that instead, without saying a word to me.

"The solicitor told me that the new owners of the house wanted vacant possession, and would be giving me notice to get out, but that I still had the option of moving into another flat in Bristol and using Raven Cottage simply as a source of income, as Eve had—but on reflection, I figured that Eve might be right about the place suiting me, and that if I had to move anyway, I ought to give it a try. The letting agents had a video of the cottage and its furnishings that they showed to holidaymakers, and it looked like a perfectly viable place to work, and as it was already fully equipped . . . well, you can fill in the rest. I packed up my books and a few personal items, and unloaded them here this afternoon, knowing nothing more about the place than I'd gleaned from cursory consultation of the web. You probably know as well as I do what that threw up: ads for the national park, the coastal path, porpoise- and seal-watching and a quote from Richard Hoare, who seems to have been too preoccupied with Druids to do anything more than register the one-time presence of an abbey on Morgan's Fork—whose history presumably came to an end in 1540 or thereabouts, with Henry VIII's dissolution."

Alexander Usher had listened to all that with conscientious attention, and summarized it by saying; "So your presence here is pure coincidence. It has nothing to do with the Murdens or . . . anything supernatural?"

"Nothing whatsoever," Simon confirmed.

"So far as you know," Megan Harwyn put in.

Simon and Alexander Usher both turned toward her. It was the clergyman whose stare she met, in a slightly pugnacious fashion. "Well," she said, "you know as well as I do that certain people around these parts think that there's no such thing as coincidence. I was warning Mr. Cannick before you arrived that he'd probably have to endure an interrogation by Cerys—although I dare say that he won't find that an unpleasant experience—but the more I think about it, the more I suspect that he'll probably get a summons to the Abbey, so that James can give him the third degree in person."

Simon had no trouble at all deducing that the last remark was intended to irritate the clergyman by provoking envy of that prospect, although he could not hazard a guess, as yet, as to the reason for the evident tension that existed between his two interlocutors.

All that Alexander Usher said in response, however, was: "Well, if that should happen, I'm sure that Mr. Cannick will find it very interesting." He turned to Simon. "You must ask James to give you a tour of the house, if you get the chance. As you're a writer, he might even let you into the library, although he wouldn't let Cerys take photographs for me in there. I deeply regret that, as there are said to be extensive family archives in manuscript form, in Latin and Welsh. Times have changed since the early nineteenth century, alas, when Seymour Murden was much more hospitable than his descendants have been."

While the clergyman was speaking, Megan Harwyn had switched her gaze to Simon. "Forgive my ignorance, Mr. Cannick," she said, "but your name meant nothing to me when you introduced yourself. Obviously, I'll look you up on the internet as soon as I get home, if I can figure out how to spell your surname, but my curiosity can't help being impatient. You write about mythology, you say?"

"I've written all sorts of things over the years," Simon said, "under a variety of names, but I've mostly used my real name—the name my adoptive parents gave me, that is—on slightly esoteric studies in a field that I prefer to think of as the history of ideas, although the ideas I've been most interested in have admittedly been sufficiently offbeat to license the Reverend Usher's description of me as 'something of a folklorist.' Thanks to Wikipedia, it's no longer a secret any more that I've also written a number of pseudonymous novels of a fantastic stripe, loosely based on my researches in mythology, legend and folklore . . . including a couple set not far from here, even though I've never actually visited the region before."

"So you assumed, Reverend, when he was introduced, that Mr. Cannick was here hunting mermaids?" Megan asked the clergyman.

"No," said Usher, calmly. "Doubtless because of my own prejudices, I assumed that he might have come to investigate the legend of St. Madoc."

"Which includes mermaids," said Megan, stubbornly.

"Which does have some mention of what you insist on calling mermaids," Usher acquiesced, with a slight sigh. "But we're being rude Miss Harwyn, are we not? Mr. Cannick doesn't know what we're talking about, it seems, and we really ought to explain it to him, rather than exchanging sarcastic banter . . . although it's a long story, I fear."

"So I've been told," Simon observed. "I'd appreciate it, though, if one of you could at least make a start, though. At present, I'm all at sea."

Megan Harwyn and Alexander Usher exchanged a slightly hostile glance. "You're the one who can start at the beginning," she observed. "Go ahead."

The historian needed no further encouragement. "Very well," he said. "Perhaps I should start by explaining my own interest. As I say, I'm a historian. Although the Church *of* England only dates back to the time of Henry VIII, the history of the Church *in* England goes back a lot further, disappearing far too rapidly into the mists of legend. Unfortunately, when Henry VIII dissolved the monasteries, appropriating their prime real estate for himself and carving up the rest between his cronies, much of the record of that previous history was erased, and what survived, in terms of architecture and documentation, suffered further catastrophes in the seventeenth century, during the Puritan revolution. All of the early religious edifices in the British Isles would have been effectively obliterated anyway by serial rebuilding and replacement, but a great many of them were violently destroyed. All that survives of most of them are scattered ruins dating back to the late Middle Ages.

"In that context, St. Madoc is of particular interest—one might almost say unique interest—to a historian. The Tine is the site of one of the earliest monasteries built in the British Isles, and there has allegedly been an edifice on the site continuously since that foundation, doubtless modified and rebuilt many times, but still a potential archeological and architectural treasure trove. Unfortunately, precisely because it has been continuously occupied, passing from being a religious institution to a manor house in the 1540s, and remaining in the hands of the same family ever since, it remains private property, its privacy very jealously guarded in recent times by the Murden family, whose reputation for eccentricity has always been . . . let's say, extreme.

"I'm not the first historian to have tried to obtain access to the house as an object of scrupulous study, but throughout the twentieth century the family refused physical access, and those still resident in the house still do. In fact, though, the Abbey had a reputation for eccentricity long before the Murdens came into possession of it, and my research suggests that if Henry VIII hadn't taken possession of it when he did, the fraternity might well have been excommunicated by the Pope. Its remote location was probably the only thing that had saved it from that fate for the previous four hundred years, during which the resident monks became notorious for their investigations in the occult sciences—investigations not unconnected with the legend of St. Madoc, although it's difficult, in observing that connection, to determine which is the cause and which the effect. Personally, I suspect that everything recorded about St. Madoc might be a product of twelfth-century Norman romance, like a great deal of so-called Welsh mythology.

"Anyway, so far as I can piece it together, the story goes that St. Madoc arrived in Wales in the late fifth century, at the same time that Saint Patrick arrived in Ireland, and probably part of the same mission . . ."

"From Lérins," Simon put in.

"You know about Lérins?" Reverend Usher did not attempt to conceal his surprise.

"Certainly," said Simon, airily. "Lérins Abbey, founded in the early fifth century by Saint Honoratus. Attracted the intellectual elite of France and became a major center of scholarship, with a huge library. Saint Patrick was said to have trained there for his mission, and the legend of him expelling the snakes from Ireland is a carbon copy of the legend of Honoratus expelling the snakes from the isle of Lérins. The original abbey was pillaged and the library burned by Saracen pirates in the eighth century, but another was built on the site and is still there, still flourishing, France still being a Catholic country."

"Very good," Usher admitted. "I can see that you really are a historian. But you never heard of St. Madoc as a fellow trainee of St. Patrick's?"

"No," Simon admitted. "My interest in Lérins came from the direction of the French Midi, and its association with various myths of that region."

"Well, as I was saying, the legend has it that Madoc arrived in Wales and built an abbey on what is now known as the Tine. The fifth-century chronology doesn't tally with the legends attached to the St. Madoc who built an abbey in Swansea, of which nothing now survives but the name, but the dating of either legend might be askew, or, this being Wales, never over-abundantly supplied with names, there might simply have been two Madocs. The one associated with our present location, however, is vaguely connected with three other supposedly ancient legends, interlinked in their association with him. The first and most notorious . . . well, let me show you."

The clergyman pulled an iPad out of his copious jacket pocket, and fiddled with it until he had brought up a photograph taken by a mobile phone.

"Cerys took this for me in the chapel adjacent to the house. Time has taken its toll, but you can still make it out."

Simon looked at the picture, which showed a design sculpted into a slab of stone integrated into a stone wall. It was, indeed, somewhat blurred by the effects of corrosion over the centuries, but, as the church historian said, the central figure was still recognizable as the probable original of the recently painted image of the pub's imitation inn-sign; it was surrounded by something that might simply have been an ornamental border, but seemed to Simon more likely to be a snake swallowing its own tail.

"It's a mermaid," Simon said, "surrounded by an ouroboros."

"Actually," Usher said, it's a morgen—that's morgen with an *e*. Nowadays Morgans Fork is spelled with an *a*, but it was undoubtedly Morgen's Fforch at one time. The sea around these parts is said to have been the location of a morgen colony, at that time associated with the island of Ys."

"The *island* of Ys?" Simon queried. "Ys was supposed to be a city off the Breton coast, which sank."

"That's true," Usher agreed "At least, that's the more famous version of the legend, and the general assumption has always been that the similar Welsh legend, attached to Cardigan Bay, is a simple transference of the Breton legend, due to the Normans, whose fondness for tale-telling provoked the transformation or wholesale invention of most of what is now taken for British mythology. In this instance, though, there might simply have been a confusion of two different traditional stories. A similarly confused transformation might have been responsible for the metamorphosis of the tale of Saint Madoc's voyage to America . . . or, at least, to the Bermudas . . . into the legend of Saint Brendan's similar voyage from Ireland and the legend of the Prince Madoc who was said to have made the same voyage in the twelfth century.

"In the version that refers to Saint Madoc, though, the voyage is intimately connected with his relationship with the morgens, and a pact that he supposedly made with them. He crossed what we now call the Atlantic to reach islands that were probably the archipelago of the Bermudas, in order to make some kind of treaty with the queen of the morgens, which had something to do with the subsequent sinking of Ys and the disappearance of morgens from the waters around the British Isles. According to the legend, Madoc never told anyone exactly what the terms were of the pact that he made with the morgens, but it involved some kind of mutual protection to extend over centuries, and perhaps indefinitely."

"Well," said Simon, "you're right about that being the sort of thing in which I'm interested. One of my old novels recycles the story of Ys—the Breton version, that is, *sans* mermaids." He looked down at the iPad again before handing it back to its owner. "Odd thing to find in a chapel, I suppose . . . but certainly no odder than many images in French churches of all sorts of monsters and demons. How old is it, do you suppose?"

"I don't know," Usher said. "All I've seen of it is that picture, although I'd come across references to it in eighteenth-century documents. Richard Hoare might have seen it, given that Seymour kept open house in those days, although he only mentions St. Madoc in passing in the *Journey*. If Miss Harwyn is right in thinking that you'll get an invitation to the Abbey, you might be able to take a look yourself, and make your own guess about the antiquity of the slab. The chapel, as a building, is probably no older than the sixteenth century, but almost certainly incorporated stones from an earlier edifice. If Richard Hoare had mentioned it he'd have been bound to attribute it to pagan beliefs wiped out by Christianity, but he had a bee in his bonnet about Druids—these matters are very subject to fashion, as you doubtless know."

"Indeed," Simon agreed. "The legend of St. Madoc would presumably have been forgotten long before Hoare made his tour, if fragments of it hadn't been scattered in Norman romance?"

"That's not entirely clear. Exoterically, yes, it had vanished from the documentary record—but esoterically . . . something certainly seems to have survived until the early fifteenth century, in the stories about Owain Glyndwr that prompted Shakespeare to make him into a wizard in *Henry IV Part I.* Do you know the play?"

"Quite well. I used to teach A-level English at one point, and there was always at least one Shakespeare play on the syllabus. Chunks of them are still engraved in my memory."

"Good. To orthodox historians, of course, Glyndwr became a warrior who led a bid for Welsh independence from England, but an esoteric tradition alleges that when he disappeared after his defeat in 1412, he took refuge in St. Madoc's Abbey, where he participated in the magical studies of the monks, and that he was taken away by the morgens, in order that he might come back one day, although it's only his ghost that is routinely seen around Morgan's Fork, along with another, unidentified phantom. Alleged sightings of morgens were occasionally recorded along the Welsh coast for another four hundred years, and there was quite a flurry of sightings in the early nineteenth century. Even in the early twentieth century, it was still one of the supposed attractions that drew people here, in spite of the inevitable steep decline in the fortunes of the parish in the latter part of the nineteenth century."

"Why was it inevitable?" Megan Harwyn put in. "I've heard vaguely that St. Madoc was a much more important place in the early 1800s, even fashionable, and that it went downhill in the later part of the century, but I can't see why that was inevitable."

"At the time," Usher told her, "the Fork formed a useful pair of deep-water moorings, albeit dangerous in stormy weather, and was home to a thriving fishing fleet. The Mermaid was a coaching inn in those days, a staging post on a route that went along the south coast of Wales, through Carmarthen, and then veered north to Cardigan. It was a good road by the standards of the day, and St. Madoc was as good a staging post as any for people traveling to Ireland. In the days when Seymour Murden and his son Rhys were still a considerable force in the land, holding court at the Abbey, St. Madoc was also a major venue for the boom in smuggling promoted by Napoleon's ill-judged attempt to isolate Britain economically with strict trade sanctions. That came to an end in 1815, of course, but the real economic damage was done later, by the double blow inflicted by railways and steamboats.

"Trade and leisure travel were increasingly focused on places where the railway went, and it didn't come here. Fishermen increasingly began to land their catches in the major ports that were connected to the rail distribution system. Steamships gradually took over passenger traffic between Wales and Ireland, which became concentrated in the ferry terminals. The tide of progress simply passed St. Madoc by. The road, which is rather mediocre by modern standards, couldn't maintain it, and once the coach route was abandoned, the village became . . ."

"The arse end of nowhere," Megan supplied, nodding in acknowledgement of the plausibility of the explanation.

"Fashions in folklore studies being what they are," the Reverend added, "the port's brief heyday as a smuggling center led to a new interpretation half a century ago of the morgen stories, and the two caves. You don't know about the caves?" The last remark was addressed to Simon.

Simon shook his head.

"There are two caves in the Central Tine—or perhaps one cave that goes all the way through. The southern one—on the left as we look from here—is known as Morgan's Cave—which is to say, the morgens' cave—and the other is known as Nyder's Cave, which is probably derived from the Welsh *neidr*, meaning snake—the sea-serpent's cave. There was a fad among folklorists some time ago for interpreting tales of monsters as scare-stories invented by poachers to scare gamekeepers and smugglers to deter revenue men. The smugglers certainly didn't invent morgens or sea-serpents, but it's not implausible that the sudden rush of sightings in that era, never repeated since, had some connection with St. Madoc's heyday as a smuggling center."

This time, Simon simply nodded, having been fed too much food for thought to be readily digestible. In the silence that fell, Megan Harwyn said: "It's my round, I think. Can I get you both another drink?"

Simon was unsure whether she was trying to prompt Alexander Usher into a gentlemanly insistence that it was really his round, but if it was a ploy, it failed. The clergyman looked at his watch, frowned slightly, and said: "I suppose I have time for one more. Bitter lemon, please," leaving Megan to follow through with her offer, while deftly laying down an excuse in advance for a later failure to reciprocate on his own part.

Megan seemed more amused than annoyed by the response.

Simon looked at his own watch, and decided that he too had time for one more before his customary bedtime. "Thanks," he said. "Same again." Then he decided that a visit to the Gents was in order. Alexander Usher pointed him in the right direction.

As he went past the four young men who were still speaking Welsh in low voices, one of them looked up and studied him, almost deciding to speak, before changing his mind and returning to his conspiratorial huddle.

Well, Simon thought, *at least that one knows I exist. Perhaps that's progress.*

III
The Murdens

When Simon returned to the table his cider was waiting for him, and the tension between Megan and the Reverend Usher seemed to have eased from hostility to mild embarrassment, although he guessed that they had not exchanged a word while he had been absent.

"Well," he said, "I'm glad I came here. I seem to have landed in an ideal spot to carry forward my idiosyncratic research. I wonder if Eve knew that when she decided to leave me the cottage?"

"She'd inherited it herself, you said?" Megan observed elliptically.

"So the solicitor said. As I told you, Eve never told me anything about the cottage—or, indeed, herself."

"When you were telling her your life story, though, you mentioned that you were a foundling?"

"Of course. Why would that be relevant?"

Megan simply shrugged her shoulders, but Alexander Usher smiled. "Because it opens up the possibility, however slim, that you might be related to the Murdens," he said. "That's why Miss Harwyn thinks that when James Murden discovers that you've inherited Raven Cottage and come to live in it, he might break what seems to have become a long-standing habit and invite you to the house instead of simply sending young Cerys to charm you."

Simon looked at Megan for confirmation of that analysis, but she simply shrugged her shoulders and stared down at her gin and tonic in order to avoid meeting his eye.

"I don't understand," Simon said, a trifle irritated by the mystery.

"We told you that it was a long story," Alexander Usher said. "So far, you've only heard fragments. Following the epoch of the monkish alchemists and the possible involvement in their magical exploits of Owain Glyndwr, there was the great upheaval of the early 1540s, when Henry VIII seized

St. Madoc's Abbey and the estate belonging to it, along with hundreds of other institutions. That's when the Murdens probably come into the picture."

"Probably?" Simon queried.

"There seems to be some suggestion, put about by the Murdens themselves, that they had been involved with the story for some time. You can see, obviously, what significance they liked, and still like to attach to their name?"

Simon did not need long to think it over. "Myrddin," he said. "Myrddin Wyllt, that is—the Welsh bard who was combined with another figure, probably of Breton origin, to make up the character of the Arthurian Merlin, as designed and greatly elaborated by Geoffrey of Monmouth."

"Exactly. It's pure nonsense, of course, but the Murden at the court of Henry VIII, who was given the St. Madoc estate, apparently liked to represent himself as a magician poet, and claimed descent from the sixth-century bard Myrddin, who, according to him, was a inheritor of magical secrets that had previously been made known to Madoc and assisted him to enter into communication with the morgens."

"Druid secrets?" Simon queried.

"Richard Hoare would doubtless have thought so. At any rate, secrets subsequently known to Owain Glyndwr. It's unclear how seriously the Murden at Henry VIII's court, who was also known as Owen Murden, took his impostures, and almost certain that Henry VIII didn't take them seriously at all. He seems, however, to have been amused by Murden, and liked having him around. Perhaps Murden was able to render him a useful service one day, but if he did, none of his contemporaries seems to have known what it was. At any rate, Henry found some reason or other to give St. Madoc's Abbey and its estate to Owen Murden, but without giving him any sort of peerage to go with it—to this day, the Murdens are simply Murdens, with not even a baronetcy to their name in nearly five hundred years. That's unusual, perhaps unique among the countless favors that Henry handed out to his supporters and friends. One way or another, though, Owen

Murden became the master of the ex-Abbey, and the custodian of the pact with the morgens.

"At that point in the story, the mystery thickens. The Murdens seem to have become secretive, preserving traditions within the family of which not a word was breathed outside—ostensibly, at least. Tradition asserts that they continued investigations in magic here, which permitted favored members of the family to acquire an extreme longevity, although skeptics suggest that they simply lied about their ages, and that sons sometimes took over the identities of their similarly named fathers as an imposture. It appears to be a habit that they never lost, and still maintain.

"The family was prosperous while St. Madoc itself was prosperous, reaching the peak of its wealth and prestige in the early nineteenth century, the era of the famous Seymour and the even-more-famous Rhys. As the fortunes of the port declined, however, so did theirs, and by 1900 the family and the estate had fallen on hard times. It was still fairly prolific at the time, with two or three brothers all claiming descent from Rhys and each having several sons of their own—but then came the Great War of 1914-18, which scythed through the ranks of that younger generation and brought economic devastation to the estate. Only a handful of male members of the family came through it, and the family appears at that time to have become an effective matriarchy, at least for a while.

"After the war, fierce quarrels broke out as the surviving males competed against the matriarchy and one another for control of the dwindling fortune. When the estate had to be broken up for partial sale, there was fierce fighting over the fragments. By the time the dust cleared, much of the farmland had gone and the remaining property in St. Madoc itself, Morpen, and along the coast in both directions, had been carved into several slices. Since then, attempts have been made to reconsolidate, it, but there are still tensions between the various branches of the family.

"Perhaps those tensions could have been sorted out decades ago if it weren't for certain confusions of genealogy and identity, which have made it difficult for the Murdens and for anyone else to know exactly who is making claims to rightful ownership of what. Over time, that has developed into a bizarre situation whereby the four permanent Murden residents of the house all claim to be very old indeed, and even the two or three servants they have left are now in their sixties, at least. The old lady always credits herself on official forms with a birth date in the eighteenth century, and James and the two female cousins all claim to be well over a hundred. The local authorities and the census bureau simply ignore what they put down on the forms, and write it off to harmless insanity. It's been going on so long that everyone simply takes it for granted.

"Over the last century, the population of the house has dwindled away. Children were still being born there as recently as the 1990s, but their parents invariably took them away, not wanting them to grow up in a madhouse. The last was Cerys, who spent her first few years there with her mother, but moved away when the time came for her to go to school, only coming back in vacations—which she continued to do when she was at university, by which time both her parents were dead. She came back again last summer, after graduation, initially intending only to stay for a few weeks, but she tells me that she doesn't feel that she can leave, because she doesn't think that James and the two women she calls her aunts can get by without her any longer. The woman she calls her grandmother—the one who claims to be two hundred years old—has been ill for a long time. There's still a cook, a housekeeper and a gardener, but they're hardly able to cope themselves. Cerys says that they were all so good to her when she was a child, and are still so kind, within their capacities, that she simply can't abandon them. I'm quite sure that she knows full well that they're all out of their minds, but she won't admit it, and I'm equally sure that she humors their follies completely, just as the servants do.

"Anyway, that's the situation—but James is still trying—or, at least, imagines that he's trying—to reintegrate the remaining immovable property of the estate, by hook or by crook, or, at the very least, to prevent any further break-up by virtue of properties being sold or bequeathed outside the family. Miss Harwyn here has been a bone of contention for some time, not only having taken Sanderling out of the family but actually living in it, within visual range of the Abbey."

"That's a matter of some dispute, as you know, Reverend," Megan put in. She turned to Simon to add: "Not that I'm living there, obviously, but that I've taken it out of the family. James hasn't addressed a word to me in sixty years, and if he ever crosses the bridge again and passes me in the street, he'll cut me dead just as he always has—but in his heart, he knows that I'm family, and that my being in Sanderling hasn't broken his precious chain of destiny. And no matter what he says and does when he finds out that you're Raven's new owner-occupier, his dearest wish will be to believe that you're family too—which, given that you were a foundling, can't be ruled impossible. He'll want to find out who this Evelyne Augerrand is—was, that is—and how she came to own Raven. Now that he's mastered the internet he'll probably succeed in that—but not before I do. I want custody of that secret first, and I want him to know that I have it before he can get it too. If there were some way to crack the other problem . . . I don't suppose, Mr. Cannick, given that we only met a couple of hours ago, that you'd be prepared to give me a DNA sample?" She blushed suddenly, and said, without a pause: "Oh shit, I'm drunk. Shouldn't have had a fourth. Forget I said that . . . I'm sorry."

Simon laughed, and shrugged. "No need," he said. "Of course you can have a sample, if there's anything you can do with it. You will give me the result of your findings first, though, won't you?"

"I honestly don't think there's any point, Miss Harwyn," the Reverend Usher put in. "Contrary to what appears to be Murden traditional belief, there are such things as coincidences. There literally isn't one chance in a million that Mr.

Cannick is related to James Murden. Do you even have a sample of his DNA for comparison?"

"No, but I've got one that's a familial match," Megan Harwyn retorted.

The clergyman shook his head, as if in compassionate sorrow.

Megan looked at Simon, while inclining her head in Usher's direction. "A man of little faith," she opined. "But still, he's right. I'll stick to searching the web for information about your mysterious benefactor—and I'll let you know if I find anything. I don't think you have to worry about Cerys stealing hairs from your hairbrush, though; James might have mastered the internet, but organizing comparative DNA tests is probably a step too far for him."

Simon felt that his situation was now more than a trifle surreal. He was not sure exactly when it had happened, but at some point since crossing the threshold of the Mermaid he seemed to have entered an alien world. Its physical trappings were all manifestly orderly—he swept the interior of the pub with a circular glance to make sure of that, and was reassured by the tables, the cream-painted walls hung with landscapes and seascapes, and the labels on the bottles behind the bar— but it had acquired an entirely new context of history and ideas with astonishing rapidity.

I ought to be glad, he thought. *All of it is virtually tailor-made for my fascination, my imagination.*

The fact was, however, that he wasn't glad. In fact, he felt oddly anxious—oddly because he would have thought that he was better equipped than almost anyone else in the world to take it all in his mental stride. That he had not known the detail of it was not surprising; in spite of his extensive reading in the fields of folklore, legend and mythology, his ignorance was only slightly less extensive than that of the average man, because the unknown always outweighed the known massively, and for years now—ever since he had been living on his own in the first-floor flat—his attention had been focused almost entirely on French sources.

He had never paid much attention to Welsh material, partly because the original documents were written in a language that he did not understand, and partly because, as Alexander Usher had pointed out, almost everything written down in Welsh had been written after the eleventh-century conquest, and it had been Normanized—rewritten or wholly invented, in the mold of Norman romance—and had thus seemed essentially fake. The same thing had happened to Breton mythology, he knew, and the authentic folklore of the Midi had been irredeemably swamped by the Albigensian Crusade, but the echoes were more prolific . . .

"You seem rather tired, Mr. Cannick," said Alexander Usher, breaking into the reverie into which he had drifted. "Hardly surprising as you've spent the day moving house. The combination of stress and physical effort is very draining. There's a little more I can tell you, in which you might be interested, but it might be better to leave it until tomorrow. I'll be here for two more nights before I have to return to England, and I hope that we'll have more opportunities to chat. Perhaps I might call on you at Raven some time tomorrow?"

"I need to try to get back into my work routine as soon as possible," Simon said, reflexively. "I'll be free in the evening, though. I could meet you here, if that's okay with you?"

"Of course."

"Will that routine still include your daily pre-lunch walk?" Megan Harwyn asked.

"Certainly," said Simon. "It won't be the same as my regular circuit of the streets of Bristol, though—just out and back along the coast road. I'll try the north-easterly stretch tomorrow, and the southwesterly the next day."

"And the road to Morpen the day after?" she suggested.

"Possibly. It might be better to avoid too much variety, at least until I settle in. By the way, I understand that the delivery van from the nearest supermarket makes its regular trip the day after tomorrow."

"Wednesday, that's right," Megan told him. Place your order by email the day before. They're very efficient, although you might find that the range of stock is more limited than it is in a big city. You don't have a car?"

"No," said Simon.

"James doesn't have one either; he sends a donkey-cart down to the bridge to pick up the delivery for the house. Mercifully, it's not a long trip—the donkey gives the impression of being as old as he is."

"In that case," said the Reverend Usher," I think I'll return to my room. "I have a little work to do before I retire."

"Googling Simon Cannick, no doubt," said Megan. "Me too. It is two *ns* and an *i*, with a *k* at the end, I assume?" she added, turning to Simon.

"That's right," said Simon.

The clergyman was already on his feet, and Simon stood up too. Megan remained seated. This time, Alexander Usher put out his hand for Simon to shake briefly.

"Until tomorrow evening, Mr. Cannick," the tall man said, his five-inch height advantage suddenly seeming slightly oppressive as he looked down at Simon. "I'm very pleased to have met you—and in case you should want to google me, it's only one *s*—I'm no relation to the notorious churchman with the similar name. Good night."

Simon contrived a polite laugh at the weak joke. When the clergyman had disappeared through the interior door, he sat down again.

"Well," he said, "that was enlightening."

"He really does have more still to tell you," Megan said, in a tone edged with irony. "I hope you continue to find it enlightening—otherwise, it might seem distinctly tedious."

"You don't like the Reverend much, I gather?"

"I don't have anything against him except that he doesn't like me. I don't have anything against churchmen in general, or even pompous pricks . . . oh God, there I go again. I've completely lost the habit of polite conversation. I'd better go home myself—it's late, and I have googling to do. There's no point in looking for me, mind, even if you can deduce the spelling of my surname. My presence in cyberspace is strictly pseudonymous."

She stood up, and Simon stood up too. "I'll walk with you," he said. "After all, we're going the same way."

He saw her gaze flick toward the conspiratorial group on the far side of the room and then to the door to the back room behind the bar, where Dai was leaning casually on the jamb, not looking at anything or anyone in particular. After a moment's hesitation, she said: "Why not?"

"I don't think it's going to compromise your reputation," Simon observed. "We're both old-age pensioners, and next-door neighbors. I don't think anyone's going to read anything undue in my walking you home."

"You don't . . . " she began, and then stopped. She was already heading for the door, seemingly having turned away to conceal a slight confusion or indecision. Once they were outside, though, she seemed perfectly relaxed again.

"Colder now than when you came in," she observed. "But considering that it's February, really quite mild. Mind you, this little corner has never had the kind of two-month snow cover that we used to see inland every year. It's said to be something to do with a tributary of the gulf stream . . . said by some, that is. Others put it down to the mermaids . . . but there's some who put everything down to the mermaids, even though no one's seen hide nor hair of one in our lifetime. You've come to a crazy place, Simon . . . may I call you Simon?"

"Of course," he said. "I'm glad."

"Glad that I'm calling you Simon?"

"No, glad that I've come to a crazy place. The fact that Bristol is so dull—unless you live in St. Paul's, which I didn't—meant that there was no distraction from my obsession, but a little surrounding craziness might do me good. I hope I do get a chance to meet the Murdens. They sound quite fascinating."

"That's one word for it," Megan muttered, but was quick to add: "Don't mind me, though. I don't have anything against them except that they really don't like me."

"Well, I hope you won't find any reason to hold anything against me," Simon said.

They were quite a distance from the nearest street lamp, so he couldn't tell whether she smiled at that.

"Well, if your story can be believed, you're kind to old ladies, even if they aren't really your friends," she said. "Who knows—I might end up leaving Sanderling to you. I don't have any heir apparent, and I wouldn't want James to get presumptive, as he probably would."

They had arrived at the gate of Sanderling Cottage. Simon made an awkward gesture part way between a nod and a bow. "Good night, then," he said. "It's been very interesting talking to you."

She laughed. "Well," she said, dryly, "like the Reverend, I still have a lot more to tell you—but unlike him, I'm here for good, so I'll have plenty of time to bore you with it without having to make appointments. Don't worry, I won't drop round while you're working—I keep regular hours myself— but we're bound to bump into one another often and anon. I really do hope that you'll be happy here. Good night, Simon."

She extended her hand but only to open the gate. She didn't look back as she took the three strides that brought her to her front door, or while she turned her key in the lock. Simon noticed as she switched on the light inside that she punched out a code on a burglar alarm key pad. Obviously, St. Madoc wasn't one of those proverbial peaceful locations where everyone left their doors unlocked because there was nothing to be feared from thieves

IV
The Raven

When Simon glanced at his watch he saw that it was quarter to ten, too close to his regular bedtime for him to bother switching on the computer, even just to check his email, but he switched it on anyway and sat down in his ergonomically-approved swivel-chair. It was not Alexander Usher's name that he googled first, however, but the word *morgen*. Wikipedia's disambiguation page gave him a dozen different references, but they did include the relevant one: a Welsh or Breton water sprite.

He cursed himself for not having recognized the Breton meaning instantly, and for not having known that Geoffrey of Monmouth had spelled the word that way, having grown accustomed to the English versions that referred to the lady of the lake as Morgan le Fay, as if it were a proper name rather than a generic term. He cursed himself doubly for having been similarly blind to the connection of the word with the legend of Ys—all the more so as he had used the legend in one of his pseudonymous fantasy novels. If he had ever known that Dahut, the princess whose lewd conduct had allegedly caused the city to be drowned, had been punished for her sins by being turned into a sea morgen, he had forgotten it.

He forgave himself a little when he realized that most of the reference books that he still kept on his shelves, for old time's sake, had simply done what Megan Harwyn and everyone else habitually did, and substituted the word "mermaid" for "morgen" in transmitting folklore referring to such entities. He took note of the fact that some Welsh sources rendered the term as murigen, and immediately wondered whether that might be the real origin of the surname Murden, and its supposed association with Myrddin merely a later improvisation inspired by coincidence.

The cross-reference between Morgens and the French legend of Melusine did not cause him to curse himself, because he was already thoroughly familiar with numerous versions of that story, and knew that there was some division between them as to whether the humanized water-spirit in question was occasionally obliged to manifest herself as a snake or a fish from the waist down. He made a mental note to ask Alexander Usher what more he knew about the mysterious caves on the Tine, one of which was allegedly named after morgens and the other after sea-serpents.

Not, of course, he thought, *that serpentine loins and a tail are any more plausible as an element of human hybridization than a fish-tail . . . and if the seductiveness of sirens goes much further than singing and putting on a show of combing their hair, they'd probably need something more closely akin to the sexual equipment of a seal than that of a herring or a viper . . .*

The train of thought was interrupted by a tapping sound.

At first, Simon couldn't tell where the sound was coming from, and thought that it might not be physical at all, but it only took him a few more seconds and a couple more taps to realize that it was coming from the window that looked out on to the street. The curtain was drawn, so he couldn't see who or what it was that was tapping, but it was a real sound, and almost ordinary.

His first thought was that it might be Megan Harwyn, although why she—or anyone else—would tap on his study window rather than ringing his doorbell was a mystery.

He stood up, went to the window, and drew the curtain.

The tapping stopped immediately, and the big black bird awkwardly perched on the window sill looked Simon straight in the eye.

A frisson ran through Simon's body, as he had the sensation, once again, of having crossed the threshold of another world—but this time abruptly, and into a world to which he could put a name of sorts: Edgar Poe.

As a matter of principle, Simon never used the middle name that had been foisted upon Poe by his literary executor, the execrable Rufus Griswold. He loved Poe too much to do that.

He never had an instant's doubt that the bird tapping on his window was a raven.

He undid the catch of the sash window and raised it very slowly, in order not to alarm the bird. It immediately hopped into the room, and flew awkwardly to perch on the back of the armchair placed in front to the television.

"I'm sorry," Simon said to the bird. "I don't actually possess a bust of Pallas. If I'd known you were coming, I'd have ordered one online."

The bid did not say *Nevermore*. Somehow, the omission appeared to Simon to be strangely tragic.

The bird did not say anything at all, in fact, for a full two minutes—which was, in rational if not esthetic terms, perfectly understandable. It did continue looking at Simon, however, in a way that he had never seen a bird look at him before. He had always held as a matter of faith the opinion that birds were a good deal more intelligent than was sometimes thought, and that it was not only owls that concealed a secret wisdom behind their limited language of screeches and songs, but he had never been able to back up that hypothesis with any unambiguous evidence.

Strictly speaking, he supposed, the fact that the raven was staring at him was not reliable evidence either—the fact that it seemed to be doing so attentively and inquisitively could easily be the product of his own imagination—but even so . . . it was, to say the least, a remarkable coincidence.

And if there really was no such thing as coincidence . . .

Suddenly, as if it had come to a decision, the bird spoke, quite clearly, in English. And what it said was: "I can call spirits from the vasty deep."

Simon's first impulse was to laugh. The bird had not only got the line wrong, but the author. It was quoting Shakespeare instead of Poe.

Almost automatically, he replied: "And so can I—but they never come when I call."

It was, of course, not the right line, but if the bird wasn't following Poe's script, Simon couldn't see why he should follow Shakespeare's.

"Time is out of joint," said the bird. "The storm is up and

all is on the hazard. And certain stars shot madly from their spheres . . ."

The temptation to laugh had gone. Simon's mind was spinning. He recognized the quote from *Hamlet*, and had a vague notion that the second phrase might be from *Julius Caesar*, while the third was definitely from *A Midsummer Night's Dream*, spoken by Oberon.

". . . To hear the sea-maid's music," he completed, remembering the production of the play in which he had once assisted, back in his teaching days.

The bird fell silent.

"Is that all?" he asked.

It seemed that it was. A minute went by, in a silence that seemed to grow more ominous by the second. And then, it seemed that if there were, in fact, such a thing as coincidence, it was going to ridiculous extremes, because while he was staring back at the uncanny bird, marveling at its size, its blackness and the impression it gave of great antiquity, he heard a voice call: "Lenore!"

That was too much. This time, Simon could not help laughing—but when he heard the hysterical tone of his own laughter, the fear finally struck him, like a dagger in the heart. What was happening was impossible. And worse than that—it was not *right*. This was not *his world*. Such things could not happen to *him*.

And suddenly doubt swept over him like a bright tide. Of course it had not happened. It was his imagination. Ravens could not talk—that was a Dickensian myth, perpetuated by Poe. And if ravens had been able to talk, they would not do so by quoting fragments of Shakespeare. It was all in his mind. The sight of the bird had triggered a hallucination. This was just a dream, breaking through the barrier that normally separated the world of consciousness, secreted in memory, from the stuff that dreams were made of, which vanished into oblivion as soon as the mind recovered its empire, its grip of the real. And what he had thought he had heard was just a chain of associations made by dream-logic. There had been mention of Owain Glyndwr in the pub, and that had made his unconscious dredge up the Shakespeare quote, and that had made him think of more Shakespeare quotes, picked at random but forming the semblance of a sequence of ideas, a message from beyond . . .

It was all fantasy, twisted dream-logic . . .

Except that the voice in the night—the voice outside, in St. Madoc's only street, really did belong to his world, and it really was calling: "Lenore!" because the big black bird—the big, black, soundless bird—was real too. It was only its voice that came from elsewhere, from the world of dreams and the manufacture of his own faithless unconscious.

"*You're* the lost Lenore!" he said to the bird—or, rather, to his own unruly unconscious. "That really is taking wordplay too far!"

Obviously, though, it was not coincidence. Whoever had named the raven was a lover of Poe . . . or, had, at least heard of him, and knew the key references of his most famous work.

But nobody any longer domesticated ravens. Perhaps they had, in the nineteenth century, even though Charles Dickens was a bare-faced liar. *Barnaby Rudge* was pure fantasy and Grip a whimsical product of the literary imagination, but that didn't mean that there weren't tame ravens in the Victorian era. But surely there were none now, if only because ravens were far too rare: an endangered species, if Simon were not mistaken. Surely no one in the twenty-first century could possibly have a tame raven, even one that couldn't talk, so surely no one would have had the Poesque idea of naming one Lenore?

Except, of course, that somebody evidently had.

Simon turned back to the open window. Because the light was on in the room and he was peering out into obscurity, he could only make out the vague silhouette of the person who had called: "Lenore," but he knew already that it was a female voice, and not Megan Harwyn's, in spite of the strong Welsh lilt.

Aware that she must have the advantage of being able see him quite clearly, Simon leaned out of the window and said, with only a hint of sarcasm: "Are you, by any change, looking for a raven?"

The woman was standing directly in front of the house, and facing it, but Simon had the impression that she had not been looking at the window, but rather at the roof.

She came right up to the garden fence, and Simon moved aside slightly in order that the light spilling out of the room would illuminate her more brightly.

She was young, not much more than twenty, and quite pretty, with dark eyes that had a kind of sparkle, and long hair that seemed raven-black—but he was aware that both the sparkle and the intensity of the blackness might be tricks of the deceptive light.

"Yes," she said. "Have you seen her?"

"She's in here," Simon told her.

The young woman's face expressed surprise. "Inside? She's come *inside*?"

"She tapped on the window until I let her in. But she hasn't said 'Nevermore' yet."

The young woman didn't smile at the joke, but surely not because she hadn't caught the implication. "I'm so sorry," she said. "I don't know what's got into her. We let her out during the day, of course, and she sometimes flies off, and usually comes here, but she's never got out at night before—not while I've been here, anyway—and she's never flown inside the house . . . not that she's had the opportunity before . . ." She stopped, evidently having become aware that there were more mysteries in the remarkable event than the raven's behavior.

"Hang on," said Simon. "I'll open the front door."

He did that, and the young woman came in. Once she was fully illuminated, he saw that neither the sparkle in her eyes nor the blackness of her hair had been momentary idiosyncrasies of uncertain lighting.

"You're Cerys Murden, I presume?" Simon said.

She seemed appropriately startled, but only for a moment. It couldn't have been hard for her to deduce that he'd talked to Megan Harwyn, and perhaps even to Alexander Usher.

"That's right," she said, as she went over to the chair facing the TV and extended her arm, like a huntsman offering her wrist to a hawk. The bird ignored the proffered limb and hopped onto her shoulder instead, still looking at Simon. When the young woman turned round to face him again, the bird did a prompt about-turn.

"I'm sorry," she said, again. "I didn't know the cottage had been let until I saw your light a few minutes ago. I didn't imagine that Lenore would have come inside. I've always thought that she sometimes comes here during the day because she's suffering from some avian equivalent of Alzheimer's, forgets where she is, and follows some ancient memory trace . . . although I have no idea what the memory might be, or why the cottage is called Raven."

"Is she very old, then?" Simon asked.

"Older than me, at any rate. According to Felicia . . . but that's not important. Are you staying long, Mr. . . . ?" Even as she spoke, she must have realized that the question was redundant, as her eyes traveled over the abundantly stocked bookshelves. She frowned slightly, in puzzlement rather than annoyance.

"Cannick," Simon supplied. "Simon Cannick." He paused briefly, to see whether there was any reaction to his name, but there wasn't the slightest flicker of recognition. "And to save any beating around the bush, I moved in today with the aim of settling here permanently. I inherited the cottage from a woman named Evelyne Augerrand. Rumor has it that the news will come as an unwelcome shock to your relatives, for which I can only apologize."

He could not help comparing the young woman's stare with the bird's, and finding a similarity between them that might have been hilarious if it had not seemed rather sinister.

Cerys digested that information. "I see you've met Megan Harwyn," she observed, in a carefully neutral tone.

"And Alexander Usher," Simon supplied. "I've just spent the evening in the Mermaid with them. That's how I was able to deduce your name. They didn't mention Lenore, though."

Cerys sighed. "Too busy banging on about morgens, Saint Madoc and the madness of the Murdens," she deduced, with deadly accuracy. "They'd have got round to Lenore if they'd had more time, and Pamphile too." She was no longer staring at Simon; her eyes had strayed to the bookshelves, and she was scanning the shelves with a certain patient care.

It took Simon a few seconds to work it out, but he got there. "Pamphile is the donkey," he deduced. "Someone in the family must be fond of quirky literary references. I approve."

"I can't claim any credit for it," Cerys told him. "They were named long before my time. Felicia was a great reader before her eyes began to let her down, apparently, and James still is. As for Grandmother . . . but you must be quite a reader yourself." She took a long stride closer to the shelves as she spoke, in order to make certain of what she had glimpsed. "Some of these books are yours," she observed. "I mean . . . you wrote them?"

"Actually," Simon said, vaingloriously, "all of the ones in that set of shelves are mine—but some of them are pseudonymous, and a lot of them are translations from the French."

He watched her gaze go from side to side and up and down, and felt an enormous surge of gratification as her features—which, now he came to think about it, really were uncommonly pretty, and would have suited any siren sea-maid—took on an expression of awed amazement.

"What, *all* of them?" she said.

"Yes," he said, proudly.

"Then how come I've never heard of you?" she blurted, bringing him down to earth with a crash.

He managed to gather enough self-esteem to say: "I fear that my work is a trifle esoteric. Even in the days when I was working in the commercial sector, it was mostly invisible. Now it's all produced on a print-on-demand basis . . . well,

I suppose you're familiar with the philosophical question about the tree falling in the remote forest."

Obviously she was. "The one that might or might not make a sound?" she countered, with alacrity.

"That's the one. The general opinion is that it doesn't, because a sound isn't a sound unless someone hears it who knows what a sound is. Well, I sometimes wonder whether a print-on-demand book that no one ever demands can really be said to be published, or even to exist."

"No one?" she queried.

"Well, not quite no one," Simon admitted. "A few people, mercifully . . . but painfully few. At least, it pains me. May I give you a present?"

Again, she was startled—and a trifle suspicious. "What present?" she asked.

Simon went to one of the boxes stacked in the corner to the right of the door and rummaged in the top one, until he found the spare copy of the book he wanted: a paperback novel published thirty years earlier called *The Bells of Ys*.

He handed it to her, saying: "The probable origin of your name: Caer-Ys. That means . . ."

"The Castle of Ys, the city out in the bay swallowed up by the sea," she interrupted, a trifle rudely but anxious to show off a little erudition. "Felicia says that it was visible from the Abbey, that St. Madoc must have seen it sink beneath the waves for the last time."

"The last time?" Simon queried.

"That's what she says. There was a big storm, and stars fell from the sky, and Caer-Ys sank for the last time . . . but one day, she says, it will come back, when the time is out of joint."

Simon felt something like a slight electric shock. "Felicia is the one who named the bird Lenore?" he asked.

"Probably. Before my time, though. She's always been a great reader. Loves Poe."

"And Shakespeare?"

"Oh, yes—very much."

"And like Barnaby Rudge, she tried to teach the raven to talk?"

Cerys laughed. "She says that it does. No one else can hear a whisper, but everyone humors her."

Simon stared at the black bird. The bird stared back, cocking her head slightly, as if to tell him that what she had said was for his ears only, and that he had better not say any more about it to Cerys, lest she think that he was mad.

"In my novel, Ys is off the coat of Brittany," Simon remarked, adding, in order to display a little erudition of his own: "The Welsh version is probably an adaptation, post-Norman conquest."

"This is you, then?" she said, just to make certain. She meant the pseudonymous by-line.

"That's right. I used pseudonyms on all my fiction, and saved my own name for non-fiction—a silly affectation, I suppose. I can't remember why I started, but once the pattern was set it just became a habit. I was young then—not when I wrote that particular book, that is, but when I formulated the policy. Does the bird—Lenore, I mean—always stare at people the way she's staring at me?"

"Don't take it personally," Cerys murmured, still looking down at the book. "I don't think she can see very well any more. Unlike Felicia and Melusine, she can't wear spectacles, so she has to look harder if something catches her attention."

"Melusine?" Simon queried. "She and Felicia are . . . your aunts?"

"I call them aunts," Cerys agreed, "but they're really great-aunts, at least, just as James is really my great-grandfather. Grandfather will be interested to see this. I'm sure that he'll have heard of you, and probably has some of your non-fiction books. He keeps the library locked nowadays, though. Mr. Usher told you about the photographs, I assume?"

"Yes. He showed me one of a morgen and an ouroboros. He said you've been a godsend . . . and coming from a man in Holy Orders, that's probably more than a casual metaphor."

"James disapproves," Cerys said, pensively, "but he had to admit that it was a reasonable compromise. He really is trying to adapt to the twenty-first century. He says that I'm a godsend too, for helping him with his computer, so that he can communicate with the scattered parts of the family and try to get a grip on the estate business, which has been stagnating for decades. Look, I really would like to talk to you about your writing at length, but I have to take Lenore back to the house, and it's very late. Could I possibly come back another time?"

"Of course," said Simon. "I've arranged to have another chat with the Reverend Usher at seven-thirty tomorrow evening, but apart from that, my time's entirely at your disposal."

What the hell am I saying? he thought, privately, wondering why he wasn't issuing the same restriction with regard to his work routine that he had imposed on Usher. He remembered, a trifle uncomfortably, Megan Harwyn's remark about his being able to tell Cerys to mind her own business if she were sent to interrogate him, but that he wouldn't do it, because she was too pretty.

Am I really that vulnerable to a glimpse of a pretty face? he asked himself, and was immediately aware that the answer to the question was decisively affirmative. *Must be my age and the force of nostalgia*, he added, by way of an apology for his weakness.

"Thanks," said Cerys. "For the invitation as well as the book. She paused on the threshold of the door to the room, and her gaze scanned the bookshelves again, before going to the computer. The raven had turned round again, so that it was still facing Simon—but even though he had been told that her eyesight was poor, he couldn't shake the impression that the uncanny bird was staring straight into his soul.

Simon accompanied his visitor to the main door of the house and held it open for her.

"Good night," he said. "I'm delighted to have met you."

She didn't echo the sentiment, but did say: "I hope you'll

be happy here, Mr. Cannick," in a tone that somehow suggested that she thought it unlikely—but that might have been his imagination.

He could have shut the door as soon as she stepped down from the doorstep on to the short garden path, but in fact he left it ajar, so that he could track Lenore's discomfiting gaze with his own eyes.

The darkness inevitably swallowed up the bird and the young woman alike, but he had the impression that the bird was still looking in his direction, still interested, even though she made no tempt to fly through the open study window again.

No need now, is there? Simon thought. *You've seen me, delivered your message—or prompted my unconscious to produce the illusion—and measured my soul. But what, exactly, did you see with your faded eyesight, and why do you care? What on earth is going on here . . . if it really is on earth that it's going on?*

The door was still ajar, and he was still lurking behind it, invisible to anyone outside because there wasn't light behind him, when he saw another silhouette run to catch up with Cerys as she made her way toward the bridge. He saw the young woman stop, and knew that a hurried whispered conversation took place, of which he could not hear a single word.

He had no problem deducing, however, that the second silhouette was that of Megan Harwyn, who was telling Cerys that she had something to tell her—but Cerys only listened for a few seconds before continuing on her way, doubtless having told Megan that she had to get Lenore back home, that it was late, and that whatever it was would have to wait for another time.

Simon closed and locked the door, went back into the study, closed and locked the window, drew the curtains and returned to his computer—but only to shut it down. There was no time for any further research tonight, if he were going to attempt to restore his usual routine with the minimum possible delay.

He knew, though, that he was unlikely to be able to go to sleep immediately, or very soon. His ever-active mind had absorbed far too much food for thought in the last few hours, and he had a nasty suspicion that he was in for a long bout of mental indigestion.

It was not until he was in bed, though, with all the lights off, that he realized how alien the environment was, with the sounds of distant traffic characteristic of the Bristolian night replaced by the similarly distant sound of the waves of the sea beating on the shore.

The phrase that sprang to mind once again, when his attention focused of its own accord on that marine pulse-beat was "the vasty deep," even though his pedantic consciousness was perfectly well aware that the vasty deep from which Shakespeare's Glendower had claimed to be able to summon spirits was not the sea but the world beyond the visible and tangible world: the world inhabited by the ghosts of the dead and other numinous entities.

Except, of course, he could not help thinking, that if the historical Owain Glyndwr really had sought refuge on St. Madoc's Abbey after his defeat by the English, and had indulged there in arcane practices with the heretic monks, the two meanings of the vasty deep might well have been confused, the sea becoming haunted by numinous entities of its own: not merely semi-human morgens but things more serpentine, and probably more dangerous.

In any case, Simon thought, *I can do that, and so can any man — and because I'm a writer, they always come when I call, and they always do what I want them to, and always are what I want them to be. In the worlds within my books, even the vasty deep is exactly what I say it is, with all the metaphors I care to use as stuffing. Poor Owain Glyndwr probably wasn't even literate, let alone a magician. He needed a Shakespeare to give him any kind of a personality after death, to keep him alive in human memory. If his ghost walks in St. Madoc, he surely owes it to Shakespeare, not to the monks of St. Madoc and their inherited Druidic magic.*

He deliberately let his mind drift, because experience had taught him that that kind of mental relaxation often spared him from insomnia, but it didn't seem to be working. In Bristol, he had never been conscious of the sounds of the night, the sounds of the city; as background noise, they were too familiar to be apprehended. But now that they were gone, their absence was obvious. It was ridiculous, of course, that an absence could be obvious, that a void could seem oppressive, but he couldn't shake the feeling that during the day, without even noticing it to begin with, he had stepped into an alien world, a world created by a different author, in which even nothing no longer had the same meaning as before, and all the metaphors had been changed, without him being notified, let alone given the key to decode them.

And he could not step back.

Anything could happen now. From the moment that the raven had tapped on his window, let alone since it had spoken to him in jumbled Shakespeare, the transition had been complete, and the rules of life had changed, without the benefit of a text-break. From now on, anything could happen, and with any rapidity. Even now, when he seemed to have time to himself, time to think, he couldn't, because the sound of the sea was too insistent, too pervasive, too inexorable. It brought to mind the metaphorical bells that he had attributed to Ys in the novel that he had given to Cerys: bells that caused no vibration in air or water but awoke a rhythm in the depths of the mind, either a tocsin or a knell, depending on circumstance.

For the moment, it seemed to him, the relentless rhythm of the waves was neither a warning nor a notification of death, but something else, something unfathomable, emanating from the Caer-Ys of Cardigan Bay, long sunk into the bed of the sea, absorbed into the rock, but still capable of reaching into the mind . . .

You'll have to get used to it, he told himself. *And you will. Two or three days, a week at the most, and it will just fade into the mental background.*

He knew that it was true, but it was not reassuring. He knew that he was uniquely sensitive to the whisper of the sea for the moment because the near-silence had brought it to his attention, but he knew that when he contrived, not merely during the day but also in the quiet of the night, to blot it out of his consciousness, it would still be there, in the background. Nor was it only the deep of the sea that was close at hand, but the other deep, perhaps even closer, which made no honest sonic vibration, not even an audible whisper, but spoke regardless, making its meaning clear even though it had no words of its own but had to borrow them from his memory and piece them together like a jigsaw . . .

That way lies madness, Simon told himself, sternly—but it was a warning that he had issued to himself countless times before in the course of his life, without it ever having had any effect. That was reassuring, in a way, given that, as yet—or so he had still been firmly convinced, only a few hours ago—he had never actually ridden all the way to that terminus.

On the other hand, he thought vaguely, as the fatigue and stress of the day finally began to take effect and liberate him from the dangerous mental drift, *there's still time . . . especially if it's slipping out of joint.*

V
The Coastal Path

Habit maintained its authority in spite of his radical geographical displacement, and Simon woke up a few minutes before five o'clock. He got up, showered, dressed, ate a rapid breakfast of Camembert on rye-bread washed down with black coffee, and was back in the swivel chair by five-thirty.

There was no difficulty picking up his work where he had left off the day before last, when he had packed up the computer ready for translocation from Bristol to St. Madoc. He plugged his earphones into the computer and switched on the machine's music player, which was programmed to select at random from his stored MP3s and play indefinitely, providing him with background music while he worked. He opened the pdf file of the text downloaded from *gallica* and resumed the translation at the point where it had been suspended. He slipped back into it almost effortlessly, allowing himself to be absorbed into the flow of his personal narrative, to the sound-track of the *Pathétique*, selected by the wisdom of chance.

It was a very comforting sensation, because it was normality. It really did not matter, he reminded himself, what there was outside the windows—what sounds there were, what population the world had—because his real home, his real life, was bounded by his desk. His own reliable reality would always be there as long as he had the computer, the monitor and the keyboard, no matter where those artifacts happened to be placed in the illusory world of Maya, which simple people, with the determined optimism of faith, called "reality."

He smiled at that thought, and hoped that he would not forget it, so that he could make use of it one day when he switched back from his translation work and his commentaries on what his translations revealed to him, to writing another novel, and savoring godly control over another petty Creation.

For the time being, though, he had to concentrate on the translation, on the reproduction of someone else's fantastic cosmos.

Simon was working on a history of French Romantic and Symbolist fantastic fiction, with particular reference to its connections with the French Occult Revival of the nineteenth century. He had already been working on it for two years and expected to be working on it for at least a further two—always provided, of course, that he contrived to live that long, given that he was fast approaching the three-score-years-and-ten traditionally set as the human lifespan.

Much of the work he did nowadays consisted of producing annotated translations of relevant texts that had not been translated into English before, which he fed to a specialist publisher as he produced them, who issued them as print-on-demand texts and then as e-books, at a rate of some thirty volumes a year. Had he been a career academic producing scholarly pulp he would have been able to content himself with simply reading the texts, but he had always considered himself a true scholar, who needed a much closer under-standing of texts than mere reading provided, but which detailed translation delivered in abundance, by placing the translator squarely in the author's shoes, providing a kind of identification even sharper and more forceful than the one provided by inventing and manipulating a character of his own in a work of fiction, precisely because the character in the translation already existed, had already been created and shaped, and his destiny determined.

In his twenties and thirties, struggling to make a liv-ing, Simon had taught English A-level classes part-time at a private college, but that had been in the days when such work only required competence and not a formal teaching qualification, and he would have been forced to abandon it at forty anyway, even if the change in his financial circum-stances following his marriage had not enabled him to do so. He had hated being bound by a syllabus that not only determined what texts he had to teach but what he had to say about them—the very opposite of authentic education, in his determinedly unorthodox opinion. Teaching texts was a kind of translation too, he supposed, but it was not real transla-tion. It was bad translation, shackled by rules and received wisdom, in which the experience of the text, the living of the text, had no role to play. It had been a great relief to him to be able to put that kind of time-wasting behind him and concentrate entirely on writing, even though he had still been forced to slant much of what he wrote, as best he could, to the requirements if the market.

Now, he was free even of that pressure, no longer required to give a moment's thought to the demands of the market and the ingrate reading public. He was a pensioner, paid per heartbeat rather than per word, and he had just enough pension left over from his teaching days and the personal pension schemes into which he had been able to pay on a desultory basis to make up his state pension to a level that permitted him to meet his routine living expenses.

That was fortunate, because his current income from his writing, even producing more than thirty books a year, would not have come close to saving him from starvation. Once his fiction had become unsaleable to publishers because his various names had all become synonymous in editors' minds with public unpopularity, he had been able to keep afloat for a further seven or eight years writing articles for reference-books, but that source of income had dried up virtually overnight when reference-books had become virtually extinct, wiped out at a stroke by the asteroid-strike that was Wikipedia. Mercifully, he had had sufficient savings to bridge the gap that separated him from the age at which he had been able to draw his various fragments of pension, even after the divorce.

Since then, he had effectively dug himself into a hole and sealed it up behind him. He had told Eve—virtually the only person to whom he had talked for the past seven years—that he had passed through all the natural phases of a writing career: that it had begun as a hobby, had then become a job, and then a vocation, to end up as a full-blown obsession.

"But not as a mental illness," he had assured her, as she listened to him meekly—or pretended to listen. "The reason that Obsessive Compulsive Disorder is problematic is because of the Compulsion. If an obsession is voluntary, like mine, there's nothing in human existence more orderly. It certainly seems to be the case that almost no one else in the world is interested in the work I do, and I don't need the fingers on both hands to count the sales of most of my books, but that doesn't mean that I'm insane to do the work. It serves its purpose—which is, in essence, to keep me sane, to feed my mind with rational argument and disciplined function, in order to prevent my innate depression from sliding into suicidal despair."

Eve, of course, had made no comment, but he had not needed any. He had not even needed the admiration and wonderment that she had also failed to supply, although he had certainly been glad to get a small measure of that from Cerys, all the more valuable as it had come from a young and pretty woman. He did not suppose for a moment that it would ever be given to him to touch attractive female flesh again, but that only made close-range visual contact with it more precious—perhaps only for reasons of nostalgia, but no less powerful for that.

He worked, as was his invariable habit, from five-thirty to eleven-twenty, at which point he backed up his work on a memory stick, put on his leather jacket, and went out for his daily two-mile walk.

As he had told Megan and the Reverend Usher, he intended to follow the coastal path to the north-east, in the direction of Cardigan, exploring that direction before trying out the opposite direction the following day. In order to join the path he had to walk to the very end of the St. Madoc's only street and then turn right opposite the entrance to the famous bridge that no one was allowed to cross in order to approach the house, and which only Cerys, it appeared, crossed nowadays in the opposite direction.

He did not pause to examine the bridge to the Tine very closely, but he did slow down somewhat and then looked over his shoulder as he changed direction, in order to contemplate it for twenty seconds or so.

It was constructed from reinforced concrete, presumably supported within by steel rods. The gap separating the central Tine of Morgan's Fork from the "mainland" was less than thirty feet across, and was a mere ditch, albeit a deep one, when the tide was at its lowest, although it had two or three fathoms of sea-water when the tide was in. The conduit carrying water pipes, electricity and telephone wires to the Tine was suspended underneath the bridge in a protective concrete tube of its own. The parapets to either side of the bridge were quite low, more likely to trip people up than to save them from a nasty fall, in Simon's opinion.

The entire construction, Simon knew, must be fairly recent, considerably less than a hundred years old. Before that, he supposed, there had probably been a wooden bridge instead—and perhaps, his imagination suggested, back in the dim and distant past, a drawbridge capable of turning the Tine into an island, at least while the tide was in.

At present, there was no defense at the nearer end of the bridge, although the hinge-posts were still in place where some sort of gate must have been suspended at some time in the past, but at the far end there was a grille comprised of six-foot metal spikes in an iron frame at intervals of three or four inches, pointed at the top. The gate was padlocked and carried a large notice saying: PRIVATE PROPERTY: TRESPASSERS WILL BE PROSECUTED. There was a bell-push to the right of the gate, which presumably communicated with a bell inside the house, more than half a furlong away. The bell-push was situated over a capacious mail-box, with a slot large enough to take books.

Once he had gone along the coastal path for fifty yards or so, Simon came to another bridge, this one over a gully, at the bottom of which ran the stream that emptied into the cleft between the Central and North-Eastern Tines. This was a stone bridge that must have been well over a hundred years old—one of a pair, matched by a twin spanning the gully that formed the inland extension of the cleft between the Central and South-Western Tines. It was equipped with much higher parapets

This time, Simon did pause to look over the right-hand parapet into the depths of the gully. The stream was flowing vigorously in spite of the abundant vegetation in the gully—surprisingly abundant, Simon thought, given the steepness of the sides and the fact that the sun hardly ever shone directly into the cleft. He wondered where the rivulet went as it snaked away through the fields. Perhaps it reached its ultimate source somewhere in Snowdonia? If so, its counterpart on the other side of St. Madoc might follow an equally meandering course all the way to the Brecon Beacons. On the other hand, it was not improbable that either or both flowed underground for much of their courses, threading a way through tunnels in the Cambrian rock that made up the body of this section of the Welsh mainland. Was it Cambrian? He thought so, but wasn't sure.

He couldn't hang around, though; his time was limited and he had to cover his two miles. He barely glanced over the other parapet, his gaze briefly scanning the sheer cliff on the north-eastern face of the Central Tine. The cave that Reverend Usher had mentioned was visible in the distance, completely cut off by the sea at present, although Simon wondered whether it might perhaps be accessible by walking along the shore at low tide. Not for long, if at all, he judged, and the approach would doubtless be exceedingly treacherous. Nevertheless he made a mental note to carry out a further observation at low tide, one day soon, and perhaps to see how close he could get to the cave by walking over the weed-covered rocks.

The path veered to the left, following the contour of the outward Tine, and he was able to get a better view of Nyder's Cave—or the neidr's cave—but could not see any detail of its interior. The cave on the other side would be less gloomy, as it had direct exposure to the sun at least some of the time, which this one never did. This was the sinister side of the Tine.

Almost as soon as he had made that mental note, he heard footsteps hurrying behind him, and turned abruptly. A young man was running along the path, obviously trying to catch up with him. He recognized him as one of the four he had seen in the Mermaid the previous evening: the one who had looked up at him as he was going to the Gents.

"May I speak with you, Mr. Cannick?" said the young man, in good, albeit heavily accented English, and with studied politeness.

"Certainly," Simon replied, "provided that you don't mind walking while you do it. I'm planning on going along the path for about a mile and then turning back, in order to be home again by noon. Will what you have to say fit into that time frame?"

"Oh, yes, easily," the other replied, falling into step with Simon and matching his stride with an insulting ease that gave him an uncomfortable awareness of the extent to which age was beginning to slow him down. "My name's Alun Gwynne. You recognize me from the pub? One of what the old woman you were with refers to as 'Cardi riff-raff'?"

"I remember," Simon confirmed.

"Well, I won't insult your intelligence by saying that I didn't mean to eavesdrop, because I was straining my ears from the moment I heard her squawk that you'd inherited Raven Cottage, and I realized that you had no connection with either her or the family. I heard a lot more, but not all of it, and there was a lot that I didn't understand, but I did hear that you're a writer, so I looked you up on the net when I got home. I realize that you aren't the kind of writer who writes for the newspapers, or even the kind who has a blog, but I also heard the woman from Sanderling saying that you might get an invitation to the house, and an opportunity to talk to James Murden face to face."

"She did say that," Simon confirmed, "but I've no idea whether it will actually happen, and even if it does . . ."

"I understand," Alun Gwynne cut in. "I'm not asking you to deliver a message. I've no right to ask you that or anything at all—but if you're settling permanently in the village, I'd like to explain our situation to you, so that you don't form your opinion of us on what you hear from people who call us Cardi riff-raff. I'm not asking you to take sides now, but I would like you to know why there are sides, and why the future of the village—St. Madoc as well as Morpen—hangs on how the argument between them works out."

"Fair enough," said Simon. "It sounds like something I might need to know."

"Well, the four of us you saw last night are all sons of former farm laborers, although we weren't actually brought up on farms, our folk having been displaced to Cardigan—that's how we know Welsh, because we learned as kids from our grandparents, not in school—and we weren't using it last night to exclude you so much as to exclude the old whore and the landlord, neither of whom speak it.

"At present, with our wives and kids, we're living in Morpen in what the DHSS calls emergency accommodation, but when the holiday season starts, we'll be moved out, to God knows where. There's a chronic housing shortage throughout the region, as you doubtless know, because virtually all the properties in the coastal villages are now second homes or investment properties.

"At present all of us are living on benefits, and that makes people call us scroungers and all sorts of other names, but we'd work if we could, and while we're in Morpen we could, at least for part of the year, when seasonal work becomes available on the local farms. Unfortunately, that's exactly the part of the year when we get moved on. We understand that what the DHSS can pay for our accommodation is less than what the owners of the cottages can get from letting them out to holidaymakers by the week, but understanding it doesn't mean that we approve. What we'd really like is to stay in Morpen all year round, perhaps for good but at least without the threat of being bounced round from one month to the next.

"Now, we don't know much about the ownership of the cottages—I've tried to get on to the Tine to see James Murden, but it's absolutely no go, and if you phone you always get one of the servants, who give you the brush-off. Rumor has it, though, that he'd buy up all the property he could if he weren't so strapped for cash himself, and that even without that, he has a lot of influence over the other owners. We'd really like to persuade him, if we could get the chance, that the village—both Morpen and St. Madoc—would do a lot more good for the area in the long run if the cottages became real homes, as they must originally have been, way back when . . . homes for Welsh people.

"I'm not saying that we've got anything against the Syrians who've been moved into two of the cottages in St. Madoc on the same kind of emergency basis as us, mind, but we can't help seeing that as a worrying development, and wondering whether we might get squeezed out to a greater extent than we already are. Most of the locals, of course, including the woman who lives next door to you, don't like the idea of anyone moving in that they call outsiders, whether they come from Cardigan, Bristol or Aleppo, and they prefer the cycle of holiday boom periods and quiet winters, because it's what they're used to—but you can understand that we don't see it that way. We think this is a place where we could belong, given a chance, and where we'd like to belong, so that we can bring up our kids in a better way than we're being forced to bring them up at the moment.

"To be honest, I don't even know whether James Murden can make that happen, but I'm pretty sure that if he can't, no one else can, and I'd like a chance to put our case to him, one way or another. We've all thought of writing him a letter, but even though we're not stupid and we can all write, we weren't sure that we could make the case persuasively enough to do it full justice. So, although I don't know what you might be able to do, if you wanted to do anything at all, I thought you ought to know what the situation is, because it affects you as well as us, and I didn't want to you hear everybody else's side without hearing ours. I think that's reasonable, don't you?"

"Eminently," Simon agreed, "and I'm glad that you've told me. I've come into this situation completely blind, and I must admit that it looks a great deal more complicated now I'm here than it did when I was looking at the letting agent's video of Raven Cottage. The more I know, the quicker I'll be able to get my bearings. I don't see why I shouldn't help you to draft a letter to Mr. Murden, setting out your case, if you think it will help. I don't know whether I will get to see him, and I haven't the slightest idea how the conversation will go if I do, but I'll certainly bear in mind what you've said, and if Mr. Murden raises the issue, at least I might be able to tell you what he thinks, and perhaps what his future plans are. I can't give you any promises, but you can at least be assured that I understand your concerns, and I'm not against you."

Alun Gwynne seemed delighted by that—perhaps naively. "Thanks, Mr. Cannick," he said.

Simon looked at his watch, and did an abrupt about-turn, heading back toward St. Madoc. He had been so busy listening to Alun Gwynne the he hadn't really taken much notice of the scenery, but the two of them had been climbing a shallow rise, and now that the ground was sloping away in front of them he took the opportunity to scan both the land to his left and the arm of sea to his right, with the Abbey standing tall on the Tine on the far side. He tried to savor the panorama as he walked.

There was a stand of oaks in the midst of the fields, itself not much larger than a football field, perhaps the remnant of one of the forests where Richard Hoare had imagined the Druids of old conducting their mysterious worship. The sea was gray because the sky was somewhat overcast, and the Abbey seemed a trifle grim silhouetted again the cloud. The house was quite tall, with a pitched roof, and the main chimney-stack was surmounted by a television aerial and a long spike that was presumably a lightning-conductor.

Now that the wind was in his face instead of behind him, Simon could feel the winter chill in the air.

"It must be beautiful in summer," Simon observed. "I can see why you don't like being kicked out and moved on when the area is coming into its prime."

"It's not good for the kids, see," said the young man, defensively. "And it's not good for the village not to have any kids, except for those who come on holiday. Morpen could be a real community, if the landowners could just see a little way past their pockets. It has no real facilities there now, but if there were a real community, there'd be a need, you see—for a primary school, a much bigger shop, and maybe even a bus terminus. It could come back to life, instead of being three-quarters dead, only interesting to people like the Reverend who's staying at the pub in St. Madoc. I feel sorry for the Murden girl. What is there for her here, if she gets stuck looking after the old folk up at the house? Rumor has it that the servants out there need as much looking after as the masters. This is a sick place, Mr. Cannick, and needs a rethink."

"It's a sick world, Mr. Gwynne," Simon said, sincerely, "and it all needs a rethink."

After a pause, the young man said, tentatively: "Will you be writing a book about the local mermaids, then, Mr. Cannick? Help put the place back on the map?"

"It would take a lot more than me writing about St. Madoc to put it back on the map," Simon told him ruefully. "If there were any substantial interest in the stuff I write, I probably wouldn't have ended up here."

"You're not famous, then?"

"Far from it. More and more books are published every year, but fewer and fewer people read them. But writing's all I've ever done, and all I ever will do, for as long as I last. I'm a species on the brink of extinction, about to go the way of the dinosaurs and the mermaids."

"But you don't believe there's anything in these old tales about mermaids, do you?" said Alun Gwynne, skeptically.

"Alas, no," said Simon. "I wish I could, but I tend to attribute them all to the imagination of people like me, who loved playing with ideas but didn't believe in any of them."

"None?" the young man queried.

"Not one," Simon confirmed.

That seemed to make Alun Gwynne oddly pensive. "I wouldn't go that far," he admitted. "Odd things happen, especially around Morpen and St. Madoc. Once you've been here for a while . . . well, let's just say that I hope I get to ask you again in a couple of years' time. It wouldn't surprise me if I got a different answer."

"Regarding mermaids?"

"Maybe not them . . . but there are stranger things in the sea than mermaids, and on the land too. Don't tell me you haven't heard about the two phantoms of Morgan's Fork? Everyone in Cardigan knows about them."

"The Reverend said something in the pub last night about the ghost of Owain Glyndwr."

"He's one of them—said to be still waiting patiently for the time to come to return from the grave and expel the English from Wales."

"And the other?"

"That's the Black Monk. Much older, apparently, from the days when the Abbey really was an Abbey. Best not to let him get close, it's said. No one who's ever seen his face—or what he has instead of a face—has ever lived to tell the tale."

Simon laughed. "I've heard of him before," he said. "Or at least, a monk of the same order." It wasn't until he pronounced that phrase that he remembered having made it before, the previous evening, when he had seen a monk walking along the single street of St. Madoc. It was on the tip of his tongue to ask whether St. Madoc was still a place of pilgrimage, possessed of any significant tomb or monument, but Alun Gwynne was already responding to his skepticism.

"I've never seen either of them myself, but I know people who swear that they have—and whatever people say about farm folk being bumpkins, they're not stupid. I've heard tales from people I trust . . . and they go back a long way, so it's said."

"They do always say that," Simon agreed, in a carefully neutral tone. "I'd quite like to meet the ghost of Owain Glyndwr. Does he talk?"

"So people say—in Welsh, mind. You wouldn't understand him."

"He probably spoke English too when he was alive," Simon observed. "He fought a war against them, so there must have been an incentive for him to understand their language . . . by his day, I think, the barons had stopped speaking French . . . although it must have been Old English, so perhaps I wouldn't understand him anyway. Shakespeare must have improvised his dialogue in *Henry IV*."

"I can call spirits from the vasty deep," Alun Gwynne quoted, to demonstrate that he wasn't uneducated, or stupid.

"But will they come?" said Simon, automatically, more to himself than his interlocutor.

"Not for me, thank the Lord," said the young man. "But for him . . . that might be another matter." Abruptly, he added: "Well, I'd better leave you now. See you soon, I hope."

And with that, he leapt sideways from the path and disappeared into a clump of bushes.

VI
The Webmistress

Simon realized when he looked ahead, at the junction where the path crossed the end of St. Madoc's only street, why Alun Gwynne had suddenly disappeared. Standing at the junction, evidently waiting for something, was Megan Harwyn. He didn't imagine that she could be waiting for anything but him.

"Good morning," he said as he approached her, having checked his watch to make sure that the greeting was still chronologically accurate. It was, albeit only by a couple of minutes

"Can I offer you that cup of tea now, Simon?" she asked him.

"I normally have a quick bite of lunch and then get back to work," he said, not wanting to encourage the practice of breaking into his schedule, lest it might become a habit.

"It won't take long," she assured him. "I'll give you a biscuit as well, if you're hungry—but I owe you an apology, and there are a couple of things I ought to tell you."

"Apology for what?" he said, but he fell into step behind her and allowed her to lead him past the gate of Raven Cottage all the way to Sanderling. She didn't reply to his question immediately, presumably postponing the explanation until she had opened the door and shown him in.

She ushered him into the room that was equivalent to the one he had elected to use as his study. He was somewhat taken aback by the sight of a massive triple computer-screen set on a huge desk littered with papers and books. It was obviously a serious work-station, and the fact that she had seemed so well-dressed for an old-age pensioner living in a tiny village suddenly didn't seem quite so surprising. While he sat down in an armchair and Megan went into the kitchen to make the tea, his eyes traveled around the furniture, the wallpaper and the shelves, measuring signs of subdued but obvious prosperity, and conscientious middle-class good taste.

When she returned she was carrying a tray with a teapot, complete with cosy, two china cups in saucers, a bowl of sugar lumps, complete with tongs, a jug of semi-skimmed milk, and a plate of digestive biscuits. He accepted the offer of a little milk, but refused the sugar.

"That's . . . very impressive," he said, waving a hand vaguely in the direction of the giant monitor, as he accepted the cup and saucer.

"Yes," she said, sitting down in another armchair, set at right angles to his, with the low table on which she had placed the tray between the two. She added: "Cerys came round this morning, and we had a long chat . . . about you."

"Is that the apology you owe me—for talking to Cerys about me?"

"Partly. Mostly, it's for not being entirely straight with you last night. But it's probably old news by now, since I saw you talking to one of the boys from Cardigan on the path. What did he say about me?"

"Hardly anything—just that you don't approve of James and his fellow property owners allowing the DHSS to use the local cottages as emergency accommodation for the overflow of their housing crisis."

"He didn't use the word *whore*?"

"Yes, once, but I thought it was just a casual insult."

"It wasn't. You didn't notice the Reverend's attitude last night?"

"I did notice a certain tension, but I hadn't speculated about the reason for it, and if I had . . ."

"You wouldn't have jumped to the conclusion that I'm on the game, given that I'm such a raddled old crone. Well, I'm not, any more. Haven't been for nearly twenty years, in fact, and trade had slackened off a lot before then, for obvious reasons—but there was a time when I only came here in the summer, renting Sanderling from . . . a friend. And, to put it bluntly, I was the village whore for the holiday season. In the winter, I moved back to the city . . . usually Cardiff, but not always. I got around a fair bit in my youth. That was a long time ago, of course, but people round here have long memories, and there's such a drastic shortage of recent gossip that old gossip lasts for decades. So, although you certainly wouldn't think it to look at me now—and you surely didn't think it when you first saw me last night—everybody who knows me here still thinks of me as the village whore. It was something of a pleasure to meet someone who didn't, so I didn't tell you, even when we said goodnight. I should have warned you, because I knew you'd be bound to hear it from someone else before today was out."

"I can assure you that no apology is necessary for that," Simon said, almost offended by the thought, and feeling that the ornamental cups and the tea cosy had become slightly surreal. "It doesn't make the slightest difference to me."

"Hang on—you haven't heard it all yet. One of the few advantages of whoring as a profession is that your working day is actually quite short, so you have a lot of spare time. At least, you do if you're not a drug addict and don't spend all your time getting drunk with other whores. I wasn't, and I didn't, so I had to have a hobby. So, way back when, at the very beginning of it all, I bought myself a new toy to play with, and got hooked: a Sinclair ZX."

"Ah!" said Simon, glancing once again at the state-of-the-art computer equipment.

74

"Exactly," she said. "So, cutting the exceedingly long story short, I upgraded my equipment every time something new came out, upgrading my skills along the way. I was a member of programming clubs even before there was an online for all that to move on to, and when the web began to grow . . . well, I was in on the ground floor. I couldn't compete with all the hot-shot nerds with degrees, obviously, but I knew my way around, so, in my small way, I was one of the pioneering website-designers in my specialized field. I still am, albeit on a much smaller scale than the people who've gone into it industrially, with massive capital and global turnover. Nowadays, I'm a little fish in a very big pond, but I get by, and my . . . associates value my understanding and my expertise."

"Associates?" Simon queried.

"I specialize in designing websites for prostitutes. Naturally, I like to think of myself as a mother goose helping to protect her goslings from as much as possible of the abuse inherent in their line of work. My commissions are extremely reasonable by industry standards, and there's absolutely nothing illegal about what I do, but in the eyes of a lot of people, I'm still living on immoral earnings. Given that I work with whores, and do business with whores, I can hardly dodge the label entirely. Not many people hereabouts have an exact idea of what it is I actually do, let alone how, but it's not hard for them to figure out that I'm not living on a minimum state pension, and they rightly figure that even though I gave up soliciting men in the Mermaid many years ago, I'm still somehow concerned with the sex trade. It doesn't take more than vague suspicion and murky rumor to generate the kind of attitude that the likes of the Reverend Alexander Usher take so little trouble to dissimulate. I figured that you were entitled to know who it was that you'd accidentally moved in next door to, just in case you wanted to start cutting me dead, the way James Murden does."

"I don't," Simon said. "I still say that it makes no difference to me."

"To tell you the truth, I had guessed that it wouldn't, after googling you thoroughly last night. It's still a relief to hear you say so, though. If I have to have a permanent next-door neighbor, as it seems that I do, I'd like it to be someone I can get along with, in a civilized manner."

"Me too," said Simon.

"Good. You're not too upset, either, about my talking to Cerys about you behind your back?"

"No—as Oscar Wilde said, the only thing worse than being talked about is not being talked about. Writers love being talked about. And I haven't told you anything in confidence. I have no secrets."

"You might think that, but there's a possibility, and perhaps a strong one, that you simply don't know that you have them—or, at least, don't know how important they might be . . . to others, if not to you. It didn't take me that long to find Evelyne Augerrand, once I started digging—it's wonderful what you can find online nowadays, without even hacking into anything sealed. I know more about her than you do now—and so does Cerys, and hence James . . . which is why I'm apologizing for breaking my semi-promise to give you any information I found first. I have my reasons . . . but as a matter of interest, you do know more than you let on last night, don't you?"

"Nothing but rumor," Simon said. "Hearing rumors doesn't constitute knowing—especially scurrilous rumors. But yes, neighbors of the house where I rented my flat did take the trouble to mention that it had once been a knocking shop, that the two old ladies who lived in the other apartments were ex-whores, and that the one who freed up my flat by dying not long before I moved in had also been an ex-whore. It didn't make any difference to me. It was a nice flat—I was very lucky to get it."

"I hate to sound like James," Megan said, "but I'm not sure that luck had anything to do with it. And if I'm not sure, you can be certain that James has got a strong whiff of the chain of destiny. We'll be able to judge when we see how quickly

Cerys comes back once she's passed on the information I've given her. Again, though, cutting the story short, as you're eager to get back to your routine, Evelyne is family—a Murden, that is—albeit a lost sheep born a long way from the Abbey. And the mother from whom she inherited Raven was, unsurprisingly, also a Murden, by the name of Lilith: the younger sister of Matthew Murden, James's father. Those are hard, provable facts, as is the fact that the person to whom Evelyne has left the house in which she lived is her natural granddaughter, via a daughter named Angela, born to her early in her career, father unknown, nowadays known as Angela Richardson. The granddaughter, by contrast, was the child of a legitimate marriage. All else, so far, is speculation—but I would like that DNA sample now."

"To compare with whose?"

"Angela Richardson's. She's in her early eighties now, but still alive. I can get that sample easily enough—thanks to my business network I have contacts all over England, including half a dozen in Bristol. You're probably acquainted with one or two of them."

"I can assure you that I'm not. I've never used prostitutes." While making the protest, Simon calculated that if Angela Richardson was in her early eighties, she would have had to have been a very young mother to have been able to give birth to him—not that he could believe for an instant that she had. Megan Harwyn seemed to be reading a lot into the coincidence that a descendant of the Murdens had left Raven Cottage to someone who happened to live in the flat downstairs.

"I never knew a man who admitted that he did use prostitutes, even while shopping for one," she continued, "but it doesn't matter. You, I'll believe. The point is that I can get the other sample."

She opened a drawer in the desk and produced a small spatula, of the kind used or taking cheek swabs, in a sterile package. She broke the sheath and handed him the spatula.

"You're serious?" he said, unable to believe it, even though he was in an alien world.

"Absolutely. No secrets, you said. Prove it."

Simon took the spatula, scraped the inside of his cheek and handed it back. Megan Harwyn popped it into a tiny test tube, sealed it carefully, and replaced it in the drawer. Simon recovered from the shock rapidly enough, telling himself that if he could cope with talking ravens, giving a sample of his DNA to a webmistress for brothel advertising was something he could surely take in his stride.

"You think that I didn't get the flat coincidentally," he said, summarizing what now seemed an obvious deduction. "You think that Eve wanted me to have it—arranged for me to have it. Did she engineer the break-up of my marriage, too, so that I'd be looking for accommodation when her former associate died?"

"I doubt it—but it wouldn't surprise me if she'd been monitoring your situation from a distance for a very long time, if she knew, or even suspected, that you were her grandson, born to and abandoned by her daughter before her marriage."

"That's ridiculous. I can't believe it."

"And you might very well be right not to. The calculus of probability is on your side. But so far as I'm concerned, the point is that James—who doesn't believe in the calculus of probability—*will* be able to believe it, and will be extremely anxious for me to test the hypothesis, if possible. And it is possible to test it, if your DNA can be compared with someone who might or might not be your mother.

"But why . . . ?"

"Why will James find it so easy to believe? Because, from his point of view, the house that your flat was in is utterly trivial, no matter what its market price might have been. You thought that leaving Raven Cottage to you was a kind of consolation prize, because Evelyne had to keep the inheritance of the house intact—in fact, you said that her solicitor told you as much. But in James's eyes, the house was the consolation prize and Raven Cottage the pot of gold. And James will want to believe, unless and until he gets proof to the contrary, that

Evelyne wouldn't have short-changed her granddaughter by giving Raven Cottage to someone else, unless she had a very good reason for doing so."

"I only talked to her when she was lonely and dying," Simon said. "I held her hand."

"And that might, indeed, be all there was to it. Rationally, in terms of common-or-garden economic calculations, you're doubtless correct. But James is a Murden, and this is St. Madoc, where a different logic applies. His calculations are of a very different order. Not to put too fine a point on it, he's as crazy as a belfry full of bats. In a way, I wish he wasn't, but he is, and I have to deal with him on that basis, if I want him to pay attention to me."

"And you're falling over yourself to humor his fantasy, even though he's been cutting you dead for the last God knows how many years?"

"Because of that. James and I have a complicated history—that's of no importance to you. I have my own reasons for dumping this on him—but I do owe you an apology for having done it behind your back. Hence the cup of tea and the chat. Refill?"

"No thanks," said Simon. "I really must be getting back to work. I'm late, and I want to reestablish my routine as soon as possible, and settle back into it. Thanks for telling me what you've found, though—I appreciate it. You will keep me informed of . . . future developments, won't you?"

"Of course." Megan smiled, perhaps simply glad that Simon hadn't taken offense, although Simon couldn't help suspecting that there was a hint of irony about the smile.

The doorbell rang as Simon was already on his way out. Although Megan hurried after him, he opened the door before she could overtake him.

Cerys Murden was standing on the doorstep. "I thought I might find you here, Mr. Cannick," she said. "I rang the bell at Raven first, but got no answer. James would like to invite you to visit him and my aunts at the Abbey."

Simon glanced to Megan, who said nothing, but whose face had *I told you so* written all over it in the language of ironic smiles.

"That's very kind," said Simon. "Please tell him that I accept with pleasure. As I told you, I have a prior engagement this evening, but I'm free the following night and all subsequent nights."

Cerys bit her lip. "James would like you to visit him and my aunts at the Abbey *now*."

"This afternoon?"

"This minute."

Simon's mouth was already open to say: *I have to work this afternoon*, but the words did not come out.

Megan Harwyn still had *I told you so* written all over her face, even more flamboyantly. Cerys, by contrast, looked manifestly anxious. She clearly did not know the extent of the power that pretty young women routinely have over nostalgic old men. She thought that the only lever she had was James Murden's authority, and was frightened that its present exercise was far too brusque.

"Very well," Simon said, eventually, trying to make it sound more like a generous concession than an inevitable capitulation. "I just have to pop into Raven for a few minutes, and then I'm all yours."

Cerys sighed with relief. Only then did she turn to look at Megan Harwyn, with a mixture of enquiry and muted resentment.

"Don't worry, dear," Megan said. "I've brought him up to date. He knows what I told you. He's not going in unprepared."

Her smile almost changed into a laugh at the idea that Simon was not going to the Abbey unprepared. Clearly she thought that, however much she had told him, last night and just now, there was no way on earth that anyone sane could be prepared for a visit to the Abbey.

VII
The Abbey

"Thanks for playing along, Mr. Cannick," Cerys said, as they walked toward the bridge. "James does get excited sometimes, but I've never seen him like this. I couldn't see anything in the message I passed on from Miss Harwyn to get excited about, and he usually freezes up if her name is mentioned, but something has really woken him up . . ."

She paused as they were about to set foot on the bridge, shook her head slightly, as if to clear it, and then she looked him in the eyes, and said: "Look, Mr. Cannick, Miss Harwyn has probably told you that James and my aunts are completely mad, and even if she hasn't, Mr. Usher might have put that idea into your head . . . and even if neither of them did, it's an idea that you might easily form of your own accord, at first glance. I can't say for certain that they're not—they're certainly very old, and they've been locked up in that old house together for a long time now. If it weren't for my visits, James having to learn to use the internet to regain some control over of the family's financial concerns—or try, at least— they could easily have lost all contact with the outside world when my mother left. But I really don't think they're mad. If they say some strange things . . . well, quite honestly, doesn't everyone? What I do know is that they're benevolent, and kind, and . . . I wouldn't like to see them upset, not because it might make things even more difficult for me than they are, but because . . . well, I don't want them to be upset. So if you could just bear with them—think of it as humoring them, if you like—I'd very grateful."

She was still looking Simon in the eyes, with a pleading expression. He still thought that she was unaware of the effect that her youth and beauty were capable of inducing, but that lack of confidence only made her concern and her appeal all the more poignant.

She didn't dare wait to confront his reaction head on. She moved across the concrete slab, taking a key from the pocket of her jeans.

"All my life," Simon told her, "people have suspected me of being crazy. Mostly, they settle for calling me eccentric, but that's just being politely condescending. And they're right, in a way. Writing is bound to seem mad in itself, as a way of life, and the kinds of writing I do are bound to seem madder than most to the average dull and materialistic mind. I'm arrogant enough, though, to think that, in fact, I'm more perfectly sane than the people who think I'm mad. When you look at how the label of madness is applied, it just means people who don't think the same way as the people who are applying it. Personally, I'm proud of not thinking the same things as most other people, and not living the same way they do, because I think the way most people think and live stinks. So, if most people—including Megan Harwyn and Alexander Usher—think your great-grandfather and your great aunts are mad, I'm far more likely to be for them than against them."

That won him a smile, but she didn't seem convinced. She pulled the padlock through the bars in order to lock the grille behind them, and then started walking toward the house at a slightly faster pace.

"I haven't had a chance to start reading the book you gave me, I'm afraid," she said. "James has it. He says that he does have some of your books, in the library, but he had no idea until last night that you wrote fiction under other names. He'd never had occasion to look you up on the internet. When he did, last night, he was already excited—this morning's excitement was on top of that, which might be why it constituted an overdose. He showed the book you gave me to my aunts. Felicia was already hyped up, and she was really impressed by the book, but Melusine pretended not to be, although she was already worked up too. Melusine doesn't like to let anything show, so she's difficult to fathom.

"This morning, when I told them what Miss Harwyn had told me to tell them, they both said that that they remembered a Lilith who had a daughter called Evelyne. I looked in the old family Bible, where all births in the family since the

1780s are supposedly recorded on the inside of the cover and the fly-leaf, and there doesn't seem to be a Lilith or Evelyne among the births recorded there, but there are more than a dozen names that have been deliberately scratched out, and one of them comes directly after Matthew—that's James's father—and could easily have been a sibling, even though James has never mentioned a younger sister in my presence. The names aren't scratched out because they're dead, I assume . . . although there are a lot of death-dates that were never filled in, presumably because the person in charge of entering them either didn't know them or didn't care."

That speech had taken them more than halfway to the house, and the manner of its delivery was suggestive of a barely suppressed nervousness.

"I'll try as hard as I can not to upset anyone, Cerys," Simon said, softly, "but I have to confess that I'm completely at sea here. I really don't understand why everyone is getting so excited . . . and whatever story Megan Harwyn has cooked up in order to make out that I might have been related to the old lady I knew as Eve, I can't believe it. I don't understand why it would be of any importance to James even if it were true, but if he thinks it is, he might be due for a disappointment."

"I don't understand either," Cerys said. "They keep me carefully locked out of some of the family secrets—literally, in the case of the library and the cellars. I was only able to consult the Bible because it's kept on the lectern in the old chapel. Mr. Usher told me far more about the family legends, as well as Seymour and Rhys, than grandfather ever has. When I asked grandfather about some of the things the Reverend had said, he agreed that he'd been told some of the same things, but he also said that the stories had been distorted, and that the truth is a lot stranger than Mr. Usher thinks."

Simon would have liked to follow that up, but they had reached the main door of the house, formed of solid planks of ancient oak. It wasn't locked. Cerys opened it herself and closed it behind them. The vestibule had a tiled floor and paneled walls. The floor had been washed not long ago and the faint reek of disinfectant fluid was still detectable, but when he looked up at the high ceiling he saw cobwebs in the corners. Evidently, whoever did the housework was more comfortable with a mop than a feather duster.

They went through another door into a carpeted hallway some twenty meters long, with four varnished wooden doors to the right, three to the left, all closed, and a staircase at the far end. The carpet was worn and the pattern faded, and Simon judged that it had to be at least as old him.

Cerys opened the second door to the left and showed him into what was now set up as a dining room, with a heavy oak table in the center of the area to the right of the door and six chairs in what Simon's inexpert mind guessed to be Queen Anne style. Although they seemed to be reproductions rather than actually dating back to the early 1700s, they too were obviously older than he was.

The first impression given by the three people who immediately rose from armchairs to the left of the door and hurried to greet their guest, however, was that they were considerably older than the furniture. That antiquity did not prevent them from moving with a certain agility as well as a certain grace. Their rapidity in claiming his attention cut off any detailed examination of the room, but he did observe a tall item of furniture behind the armchairs, presumably custom-built, designed to provide a head-high perch for a bird of substantial dimensions. Lenore was sitting there, seemingly unmoved by the sudden flurry of activity, and perhaps asleep, or entranced.

Cerys stepped forward in order to make the introductions, but the privilege was smoothly usurped by her great-grandfather.

"Mr. Cannick!" he exclaimed offering his hand. "It's a great pleasure to meet you. I know your work. When I heard that you had moved into the village to become a permanent resident, I was utterly delighted. You can't imagine what a pleasure it will be to have a man like you as a neighbor. I hope you'll forgive the urgency of my invitation, but a man of my age doesn't like to put off until tomorrow what he can do immediately, lest tomorrow never comes. We've taken the liberty of preparing a little lunch for you—just a cold collation, I fear, but you've probably found out already about the delivery problems we have nowadays. But I'm getting carried away. Might I introduce my sister, Felicia, and my cousin Melusine? Felicia will be particularly glad to have you in the village. She's always been a great lover of literature."

Melusine was almost as tall as James—only an inch shorter than Simon—but Felicia was several inches shorter. Although both were white-haired, and Felicia and Melusine both had their hair neatly tied back in a bun, there would have been no obvious family resemblance between them even had they been the same height. Felicia's eyes, behind spectacles with brown plastic rims, were blue, her nose was a trifle snub, and she was wearing red lipstick that, although by no means garish, did give her a slightly coquettish air. Melusine had gray eyes, her nose had a more prominent bridge, her lips were pale and her spectacles had metal rims. If she was wearing any make-up at all, Simon judged, it was only a carefully applied concealer. In spite of that lack of concession to conventional femininity, however, she did not seem in the least masculine, or even stern.

Both women, Simon presumed, had been beautiful in their youth, and they still retained the vestiges of that beauty in their attitude and their stance. They were not stooped, and they were not stout. Time had worked on their features inexorably, but not cruelly. It was impossible to tell how long ago that glorious youth had been, but they gave the impression of being older than Megan Harwyn. They were both wearing full-length dresses with high neck-lines, Felicia in pale blue and Melusine in a color somewhere between amber and chestnut brown to which Simon could not put a precise name. Both were looking at him with extreme attention—and, he thought, affection.

James Murden, not entirely to Simon's surprise, seemed to have aged just as well. He too stood upright, without the artificial stiffness sometimes affected effortfully by old military men; his straightness seemed relaxed. His eyes were blue too, but a less intense blue than Felicia's. His hair was neatly but simply trimmed, with a parting on the left, thin without the hairline receding too obviously. He wore a thin moustache and a trimmed beard, as white as his hair, and his complexion was also very pale. He was wearing a black suit, but his beige waistcoat and white shirt dispelled any suggestion of an undertaker or a clergyman, and the suit was slightly ill-fitting. Slim without being skeletal, he gave the impression that he had once been not merely handsome but dashing—a very long time ago.

Simon bowed to each of the women in turn, once James Murden had released his hand, noted that Felicia's smile in reply seemed even warmer than Melusine's, and said, more than a trifle awkwardly: "It's very kind of you to invite me, Mr. Murden."

"James," said the old man. "And we shall call you Simon, if we may. It's informal, I know—I'm sure that in the old days, the legendary Seymour Murden always addressed his famous literary guests as Mr. Peacock, Mr. Shelley and Mr. Southey, but time has moved on, has it not? Sit here, will you, to my right, opposite Felicia."

Simon took the place indicated. The "cold collation" set out on the table was, as James had said, quite simple, consisting of an elementary salad with cheese, hard-boiled eggs and sliced ham, and a large basket of bread rolls. It had already been served on to individual plates, and the lettuce was a trifle wilted. The cutlery was silver-plated and the glasses crystal.

"Will you have a little wine?" James asked, picking up a decanter containing white wine of anonymous provenance.

"Please," Simon answered. Normally, he only drank water with his midday meal and his evening meal, but he thought that a little fortification might be helpful.

He did not notice until Felicia and Melusine had taken the seats on the far side of the table, that Cerys had slipped out of the room, and that only four places had been set, leaving the chair to his right and the one at the far end of the table, opposite James, vacant.

"Did the Reverend Usher tell you, Simon, that the house had been host to eminent litterateurs in the Georgian Era?" James asked, as Felicia and Melusine began to ply their forks nervously, setting an example. James got the impression, however, that they were both listening avidly, and studying him covertly with an intense curiosity.

"He did say something about your ancestor entertaining notable people back then," Simon recalled, "but he didn't mention any names."

"No sense of priorities," James said. "He thinks me rude, I suppose, for refusing to receive him in the house, but there are good reasons for that. Yes, Seymour was a great lover of literature, as Felicia is—and so am I, in my own way, although I must admit that I take more after Rhys the Engineer than Seymour. Seymour was fortunate enough to entertain some of the luminaries of his era, although he was never able to entice Lord Byron, and Mr. Coleridge was unable to accompany Mr. Southey. We have made our slight contribution to the heritage of English literature, though. You've written abundantly about the Romantics I understand?"

"I've done an enormous number of reference-book articles," Simon admitted, "including pieces on a great many nineteenth-century writers, but nothing out of the ordinary. I taught English literature part-time for nearly twenty years to A-level students, but the syllabus was very restricted—Shelley was included, but not Peacock or Southey. They actually stayed here, then?"

"Oh yes—Mr. Southey had a room in the house, but Mr. Peacock stayed in one of the cottages on three or four occasions. Once—the second time, I believe—he brought Mr. Shelley with him. That would have been in 1814, I believe."

Simon looked around the room, as if suddenly equipped with new eyes. "By your *contribution to English literature*," he said, "you mean that *Nightmare Abbey* is based on St. Madoc's Abbey?"

James laughed. "Exceedingly loosely, if so," he said. "In fact, I was thinking more of *The Misfortunes of Elphin*. But yes, I can confess it to you, since you're a writer and will understand, there was an unfortunate incident during that second visit, of which there is an echo of sorts in *Nightmare Abbey*."

"Concerning Scythrop's encounter with the supposed mermaid?" Simon suggested.

"Precisely. Mr. Shelley was an impressionable young man, I understand, and he was in a state of some distress at the time of his visit. Very interested in the folklore associated with the Abbey, as might be expected, and having taken laudanum to soothe his agitation, he suffered an unfortunate hallucination. Seymour and Mr. Peacock had some difficulty calming him down, I fear. Mr. Peacock visited again, but not for some time; he could not bring Mr. Shelley with him, alas."

"He was dead by then?"

"Tragically."

"But Peacock had already published *Nightmare Abbey* by then, modeling Scythrop on Shelley, somewhat less respectfully than the earlier satirical portrait of him in *Headlong Hall*?"

That won a nod of approval from Felicia and a sympathetic smile, but she remained silent, while James continued: "That's correct. It was probably coincidence, of course."

"I'm sorry," Simon said, having lost the thread slightly while focusing on Felicia's apparent sympathy. "What was probably coincidence?"

"Shelley's death by drowning."

Probably coincidence? Simon thought—but the implications opened up by that remark were not something that he wanted to investigate for the moment, while the conversation was proceeding in a sane and civilized manner that he had not expected.

Apparently, he was not the only one who felt that the subject ought to be changed, because Melusine said, abruptly: "You knew Lilith's daughter Evelyne, I understand, Simon. That's the real reason you're here, as I'm sure Cerys explained. James is quite right to say that it's an honor to have a writer of your stature in St. Madoc, but what excited us in particular was the possibility of having news of Evelyne. She's by no means the only family member of whom we lost track during the turbulent twenties, but . . . it was so long ago, as you'll understand, that it's more a matter of research than memory for us, but there might be reasons for thinking that the estrangement of Evelyne's mother was a particularly serious loss, or was felt as such. When you meet Grandmother . . ."

Perhaps annoyed at the interruption of his own line of discourse, which must have been carefully planned, James cut her off.

"I fear, Melusine, that you're anticipating a little too much. Grandmother is very unwell, and I fear that it might not be possible to introduce Mr. Cannick to her for some time—certainly not today, at least."

"But as you said yourself, James," Melusine put in, her voice heavy with irony, "it's as well for people of our age not to put off till tomorrow what ought to be done today, lest the grim reaper arrive before the dawn."

Simon could see that James was having to make a prodigious effort not to let his redoubled irritation show, but he succeeded, after a fashion.

"All in good time, Melusine," he said. "The grim reaper, as you call her, has long had an understanding with dear Ceridwen. But you're probably right to chide me for talking about literary matters, when we should be more concerned with . . ." He turned slightly in his seat to emphasize the fact that he was addressing Simon. "You must already have been informed, albeit in a confused and probably mistaken fashion, that our family history is somewhat troubled. Frankly, I don't understand the detail of what happened in the aftermath of the Great War, because I was too young at the time, and Grandmother's memories are . . . confused. Suffice it to say that I—we, that is—are not only excited by your arrival in the village because of your intellectual status, but because you inherited Raven Cottage from a daughter of a family member who was once reckoned very precious, by *all* of us."

The manner in which he stressed the word all suggested strongly to Simon that there had been, and perhaps still was, some dispute regarding that preciousness. Melusine was still looking at him expectantly, whereas Felicia's expression was more sympathetic, as if she, at least, would have been perfectly happy to continue discussing "Mr. Peacock" and "Mr. Shelley."

"I'm not sure that there's anything much I can tell you," he said, apologetically. "I only knew Eve—that was the name by which I knew her—as a neighbor. In the last few months of her life, I helped the care workers who were looking after her to make her a little more comfortable. I did her shopping, and I kept her company in the evenings. She could still speak clearly enough to make herself understood, but it was an effort, so I did almost all the talking, and she really didn't tell me anything about her life, or her feelings. I didn't even know her full name until the solicitor came to tell me that she'd left Raven Cottage to me, and that was a complete surprise. She never mentioned St. Madoc, or the name Murden. I'm sorry."

"But you held her hand," Melusine put in. "Cerys said that you held her hand."

"Yes, I did," Simon agreed. "The care workers did an excellent job of attending to her needs, but they had other clients, and were always a little hurried. I had time to spare, so I was able simply to sit with her, and to provide a little extra human contact. Really, it was almost nothing—certainly nothing that merited a mention in her will. I felt a little guilty about accepting it, to be honest, but as I was going to be turfed out of the apartment, and the general level of rents had gone up so much while I was living there, it would have been difficult for me to find other accommodation in Bristol, and it was a case of any port in a storm."

James Murden was frowning. "But surely," he said, "you must be quite well off. All those books . . ."

"I fear not," Simon said. "As I explained to Cerys last night, it's very easy nowadays to publish prolifically and earn next to nothing. I'm very flattered to discover that you've read some of my books, all the more so because so few people have. The ones you have were presumably published in the days when I was still clinging to a marginal existence in the commercial sector, but they were published in editions of two or three hundred, almost all of which went to libraries, and have probably have been discarded by now—my PLR returns certainly suggest that that's the case. My more recent publications wouldn't bring in enough to pay for the paper and printer ink, if I still had to produce an actual typescript—mercifully, everything is electronic now, so my running costs are negligible—but I actually live, quite frugally, on my bits of pension. Such savings as I accumulated during the years when I was making reasonably good money were wiped out seven years ago, in the aftermath of my divorce."

James took all that aboard effortlessly, nodding as if it explained things that had puzzled him. "I'm sorry," he said. "Cerys did tell me what you'd said to her, but I hadn't quite grasped the import of it. You were actually in need, then, when Evelyne took you in?"

"She didn't *take me in*. I simply went to the local letting agent when my wife threw me out and asked what flats he had available. I took the one that seemed most affordable. I paid the rent to the agency. I had no idea that Eve was my landlady until the solicitor told me. I know that Megan Harwyn wants to read something into that, but I think she's misrepresenting the situation, for some motive beyond my understanding. I don't want you to be deceived into thinking that I'm something I'm not. It really was just a coincidence that I happened to end up living downstairs from Eve, and it really was just an act of kindness for her to leave me Raven Cottage, presumably because she knew that I'd be given notice to quit the flat I was in and knew that I'd be in difficulties thereafter."

"It's not as simple as that, Simon," said Melusine. "There are other things to be taken into account—especially Lenore."

"Lenore?" Simon queried.

"Yes. Surely you can see that it's . . . unusual that she came to tap on your window last night."

Simon hesitated, remembering the illusion that had convinced him, briefly, that the bird had spoken to him, but then he simply conceded: "Very unusual—but I don't know what you might be reading into it."

"That is a problem," Melusine agreed, "and a bush that James is being very careful to beat round, perhaps for good reasons . . . but as you've spoken to the Reverend, who has been kind enough to tell Cerys at great length about the results of his research into the history and legendry of our family, and obviously loves talking about it to anyone who shows a flicker of interest, you probably find James's reticence as frustrating as I do. Wouldn't you prefer it if we simply laid our cards on the table, even at the risk of your thinking that we're all insane?"

James was pale in any case, but Simon had the impression that he would have gone white with suppressed fury had there been any margin for him to do so. All he actually said was: "That really isn't called for, Melusine," in a tone in which he contrived to maintain a conspicuous mildness, but he turned to Simon then, and said: "Melusine is right, of course. I *am* beating around the bush, but with good reason. I feel at something of a disadvantage, not knowing what the Reverend Usher and . . . Miss Harwyn might have told you about us. All I know for sure is that it was probably highly misleading . . . but you're an imaginative man, and, more importantly, a skeptical one. I hope that you haven't have taken what they told you too seriously, and that you'll have time enough, as you get to know us, to form your own opinion of us."

All that Simon could think of to say was: "I have an open mind . . . and, for the present, one that's lost in confusion."

"Eventually," Melusine said, mildly, "we shall have to make the attempt to clear up that confusion, whatever the risk, and however Megan Harwyn's machinations play out. Don't you think James, that we ought to take the opportunity to start now?"

James had obviously not intended the conversation to take that direction so soon, but he capitulated. "Of course," he said. "If only I knew where to start . . ."

"Perhaps it would help," Simon suggested, "if I asked one or two questions, which might help to clarify some of the issues that are puzzling me."

"I'm not certain that it would," James opined, "but I can understand that you feel entitled. What would you like to ask?"

Simon cleared his throat. "I hope you won't think that I'm being indelicate," he said, "but you did mention, just now, that you were too young in the 1920s to understand the details of what the Reverend Usher calls the Great Murden Schism . . . which implies that you're well over a hundred years old. And you refer to the invalid to whom I might or might not be introduced at some stage as your grandmother . . . which implies that she might be nearer two hundred. Is that really the case?"

James only hesitated momentarily before shrugging his shoulders and saying: "Yes it is. No one seems to be prepared to believe it, but it's true. There are complications, but the simple fact is that certain members of the family, for whatever reason, are extraordinarily long-lived. Do you find that impossible to believe, Simon?"

"Actually, no," Simon said. "In some ways, if one thinks about it from an objective viewpoint, there's more mystery in the fact that bodies wear out and decay at such a rapid rate, when there seems to be no physical reason why they shouldn't continue to renew themselves indefinitely. The modern fashion is to take anecdotal accounts of extraordinary longevity among animals with a pinch of salt, but there's no doubt that the lifespans of some bird species vary enormously, and that accounts of parrots living to well over a hundred can't be discounted." He glanced significantly at Lenore.

James Murden emitted an enormous sigh of relief. "You have no idea, Simon, how glad I am to hear you say that. I have to confess, though, that the rest of the story might be a lot harder to swallow. I've ordered copies of a number of your works of fiction from amazon, and I've almost reached the end of *The Bells of Ys*, but so far, all I really have to go on are the titles. I notice that there's one called *The Seventh Element*, and I wanted particularly to ask you about that one. Would you mind explaining the title?"

"Of course. Plainly, it doesn't refer to elements in the modern sense of the periodic table, but to the four elements acknowledged by the ancients, which are really the three familiar states of matter—solid, liquid and gaseous—and the agent primarily responsible for the familiar transitions between them: electromagnetic energy, manifest as heat. The story plays with the idea that there might conceivably be other, rarer, states of matter, and other agents of transition . . . or transmutation, if you prefer that term. It was published as science fiction, because that was the label most convenient for marketing, but I prefer to think of it as metaphysical fantasy."

James was nodding fervently. "Yes," he said, "I guessed as much." Melusine still seemed annoyed, presumably because she thought that James was going about his project in the wrong way, but Felicia's silent sympathy seemed still to be growing stronger.

"It's just playing with ideas," Simon stressed. "It's not something I *believe*."

"Of course, of course," said James, "but you had the idea. You've had a great many ideas, in the course of your career. More than eighty novels, in all."

"That's the current total," Simon agreed. "Most of the early ones are hack space opera, though, because that was the softest market at the time, and for a long time, my principal motive for writing fiction was simply to produce something saleable. It was only when the job turned into a vocation that I began to develop the metaphysical fantasy, for which there was never any conspicuous market demand, and even then I mostly stuck to conventional motifs—vampires, werewolves and ghosts—for a while, because editors and readers found them familiar, and they went through waves of fashionability. *The Bells of Ys* and *The Seventh Element* belong to the beginning of the third wave of my career, when the commercial sector had effectively given up on me, which meant that I was free to write whatever I liked . . . as long as I didn't expect to make any money from it."

"Would you mind telling us a little about your attitude to ghosts?" James asked, swiftly. "Just as a matter of playing with ideas, obviously . . . unless, of course, you actually do believe in such manifestations?" He was determinedly ignoring Melusine's ostentatious sighs of frustration.

"The ghost of Owain Glyndwr, for instance?" Simon countered, feeling that he was entitled to a little teasing retaliation. "He's sometimes seen around these parts, I gather? Have any of you seen him yourselves?"

James exchanged glances with both Felicia and Melusine.

"We all have," said Felicia, breaking her silence at last.

"And so might you, if you stay here for long," said Melusine. "Certainly, if you are, in fact, related to us."

"But the matter isn't as simple as people generally assume," James was quick to put in. "That's why I'm asking you about the ideas you've . . . played with. I really would like to know."

"I've written numerous stories in which ghosts play some part," Simon said, obligingly, "including *The Bells of Ys*, where the bells are ghostly presences of a sort, emanating from the seabed where my version of Ys was absorbed, although they only ring within the mind. Mostly, my assumption is that all apparitions, sonic or visual, are in the mind of the hearer or beholder, requiring psychological explanation rather than any kind of physical explanation, but I have occasionally redesigned the universe speculatively in such a way that personal residues of a kind can survive the death of the body, involving some alternative state of matter like the ones featured in *The Seventh Element*. There's a conventional notion, almost a cliché, that posits that ghosts that stick around, the haunting kind, have some kind of unfinished business to which they're endeavoring to attend—missions to complete. That's an idea I've played with on more than one occasion, involving ghosts that have to be deliberately generated, using some kind of necrological magic, either preliminary, on the part of the individual who becomes manifest as a ghost, or retrospectively, by another interested party."

"Good, good," said James, evidently very satisfied by that summation. "And what about the Sargasso Sea?"

Simon blinked, not having expected that abrupt change of subject. "That's not a notion I've employed in my fiction," he said, "although I've had occasion to refer to it in my nonfiction, especially in reference-book articles on William Hope Hodgson. It's an interesting myth."

"Myth?" James queried.

"Well, not in the sense of being entirely invented. Obviously, ships did have problems at one time with floating weed in the Atlantic, especially in the area that later came to be called the Bermuda triangle, although the travelers' tales relating to it were exaggerated. And there's the matter of the eels' spawning-ground, obviously: seriously weird, but nevertheless true. Why all the eels that migrate to freshwater habitats all over the Atlantic coast in the early spring return in autumn to a particular area of the seabed in order to breed is a genuine mystery."

James nodded his head, seemingly having become pensive. Simon thought that it might be time to take the initiative again, and said: "Are you carefully refraining from asking about mermaids, or are you just saving it for last?"

James was now sufficiently relaxed to smile at that. "I was coming to the morgens and the neider," he said, "but as I told you, the matter is complicated. Before I start playing with ideas myself . . . well, since you've brought it up, perhaps you'd like to play with that idea yourself?"

"Again," Simon said, "it's not something extensively featured in my fiction, but I have written a couple of stories about sirens, concentrating on the singing rather than their supposed hybrid physique—although, as with the bells of Ys, the siren songs in my stories are inside the minds of their hearers rather than constituting vibrations in the air. I must confess, though, to an enduring fascination with the evolutionary fantasies set out in *Telliamed* and Restif de la Bretonne's work—something of a hobby-horse of mine—and the role played in their scheme by marine humans."

James was nodding furiously, but Melusine leaned forward and said: "You've lost me, I'm afraid. Those references are completely unfamiliar to me."

Felicia nodded, to signify that she too was unfamiliar with them in spite of being "a great reader."

Simon exchanged a glance with James, whose expression invited him to do the honors.

"*Telliamed* is a book by an eighteenth-century French geologist called Benoît de Maillet," he explained. "Struck by the observation that many rock strata, including some in high mountains, were full of fossils that he correctly identified as the remains of mollusk shells, he realized that the Earth's surface had undergone enormous upheavals in the past, which had raised up what was once the bed of the sea to create continental lands. He also realized that the strata in question were sedimentary rocks that must have taken millions of years to deposit. He came up with a theory of evolution that suggested that all land animals, including human beings, must have developed from marine animals by some kind of metamorphic process extending over many generations, and he tried to find evidence for that in accounts of hybrid creatures—among which accounts of mermaids featured prominently. His ideas were regarded as dangerously heretical in an era when the Catholic Church still held it as a dogma that the six-thousand-year Biblical chronology was true, and his work was only published in bowdlerized form—the full text was only restored in the twentieth century. His thesis won one enthusiastic convert, in Nicolas Restif de la Bretonne, who produced his own modified versions of it in both fictional and non-fictional works."

"I have *Telliamed* in the library," James supplied.

"And Restif's works are now available in English translation," Simon supplied.

"But that's not what morgens really are," Felicia put in.

"We're just playing with ideas, Felicia," James said, keeping his voice conspicuously mild. "That's all we can really do, since none of us have actually seen a morgen or a neider in the flesh, and even we can't be absolutely certain that such things do exist."

Even Felicia seemed annoyed by that, as impatient as Melusine with James's apparent insistence on pandering to Simon's skepticism.

"*We* meaning those present in the room, of course," was Melusine's murmured contribution, as if it were a significant correction.

"*Neidr* is Welsh for snake, isn't it?" Simon queried. "But what you mean by it is some kind of sea-serpent, I presume?"

"We spell it with a second *e*," James said, "and yes, the neider, as in the neider's cave—although the English spell it with a *y* rather than an *ei*—is a kind of sea-creature, akin to a morgen, although exactly how . . . but that's a matter of pure speculation, of course, as we're just playing with ideas."

"It seems to me, James," Simon said, "that you're protesting a little too much. As Melusine said, a little while ago, your cards are going to have to be laid on the table eventually. If you do take all this seriously, you might as well simply say so."

"The problem is, Simon," James replied earnestly, "that we don't know ourselves how seriously we can . . ."

He cut himself off in mid-sentence because the door to the corridor had opened, and Cerys came in. James hardly had time to frown before she was beside him, whispering in his ear. The frown disappeared, but the expression that replaced it was deeply anxious. "I don't . . . " he began.

"We know you don't," Melusine cut in. "But it's a battle you can't win." To Simon, she said: "What Cerys is telling my cousin, without any real need for the show of secrecy, is that Ceridwen, the ancestor we call Grandmother, wants to see you. And she wants to see you *now*. That was inevitable, in fact, the moment that James made the decision to summon you to the house. How he can have thought otherwise is beyond me."

"I didn't . . . " James began.

Melusine cut him off again. "Obviously not," she said. "But the cat's out of the bag. I'll go up with him."

"She wants to see him on her own," Cerys announced. "She's out of bed. And before you all pitch into me, it wasn't me who told her, and it wasn't any of the servants."

"Then how . . . ?" James began, but stopped, and then groaned. "Oh, that *bloody* woman! Take him up, then, Cerys, and come straight back down again. Don't worry—we're not going to tell you off, but we do need to have a serious family conference."

Cerys escorted Simon along the corridor to the staircase.

"I hope you're not in trouble," Simon remarked.

"We all are," Cerys muttered. "You included—but it's not your fault. And it's no good asking me what's going on, because I don't have a clue."

"Any advice, then?" Simon asked, as they went upstairs.

"She won't bite," Cerys assured him. "Just bear it in mind that you're the first stranger she's seen in the flesh for at least as long as I've been alive, and I doubt that she's got out of bed in all that time. I don't understand why, but you're one hell of a special case."

There was no time for her to add any more. Ceridwen Murden's room was on the first floor, not far from the head of the stairs. Cerys rapped on the door, opened it, and stood aside to let Simon in, before closing it behind him.

VIII
Ceridwen

Two armchairs had been stationed to either side of a hearth on the opposite side of the room to a huge four-poster bed with drawn curtain, but the "fire" in the grate was an electric heater whose "flames" were painted on a transparent plastic cover with a light bulb inside.

An old lady was sitting in one of the chairs. She was tiny and wizened, and it did not require too much of a stretch of the imagination to think that she might, indeed, be far older than any human being had a natural right to be. She was wearing a royal blue ankle-length dress with the same kind of high neck as the ones that Felicia and Melusine were wearing, but she also had a kind of flower-patterned shawl around her shoulders that looked like silk.

"Please forgive me for not getting up, my dear," she said to Simon, extending her right hand toward him, obviously intending him to take it.

As he stepped forward, he noticed that her left hand was clutching an iPad.

Her hand was slender, but not as weak as he had expected. Her grip seemed firm, and she did not let go. Instead, she raised the iPad, and said: "Wonderful devices, these? Do you have one?"

"Actually, no," Simon admitted. "I don't even have a mobile phone. I'm something of a technophobe, I fear. I work on a computer nowadays, obviously, but I still think of it as a glorified typewriter, albeit one equipped with a visual display and music." He deduced that it was via the iPad that she had been notified of his presence in the house, and realized, a trifle belatedly, that the "bloody woman" to whom James had referred in his exasperation must be Megan Harwyn.

"But you use the internet, and Skype?" she queried.

"The net, yes—I couldn't do without it. Skype, no—I don't have anyone to talk to, alas. I have a lot of MP3s stored on the machine, though, to provide background music while I work."

"What sort of background music?" she asked.

"These days, my soundtrack consists entirely of popular classics—Beethoven, Tchaikovsky, Vivaldi, etcetera. In my youth I went through a heavy rock phase, and as late as the nineties I was still into Gothic Rock, but when I cleared out all my vinyl and got rid of all my CDs, I found that that kind of music had become too intrusive and I left it off the playlist on the computer and banished lyrics entirely. I think it was the headphones—they're more intimate, somehow."

Simon was uncomfortably aware that he was rambling, but the old woman seemed rapt with attention, as if she really cared about the nature of the soundtrack to his work. She nodded her head, in apparent satisfaction.

"You can get the weather forecast, you know," she said, letting the iPad fall back slightly, as if its weight were becoming too much for her feeble arm, "five days in advance . . . and accurate too. Isn't that marvelous?"

"Meteorology has made great strides," Simon admitted, remembering what Lenore had said—or seemed to say—about a storm coming.

"But it's all changing, isn't it? It's only the end of February and spring is already here. Global warming, they say—you know about global warming?"

"Yes."

"And the gulf stream—you know about that?"

"A little," Simon agreed, thinking that the conversation was becoming positively surreal.

"It's all so marvelous," the old lady opined. "And all so strange. But there's a lot it might explain. Melusine's beginning to understand, I think, but James is just Rhys all over again: pedantic and always quibbling. He didn't want you to see me, did he?"

"He seems concerned for your state of health."

"For my state of mind, more like—he's afraid I'll talk too much, tell you things you won't be able to believe and scare you off. But if you really are family . . . and Felicia's convinced, although she does get carried away sometimes . . . anyway, if you are, you won't be scared off, and if you aren't, it doesn't matter what you think."

The old lady was still holding his hand, and she suddenly seemed to realize that he found the continued contact slightly unusual. "Forgive me, my dear," she said. She handed him the iPad, open at the email address book. "Could you possibly type in your email address for me," she said. "Your fingers are probably more nimble than mine. Isn't the virtual keyboard marvelous?"

Simon did as he was asked, but when he handed the iPad back to her, she seized his hand again. "Humor me, please, for a few moments longer. It's been a long time since I've been in the presence of anyone except the permanent residents of the house, and I'd like to make the most of it. Not that I'm a prisoner, you understand—the isolation has been voluntary, to the extent that it hasn't been forced by the inconveniences of old age. But I feel much better today—*much* better."

She let go of his hand for a second time then, and used her forefinger to indicate the second armchair. "Please sit down, my dear. May I call you Simon?"

"Of course," said Simon, sitting down.

"Everybody else calls me Grandmother—would you mind very much doing the same?"

"Not at all," said Simon. "Although I understand that at least a couple of greats ought to be added on to the title."

The old lady sighed slightly. "There comes a time when the generations become confused," she said, "and the matter is a little more complicated than it seems. Would it trouble you to think that I might actually be your grandmother, with a few greats added on, or at least a great-aunt?"

"Did Megan Harwyn tell you that when she emailed you to tell me that I was here?" Simon asked.

"She does have a certain interest in making me think that it might be the case," the old lady said, "so I suppose I shouldn't take her word too seriously. Would you mind if I were to investigate the question in my own way, given that I have no faith in her DNA test, or the likelihood of her telling the truth about the result?"

"What way would that be, exactly?" Simon asked.

"Oh, nothing arcane, I assure you," she said. "I'd just like to get to know you. If I were to ask you to come back and see me again from time to time, in order to do that, would that be all right?"

"Yes, of course."

"I won't be the only one to make the request of you, I suspect—but it won't cost you anything but time, and perhaps a little frustration. Feel free to say no—to any of us. No one means you any harm, I assure you. But I ought to warn you that, although you have a thousand questions, James is right to judge that it might not be wise for us to answer all of them right away, without first laying adequate foundations. I have a lot of questions myself, and I couldn't hold it against you if you took the view that they're too intrusive, but I hope you won't."

"As I was explaining to your . . . grandchildren a few minutes ago, I really don't know anything about Evelyne, or her mother, and I don't have any information at all about my biological parentage."

"So I gather. And I dare say that James will mount an exceedingly thorough investigation of your writings, so I'll leave that to him. But before I get to serious matters, might I ask you what your impression is of Alexander Usher?"

Simon might have been startled by that under other circumstances, but he was becoming so used to the unexpected by now that the change of subject seemed perfectly normal. "I only met him for the first time last night. Cerys can surely give you a much more informed opinion than I can."

"Cerys is an innocent, and Megan is untrustworthy. The reason that I'm asking is that the family has had difficulties with Churchmen in the past, and I'm a trifle anxious that the agenda of his present investigation might have a hidden element."

"He's a college chaplain in the C-of-E," Simon said, "not an old-fashioned Dominican Inquisitor. He struck me as being a typical antiquarian, fascinated by his subject and eager to explain it to anyone who might constitute an audience. I can understand the mentality, although I hope that I'm a little less obvious."

"The Abbey's troubles didn't come to an end when it was deconsecrated in the sixteenth century," the old lady told him. "The Puritans didn't like us any better than the Catholics, and in my own time, some Methodists have looked at us with a distinctly jaundiced eye. We might be living in a new world"—she lifted the iPad again—"but the old one hasn't been entirely effaced, and this new technology brings new threats as well as wonderful opportunities. That's a minor matter, though, and I don't want to waste any more time on it. You first came into contact with Evelyne, I believe, following your divorce?"

That change of tack seemed more disconcerting. "That's correct," Simon said, warily.

"But you're not comfortable talking about that?" she diagnosed, immediately.

After a momentary hesitation, Simon shrugged. "I don't mind," he said, "but I don't see what relevance it can possibly have."

"Humor me, please," said the old lady. "You have no children, it appears?"

"No. I married quite late, and my wife was already in her forties, a year or two older than me. Children weren't on our agenda."

"Nor mine—but things don't always work out as we plan them. I had four, by three different fathers—which, in retrospect, might be reckoned at least two too many. I didn't regret it at the time, though. Motherhood does strange things to a woman, no matter what the circumstances are. What was your agenda, then? And what went wrong?"

Simon pursed his lips, but there didn't seem to be any reason to refuse to answer the question, whatever the old lady's motive for asking it might be.

"I started writing in my teens," he said. "It was all I ever wanted to do. I told Eve, glibly, that it started out as a hobby, and then became a job, and then a vocation and ended up as an obsession, but I guess it was always an obsession. It was always the focal point of my life and thinking. I didn't want to be a monk, though. I always wanted to have a personal life as well—just one that fitted in with the writing. While I was teaching, it was easy enough to meet women, and not too difficult to form relationships. I had several girlfriends in my twenties and thirties, including a couple of relationships that lasted for years, but they didn't lead to marriage. To be honest, looking back, I'm not entirely sure why they didn't. I guess it was just that the way the relationships were suited me perfectly—but it didn't suit my girlfriends as well. They wanted more—not marriage, specifically, but they wanted to be the center of my attention, instead of my work.

"If either of the women with whom I had long-term relationships had pressured me into marriage, I would have gone along with it, but they both figured out that I wasn't going to change, and let go instead. Marilyn—that's my ex-wife—was a bit more stubborn, or a bit more deluded. She thought she could handle it—handle my obsession, that is. For a long time, I thought she was right, and the arrangement still suited me perfectly all the way to the end—but she got tired of it, and eventually traded me in for someone who did want to make her the center of his existence and the focal point of his obsession.

"She'd been much more prudent than me in her youth, and had bought a house back in the days when that was still possible for single people. When we married I gave up the flat I was renting and moved in with her. The house was always in her name, so when she filed for divorce, she simply threw me out. Maybe I could have got some kind of payout from the increased equity in the house, if I'd hired a solicitor to fight it through the courts, but the odds are that the lion's share of the money would have gone to pay off the competing solicitors, so I didn't fight. I got the new flat with no trouble. I moved in, and just focused on my work. The break-up broke me too, in a way, because I really had got a lot out of the marriage, but such is life. Does that answer your question?"

"Yes," she said. "It does, quite adequately."

"But why on earth did you want to know?"

"I want to know you. I want to know whether you are, in fact, my descendant . . . and I want a more reliable guide than the results of an alleged DNA-comparison reported by Megan Harwyn. I've always been more than willing to accept that she's a descendant too, mind—I don't have James's capacity for denial, and I really don't care how she's made her living—but the fact remains that if she has an incentive to lie she'll lie. It's not her fault, really, any more than it's James's fault that he won't ever admit that he's her father, even under torture."

"But nothing I just said can possibly count as evidence that I'm your descendant," Simon objected.

"Not is a legal sense," the old lady agreed. "Let's just say that I imagine that I have a talent for reading between the lines, shall we?"

"All right," said Simon, "let's say that. What was it that you read, then, exactly?"

"It's not an art that permits exactitude. It also takes time. That's why I'd like you to come back, if you will. Think of it as an act of kindness, like the one you rendered Evelyne . . . but I won't ask you to come back every day, or every evening. And eventually, one way or another, I will explain, if Melusine's impatience doesn't make her jump the gun before James has even said 'Ready.' If she does, by the way, don't take what she says too seriously—I'm the one and only reliable source, and I even have doubts about my own memory sometimes. The children all have their own pet theories, but they haven't had the chance to see what I've seen or feel what I've felt. Rhys's engineering has a lot to answer for . . . although now that I know about global warming and the gulf stream, it was obviously only a contributory factor. Even if Melusine can contain herself, you'll probably see . . . well, something. It might be kinder of me to hope that you won't see anything, but I can't do that. I need you to see. We all do, including you . . . especially you."

"You're talking in riddles, Mrs. Murden."

"Grandmother," she corrected. "And if you can't bear to call me that, Ceridwen. Or, if you really must, it's *Miss* Murden, just like the other female members of the household. I've never been married, or even in the kind of long-term relationship you seem to have enjoyed. Scandalous, I know . . . even more so at the time. And if they'd known the whole truth . . . but let's not get ahead of ourselves. Nobody knows that."

Her blue eyes seemed suddenly intense, but not because she was looking at Simon, and for a moment, her thoughts seemed to drift away—but she brought her attention back with a sudden effort. "I'm afraid that might be enough, for now," she said, reluctantly. "The effort has taken more out of me than I assumed, I fear. They'll want to know what we've said to one another, of course. You can tell them, but if you want to tease them a little, feel free. They certainly won't hesitate to tease you. But be kind to Cerys and Felicia, please. When can you come again?"

"Evenings are better for me," Simon said. "I'm trying to get back into my work routine, although I can see that it won't be easy."

"Evenings are fine. You won't hold it against me if I receive you in bed, I hope . . . I might have overstretched my resources a little today. Shall we say the day after tomorrow—Friday, that is—at seven-thirty? I'll have a bottle of good port sent up."

"Fine by me. I'll look forward to it."

"Excellent. May I ask one more thing of you?"

"What is it?" Simon parried, unwilling to commit himself without knowing.

She set the iPad down to her lap and held out both her hands. "Would you mind taking both my hands, and kissing me on the forehead, as if you really were my great-grandnephew?"

"I can do that," Simon said—and did, albeit very lightly. He didn't feel the slightest sense of kinship, but he didn't feel the slightest resentment either. In fact, the idea of being a Murden, absurd as it might be, didn't seem as horrific now as it had while he was being grilled by the redoubtable James.

When he let go of the old lady's hands, he saw her relax abruptly, and realized that she really had been making a considerable effort simply to sit there and talk to him. He felt a sudden pang of guilt then, profoundly unsure that he was deserving of so much effort on the part of someone so frail, no matter what hopes she might be entertaining of him.

"Thank you, Simon," she said, in a voice hardly above a whisper. She raised her head again, however, to say: "I was born in the year of the French Revolution. Seymour Murden was my mother's husband, and gave me his name, but he wasn't my father. I've met the Duke of Wellington, Queen Victoria, Tom Paine, Thomas Love Peacock, Robert Southey, and poor Percy Shelley. I've seen morgens by the score and slept with the neider, and I'm on intimate terms with the ghost of Owain Glyndwr—and he's not the only spirit I can summon from the deep, by any means. But if you're wise, you won't believe a word of that as yet, because if you try, people will think you're mad. That's all I can do, for now . . . but this is just the beginning, you poor lamb, and the warm-water storms are coming early this year, according to the forecast, as well as the elvers. If you go home now, you can get back to Raven well before dusk. If James or Melusine tries to stop you, tell them I've given you permission to go."

When she stopped, it was as if she had run completely out of breath. Her head slumped again, and for a moment Simon wondered whether he ought to stay, or call for help. Then she raised her eyes to look at him again, and nodded, to tell him that she would be all right. He bowed, and said, "Thank you, Miss Murden," and went to the door, closing it quietly behind him.

He went downstairs and returned to the dining room. The table had been cleared, and his four hosts were sitting in the armchairs again. All four stood up as he came in, and Cerys immediately moved aside to offer him her chair.

"Thank you," he said, "but I think I'd better leave now. Your grandmother has given me permission to go."

"Cerys will walk with you," James said, immediately, seemingly not even giving a thought to the possibility of challenging his grandmother's decision, and knowing full well that her "permission" was an instruction.

"You must come again," said Melusine. "I'm sure you have a thousand questions to ask us."

It was on the tip of Simon's tongue to say: *To which you seem to have no intention of giving me a straight answer*—but he refrained. Instead he said: "Thank you for lunch. It was very kind of you to invite me—and it was a great pleasure to meet your grandmother. She's a remarkable woman."

"Yes, she is," said James, colorlessly. Simon almost turned away, but he was gripped by a sudden whim. "By the way, Mr. Murden" he said, "I met a young man named Alun Gwynne this morning. He's one of the emergency housing tenants in Morpen. He has some serious concerns about the future welfare of his family, and would really like to know what your plans are for the future of the estate. It would be a great kindness on your part if you were to open communication with him—by telephone or email if not in person."

James seemed profoundly surprised, but he simply nodded his head. "Thank you for letting me know," he said. "I'll look into it." He offered Simon his hand.

Simon shook it, and then moved toward the door, but it wasn't that easy. Melusine came to shake his hand, and whispered in his ear: "I need to speak with you in private. I'll email you."

Felicia shook his hand too. She said nothing except for a muttered: "Thank you for coming," but Simon got the distinct impression that it was only with reluctance that she refrained from trying to arrange an assignation there and then.

He paused on the threshold to look at Lenore. The bird immediately raised her head, and flicked her wings, as if in a gesture of farewell, but did not attempt to produce an apposite Shakespearean quote.

As soon as they were outside, Cerys said: "First of all, it's still no use you asking me what's going on, because I still haven't got a clue. Secondly, James has told me to stick to you like glue and find out exactly what Grandmother said to you, and what you said to her. He seems to think that my feminine wiles would be adequate to the task, but to be perfectly honest, I'd rather stay out of this, whatever it is, so if you don't want to tell me anything at all, feel free." Almost as an afterthought, after a slight pause, she added: "I do have a few questions of my own that I'd like to ask you, though, if you wouldn't mind?"

Simon laughed. "Well, you seem to have been given the first place in the queue, so you might as well take advantage of it. But I wouldn't want to expose you to James's annoyance so I have no objection at all to telling you what your Grandmother said to me. She showed me her iPad, disapproved of my own technophobia, and extolled the wonders of the long-range weather forecast. Then—I have no idea why—she asked me to tell her about my divorce—not because the details were of any importance but because she wanted to 'read between the lines,' as she put it. I think she meant that she wanted to figure out what kind of person I am. Looking back on what I said, I suspect that that I didn't make myself look good. She asked me to come to see her again on Friday evening, and strongly implied that she wanted such visits to become a regular thing, at least until she feels that she knows me. I feel rather as if I'm being subjected to an examination, to see whether I'm worthy of admission to the family . . . which, meaning no offense, looks for the moment to be a slightly dubious privilege."

"Couldn't have put it better myself," Cerys replied. "I feel that I've been subjected to the same examination for the last six months, and certainly haven't passed yet. I really don't know whether I ought to be sorry about that, or profoundly grateful. But you got Grandmother out of bed, which is more than I've ever done, and taking an interest in something other than her dreams and delusions, which can only be good, provided that the effort doesn't give her a heart attack. Come to that, I've never seen James so animated before, or Melusine, and if Felicia weren't so timid, I'd swear that she'd be setting out to seduce you before the weekend. If Megan Harwyn wanted to stir things up, she's certainly succeeded."

"Your grandmother also mentioned that James is Megan Harwyn's father—but you might find it more diplomatic not to pass that tidbit in to him."

"I might," Cerys agreed. "He denies it, obviously . . . but now he knows that Grandmother's in contact with Megan via the iPad, he might find that simply continuing to ignore the issue won't work."

They passed through the gate, and Cerys locked it behind her carefully before continuing to walk with him.

"Anything else you care to pass on?" she asked him.

"She asked me to be kind to you and Felicia."

"That's nice of her."

"Not really, if you read between the lines. Asking me to be kind to you and Felicia is tantamount to giving me permission not to be kind to James and Melusine, which implies that I somehow have the option of not being, and that they might care."

"I think you might be overthinking that," Cerys suggested.

"Maybe so," Simon agreed, meekly, convinced that he was not, and that he had read the old lady's meaning precisely. As they arrived at the gate of Raven Cottage he looked at the window of Sanderling, but could not see anyone there. "What was it you wanted to ask me?" he added.

Cerys turned her head in the same direction in which his own gaze had gone, and did not seem reassured by the absence of any evident presence. "Not here," she said.

"You'd better come in then," he said, suppressing a sigh and writing off the entire afternoon from the viewpoint of getting any further work done.

They went inside. "Would you like a cup of coffee?" he asked, for the sake of politeness.

"Yes, please," she said. "Black, no sugar." Without waiting for any indication as to where she ought to go, she went into the study, and made a beeline for the bookshelves.

When he came back with the two mugs of coffee, she was studying a copy of *The Seventh Element* intently.

"James has ordered a copy from amazon, apparently," he said, "but if there's likely to be competition among potential readers, I can let you have a spare. As many titles as you want, in fact—I hang on to the complimentary copies, but they're really just cluttering up the place. You're welcome to look through the boxes in the corner and take whatever you like."

"Thanks," she said, "but I didn't come fishing for freebies. I really wanted some advice . . . about writing."

This time, Simon didn't suppress the sigh. "That's a pity," he said.

"Why?"

"Because there isn't any advice I can offer would-be writers any more except: 'Forget it.' There isn't any money to be made, and precious little satisfaction from seeing yourself in print. For an old wreck like me, with nothing between him and the grave but his obsession, it fills in the time adequately—but you're young and beautiful. You can get a life—anywhere but here, at least. Or, if you really are desperate to write, search the internet for advice on how to lay out a script for TV, and information about the submission process. The odds against success are high, but at least there's still a possibility. I don't know any more about it than the next man, though, so there's no use asking me about it."

She seemed surprised as well as hurt. "And that's your idea of being kind, is it?" she commented.

Simon felt guilty. "I believe I did throw a compliment in there, including the word 'beautiful'—but you're right; it's wasn't kind, and I won't take refuge in the weaselly old saw about sometimes having to be cruel to be kind. Just put it down to my bitterness, and forgive me, if you can."

Without being invited, Cerys pulled the armchair from in front of the TV around; it moved easily on its castors. She sat down in it. "Is it really that bad?" she asked.

He sat down in his swivel chair, swiveling it to face her.

"Yes," he said—but promptly added: "Probably not. I've got no grounds for complaint. I'm a completely self-made failure. Ignore me. I suppose it's just that when your grandmother tried to weigh me up by asking me about my divorce and then explaining that she was reading between the lines, I had to weigh myself up and try to read between the lines, and I didn't look good in the balance pan. Young people like you shouldn't come to battered old wrecks like me for advice—they should go to successful people full of verve and zest."

"And where am I going to find one of those around here? The Mermaid? Next door?"

"Fair point," he admitted. "To be perfectly honest, though, from what I saw today, your elders up over at the Abbey are far from helpless. They can get by without you."

"It's not as simple as that. And in order to go, I'd need somewhere to go to. I've been applying for jobs online for months, and even if I could get one, it would hardly pay enough for me to be able to rent a flat—unless I get Miss Harwyn to design a website for me. Even she reacts with utter horror to that suggestion—not that it was serious, I hasten to add. That branch of the family tradition doesn't appeal to me at all. Mind you, I don't suppose it appealed to Megan either, to begin with, or to your Eve. It's a last resort sort of thing, and for the time being at least, I'm not yet there."

"Can't your parents help?"

"That would be parent, singular. Why do you think I have my mother's surname? And no, she can't help. She's always had difficulty making ends meet herself—although, at least as far as I know, she never got to the stage of asking Megan to design her a website, and it's probably too late, now she's way past forty."

"She never married?"

"Do Murden women ever marry? Well yes, obviously some do, but not the majority. One way or another, most seem to end up like Melusine, Felicia, Megan and your Eve. All misses—not a hit among them, unless you count the occasional by-blow . . . and if Megan's right about you, some of those just get dumped in the street."

She looked at him, in order to see what effect that remark had on him. She wasn't being kind.

"It doesn't bother me," he told her. "It hasn't left me with a traumatic desire to confront my biological mother and beg her to tell me why she didn't want me. If Megan Harwyn's fantasy turned out to be true—which it won't—and this Angela Richardson person were my mother, I really wouldn't care. I wouldn't rush off immediately to meet her and the half-sister who had to split Eve's inheritance with me. And you certainly don't have to worry about me stealing part of your inheritance."

Cerys laughed at that. "Feel free," she said. "James has already explained that I can't inherit the Abbey or the cottages, because of the conditions of the entail, and there isn't a penny left apart from that, so far as I can tell. The Murdens might have been prosperous back in Old Seymour's day, but we're on the rocks now—and believe me, it's for families like ours that the word dysfunctional was invented."

The memory returned to Simon's mind of the aged Ceridwen's confession that she had had four children by three different fathers but had never married . . . and that even that wasn't the whole truth.

"According to Alexander Usher, though, there were plenty of men in the family before the Great War."

"Sure," said Cerys. "Men like James, probably, who screwed the servants, then denied any responsibility for the consequences, and were then so overwhelmed by pathological remorse that . . . but it's not my place to speculate. The simple fact is that we're cursed. I doubt that it's because our remote ancestors really made a pact with the Devil, but one way or another, we're cursed . . . me included . . . and you too, if Megan's not just trying to put one over on James to pay him back for a lifetime of insult and humiliation."

"I thought Saint Madoc was supposed to have made a pact with the morgens, not the Devil?" Simon queried. "And don't you trace your name back to Myrddin Wyllt the mad bard, not Saint Madoc, who presumably didn't have any children?"

"Maybe. It's all nonsense anyway. Even James knows that, deep down. Grandmother seems to believe it, but she thinks she's met Queen Victoria, screwed a sea-serpent, and holds regular necromantic communication with Owain Glyndwr, so how reliable can her word be? Sometimes, I wish she wasn't so sweet and frail, so that I could just say to hell with her . . . but I can't. Even James . . . he really is good, and generous. He was the one who paid to put me through a decent school and uni, you know, not Mother. She didn't run away with me—he sent her away, for her own good, or at least for mine . . . and if there was a bit of cruelty in that, he really was doing it in order to be kind. And take it from me, if you think that Grandmother was telling you to be unkind to him by asking you to be kind to me, you really are overthinking things. Dysfunctional we may be, and quarrelsome, but we really do love one another. Maybe that's part of the curse."

"Is it really that bad?" he asked, with an ironic smile.

She formed a similar smile of her own. "Probably not," she said. "Put it down to my bitterness, and forgive me if you can. Did you mean it about taking some books? James has amazon, but Felicia hasn't learned to use the computer yet, and she really will be extremely grateful if I can take some for her. As I say, she'd have been fawning over you earlier, if she wasn't so timid, or afraid of what Melusine might say. And I really would like to read them myself, obviously . . ."

115

Simon had already opened the top box in the stack. "Here," he said. "Try this, and this . . ."

He continued picking out copies of his old novels and handing them to her, until she had a stack of ten.

"That's all I can carry for now," Cerys said. "I might come back though—and since Grandmother got out of bed, I wouldn't be entirely surprised if Felicia were to cross the bridge. James surely will, now that he has a reason again. You'll probably have to start screening your telephone calls and ignoring your doorbell."

She turned toward the door of the room. She really was very pretty, Simon thought. "You can email me some of your work, if you like," he said, in a surge of generosity, "but be warned—I'm a harsh critic."

She beamed at him. "You read my mind," she said. "Perhaps as well, as I didn't dare ask. And I can take criticism—but do be kind to Felicia, if she assumes that the permission extends to her. She might be more fragile."

Simon's heart sank slightly, but he put on a brave face as he bade farewell to the young woman, and closed the door behind her.

There was no time left to get any serious work done, but he sat down at the computer to check his email. There was one from Melusine, asking him for a private meeting "as soon as possible" at a time and place of his choosing, in order "to give him some information that he would undoubtedly find interesting." He wrote back to say that he would be happy to see her the following evening, at seven-thirty, at Raven Cottage, if that were agreeable to her.

Then he made himself a rather frugal meal, thankful for the fact that the supermarket delivery truck was due in the morning, even though he would have to interrupt his work in order to receive and unpack the consignment.

IX
The Weather Forecast

When Simon stepped into the Mermaid a few minutes after half-past seven he found the same four customers sitting at the same table to the left of the door, while the Reverend Alexander Usher was leaning on the bar on the far side of the room. Simon turned to the right, but Alun Gwynne immediately bounded out of his seat and came to intercept him.

"Thank you, Mr. Cannick," he said, effusively.

"For what?" Simon asked.

"James Murden emailed me an hour ago and said that you had mentioned me to him. He's invited us to meet him here tomorrow in order to listen to what we have to say. He says that he can't make us any promises, but that he'll hear us out. That's quite something if, as I understand, he hasn't come into the village for years. We're very grateful to you."

"It might be unwise to get your hopes up too high," Simon said, carefully, "but it is something. I'm glad to have been of some assistance."

"Can we buy you a drink?"

"Not now, thanks—I have an appointment with the Reverend. Another time, perhaps."

"For sure. Thanks again," the young man said, returning to his seat. Simon had time to notice, before joining the Reverend, that they were now speaking English.

"May I buy you a drink, then?" the clergyman asked.

"Of course," said Simon. "Dry cider please."

Dai nodded to Simon in a fashion that was distinctly respectful, as he served them both,. Afterwards, he retired to the back room again, where the television could be heard.

Simon and Alexander Usher took their seats at the same table as before. Simon looked at the empty chair that Megan Harwyn had occupied the previous evening. "To be honest," he said, "I'm a little surprised that we haven't been gatecrashed."

"Miss Harwyn has a car discreetly garaged on the far side of the village. She left in it shortly after you and Cerys set off for the Abbey. You can probably make a better guess than I can as to where she's gone."

"Probably Bristol," Simon said, and left it at that.

"You put in a word for the young men at the Abbey, then?" queried the clergyman, nodding in the direction of the other group.

"I mentioned in passing that they'd like to see him. I didn't realize I had that much influence, to tell the truth—but I suspect that James might have intended to cross the bridge anyway, in order to visit me. It will disrupt my work, but I admit that I'm quite keen to hear what he might have to tell me, even though he seems insistent on doing it in an annoyingly roundabout fashion. We were interrupted this afternoon."

"Really. How?"

"I was summoned upstairs by the grandmother."

"Indeed? That is an honor. They took what Miss Harwyn told them very seriously, then? They really do think that you're a long-lost member of the family?"

"Apparently. If Megan's attempt to prove that I might be obtains the opposite result, though, their delight might disappear in a trice." He didn't mention the possibility that Megan might lie about it, as Ceridwen Murden seemed to suspect.

"What did the old woman say to you?" the Reverend asked, apparently unconcerned with the possibility that the question might seem indiscreet.

"That she wanted to get to know me. We chatted about this and that: her new iPad, the weather forecast, global warming . . . and then she asked about you."

"Me? Why me?"

"She wanted to know my impression of you. Unfortunately, I hadn't really formed one. She knows all about your project, of course, from Cerys, so there wasn't anything I could add to that. She seemed anxious, though, that you might have a further agenda."

"I don't—doubtless the whole family has got the impression that I'm prying, and far too inquisitively for their liking, but my interest really is purely academic."

"That's hardly possible," Simon observed.

"What do you mean?"

"You're a clergyman."

"Yes—but I'm C-of-E, not a Dominican heresy-hunter in quest of evidence of diabolism."

"That's I exactly what I said. It didn't seem to put her mind entirely at rest—but I'm going to see her again on Friday. You'll be gone by then, I understand?"

"Yes, I need to get back to Bristol myself."

"But you have plans, presumably, to write up what you've discovered—not just about the architecture of the Abbey, but about the legends associated with it . . . including those attached to its more recent history?"

"I might," the Revered agreed, warily. "It's a fascinating subject—but folklore is folklore; I certainly won't be trying to stir up any trouble for them. If I see James before I leave tomorrow, I'll offer to let him see anything I write before publishing it. I'd have made the offer anyway, by email, but I really ought to introduce myself in the flesh, if I can."

"That will probably set their minds at rest," Simon agreed. "But just to set my mind at rest, might I ask you an impertinent question? You believe in God, obviously, and the divinity of Jesus Christ, and, I presume, in the miracles of the New Testament—but do you believe that miracles still happen, in the modern world?"

"I don't rule out the possibility, in principle," said Alexander Usher, still wary, "but in practice, I would always look for a natural explanation for any event, in the first instance, in preference to a supernatural one."

"What about the Devil?"

"How do you mean?"

"Do you believe in him?"

The clergyman thought about that for a moment before saying: "That's not an easy question. If you mean, do I believe in an active force of temptation and evil delusion, yes, but not as a material personality. I believe that there's a force of evil, but it exists in our souls, provoking and attempting to guide our passions, undermining the force for good, which is Jesus. There is a spiritual battle, in which we're all engaged, in which Jesus is our ally against a real enemy."

"When you use the phrase 'evil delusion,' does that mean that you believe that all delusions are evil, or that some are and some aren't?"

Again, Usher paused for some time, before saying: "I certainly wouldn't say that all delusion is diabolical, or even necessarily a bad thing—but on the whole, I think it's better to see things clearly, rationally and virtuously. Exactly what delusion do you have in mind, Mr. Cannick? The existence of morgens?"

"Principally, yes. Also the ghost of Owain Glyndwr, and possibly the conviction that one is more than two hundred and thirty years old."

"Ah. Well, if those really were delusions rather than, for instance, errors of perception or simple lies, I wouldn't be in a hurry to categorize them as diabolical, but I would probably suspect strongly that they might be harmful, and better cleared up, if possible. On the other hand, I can see why people might want to humor such convictions, in certain circumstances, and I wouldn't automatically judge it a bad thing. I can see that it might even qualify as an act of kindness. Does that set your mind at rest?"

"Oh, my mind's already at rest," Simon assured him. "I just wanted to get to know yours a little better, in case anyone asks me for my opinion of you in future."

The clergyman contrived a wry smile. "Fair enough," he said. "May I ask you, in exchange, what your opinion of Ceridwen Murden is?"

"I've decided, after due reflection, that I like her. Perhaps more to the point, although it reveals me to be a trifle egotistical, I find myself caring whether or not she likes me. Obviously, I prefer everyone to like me, but there are always going to be people whose opinion one cares about more particularly, for one reason or another. On the other hand, I'm not sure that I want her to like me just because she's under the delusion that I'm her long-lost great grandson, or great nephew, and not at all sure that I ought to encourage that delusion as a means of currying favor. But that's entirely my problem. The point of our meeting tonight was for me to seek a little more information about the situation I seem to have walked into. I have to admit that today's encounters have thrown up far more questions than answers, and I really would like to ask you whether you can cast any light on some of the puzzles that have cropped up. May I consult your expertise?"

"Of course," said the Reverend

Flattery, Simon thought, *will get you anywhere.* "Mention has been made a couple of times of a Rhys Murden, who was the head of the family after Seymour, presumably in the mid nineteenth-century. Do you know anything about him?"

"Rhys the Engineer? Oh, yes—he was famous in his day, not just in West Wales. Perhaps the greatest benefactor St. Madoc, Morpen and the associated farms ever had—but nothing whatsoever to do with the folklore of the morgens."

"Benefactor in what sense?"

"Primarily in terms of public hygiene, and perhaps from an environmentalist point of view too. In Seymour's day, you see, the villagers and the farmers thought nothing of simply dumping all their wastes and excrements into the streams that flow to either side of the village and into the bays between the Tines of Morgan's Fork. That was common practice at the time and nobody thought anything of it. Rhys, however, thought it unsanitary and a cause of disease, as it surely was. He excavated a network of underground pipes throughout St. Madoc and Morpen, and directed all the excrement of the villages, including animal excrements from the farms, into two large underground cesspits, which were emptied on a weekly basis so that the material could be carted to a specialist sewage treatment center—the first in South Wales.

"The cesspits are still in use, and the waste still gets transported, in a tanker. You might see it tomorrow, if you're out and about when it comes—Wednesday is the day when the wastes are collected as well as the day when the supermarket delivers food supplies. A nice symmetry, in a way. As a result, the village's water supply became far healthier, and the two streams much cleaner. It became possible to bathe in either bay without the risk of catching something nasty. The tourist industry that developed in the twentieth century wouldn't have been possible otherwise. The eels probably appreciated it too."

"Eels?"

"Yes. I was down in the southern gully this morning, and I saw elvers in the stream. That's unusual, as eels don't usually return to rivers until the spring—but spring seems to be getting earlier every year now, and after the boost to the general increase in the atmospheric temperature caused by last year's El Niño event, this year might set another new record. A new era is beginning, it seems."

"The time is out of joint," Simon murmured. "The old lady mentioned something about the Gulf Stream."

"Did she, indeed? That's interesting. A long way from the morgen folklore, obviously . . . but maybe not entirely. She didn't mention the Sargasso Sea too, by any chance?"

"James did. He asked me what I thought about it. It seemed a very strange question at the time, but I think I'm beginning to see where it might fit into the jigsaw, given that St. Madoc is supposed to have sailed to islands in the heart of the Sargasso Sea in order to make his pact with the morgens, and that Felicia thinks that Caer-Ys might have risen and sunk more than once . . . and might yet rise again."

"The floating island hypothesis—as in the episode in the tale of Sinbad the Sailor. Yes, you might be able to fit that into the story . . . if, as I assume, you're thinking about this in terms of concocting a story. It's not my field, obviously, but I have come across suggestions that St. Madoc is the end-point of one of the tributaries of the Gulf Stream, like Findhorn in Scotland. If it's true, it might help explain why the two streams used to provide such abundant eel-fishing, so early in the season—and why the weather is reputedly so bad."

"Bad? Why bad? I thought the Gulf Stream water was warmer than that of the ocean through which it flows."

"It is. That's why its tributaries act as guides of a sort for storms that form in the Caribbean and track across the Atlantic. You've been lucky since you arrived, but St. Madoc has a higher average annual rainfall than Cardigan or Fishguard and there's something about the topography of Morgan's Fork that seems to have a tunneling effect on the wind, and compresses the tidal water. You'll soon learn that if there's a bad storm, you shouldn't risk going outside at all, let alone walking along the coastal path, especially the section that curves around the edge of the northern Tine."

"The storm is up and all is on the hazard," Simon muttered.

"Pardon?"

"I think it's from *Julius Caesar*. I must look it up. I must have heard it in my teaching days and it stuck in my unconscious. Sorry—it sprang to mind last night, and I couldn't work out why. Can you get the five-day weather forecast on that iPad of yours?"

"Of course." Alexander Usher pulled the device out of his pocket, called up the five-day forecast and showed the screen to Simon. There was a storm brewing in the Caribbean, scheduled to reach the British Isles in approximately forty-eight hours time, on Friday evening. The Met Office was already issuing weather warnings to southern Ireland and West Wales.

Simon nodded. "That's what the old lady was looking at when I went into her room," he said.

"Well, if that's when you're going to see her," said the clergyman, "I hope you've got a good raincoat. An umbrella won't do you any good—it won't survive the walk without getting blown away."

"I'll take care. When you mentioned the caves in the flanks of the Tine, you said that the Nyder in Nyder's Cave really ought to be *neidr*, referring to some kind of sea serpent. Do know any more about that item of folklore?"

"Nothing. The word is used in that context, but its meaning is unclear. It might be relevant that it was only discovered that eels were fish in the nineteenth century. Before then, they were often thought to be more closely related to snakes—understandable, given that migrating eels sometimes travel overland for considerable distances. In this context, an eel might have been called a *neidr* in the past—but that's pure speculation on my part."

"That's plausible. Can I get you another bitter lemon?"

"Why not? It's my last night—might as well splash out."

Simon went to the bar and waited for Dai to materialize, which he did with his usual promptitude. "You're a member of the family, sir, I believe?" the landlord said, breaking his habit of taciturnity.

"That's yet to be determined," said Simon. "We're all on tenterhooks. I've met them all, though, except for the ghost of Owain Glydwr."

Dai's hand stopped in mid-gesture but continued almost immediately, completing the process of emptying the bottle of cider into Simon's glass.

"You won't understand him if you do, sir," said the landlord, by way of a joke. "He only speaks Welsh. Can't do that myself, shameful as it is for a man in my position."

Simon carried the drinks back to the table.

"Always a slightly touchy subject, Glyndwr," commented the clergyman. "The ghost is taken very seriously around here. Even the Syrian refugees have got to hear about the local ghosts, although there seem to be only two of them who even speak broken English, and it's not as if anyone's rushing to make friends with them. Nothing travels faster than that kind of rumor."

"Do any of the alleged sightings give any clue as to why Glyndwr's ghost is hanging around here?"

"Not really. The conventional explanation is that persistent ghosts have unfinished business, but if Owain's waiting for his chance to drive the English out of Wales, he'll have a very long wait. The Murdens mentioned St. Madoc's ghosts, then?"

"Yes. They all seem very familiar with Glyndwr, although they don't seem to be on such intimate terms with the Black Monk. Hence my remark to Dai about Glyndwr being practically one of the family."

"Odd, if so. When Glyndwr allegedly hid out in the Abbey it really was an Abbey, more than a century before the Murdens took it over."

"How about the other ghost—the Monk. Who is he supposed to be?"

"Nobody in particular, so far as I know. It's not even certain that he's a monk. He wears a black hood, apparently . . . but that might not mean anything. If Richard Hoare had bothered to record any sightings of the apparition, he'd undoubtedly have suggested that he must be a Druid, haunting the location of the ancient woods, looking for mistletoe. The eye of the beholder always contributes more than is actually there."

"Of course—thanks."

"No problem." Alexander Usher handed his iPad over again, this time open to the address page. "Would you mind typing your email address in there?" he asked. "We really must keep in touch. I wish I could stay another couple of days, to see how things work out . . . and to hear what the Murdens can tell you about their own investigations of the family folklore, given that they seem to have access to archives that they're determined to keep out of sight. Getting to chat with the old lady is only half the battle ahead of you—the real prize will be getting access to the library, if you can."

"Perhaps so," Simon agreed. "I do get the impression, though, that James and the two aunts have different theories of their own—there's a certain tension between them, although they seem to fall over themselves to avoid actually quarreling, at least in front of strangers. I'm not sure how much older than me they really are, but even if they're as old as they say they are, they're in much the same situation as you are, trying to make sense of ancient documentary sources that might be entirely fantastic. Even if they do have family archives going back centuries, they can't just assume that they're reliable. The old lady seems to be the only one who actually claims to have seen morgens in the flesh, and the others give the impression that they have doubts about her testimony too. Felicia seems to be a creative writer, and James obviously thinks of himself as an authentic scholar, insistently unconvinced that he's doing anything more than playing with ideas. They might have more in common with me than I first thought—although I still can't quite fathom why they're all so keen to talk to me, on the off chance that I might be distantly related to them. There must be something I'm missing."

"I do envy you," the clergyman confessed, with a sigh. "They've avoided meeting and talking to me with the utmost care, only letting Cerys take a few photographs for me as a kind of sop—but you turn up out of the blue, and all of a sudden, they're willing to change their habits overnight and start crossing the bridge again. At low tide tomorrow I might make one last attempt to reach Nyder's Cave, in order to take a quick look inside before I have to head home . . . but you might even get to go down the other way, from the crypt of the chapel."

"You think the chapel's crypt communicates with the caves?"

"I have no idea. No one knows, except the family—and even Cerys isn't allowed down there. I've tried to get local boatmen to take me into one of the caves while the water's high, but they won't even go close. Very frustrating."

"Nobody mentioned the caves, and I didn't ask. What time is tomorrow's low tide?"

"Eight-thirty in the morning. Do you want to come with me?"

"No—I'll be working. And as you say, if my credit with the family lasts I might get to go down the easy way . . . the safe way, that is. Be careful, won't you."

"Oh, I'm certainly not going to risk my neck purely for the sake of idle curiosity. It's hardly of any architectural significance."

"True. By the way, what's the C-of-E's position on necromancy these days?"

"Disapproving, obviously . . . while simultaneously holding, of course, that it doesn't work."

"Their model being the conjuration of the spirit of Samuel by the witch of Endor in the Old Testament?"

"That's how necromancy is traditionally supposed to work, with only slight variations in the way Spiritualist mediums operate. Do you have another model in mind."

"I've played with others in my fiction, in the interest of avoiding cliché."

"We're back to the ghosts of Owain Glyndwr and the Faceless Monk, I presume? You're . . . playing with the idea that Glyndwr's ghost might be summoned rather than appearing spontaneously? That if it has a mission it might be someone else's rather than his own? If so, whose? The old lady's?"

"Perhaps. She quoted Shakespeare's line about being able to summon spirits from the vasty deep—but she's not the only person to have done that today and that line does seem to strike a chord in people's minds whenever the name of Glyndwr is mentioned. Some lines stick like that."

"Like *Quoth the raven, 'Nevermore.'*?"

"Yes. You heard about my visitation, then?"

"Yes. Word travels fast in a gossip-desert. But the bird quite often flies to the cottage, I understand—it's just that there isn't usually anyone to let it in if it should tap. Most people probably wouldn't. It was taking a risk flying at night, though. There are still owls in these parts, even though the oak-woods where the Druids allegedly used to worship have all been cleared to make way for agriculture, save for a few derisory stands. Maybe it saw your light, and remembered someone else who used to let it in. It's very old, according to Cerys."

"So she said, when she came to collect it—and it certainly looks old. It has a disconcerting stare, at close range."

"But it doesn't say 'Nevermore.'"

"No, Simon agreed. 'It doesn't say 'Nevermore.' Look, I'm sorry to run out on you so soon, but I had a late night yesterday, thanks to the bird, and I've had quite a hectic day, thanks to Megan Harwyn's whims and the hare she's started. Maybe I'll see you again tomorrow, before you leave, but if not, I hope you have a good journey home, and that your excursion here has been sufficiently profitable. As you say, we'll keep in touch. I dare say we'll both have further information of interest to exchange."

Simon had stood up while speaking, and he extended his hand. The clergyman stood up too, towering above him once again, and shook his hand amicably.

"I wish you the best of luck too," he said, "however this strange little drama plays out. Do let me know, won't you? And sleep well."

Simon gave Alun Gwynne a friendly wave as he left, but hurried on lest he get trapped in conversation. He moved along the street swiftly, reaching Raven Cottage in less than a minute. He opened the door and was about to turn right into the study when he noticed a glimmer of light coming from the floor above, which seemed to be emerging from the direction of the bedroom overlooking the back of the house, as if there were a light on in the room and the door were ajar.

He could not remember having switched the bedroom light on, let alone having left it on. His first thought, although he chided himself for it immediately, was that it might be a supernatural visitation of some kind. Once again, as he pricked up his ears, the sound of the sea's patient waves became audible. He had been able to ignore them all day, but they seemed to be reminding him now that they had never been away . . . that the deep never went away, no matter how skilled the human mind became at blotting it out of consciousness.

Although he knew that the sound of the front door opening and closing must have been audible to anyone upstairs, given the relative exiguity of the cottage, he went upstairs on tiptoe. He pushed the bedroom door—which was, indeed, ajar—carefully.

The light was coming from the bedside lamp. Sitting up on the bed, fully dressed but perfectly relaxed, Felicia Murden was reading a copy of *The Seventh Element*.

X
Felicia

"How on earth did you get in?" was all that the flabbergasted Simon could think of to say.

"Getting in was no problem," she replied, serenely. "There are duplicate keys to all the cottages at the Abbey. The only problem was getting out of the house undetected. With Melusine having arranged to meet you tomorrow night and James now determined to anticipate her during the day, they might have been a trifle upset had they realized my intention of anticipating both of them. I hope you don't mind."

"Not at all," Simon assured her, sarcastically.

"I didn't want to wait in the study in case someone saw the light from the street. This room has thicker curtains and faces a direction from which no one was likely to see it. In any case . . ." She stopped, becoming hesitant. "It is a liberty, I know, but . . . I felt that I needed to do it."

"You're clearly not the only one," Simon observed still standing on the threshold, reluctant to take a step forward. "I don't understand why, though. Even if there is a slim chance that I might be distantly related to you all, I don't see . . ."

"Oh, it's not a slim chance," Felicia told him. "We all knew what you were last night, if not exactly who, long before poor Megan decided to play her little game. We had to send Cerys to find out what she'd discovered on the web, though. James isn't nearly as clever with computers as she is. He's terribly jealous of that—it makes him furious. But James gets furious very easily, where Megan's concerned. Do come in. There is a chair here if you don't want to sit on the bed."

Simon went into the bedroom, and sat down on the chair beside the bed, after moving it so that he could face her, at what seemed to be a respectful distance.

"How did you know . . . what I am?" he asked.

"Lenore told us—at least, she told me. The others don't really believe that she can talk—but the mere fact that she's come to the cottage at night and tapped on the window was enough to make them ready to believe me. Do *you* believe that she can talk?"

Simon hesitated for some time before eventually confessing: "I did think I heard something, but I thought then, and still think, that it was an illusion produced by my own mind."

"That's possible. What did she say to you?"

"She quoted Shakespeare—from three different plays. She said that the time is out of joint, that a storm is coming, and that stars are going to fall."

Felicia nodded, as if that were only to be expected, from such a wise bird, but Simon got the impression that she might just as easily have laughed at the whim of his unconscious mind, which had chosen, in that strange moment, to select the phrases remembered from thirty or forty years ago, fragments of Shakespeare, as the building-blocks with which to construct the message, in order that he might receive it. Why had he not employed his own words? Was he so dissatisfied with himself, as a composer of ideas, that he had only been able to borrow, clinging desperately to something known and half-familiar, something respectable?

To Felicia, he said: "You say that you know what I am, if not exactly who. By that you mean a Murden?"

"Yes—but it's more complicated than that. Not all Murdens are alike. James and Melusine are morgens. Lenore and I are neider. So are you. That makes you even more important, although none of us is exactly sure why."

It seemed to Simon that something stirred within him, as if awakened from a torpor, and almost uncoiled, but that was it was paralyzed; it did not know how to uncoil, or what to do next if it did. But that had to be pure imagination . . . if there was any purity left in his imagination, which had been corrupt for a long time.

"I'm entirely human, I assure you," he said.

"So am I," she told him. "But Murdens have more than one entirety. James has a theory, and so does Melusine, but we don't really know. There are different degrees too. Melusine's more morgen than James is, and you're more neider than me, or Lenore.

Completely out of his depth, Simon said: "I thought a neider was a snake . . . or maybe an eel."

Again, Felicia nodded, patiently. She was humoring him, trying to coax him.

"So it's said, yes," she said, "but that's just the way people used to see it, when they could still catch glimpses. The carved stone in the chapel represents it as an ouroboros, but I don't think that's right. Grandmother's the only one who's made direct contact with it, and she says that it's more like a hydra that can detach its tentacles, which then give the impression of being snakes or eels. She thinks eels might be distant offspring of the neider, in fact, and perhaps morgens are too, having transformed their nature as well as their form. She says that lots of species might have originated the same way in the very distant past, long before the day of the Caer-Ys, but that Murdens are much more recent—hybrids of a different sort. She'll probably explain it to you, as she sees it, in time, but if James and Melusine have explained it first, as they seem to be desperate to do, it will undoubtedly seem very confused. And I'm not helping, so I really ought to shut up. That's not what I came for."

Simon did not move. Indeed, he felt that he could not move. He needed to understand—but she was right; she wasn't helping, and he was already utterly confused.

This way, madness lies, he told himself, again. But he knew that, and he knew that reminding himself never stopped him from following the signposts. He knew only too well how obsessive he was in that regard—but he had only been playing with ideas, striving to understand the sickness and incompleteness of everything by means of fanciful hypotheses. He had only been playing solitaire, in the cozy privacy of his own imagination. Now, there was a strange old woman in his bedroom—in his bed—not playing with words but playing with him. And she was only one of four . . . five, counting Cerys, six, counting Lenore.

The game was no longer solitaire, but something competitive, whose rules he did not know.

"But it's impossible," said a voice, which was his own, but suddenly sounded alien, as if it belonged to a personality that was only a disguise, essentially false, but which he had been living for so long—longer than his present incarnation—that it had almost taken him over completely.

Almost—but not quite. Felicia knew. Felicia had recognized him, and she was trying to help him . . . not to remember, because it wasn't a matter of memory, but to discover . . .

"I'm afraid it's true, Simon," she said, sympathetically. She almost added something else, and it leapt to his mind that she wanted to assure him that it was also *good*—to assure him that it was good for him, although what she probably meant was that it was somehow good for her, good for her brother, her cousin, and the marvelous little old lady who had been clinging to the vestiges of life for two hundred years, waiting . . . not necessarily for him, but for *something* . . .

But then the sense that he was hovering on the brink of madness dragged him back to earth. Not down to earth—quite the opposite, in fact—but back to the fake reality, back to the *precipitate.*

"I don't believe you," he said. It was all he could do to refrain from adding: *You're mad.* "How can you possibly know?"

She sighed, exasperated. Immediately, though, she softened again, attempting to be soothing and—in spite of the fact that she was more than a hundred years old—seductive.

"The essential fact is," she told him, "that we're not in doubt—not any longer. Lenore's testimony was only conclusive for me, at first, but when grandmother had confirmed it, that was the end of all doubt. James was furious, of course, because he wanted to manage things his own way. You'd think he'd have learned by now, but no . . . I can't blame him, though. I want to manage it my way . . . but I have grandmother's blessing, or at least her permission. It's the best way, I think, even if Melusine will be furious too, and not just out of jealousy. I truly believe that it's the best thing to do, to go behind their backs. This isn't the sort of thing that can be settled by one of James's family conferences. But we're wasting time."

"Are we? You're explaining—isn't that what you came here to do?"

"Heavens, no." She tried to laugh, and added, with a strange smile: "I just told you that it wasn't."

"Why did you come, then?"

It seemed like a natural question—but he could tell from the sudden tension in her expression that for her it was a kind of hurdle: an intimidating hurdle.

"I came because I want to sleep with you," she said, flatly.

"What!" Every time Simon thought that he was beyond the reach of amazement, events proved him wrong.

Felicia was still trying to contrive a smile, impishly, as if she thought that it might make it easier for him, or for her, if she pretended for a few seconds more that it was just a joke, when it plainly wasn't.

"That's not a very flattering reaction, Simon. Perhaps it will set your mind at rest if I add that I'm speaking literally. I'm not asking to have sexual intercourse with you, although I'd certainly have no objection. But I do want to sleep in this bed with you, lying beside you, all night long."

133

Simon pressed his spine into the back of the chair, in order to reassure himself that it was still solid . . . it, rather, that *he* was still solid, although he couldn't . . . literally couldn't . . . imagine what else he could be.

The only question his mind could form was: "Why?"

"Because I want to share your dream . . . and to share my dream with you. I want us to dream together."

"And you can make that happen?" He was genuinely curious.

"I'm not at all sure that I'll be making it happen, but it will happen. I can't guarantee the nature of the dream, obviously, and I can't guarantee that you'll remember it after you wake up, although I can guarantee that I will, and I think there's probably a good chance that you will too. Either way, it will be useful practice for Friday."

"Friday?"

"Yes. You'll be staying overnight at the Abbey . . . if you agree to it, obviously. You have to want to, just as you have to want to sleep with me now. Grandmother told you to be kind to me, I know, but if it's to work, there has to be more than kindness. At least, that's what I think. Kindness doesn't hurt, mind. You were kind to Lilith's daughter apparently. That *was* necessary, because she can only have had the vaguest idea what she was doing, and why."

"She was way ahead of me, then," muttered Simon.

"And yet, you're here. And you heard what Lenore said to you. Don't worry about the explanations, for now—James knows that Melusine intends to lay her cards on the table, so he's bound to lay out his. This time tomorrow, you'll have explanations coming out of your ears. Whether you can make sense of them is a different matter. It might even be better if you didn't try . . . but I honestly think that it will be better for you as well as for me if you dream with me first. You might enjoy it—it's not unknown."

"You've done this before, then?"

"Shared dreams? Oh, yes. I've had sexual intercourse before too, although it was a long time ago now, if that's what you meant. I haven't had the opportunity to sleep with a neider before, though, so I suppose it will be my first time in that sense. Actually, you've probably done it lots of times yourself, without knowing it and without remembering it—dreaming together, I mean, not the sexual intercourse . . . although you've done that too, obviously."

Again, Simon felt reality—or sanity, at least—slipping away, although he was not sure that it had ever returned, since Lenore had warned him that a storm was coming. Obviously the clever bird knew about double meanings as well as meteorology.

Felicia closed the book that she had been reading while she waited for him. She placed it carefully on the bedside table. Then she removed her spectacles, and placed them on top of it. Then she looked directly at him, her blue eyes seeming slightly green in the lamplight. "I don't know if I can do this properly," she said, apologetically. "I know that I'm not. . . well, not Cerys. But I need to try. I need to try to make you want to. Will you come and sit on the bed, please, Simon, and at least take my hand? Out of kindness, if that's all you can manage . . . although it would be so much better if you could really . . . feel something."

Her voice was no longer attempting to sound flirtatious. It had become more serious, as if she were trying to drop the act she had been putting on, the human mask that she had been wearing, which did not quite fit, and never had, in a hundred years and longer.

Simon could no longer feel the back of the chair against his vertebrae. That was because he was leaning forward. He took the hands that were reaching toward him, and allowed them to pull him on to the bed. Felicia moved sideways, to make room for him, and slithered toward the bottom on the bed, so that she could lie full length, with her head on the pillow. He slithered too, until he was lying beside her, facing her. They were both fully dressed, but he knew that it didn't matter.

She was still looking into his eyes, but he knew that without the corrective lenses she wouldn't really be able to bring his own face into focus. He also knew, however, that it wasn't his face that interested her—how could it?—and that the image formed on her retina wasn't really what she was striving to behold. She wasn't trying to see him at all. She wasn't trying to make sense of him. She was a great reader, but *The Seventh Element* wasn't the only broth of words that she had put away for the moment, and the glass lenses with the brown frames weren't the only focusing device she had set aside.

He felt slightly guilty about the fact that he wasn't being kind, or loving. He felt, in fact, that he was merely curious, because that had always been his primary vice, his primary passion. He was sure that she was being honest, that she really did want to sleep with him . . . to abandon rational thought and let her consciousness drift into a vasty deep of disconnection.

But that wasn't what he wanted. Whatever he was, he told himself, he couldn't be the same kind of creature as her. But she was right in thinking that kindness wouldn't have been enough; he really did need to want to be there, if he were ever going to arrive at that particular terminus. And he didn't. Not because she was an old lady, perhaps even old enough to be his mother or his great-aunt, because he thought, in fact, that she wasn't physically unattractive. What he didn't want was to let her into his dreams, because he didn't think that they were any place for a decent old lady like her to be.

Fortunately, he was certain that he wasn't going to go to sleep, and although he wasn't sure that wakefulness would guarantee that he was safe from dreaming, he thought that it would at least assure him of a degree of control over any dream he had, and thus protect Felicia from the wilder excesses of the unfettered imagination.

He did want to protect her. He didn't know her yet, so he couldn't tell whether he liked her, or how much, but he did want to protect her, as Cerys and Ceridwen had both urged him to do. He wanted to be kind to her, within limits.

He thought perhaps that he ought to be glad that it was Felicia who had come to him first, before James the scholar or Melusine the morgen. Logically, perhaps, it ought to have been the other way around, and Felicia should have been the last, after the siren song and the scholarly account . . . but the whole point of this bizarre revelation, if it had any point at all, was to drive home the awareness that everything was topsy-turvy now, and that it would be infinitely more convenient and satisfactory for him if he could *feel* his way to a sense of who and what he really was, given that he was, as yet, unborn, or at the very least untransformed, still in his human chrysalis, not even dreaming, as yet, of fulfilling his real biological destiny . . .

Perhaps, indeed, he ought to be glad . . . but he wasn't. He couldn't be. Wretched as his self might be, he was what he knew, what he was accustomed to, and his instinct was to cling to it with all his might.

Felicia let go of his hands and wrapped her arms around him, pressing her body against his from the tips of her tiny feet all the way to her soft, frail breasts. He put his arms around her, and became sharply aware of the extent to which he had missed that human contact in the last seven years. He had missed the sex, obviously, but intercourse, when viewed retrospectively, from the objectivity of the long aftermath, was brief, spasmodic and egotistical—impersonal, even— whereas bodily contact of a less hectic kind, calm, unfeverish and close, was authentically intimate, authentically soothing, authentically rewarding . . .

He realized, very belatedly, that what he had appreciated most about his relationships with women, had not been the sex *per se*, but sleeping with his partners, in the literal sense. But he had not shared their dreams. That was impossible, and absurd.

He wrapped his arms around Felicia—very carefully, because she was an old woman—and kissed her very softly on the forehead, not in the manner of a grandchild kissing a venerable ancestor, but in the manner of someone who knew that, for the moment, the mind was more important than the lips, and the idea more important than the flesh.

She already seemed to be asleep, already released into the deep beneath the surface of consciousness, adrift in an element beyond the known spectrum of material possibility.

He had vaguely assumed, when Felicia had first mentioned sharing a dream, that that meant sharing the images of a dream, seeing the same hallucinations, strolling hand in hand through an Eden of the imagination. Perhaps, with someone else, that might have been possible, but Felicia, he knew, was a great reader. Like his, her imagination was not primarily orientated toward visual imagery, and her dreams were not cinematic.

Reading, Simon knew, was a perversion of sight; it switched off the normal functions of visual interpretation in order to turn the optical process into a kind of deciphering device. What the eye *saw* was a long series of symbols on the page, but what the mind *consumed* was the meaning of those symbols. It was a form of translation, and when done with full engagement, cutting narrative distance to a minimum, it could simulate, and perhaps even achieve, a kind of identification with the meaning of the text. A true reader—an expert reader, a talented reader—could almost enter into the text, ignoring the world outside and living in the world within the text instead. Reading, when done wholeheartedly, was an altered state of consciousness, more closely akin to sleep than wakefulness. It was an emotional state of mind at least as much as an intellectual one.

Reading was certainly food for thought, but it was also food for feeling, and if it educated thought, as it surely could, if only rarely for the kind of reader who liked formularistic plots and formularistic denouements, it did so primarily by way of feeling. When readers entered fully into books, when they became real translators rather than mere skimmers, they opened up the well of the emotions. Simon knew that better than anyone. How many times, while translating, had he been in floods of tears, hardly able to focus on the page of text that he was translating?

Felicia had put down the book she had been reading, but only so that she could read the author instead of the book, in order that she could translate the text of his inner being instead of symbols on a printed page. That was her talent, her expertise, her genius. And her interest was not primarily intellectual. The quest for food for thought was not uppermost in her motivation. What she really craved was feeling, shared emotion.

That was unwise, he thought—or at least, it was unwise for her to want to sleep with him for that purpose. He had learned long ago to hide his feelings from people, even to the limited extent that they might perceive them in his speech. People did not like that aspect of him, that element of his personality.

But there was a part of him, too, that wanted her to do it. There was something in him that wanted to be read, and read by Felicia, even though he knew nothing about her, and did not even know as yet whether he liked her. There was a part of him that would have liked her to know him, and to love him—and for precisely that reason, he wanted to protect her, and to be kind to her.

His body, lying on the bed, was still fully clothed, but he had an uncomfortable sensation that his mind was naked, as it was when he was fully committed to a translation, having entered as intimately as possible into the text he was translating. It was his imagination, obviously; he had no intention of endeavoring to translate Felicia, even if that were conceivable as a mental process, and he had no intention of allowing her to translate him. That kind of mutual penetration was far beyond the scope of his meager imagination. It would be no mere insertion, no mere friction, no mere stimulation aimed at spasmodic release. It really would be a kind of sharing, a kind of sharing that would need to be as necessary for him as for her, if that were possible. But it was not. He knew that he had never been able to see himself clearly from within, and that it was a mercy, for himself at least, that that was the case.

In order for eyes to look at themselves, Simon thought, subvocally, *they need a mirror, but the mind's eye has no mirror.* Even now, his mind's eye had no mirror; it could not simply look at his soul and evaluate its true dimensions, its true species and its true identity. Perhaps, if he really had been able to share Felicia's dream, he might have been able—at last—to see himself from a different point of view, to obtain a more distanced and more accurate sense of himself, of what he really was.

But that was impossible.

Mercifully.

James, he realized, would probably give him the words, would allow him to get a mental grip of whatever he was supposed by the Murdens to be, and why it might be important for him to be whatever that was at this particular point in time. Melusine might attempt to inform him, and perhaps help him to comprehend, what the morgens had once enabled St. Madoc to see, in order to seduce him into the pact that he had made. But Felicia was surely the only one of the three who could might have been able to make him sense himself, to know himself, to be at one, not merely with the identity he had forged for himself so ineptly in the past—the ridiculous artifact that he had made of Simon Cannick, writer and abysmal failure as a human being—but with his real self, the neider that he really was.

She might, had such a feat been possible.

It was a pity, he thought, that he could not really be some kind of bizarre sea monster, some fabulous hydra with snaky tentacles. After all, he had never been fitted for human life. Almost as soon as he had become conscious of being, he had become conscious of being wrong . . . not merely different, but *wrong*.

His adoptive parents had never tried to pretend that he was really their child; they had always been honest with him. His mother had wanted a child, desperately, and had wanted to love that child, dearly, but she had not been able to bear one, physically, because of some defect in her flesh. So she had adopted one, more or less at random. He was a foundling, and she had been fortunate enough to find him, and for her, that had been an enormous privilege, an enormous stroke of luck, because she had been well aware of what a privilege and what an enormous gift of fortune it was to have a child, she had loved that child more than many a mother did for whom pregnancy had simply been something that had happened to her, and her child simply something that had dropped out of her entrails, painfully, when she could no longer hold it in.

But it had not been anything personal. He could have been any child, any foundling. What she had loved in him was *what* he was, not *who* he was.

Because she had been fortunate, so had he. He knew that. He had been loved. She had been lucky, too, in having a good and careful husband, who had thus provided Simon with a careful and responsible father. He had been cared for, responsibly. He had been lucky—far luckier than many.

But still, he had been *wrong*. He had been wrong for the part. He had been miscast. He was a changeling. He had never been fully equipped to be a human being. Before he had cut his first tooth, learned to smile, learned to crawl and learned to talk, he had been a misfit. And once he had learned to read, he had had a way out of that world, where he felt so uncomfortable, into another, into an infinite number of others. And once he had learned to write, he had had the tools necessary to build worlds of that kind, to become a creator as well as a user of worlds made out of words. He had had a license to play with ideas.

He had never had a talent for it. He was painfully aware of that. He had been a very slow learner, serving a very long apprenticeship in the use of those tools, and he had never become a master, never produced the masterpiece that would have allowed him to think that he was authentically qualified. Part of the reason for his obsession, he knew, was the simple fact that he was not very good at what he did. Part of the reason why he was such a stubbornly esoteric writer, so stubbornly contemptuous of what the majority of readers actually wanted to read, was because he knew that, no matter what efforts he made, he would not have been able to please them anyway, because he simply was not very good at the one and only thing he had ever wanted to do, the only thing that he had ever been able to do . . . after a fashion.

Even there, he was wrong. Even though there was nothing left of him now but the translator and writer, who made a point of slaving over a keyboard for eleven hours a day, and would gladly have made it twelve if he had not grown so tired that his mind and his typing eventually collapsed into weary incoherence, he was not very good at what he did, not very good at being what he was, and no good at all at being *who* he was. Not that he ever let on, of course. Of all the feelings he hid, that was perhaps the most intimate. People glimpsed it, obviously. They sensed it. But they could never be certain of what it was they sensed; there was always doubt, always dissimulation.

He had contrived to avoid many of the things that he had known that he would be no good at. He had never learned to swim. He had never learned to drive a car. But those were avoidable, other things were not. Children had been avoidable, and he had contrived to avoid imposing on any he might conceivably have fathered the penalty and the burden of having him for a father. Human relationships had not been avoidable, nor had he wanted to avoid them. He had wanted to love, and, if possible, to be loved, even though he had always known, in his heart of hearts, that he would not be very good at it. So he had had relationships. He had even contrived—Heaven only knew how—to get married. But he had been a lousy husband. He could no more measure up to the desires and expectations of a wife than he could measure up to the desires and expectations of the reading public. He knew that, although it hadn't made the divorce any less easy to bear, or the seven lonely years that had followed, when he had recognized the simple impossibility of trying to form any new relationship with a comparable level of intimacy.

It could never have succeeded, because he was simply *wrong*. Even his writing could never really have succeeded;

the best he could ever have hoped for was to scrape by, and he was fortunate to have been able to do that, to have been able to find a hole to hide in, in order to cut himself off from any meaningful contact with the human world.

He had not been able to avoid being a human being, living a human life, but the simple fact was that he was not very good at it.

Perhaps it would have made him feel better to know that he really was a changeling, that he was really a neider—but how could it? The word existed, apparently, although he had not even known that until today, but its meaning was unclear and he still knew, no matter how hard he tried, in the grip of Felicia's ancient arms, that whatever it was supposed to mean, it was impossible that he or she could be one. No matter how hard he tried, even if he were able to attempt it as a *folie à deux*, he knew that he was not going to be any good at this either, whatever it was. No matter how persuasively James Murden explained it, and no matter how seductively Melusine allowed him to see it, he was not going to be able to believe it. He was wrong for the part.

He was only human. He could play with ideas, but he was no good when it came to letting ideas play with him. He could write books—mediocre books—but he would be no good at all at being in one. He was not cut from the cloth of a hero, a villain, or any kind of character with whom readers could actually engage. And who could possibly want a fate like that anyhow? Who could possibly want to be a figment of someone else's imagination, obliged to follow whatever fate had laid down for them by their scheming, likely to be astonished and betrayed at any moment by the whim of their wayward inspiration, bound by no natural law, or even by any reasonable standard of plausibility?

Oh, no. As a writer himself, that was a fate he would not wish on anyone. Better to be real, no matter how incompetent one was, no matter how doomed one might be to ignominious failure. It was far better to be real than even the most favored of protagonists, the most fortunate beneficiary of a *deus ex machina*. Better to be real—except that the world was such a shitty place, and life such a travesty of reason and justice. At least it was impossible to believe that reality had a writer. No one could be *that* bad.

He wondered, now, whether he had ever had a real relationship in his life, with anyone. Had he even had a real relationship with his biological parents, whoever they were, and all the ancestors from which he had been descended? Did he even really exist, in any meaningful sense?

He knew, of course, that in the cosmic perspective, he was not what he thought himself to be, any more than anyone else was. He was merely an abortive attempt at a reproductive device with delusions of grandeur.

Real biological entities, he knew, were immortal. They reproduced themselves infinitely. The entities that appeared to the human eye to be individuals, to be creatures, were merely artifices that egg cells used in order to make more egg cells. Complexity, beauty and intelligence were simply ploys in the manufacture of more egg cells, hopeful experimental attempts to design better processes of replication. And most of them failed. He was not alone, by any means, in being utterly useless within the context of the great cosmic design. The vast majority of organisms gave rise to no offspring at all. The overwhelming majority were eaten by other avid organisms before they ever got a chance to reproduce.

Of every million elvers hatched in the murky depths of the Sargasso Sea, he knew, only one, if that, actually made it through the bizarre ritual of swimming across the Atlantic, finding a river, swimming up it, growing to adulthood, and swimming all the way back again in order to lay a million new eggs. Why did they do that? What bizarre freak of natural selection caused them to indulge in such utterly absurd behavior? No one knew; no one could even imagine a reason. But the fact was that they did it, and that for every one that succeeded, at least a million failed. At least they died trying. They died doing what it was that cruel biological destiny had shaped them to do. If they didn't get eaten on the way, they did what they were supposed to do. Elvers that survived their extraordinary odyssey and grew up to be eels, difficult as that was, were presumably good at being eels. They were good enough to do their bit in making more eggs, in securing the immortality of their single-celled creator.

But he had not. Within the great cosmic scheme of things, he had done nothing. He had not swum the Atlantic, he had not made his way up a river in quest of its source, he had not turned around and gone back again, swum the Atlantic for a second time, and spawned. Instead, he had written books— hundreds of the damned things. And not very well. They were wrong for the part, miscast, just as he had been miscast as a human being. He was far more of a freak, far more of a monster, than any eel, morgen, sea serpent or giant disintegrating hydra. His was the truly bizarre existence.

And if he really had been a neider, whatever that was, what difference could it possibly have made?

Not only had he not done anything for the cause of his own single-celled creator, he knew, but he had not even done anything to assist other human organisms to fulfill their function, after the fashion of his foster-parents, who had at least tried, when they knew that they could not have a child of their own, to bring up an abandoned and unwanted child, in the hope that he might become an effective reproduction machine. They had done it for egotistical reasons of self-satisfaction, but they had done it. They had been heroic, in their own limited fashion. What had he ever done, even by way of acts of kindness, except hold the hand of an old lady who was dying, for an hour or two in the evening? And he had only done that because he had had nothing better to do, because he had simply been too tired to go on working effectively.

Had even that been a true act of kindness? No, of course not. He had got infinitely more comfort out of it than poor dying Eve. She had not even been able to talk, whereas he had had all the opportunity that he could possibly have wanted to tell her about himself, about his so-called work, and to feel virtuous in doing it. He had not been able to hear her confession, to grant her absolution for her real or imaginary sins, or to console her with some fantasy of life beyond death . . .

No, that wasn't strictly true. He was being too indulgent with his self-flagellation and his self-pity. He had made some attempt to console her. He had talked to her about the possibility of some kind of life after death. But he had only done so in the context of his own playing with ideas. He had never offered her a glimpse of paradise, any idea of existence beyond her present wretched, expiring life that could possibly make the prospect seem attractive. He had never attempted any magic, real or delusory, that might spare her the tiniest parcel of regret.

Poor Eve! At least he had always been able to make a living selling his soul; she had been forced do it by selling her flesh. Perhaps she had been good at it—she must at least have been successfully meeting a demand—but even so . . . and yet, from a cosmic perspective, she had contrived in spite of everything to fulfill the mission of her single-celled creator. She had given birth to a daughter she had named Angela, and that daughter had given birth to a daughter in her turn . . . and perhaps, although he still could not believe it, and would not believe it no matter what Megan Harwyn claimed that her DNA-comparison implied—a son as well, whom she had heroically abandoned, in order to give him a chance of a better life than she felt capable of providing at the time.

Had she—Eve, that is, not her daughter—obtained any satisfaction from that eventual result? Had it made her life seemed worthwhile? He hoped so, but he couldn't imagine that it had. Even if Megan Harwyn's fantasy were true, and she really had taken him in, lent him the flat in Bristol, and then given him Raven Cottage, because she felt a sense of empathy or distant kinship with him, had that improved the quality of her life in any significant degree? Had it really made any difference to her that he had sat by her bedside for a few hours while she was dying, and held her hand? And would it have made any more difference if he really were her grandson, than if he were a random stranger who was only holding her hand because he had nothing better to do?

He remembered, suddenly, that he was supposed to be sharing Felicia's dream. She had slipped out of the Abbey and had come to the cottage to wait for him, in his bedroom, with the intention of putting her arms around him, of holding him closely, and reading him, and taking him away into a dream-dimension, and he had not even spared her a thought, had not even tried to catch the slightest glimpse of her dream! She had come to him intent on some kind of intimate collaboration, but what was she getting? Nothing. But what would he have been capable of giving her, if it had been possible to give her anything at all? An exaggerated misery memoir, it seemed: an orgy of self-pity? Whatever she had wanted, surely it could not possibly have been that. Surely she had expected far more of his imagination than that. How disappointed she would have been, if the kind of collaboration of which she had dreamed had really been possible! And she had guaranteed that when she woke up, she, at least, would remember what they had dreamed. Poor Felicia! At least he had spared her that. At least he had kept his depression to himself, had preserved discretion, decorum and silent decency.

Had her life, he wondered, been any more rewarding than Eve's? She had been cooped up in that house with her crazy brother, her crazy cousin and her even crazier great-grandmother for the last fifty years or more. She had never married, had never had children. She had, it seemed, been intimate with men before, had even had sexual intercourse with them, although the dismissive manner in which she had made that reference had suggested strongly that she had obtained no great fulfillment from it. Mostly, it seemed, she had read. She had read Poe, she had read Shakespeare, and doubtless hundreds of other writers infinitely more rewarding than Simon Cannick. But he could not imagine, though, that that had been enough to constitute a life worth living for a hundred years and more, for a human being.

Except, he ought not to forget, that she was not entirely human. Apparently, she did not know exactly what it entailed, but she was convinced that she was a neider as well as a human being. What could that possibly mean? What possibilities were attached to it, not merely for her but for him, in her mind? What did she expect of him in consequence? What did they all expect of him?

There was still something he was missing about this whole business, about its history, its present and, perhaps most importantly, its possibilities for further development. Evidently, Felicia and the other members of her family felt that there was something they were missing too, because they too were still trying to understand, but they thought, for whatever reason, that he might be able to play a part in helping them to do it. They had far more of the jigsaw-pieces of the mystery in their possession than he had, but still they could not quite fit them together. His advent had excited them all because it was not only an extra piece to be slotted into the jigsaw, but because they thought that it might lead to further revelations. They had been waiting for a long time, not necessarily for him, but for *something* . . . something perhaps as mysterious to them as it was to him for the moment, but something potentially hopeful.

And all they had got, alas, was him. He knew, in the utmost depths of his soul, that whatever they wanted of him—whatever they wanted him to do, or say, or dream—he would not be any good at it. He knew that he would simply not be up to the task, whatever it might be. And for that, he felt remorse—twisted remorse, perhaps, but remorse nevertheless. Not so much for James or Melusine, but for frail old Ceridwen, and most of all for Felicia, who had wanted to sleep with him and share her dream with him.

He felt that he was letting her down badly, and he regretted that. He liked Felicia. He was grateful to her, because she had wanted to put her arms around him, and he was grateful to her, too, for having wanted him to put his arms around her, and for permitting him to do it. She was an old lady, not a beautiful young woman like Cerys, and he felt no particular lust for her body, but for *her*, for her true self, he felt a definite affection, and more.

He would have liked to have given her more. He would have liked their collaborative dream to have been Shakespearean, or at least Poesque. He would have liked it to be well-written, well-imagined, beautiful, or even awesome. But it wasn't. He knew that. It was just him. It wasn't even an amusing game of ideas. It was just the way he really felt, which was awful.

He hugged her a little more closely, and tried to tell her, telepathically, how truly sorry he was.

He felt moisture on her face, and thought for a moment that she was weeping, but he realized that the tears were, in fact, his.

Well, he thought, *if this is what my human existence amounts to, perhaps I ought to wish that I really were a neider, whatever a neider is. Perhaps I ought to wish that I were a snake or an eel, or a hydra, or some other kind of sea creature. But I can't even believe in the etymology of the word. It's not neidr, it's* neither, *or* nada. *It's* nothing: *a void of understanding, a sign with no referent. That's the whole problem. I'm a hybrid, but I'm not half-human and half-alien, I'm half-human and half-non-existent, half-abortion and half-black hole . . .*

The train of thought presumably ran on, and on . . . but when he eventually woke up, evidently having escaped into sleep, that was all he could remember.

XI
Dawn

When Simon woke up, it was still dark. The bedside lamp was still on. Felicia was no longer in his arms, nor he in hers. She was standing beside the bed, reaching out for the book that she had put down on the bedside table. He realized that she must have slithered down to the bottom of the bed and made her way around it, in an attempt not to wake him. When she saw that he was awake, a slight grimace appeared on her face, and he inferred that she had intended to slip out silently.

"I have to go now," she said, "or I'll be missed. But thank you. I needed that. And I'm truly sorry."

"Sorry?" he queried, uncomprehendingly.

"Yes. I really hadn't intended to dump all that on you. I really hadn't expected it . . . I simply hadn't realized how . . . well, I honestly didn't know what would come of it . . . it's been such a long time . . . but I really didn't expect that. I haven't done you any favors, I'm afraid. I'm sorry . . . I've been very selfish."

He sat up, abruptly. "But I'm the one who should be apologizing," he said. "I failed you. I'm the one who . . ."

She reached not with her hand and placed her forefinger over his lips.

"Don't think that," she said. "It's confusing, I know, but it really wasn't you. It was me. I hadn't realized . . . I'm older than I thought, obviously. I thought that although my body had aged, my mind was still young. Self-delusion. I needed it, but it wasn't fair to you. Please don't think that it was your fault, because it wasn't. And it won't happen again. James is all talk, and whatever Melusine tries, the result will be kinder than that. I'm a wreck, I'm afraid, but she's still strong. There's far more morgen about her than neider in me. And whatever grandmother has in mind for Friday . . . well, I can't believe that it will involve begging you to lie down with her and letting her into your dreams. She's too wise for that. Even she doesn't really know what the pact involves, but I'm sure that she must have a better idea of what's actually inside the vitreous cocoons than James or Melusine. Don't ask me about that now . . . James will explain it, or Melusine will, if he still wants to eke out his secrets. Remember, though, that they don't really *know*. They're convinced they've thought it through, but they can't have, really, or they wouldn't have reached different conclusions. I really do have to go, though, and I truly am sorry. Please forgive me, if you can."

150

And with that, she slipped through the doorway, where the door still stood open, and disappeared. He heard the key turn in the lock on the front door, and the door click shut again, as she closed it, as quietly as she could.

He didn't know what to read into what she had said. Had she, then, picked up empathically on the undercurrent of his dismal train of thought? And had she mistakenly thought that she was really feeling it, on her own account?

No. That wasn't possible. He didn't want it to be possible. And they had been his tears, not hers.

He lifted the curtain, and looked out of the window, which faced south-eastwards. A pre-dawn pallor was just beginning to tint the sky.

He got up and went into the bathroom. He undressed, had a shower, and then came back into the bedroom, leaving the clothes he had been wearing in the laundry basket. He put on clean ones, and then went downstairs. By the time he put two slices of stale bread into the toaster, dawn was breaking, but from the kitchen window he could not see the leading edge of the sun peeping over the horizon.

He did not know what to think. He was no longer sure, in fact, what he had been thinking. The train of thought still seemed clear in his mind, but he was no longer sure that he had actually thought it. Perhaps he had dreamed it. He knew from long experience how easy it was to dream that he was translating. It had to be just as possible, just as likely, that he might dream that he was thinking. But wasn't thinking itself a kind of lucid dream? What was the difference, then, if any, between dreaming that he was thinking and actually thinking?

It had all been true . . . but he was no longer sure that the feelings reflected by the thoughts had simply been a kind of emotional backwash. Perhaps, in fact, it had been the feelings that had prompted the thoughts, rather than the thoughts that had prompted the feelings.

What if, in fact . . . ?

But no.

Even so, he thought: *Poor Felicia!* And he wanted to hug her again, to tell her that there was nothing to be forgiven, nothing for which she needed to feel sorry, that he had needed to see himself as he had seen himself the previous night, at least as much as she had needed the closeness and intimacy that she had wanted him to provide for her, and seemed to think that he had provided for her, although she must surely have been dreaming her own dream, with its own intimate images, regrets and twisted remorse . . . and had been afraid that she might somehow have inflicted some kind of overflow on him.

Poor Felicia! He certainly had no need of any portion of her self-dissatisfaction to stimulate his own. He would have to reassure her as to that, next time he saw her.

He wondered, however, what he . . . what they . . . might have dreamed after he had fallen asleep, and which he had now completely forgotten . . . if any such sharing were, in fact, possible . . .

He wondered, too, what on earth the "vitreous cocoons" might be. That was a phrase that had never cropped up before. Apparently, however, he would probably have the explanation before the day was out.

The kettle boiled, and he poured hot water on to the instant coffee in a mug. He buttered his toast and spread marmalade on it. The toast was brittle, as toast made with stale bread invariably was, but he ate it with a certain amount of pleasure and satisfaction. The caffeine in the coffee seemed to take almost instant effect, but he knew that it was probably an illusion, an effect of psychological conditioning.

He went into the study and switched on the computer. He was late for work, he realized. He had slept way beyond five o'clock. Dawn, at this time of year, was nearer seven, and the computer's time display told him that it was now after half-past. His routine was already wrecked. He downloaded his email, reflexively, but there was nothing but junk. Then he checked the weather forecast.

The Met Office had named the storm that was brewing in the Atlantic Storm Deirdre, which signified that they thought that was going to be violent. Given the current position of the jet stream, it was scheduled to track across the sea south of the coast of Ireland and run straight into Saint David's Head before skimming the coast all the way to Cardigan Bay, veering landwards in the vicinity of Morgan's Fork at approximately eight o'clock on Saturday evening. Flood warnings had been posted, and gale-force winds anticipated, but there was no mention of stars falling from the sky. Such anomalous phenomena were not within the Met Office remit.

Simon put on the headphones, switched on the background music, found the pdf file of his current translation, and opened the document—but summoning up the enthusiasm required to plug on with the translation was more difficult, and when he had started, his mind kept wandering. He cursed himself for not being able to reconnect with normality, because he felt the necessity of doing so even more keenly than he had the previous day.

The knowledge that he couldn't possibly reach his wordage quota for the day, having started two hours late, nagged his consciousness like an illusory toothache, made worse by the fact that he had lost an entire afternoon the day before, and was highly likely to lose a similar amount of time later today.

Rather than the annoyance it would normally have been, it was almost a relief when the doorbell cut rudely into Rimsky-Korsakov's *Scheherazade*.

He assumed, as he went to open the door, that it would be James Murden, but it was actually a van driver with his consignment of groceries. It was a large consignment, and there were two heavy boxes to carry through into the kitchen and unload. The distribution, between the refrigerator, the freezer, the larder and the dresser, took a full quarter of an hour. By the time he had made himself another cup of coffee and returned to the computer it was half past ten, and the fifty minutes remaining before his scheduled walk seemed entirely inadequate to any serious accomplishment. He used every minute of it, with grim determination, but once again, it was a relief to close the documents, slot in the memory stick, back up the document, put on his leather jacket, and step out of the front door of Raven Cottage.

The sky was heavily overcast again, but it wasn't actually raining—at least, not yet. He turned left at the end of the street and headed for the one bridge that he had not yet crossed.

Megan Harwyn was standing in the middle of the bridge, evidently waiting to intercept him.

"Do you mind if I walk with you?" she asked. "I can keep up."

"Feel free," he said, curtly, hurriedly checking his watch without pausing in his stride. He wondered whether he was going to have company every time he went for a walk in the arse end of nowhere. At least no one had taken the slightest notice of him in the civilized streets of Bristol.

"I've just had a visit," she said. "Well, two actually, but I don't really count the one from the Reverend, although I suppose it required a bit of an effort on his part to pay a courtesy call on a scarlet woman. I mean a visit from James."

"Really?" said Simon. "Is he so very anxious to hear the result of your DNA-comparison, or does he finally want to acknowledge you as his daughter?"

"Who told you that?" she said. "No . . . obviously not— and I won't have the result of the comparison for at least a week, probably a fortnight. I gather, though, that I'm no longer keeping anyone at the Abbey in suspense. James said he wanted to save me the trouble of any more searching for information and any more . . . *machinations* was the word he used. Actually, I suspect he just wanted me to know that he'd crossed the bridge. He says that he's meeting a delegation of emergency tenants from Morpen this afternoon to discuss the possibility of letting them stay on longer. He mentioned that you had something to do with that."

"I just passed on a request for a meeting when I was invited to the abbey yesterday."

"From that Cardi who buttonholed you when you went for a walk yesterday?"

"Yes."

"You've got a bit of a nerve, sticking your nose into our business before you've been here forty-eight hours.

"I didn't stick my nose in. I was grabbed bodily as soon as I arrived—by you among others. In any case, I had no idea that James would actually grant the request for a meeting, let alone consider the DHSS tenants' case seriously."

"I doubt that he is. Your arrival certainly seems to have stirred him out of his torpor, but I think he was just trying to annoy me, to pay me back for the DNA-test business. Anyway, he's reassured me that he'll do everything he can to keep the St. Madoc cottages as holiday lets, at least for the present season. He seems to have been emailing the other landlords furiously, though. I wouldn't be at all surprised if we don't both get summoned to some kind of mass meeting to debate the future of the villages. It's a pity he ever got that damned computer—everything was much quieter when the agents handled everything."

"Everything changes," said Simon, philosophically. "The twenty-first century was bound to reach St. Madoc eventually."

"It already had," she retorted, bitterly. "It's just that I used to be in sole charge of it. Now even the old witch has a bloody iPad."

"You were glad of it yesterday when you tipped her off that the younger generation had invited me over for a chat."

"And even that backfired! James was positively gloating when he called. I didn't realize how well off I was when he wasn't talking to me."

"If it's any consolation, he was seriously chagrined for at least thirty seconds when I got the summons from upstairs."

"There's no need for you to gloat too. I suppose you'll be siding with them against me from now on. And I have to live next door to you." After a pause, she added: "It was her, wasn't it?"

"Who? And what?"

"The old lady—she told you that James is my father. The aunts wouldn't have dared, and I'm not even sure that Cerys knows."

"Does it matter?"

"No, of course not. I just wonder what she's up to, that's all. I don't suppose you'd consider telling me what she said to you?"

"Mostly, she just asked me personal questions. Have you seen the weather forecast, by the way?"

"There are subtler ways of changing the subject. No, but it doesn't take a genius to tell that it's going to rain. We should be able to get back before it starts, though."

"No, I mean Friday's forecast—Storm Deidre."

"Oh, don't worry about that. We get them all the time, at least in winter. You'll soon get used to it. It's something to do with the gulf stream, apparently. The cottages are solidly built, and you've seen how deep the gullies are—there's no danger of flooding in St. Madoc, although Raven does get spray from the funneled waves when the tide's in and it's blowing a gale. Water piles up between the tines, you see, and there's a big splash where the two surges collide, near the bridge. Stay indoors, or you could get drenched."

"It might be unusually bad, apparently," Simon persisted. "The tributary of the gulf stream isn't the only factor. The atmosphere is unusually active because of the combination of global warming and last year's El Niño, and because the jet stream, which has been counterbalancing the gulf stream effect for most of the winter, has settled into a position where it will supplement it this time."

Megan waved a hand dismissively. "Seen it all before," she said. "Trust me, it blows over soon enough. And lightning never strikes the cottages. The Abbey's quite a target, mind—that lightning conductor's the third one James has put up since I started wintering here. So much for it never striking twice in the same place—but they seem to work, once at least. Do we really have to talk about the weather?"

"No, of course not," Simon said. "What would you rather talk about? Nineteenth-century French fantasy or web design?"

"For five minutes yesterday, you know, I actually quite liked you," she said. "I thought that, as next-door neighbors went, you might be better than most. I suppose it's my own fault, though, for bringing you to James's attention. I only wanted to give him a little poke—how was I to know that it would turn the whole world upside down?"

"You didn't."

"What?"

"You didn't bring me to James's attention. You just provided him with a little supplementary information. He would have invited me to the Abbey, and everything would have been turned upside down, even if you hadn't said a word—but don't ask me why, because I don't know yet."

She stared at him. "The bloody Reverend!" she guessed.

"No. It was Lenore."

"Lenore? Felicia's pet raven?"

"Apparently. When she came tap-tap-tapping at my window I assumed that she'd been reading Edgar Poe and knew that I was a fan, but the Murdens apparently read something far more significant into it."

"That's bizarre!"

"True. Almost as bizarre as what the bird said to me—but that was my imagination running away with me. It's been doing that a lot over the last two days. You know, I suppose, about the curse on the Murden women?"

"What curse? The Reverend didn't say anything about a curse in the pub . . . but you saw him again last night, I gather?"

"Briefly, but it wasn't him who mentioned it. The information you provided about Lilith and Eve seems to have added further examples of Murden women who never married . . . in addition to Ceridwen, Melanie, Felicia and you, that is."

"And you think that's a curse?" Megan's lip was curled. "Anyway, the old lady, or the person she pretends to be, must have been married—she had four kids, according to the Reverend."

"He was probably being delicate in not mentioning that they were all born out of wedlock. You don't find the idea of a curse plausible, then?"

"Of course not. Anyway, I had offers. I could have been married if I'd wanted to."

"But you didn't?"

"No," she said, curtly. "You can figure out why, if you put your mind to it. Your mother was married, though . . . after she dumped you in the shopping center, admittedly . . . if Angela Auguerrand, as she must have been then, really was your mother, that is."

"I suspect that some might think her a rare exception. Of course, it might not just be the women. James and I aren't exactly shining examples."

"You've been married."

"Unsuccessfully. To tell you the truth, if I thought I were the victim of a curse, it might make me feel a trifle better about my many failings."

"Bollocks. For one thing, you don't believe in anything. For another, it would be as likely to make you feel worse as to make you feel better. I should have settled for talking about the weather, shouldn't I? Will you give me an honest answer to one question?"

"What is it?"

"Do you think he might?"

"Who? And what?"

"James, of course. You brought it up—do you actually have a reason to think that he intends to acknowledge that I'm his daughter?"

"Oh," said Simon, slightly embarrassed. "No—I'm sorry. I was just being flippant. That was insensitive; I should have realized that it's a big deal for you."

"I can prove it, you know."

"I know—and so does he, now you've kindly drawn his attention to the utility of DNA comparisons. But that's really why you chose this particular way to give him a poke, isn't it? It was a veiled threat."

"What was that you were saying about being sorry for being insensitive? Oh, never mind. I've got a thick skin. Yes it is. But I'm not trying to muscle in on the inheritance. Cerys can have the Abbey and the entire estate, for all I care—or you, if it comes to that. I don't even care whether she, or you, or anyone else surrounds me with Syrian refugees and Cardi riff-raff in my twilight years. I just want him to say he's sorry before he kicks the bucket. Is that so much to ask, after seventy fucking years of bare-faced lies? I just want him to admit that it was all his fault. Tell him that, if you like—in fact, I'd be grateful to you if you would, even if it's just to commiserate with him about how much sharper than a serpent's tooth it is to have a thankless child."

"I'll mention it when he comes to see me," Simon said, mildly. "*Sans* commiseration. And for what it's worth, I have absolutely no designs on the Abbey. If the members of the present older generation ever bother to die, and you succeed in proving your claim, you're more than welcome to it—but please don't leave poor Cerys destitute. She really would believe there's a curse then."

Megan took time out to draw breath. "Sorry about that little outburst," she said. "Don't even have the excuse of being drunk, do I? Here am I casting aspersions on your qualities as a neighbor, and I'm turning myself into the batty old bitch next door. I really should have let you run with the weather."

"No problem. What did the Reverend have to say when he came to see you?"

"Just goodbye. He hesitated over ringing your doorbell, but he thought you might not appreciate being interrupted at work. He asked me to give you his best wishes. He didn't manage to reach the cave, by the way. I had told him that it's inaccessible at low tide, but he had to see for himself and get his boots muddy all the way up to the knee. He'd already tried to get one of the local boatmen to take him inside at the point when the water level's just right, but none of them would risk it. No guts, he says—according to him, the old smugglers used to slip in and out like eels, although the revenue men came to grief more than once. He's not a bad fellow, for a rev—and he's a real mine of useless information. I learned a lot the night before last, thanks to you. He wouldn't even have talked to me if you hadn't been there."

"Not very Christian, considering that Jesus made a point of being kind to prostitutes."

"Perhaps they gave him a discount. Not that I'd have made that suggestion to the Reverend, mind, even when drunk. I always treated them with respect, even back in the day. Real gentlemen, for the most part—the ones who preferred whores to little boys, that is. But we're almost back to the bridge again. I swear I won't be lying in wait for you tomorrow, no matter how eager I am to find out what James has to say to you—or as much of it as you might willing to divulge. I'll just hunker down and wait for the storm to pass . . . and if lightning should strike, I'll do what I can to help. I should never have dragged you into my petty quarrels in the first place, but I hope you can forgive me. Jesus would, apparently. See you, neighbor."

And with that, she hurried off ahead of him, without offering him a cup of tea. He decided to attribute that to consideration for his busy schedule, and thought that, on the whole, the conversation and the walk had restored his sense of normality to an acceptable level.

While Megan Harwyn was letting herself into Sanderling, Simon turned into his own garden path, and pulled out his door key, feeling that he was ready to do full justice to a spot of lunch.

XII
The Seventh Element

"How did your meeting at the Mermaid go?" Simon asked James Murden, when he had invited him to sit down in the armchair in the study. James had refused tea, coffee and alcohol, and even though his eyes had scanned the room mechanically, taking in the bookshelves and the computer, they had done so absent-mindedly, as if his mind, focused on his mission, had not attention to spare for trivia.

"Not well, I fear," he said, in answer to the question—and might have left it at that if he had not realized, a trifle belatedly, that Simon was curious to obtain more details. "I explained the ownership of the cottages in Morpen as best I could, and my own financial situation," he continued, "but there's nothing I can do to relieve their problems for the current year except to attempt to convene a meeting of landlords and tenants—which might not come to anything if a substantial fraction of the landlords refuse to attend, as they might."

"Really?" said Simon. "I thought they were all family members—cousins, I assume."

"Indeed—and family disputes are extraordinarily long-lasting and spiteful. Because they're relatives, the tenants seem to assume that I must have influence over them, but it's more a matter of stubborn hostility. I fear that I left everything in the hands of the agents for far too long, rather than trying to reorganize things myself, but . . . well, to tell you the blunt truth, I didn't expect to live as long as I have. I assumed for a long time that the problem would be sorted out by someone else, and was content to wash my hands of it by postponement . . . although, if I had died, the inheritance would have been complicated. The entail specifies that the Abbey and the remainder of the estate have to go to my nearest surviving male relative, and that calculation might be subject to dispute . . . and perhaps subject to challenge."

James looked at his interlocutor sharply.

"It must be a worry," Simon said, in a neutral tone. He did not want to keep his promise to Megan just yet. He wanted to hear James's explanations first.

"I'm sorry that we were interrupted yesterday," James said, apparently quite happy to pass on. "The delay must have been frustrating for you, especially as whatever my grandmother said to you is likely only to have confused you further. Evidently, you will have no idea what to believe, and it will be little consolation to you to know that I have the same problem myself. You gathered yesterday, of course, that Melusine and I do not see eye to eye on the matter, and that we were not in agreement as to how to explain it to you?"

"Indeed," said Simon, nodding his head.

"Doubtless she will give you her own interpretations this evening, but I really do think that you and I might find it easier to achieve a measure of understanding between the two of us. In any case, we have already crossed the first obstacle. You are at least prepared to accept, for the time being, our assertions regarding our ages?"

"Yes."

"For a long time, I had my own doubts regarding my grandmother's claims, which I thought fantastic, but now . . . you can see how they became more plausible once my sister, my cousin and I had all passed our hundredth year, while still remaining reasonably active and, I hope, completely *compos mentis*?"

Simon was content to signify assent with a nod of the head.

"Good. As you can imagine, the attempt to explain our own longevity has been one of the factors guiding my research. My inclination for many years was to treat all the family legends and much of what is recorded in the archives as pure nonsense, as my grandfather, Rhys the Engineer, did. His equally celebrated grandfather, Seymour, seems to have been more open-minded, although he seems to have been insistent that what had happened to Mr. Shelley was a subjective hallucination, and he discounted his encounters with Owain Glyndwr's ghost in the same way. Grandmother, however—who, if she really was Rhys's mother, is actually my great-grandmother—is not unpersuasive, once her extraordinary antiquity is accepted as a given, and over time, I have begun to take her ideas a little more seriously, as puzzles to be solved if not as reliable assertions.

"I have other reasons for taking the legends associated with Prince Madoc seriously, which I shall get to shortly, but first I should like to talk to you about what you call the seventh element, and the Sargasso Sea, as I tried to do yesterday. It still seems to me to be the best avenue of approach. I wanted to read *The Seventh Element*, but the copy I ordered from amazon has not yet arrived, and Felicia took possession of the copy that Cerys brought home and locked herself in her bedroom with it, all night. I know that your story is pure fiction, but would you might explaining the logic of its title to me, so that I can see how closely it compares with my own reasoning?"

"Not at all. As I said yesterday, the four elements of the ancients refer to the three commonplace states of matter and the principle visible item governing the transitions between them—fire, in their terminology, although we would broaden it to all kinds of electromagnetic energy. In modern times, physicists have already discovered that there is a fourth state of matter, beyond the gaseous: the kind of plasma found in the heart of the sun, which is the state that matter acquires at extremely high temperatures. Recently, physicists have suggested that there might be at least one more distinctive state that can only exist at extremely low temperature: a variant of solidity. When I wrote the novel, however, I didn't know that, so, in order to extend the spectrum hypothetically, it seemed logical to me to invent a new state of matter that was beyond solidity in a different sense, and an imaginary force capable of governing transitions between that new state of matter and the solid state, thus adding up to seven."

"Admirable logic! Yes, Mr. Cannick, the hypothesis that I have developed is based on much the same thinking. I think that a great deal of the legendry associated with St. Madoc can be explained in those terms, including the pact that he is said made with the morgens, or perhaps inherited from the so-called Druids who substituted for priests in the pagan religion of ancient Wales. At any rate, it might help to make a sort of sense of certain corollaries of the pact that, at least according to Grandmother, are still relevant today . . . perhaps more so today than at any time in the last seven centuries. Can you accept, if only for the sake of argument, that there might be some truth in the legends, and there really might be such entities as morgens, which are responsible for the rich mythology of marine humans, of which Benoît de Maillet made so much in his evolutionary fantasy?"

"Go on," said Simon.

"Very well. I accepted, hypothetically, the proposition that St. Madoc really did make contact with sentient sea creatures in the vicinity of what is now called Morgan's Fork, and was indeed taken or guided by them to a distant region of the Atlantic, where he visited what appeared to him to be islands. I suspect, however, that they were not projections of the sea-bed protruding above the surface of the sea, but massive organic entities, which might have rested on the sea-bed, but were nevertheless capable of motility. I also believe that at least one such entity was once present off the shore of Brittany, and that others could then be found off the western shore of Scotland and in the Irish Sea—specifically, in Cardigan Bay. Those entities, I believe, were known as Caer-Ys—a term that I suppose to be plural rather than singular. More than one, I suspect, was colonized, and fortified, but the populations of those reckless colonists must have been wiped out when the Caer-Ys altered their shape in order to change location, as they must have done at intervals, albeit intervals of several decades, and perhaps centuries.

"The Caer-Ys must have had an elaborate associated flora of fauna, necessarily amphibian and able to endure periodic submersion. Those ecosystems, I believe, included species that can be considered as marine humans—morgens—

although their precise relationship with the human species seems to be complicated. The Caer-Ys must, of course, have become extinct many centuries ago, although not as long ago as modern scientists are ready to assume, extrapolating backwards from the axiom that the continents, the seas, and what lies beneath the sea, must have been very similar to what it is now for millions of years, save for the exceedingly slow process to continental drift. My assumption is that although they had been in decline for hundreds of thousands of years, and were on the very brink of extinction in the fifth century of the Christian Era, they still existed at that time, including one or two on the European continental shelf, although their last substantial refuge was the Sargasso Sea.

"I suspect that substantial remnants of the Sargasso Sea ecosystem still existed in the seventeenth century, and perhaps the eighteenth, although the extinction was virtually complete by the nineteenth. I say *virtually* complete, because I know for a fact that certain vestiges still remain. In fact, 'vestiges' might be a misleading term, because they are not mere accidental survivals. My thesis supposes that the intelligent species within the Sargasso Sea ecosystem anticipated their extinction, as a result of certain catastrophes, and attempted to make provision for their survival of the extinction event and their potential return at a later date. Many of the measures they took must have come to nothing, because the locations that they chose in which to make their deposits were annihilated. One that was not, however, lies directly beneath St. Madoc's Abbey, and access to it is still possible. If my hypothesis is correct, that was a key clause of the pact that St. Madoc made with the morgens: he became its custodian, and undertook to transmit that custody over the human generations.

"Unfortunately, human generations appear to be much shorter than morgen generations, and far more vulnerable to forgetfulness and upheaval. In seventeen centuries, it has sometimes proved difficult to maintain that custody, and for the inheriting generations to believe in the traditions they inherited regarding its nature. That difficulty has been intensified, obviously, by the almost total disappearance of the Sargasso Sea ecosystem, and it is in its speculations regarding the nature of that ecosystem and its disappearance that my hypotheses are forced to become far more exotic, and hence more dubious."

"And that's where the seventh element comes in?"

"Yes. In order to accommodate the existence of an ecosystem as exotic as the one I envisage existing in the Sargasso, with extensions accumulated at the ends of the various tributaries of the gulf stream, it is necessary to make substantial adjustments to the presumed history of life on earth and its evolution. Clearly the ecosystem in question has left no identifiable traces in the fossil record. We know, obviously, that countless soft-bodied organisms have probably left little or no such traces, and that the story of life as constructed from the fossil record is very largely the history of hard-bodied entities, creatures with shells and skeletons. Logically, however, there must have been paleontologically invisible species living alongside those of which we have a record."

"But that doesn't require a seventh element?"

"No, but I'm sure you can follow the argument easily enough. If there were a fifth state of matter, distinct from the ones we know, and a second agent of transition between the states, in addition to heat energy, we are obliged to hypothesize that the existence of that extra state and extra transitional force must be invisible, not simply in the observations we routinely make at the earth's surface of solids, liquids and gases, but also invisible in geological strata and any fossils contained therein.

"You mentioned just now that physicists have recently discovered further states of matter at exceedingly low temperatures. Obviously, those have left no trace in the geological record, because those exceedingly low temperatures never existed in nature before being produced in the laboratory, any more than plasma existed at the earth's surface before being discovered in the core of the sun. The fifth state of matter that I hypothesize, however, is invisible for other reasons than the non-existence of certain temperature ranges, because its relationship with the other states of matter is governed by a kind of energy quite different from heat. You're aware, obviously, that the ancients already had a fifth element long before plasma was discovered, and that physicists did not discard it completely until the early twentieth century?"

"Aether."

"Exactly. The ancients invented aether to supply the heavens, as they imagined them, with a constitutive element distinct from air, but physicists brought it down to earth, as it were, for various theoretical purposes, notably that of providing light with a medium in which to travel. Eventually, however, they decided that no such medium was necessary, and the luminiferous aether was simply allowed to disappear, to become a void."

"*Nada*," murmured Simon.

"Precisely. The aether became nothing, because it was undetectable by measuring devises adapted to evaluate solids, liquids and gases, and it no longer had any hypothetical function in contemporary physical theories, which seemed to work tolerably well without it. I have hypothesized, however, that an element in some ways analogous to the ancients' aether might indeed play a role in events at the surface of the earth . . . or, more pertinently, *beneath* it. Instead of making the aether the quintessential element of the heavens—although I do not deny the possibility of another state of matter playing a role there—my fifth state of matter is principally active in the Underworld."

"The Underworld?" Simon queried.

"Yes. The ancients imagined an Underworld too, of course, as a location for the abode of the dead, which became, in a later historical period dominated by Christian ideas, the Inferno. There is a rich mythology of descents into that Underworld, as well as a rich tradition of modern fiction and scholarly fantasy imagining that the Earth might be hollow, or at least contain cave-systems large enough to qualify as subterranean worlds, with continents and seas. My theory accepts that there might be a basis of truth in that body of folklore, but that the experiences of the rare humans who were able to make such descents were misinterpreted within the framework of the conventional theory of the four elements rather than a more elaborate schema."

"That seems a trifle far-fetched."

"Yes, it does, at present. It will seem less so when you have made your own descent."

Simon sat up straighter. "You've been into this Underworld?"

"Yes. So have Melusine and Felicia, although Cerys has not yet been initiated into the secret. It made a deep impression on both of them, but not an identical impression. It is, to say the least, a confusing experience. I have been down several times, but I confess that I found it hardly less disconcerting the last time than the first. I will be interested to see what you make of it. My ancestors have left various interpretations in the archives, but most of them, inevitably, did so in the context of religious thought, as St. Madoc must have done, and Owain Glydwr did. Rhys might have been the first to reject entirely the idea that it was some kind of divine revelation—a visionary glimpse of paradise—and to insist that it must be a natural phenomenon. His attempts to come up with a theory of his own, however, were hindered by the limitations of nineteenth-century physics. He construed the light of the Underworld as an electrical phenomenon, and tried for years to duplicate it in the laboratory, without success.

"My own father, Matthew Murden, had no idea what to believe, and any attempts he might have made to investigate it were cut tragically short when he was killed on the Western Front. Rhys died before I was born, and my father while I was a babe in arms, along with the other male members of his generation. My great-grandmother assumed the responsibility of my education, but I fear that I lacked respect for her ideas—she claimed to be over a hundred even then, and I was frankly skeptical. She often described me, and still does, as

'Rhys all over again,' although I think the comparison inapt and her use of it as a term of derision equally inappropriate. She seems to have transferred certain resentments against his father to him, but I don't know the details."

"But modern seismological data offer no evidence for the existence of any such Underworld," Simon objected.

"Modern physicists, basing their assertions on seismological evidence, have indeed constructed a moderately elaborate map of the Earth's crust, mantle and core, which leaves little scope for vast lacunae of the kinds envisaged by Hollow Earth theories. But that reasoning assumes that the solid matter detected by seismic waves beneath the surface is stable and invariant. Such reasoning cannot take account of the notion of a fifth state of matter, whose interactions and transitions with solid, liquid and gaseous states are determined by an exotic agent: an underworld that no more needs vast lacunae of the kind imagined by Hollow Earth theories than aquatic life requires vast lacunae under the sea.

"Suppose, hypothetically, that entities composed of the fifth state of matter could move through solids in much the same way that solid entities can move through liquids and gases. In that case, entities composed of the fifth state of matter could form hybrids of a kind with solids, in much the same way that the other states of matter can form such hybrids as colloids, gels and aerosols. In that case, the hypothetical possibility arises of hybrid biological entities that do not merely consist of solids, liquids and gases in complex association, but have components of the fifth state of matter, which might be capable, by virtue of that combination, of transformations of which simple entities composed of the familiar three states of matter are incapable. You can extrapolate the argument, I assume?"

"I can," Simon agreed. "Doubtless not as far as you, for the moment, but I can see how it might be used, hypothetically, not only to explain an exotic ecosystem originating from a nucleus on the bed of the Sargasso Sea, but also some kind of life-containing Underworld beneath it. I'll need to give it further thought, though."

"Of course. And when you do, I'm confident that you'll begin to glimpse the kinds of experiments that the alchemist monks of St. Madoc began to carry out in the Middle Ages, probably following in the footsteps of pagan magicians—experiments that appear to have given rise, among other things, to the entity nowadays known as the ghost of Owain Glyndwr. We can be certain, at any rate, that some such experiments have given rise to strange heredities, producing humans capable of unusual longevity and perhaps certain exotic metamorphoses."

"Metamorphoses into morgens, you mean?"

"Probably. There are accounts of that kind of metamorphosis in the archives."

"And others?"

"Perhaps—the accounts are unclear, and seem to be polluted by a great deal of speculation."

"But you accept that there are hybrid humans potentially capable of such metamorphoses—of which you are one yourself?"

"The accounts in the archives only speak of female morgens—but that might be a misinterpretation. Grandmother has said that I will never be able to change, in spite of being morgen as well as human, but that Melusine might, under the right circumstances. I doubt that she can have good grounds for that assertion, however."

"And does she believe that Felicia might metamorphose into a neider?"

"She says not." For the first time, James gave the impression that there was something he was not saying. Simon could follow the esthetic logic well enough to deduce what it might be. "But she thinks that I might?" he said.

"I repeat: she cannot have any grounds for that assertion, and I have no faith in her intuitions, in spite of her antiquity. Indeed, I long ago lost the conviction that she confides her intuitions to me honestly. Sometimes I think she just teases me with hyperbolic suggestions, and keeps her real ideas to herself."

"She did give me permission to tease you," said Simon, reflectively, "and Melusine too. But she asked me to be kind of Felicia and Cerys. Can I take that to mean that she identifies Cerys as a neider too . . . and, for that matter, that all such identifications are based on her intuitions?"

"You can. But I hasten to say that, although I have no faith in the accuracy of her intuitions, or even her honesty in reporting them to me, I am not prepared to dismiss them completely, as Rhys probably did. She has certainly seen and felt stranger things than I have, and her assertion that she still receives communications from certain Underworld entities is probably true. It is her interpretations that I doubt."

"You mean that she communicates with neiders."

"The use of the plural might be inappropriate—she never puts an s on the end of the term, but whether that is because neider can be used as a plural as it is, or whether she imagines that there really is only one, I can't tell."

"But you do accept the claim, even though it initially came from a tame raven that can only talk to Felicia, that there's more to me than meets the eye . . . that I have a ghost of sorts lurking within me: a neider ghost?"

James pulled a face. "That is, indeed, the nub of the matter, Mr. Cannick. Yes, Grandmother does believe that you're a neider. I don't know what you said to her yesterday, but whatever it was, it seems to have confirmed her in that belief, and in the belief that the timing of your arrival in St. Madoc is highly significant. As to whether I can believe it . . . that might be a different matter, but I'm not prepared to reject the notion out of hand. What I don't know, because she has not yet told me, is what she expects of you in consequence. Perhaps nothing, except that you might join our little community, but probably more than that."

It was in the tip of Simon's tongue to ask about vitreous cocoons, but James seemed to be unaware of Felicia's nocturnal excursion, and he wanted to keep her secret, so he refrained. He did, however, think it safe to say: "And there's a fragment of an underworld beneath the Abbey, to which access can be gained via the crypt? And in that underworld, there are . . . what? Seeds or spores of some kind? Long-dormant morgens, or a neider . . . perhaps even an entire Noah's Ark of the ancient Sargasso Sea ecosystem, complete with Caer-Ys, which Felicia appears to have told Cerys, not entirely in jest, might some day rise again?"

"Bravo," said James. "That really is impressive, Simon. With every passing hour, I become more convinced that you really are not merely a member of the family, but might be a valuable one. Yes, that is precisely my thinking: a Noah's Ark of the Sargasso ecosystem. Unfortunately I have no way of knowing exactly what it contains, or what proportion of its contents might still be viable. In the days when morgens visited the caves beneath the Abbey occasionally, the basis for communication on that and other issues must still have existed, but it has been a long time, as you know, since the last such visitation, at which time Rhys was still a child. It is not entirely surprising that when he became an adult, he began to doubt their reality."

"But what you have deduced from your research in the family archives is that such visits often accompanied storms guided across the Atlantic by the gulf stream?"

"There is anecdotal evidence to that effect. I have no firm basis, obviously, for thinking that Storm Deirdre might bring us some such visitation, but what Grandmother seems to be hoping—and I would be delighted if she were proved correct—is that your presence here might provoke a visitation, or facilitate some kind of communication if one were to happen. You have obviously deduced already that she had an ulterior motive for asking you to visit her on Friday, not long before the storm is forecast to peak."

"Indeed," Simon agreed. "Doubtless you will be very interested to see what happens, if anything does, if only because it will provide a test case of sorts for your grandmother's intuitions."

"Exactly. I'm delighted that you have followed my arguments so accurately. I confess that I wasn't certain that you would, even though I was convinced that my approach to explaining the situation to you was the best one. I hasten to add, though, that I do not expect you to endorse my conclusions until you have seen more evidence. Indeed, I would be disappointed if you did. Thus far, from your viewpoint, it can only be a matter of playing with ideas."

"Until I see the Underworld?"

"That, at least . . . and until you have seen whatever happens, or fails to happen, on Friday night. It might have been better, of course, from my own viewpoint, to withhold any mention of the Underworld until Saturday, at the earliest—but Melusine is determined, as she puts it, to put all our cards on the table, and Grandmother has apparently encouraged her to do so, so my hand was effectively forced. I felt that I had little alternative but to tell you everything."

"I'm grateful to you for doing so," Simon said.

"Excellent. I'm so pleased that this has gone smoothly. I can't guarantee anything at all, naturally, and there must remain a possibility that all my speculations are mere moonshine . . . but even if we regard it as mere playing with ideas, it is utterly fascinating, is it not?"

"Utterly," Simon agreed. "But may I ask a few questions?"

"Of course."

"Would you explain to me exactly what a neider is, in the context of your theory, and what your great-grandmother has told you about her alleged encounter with one?"

"Certainly. It seems to me that two species in the Sargasso ecosystem that migrated from the Underworld either already were or became sentient in the process of their adaptation to life in the sea. The morgens eventually stabilized in a physical form intermediate between humans and seals, retaining some ability to metamorphose into one or the other. Perhaps that form was deliberately chosen, or perhaps it resulted from an actual process of hybridization; at any rate, the form was equipped with humanoid hands and a humanoid throat, rendering it capable of speech, and hence of vocal communication.

"The other, the neider, appears to have been much more massive, with a central trunk and tentacles, which could produce independent eel-like entities by fragmentation. Perhaps that was its natural mode of reproduction, and perhaps the morgens, and eels, were initially produced from the neider by that kind of fragmentation, although the morgens seem to have become capable of independent reproduction, giving birth and suckling young in the mammalian fashion. Abundant reports suggest that morgens are capable of speech and song, and of learning human language, but I have not discovered any reports of neider speech. The species is, however, said to be capable of a kind of communication that involves the transmission of feelings—what some modern writers call empathy, or telempathy. It requires close physical contact, and Grandmother claims that the neider coiled itself around her in order to achieve it.

"Human neider are allegedly capable of a similar communication; Felicia certainly believes that she can do something of the sort, and might well invite you to experiment with her to that effect. Grandmother seems to have encouraged her in that purpose, but Felicia is rather timid by nature, and it might be some time before she plucks up the courage. Do try it, if she does make the request—I'll be very interested to hear your impression of the result, if any. I fear that I seem to be a poor subject, but Melusine has given more enthusiastic reports. We have agreed that it would be inappropriate, as yet, to involve Cerys in any such procedure.

"Between the neider and other organisms from its own ecosystem, that kind of communication is presumably wordless, but information of a kind can nevertheless be achieved by virtue of a kind of temporarily shared mental identity. It seems probable, however, that when neider form such an association with morgens, the sharing process enables the neider to parasitize, as it were, the vocalized thoughts of the morgen. The principal effect of that, so far as I can deduce from the confused and rather gnomic reports in the family archives as well as Grandmother's personal testimony, is that the morgen's thought-processes are infected by the neider's wordless empathy, although the neider might experience the same thought processes as near-gibberish, having no capacity to decode it as language.

"The morgens already had the capacity for that kind of empathic communication, I assume, but not nearly as highly developed as it was in the neider, although it became much more so in a few morgen who had frequent . . . intercourse with the neider. Those morgens, I suspect, played a particular part in entering into communication with humans, perhaps as a side-effect of their intercourse with neider. When I say intercourse, with respect to any kind of interspecific coupling, of course, I do not mean sexual intercourse of the kind that humans have. Natural morgens appear to be female, giving birth parthenogenetically, and the variation of offspring that creates scope for natural selection and evolution arises from their metamorphic capabilities, not from genetic crossing. That is of some importance with regard to the rare human beings who became hybridized with morgens or neider in the special sense that exotic matter became incorporated into their physical make-up, their hereditary, albeit in a somewhat haphazard manner, via female ova but not, so far as I can tell, via male sperm."

James took out a thickly padded wallet, opened it, ferreted through one of the pockets and produced two old photographs. He handed them to Simon one by one, saying: "My mother, circa 1922. My sister Felicia, in 1946."

The two photographs were not absolutely similar, but the two women might have been identical twins.

"Your mother gave birth to Felicia parthenogenetically?" Simon queried.

"Apparently. Unlike me, she appears to have had no father, and that is presumably why, although we really are brother and sister. Oddly enough, however, Grandmother finds no difficulty in identifying her as neider, and me as morgen, although one might have expected it be the other way around, unless neider also reproduce parthenogenetically. Family portraits reveal several earlier instances of apparent parthenogenetic births—including Melusine, of course. But Melusine inherited her mother's seventh element, and is morgen as well as human, albeit an exotic morgen long detached from her kin and devoid of their culture. Felicia, meanwhile, claims to have a degree of empathic communication of a specifically neider type, which allows her to communicate with Lenore as well as other humans, especially those with a second neider self."

"And that has happened frequently in the course of your family history?"

"It's impossible to tell from the archives exactly how many parthenogenetic births there have been, but I suspect that they have been numerous, over the generations."

Simon did not know what to make of that information, and filed it away as a mere oddity for the time being. He moved on to his next question. "And the specters generated, or preserved, in the course of the Medieval experiments carried out by the monks of the Abbey and continued by the Murden occult scientists also incorporate exotic matter derived from morgens, in your view?"

"Exotic matter, yes, but not necessarily derived from morgens. Over the centuries, in any case, almost all of them have disappeared, with two celebrated exceptions. One was derived from the flesh of Owain Glyndwr, who was passionately desirous of survival after death and readily lend himself to my ancestors' experiments . . . although death seems to have changed him to a far greater extent than he had anticipated. The other I have barely glimpsed, and even Grandmother has had little success in evoking him. What agenda he had that caused him to participate in the experiment that rendered him a sort of immortality, I don't know, nor do I know how death transformed that agenda. No one, so far as I can tell, knows his name and no one has ever seen his face, for he only becomes visible clad in a monk's cowl, arranged so as to hide his features."

"Do specters have any way of communicating exotic matter, as humans-cum-morgens apparently can?"

"Possibly, if legendary accounts of incubi and succubi have any factual basis, but I doubt it. I find it difficult to believe that spectral sperm could fertilize female ova, or that spectral ova, if there are such things, could be fertilized by living sperm. The kinds of empathic intercourse of which the neider are capable might, I suppose, be capable of communicating exotic matter, but I find that hard to believe too."

"But if it were possible, humans—or morgens, for that matter—could, as it were, be *possessed* by neider. I use the term by analogy with the legendry of demonic possession, obviously, but I hasten to add that I mean no moral judgment."

"It's conceivable," James admitted, "but purely speculative. If you are trying to understand your own situation, I do know that Grandmother considered my Aunt Lilith to be a neider, and if that was so, she might have passed that component down to her daughter and granddaughter."

"So you don't consider me to be a victim of possession?"

"Oh, is that what's worrying you? No, I don't—but even if it were the case, as you said yourself, we're using the word in a morally neutral context. There wouldn't be any reason to think of it as inherently evil."

"Alexander Usher might not agree."

"Which is one reason that we didn't want to let him anywhere near the family archives. Even if he had no secondary agenda when he came here, he might have developed one had he explored the family secrets further."

"However I acquired the human/neider identity you seem to believe that I have, though," Simon persisted, "the latter part certainly sees to have been dormant all my life. Can I presume that your plans—or, at any rate, Ceridwen's plans—involve some kind of awakening?"

"You'll have to ask her on Friday what her plans are, if she has any—but don't discount the hypothesis that the process has already begun."

Simon frowned, but realized quickly enough that he meant Eve, and the evenings that he had spent holding her hand. "Before I even arrived here?" he queried, just to make sure.

"Before you were impelled here," James corrected. "Whether your next-door neighbor is right or not about Lilith's daughter having kept track of your movements after her own daughter had abandoned you, and whether or not Evelyne was aware of what she was doing in seducing you . . . let's call it seduction, although I'm not implying that there was anything sexual in your relationship . . . the end result seems to be evident. Or, to be more accurate, the end result seems to be on the point of becoming evident. As I say, I don't know what Grandmother intends, either because she's not entirely sure herself what she intends or because she simply likes to tease me by maintaining her secrets, but she is certainly hoping that the gulf stream will not only bring Storm Deidre to Morgan's Fork on Friday, but morgens, and she is probably hoping that your presence will facilitate communication, with the morgens, or with the neider, or both. Communication concerning the deposit left in the custody of the Abbey in the days of St. Madoc, that is. I hope that she might be right, but perhaps not for the same reasons."

"What are your reasons?"

James Murden only hesitated momentarily before saying: "I'd dearly like to be rid of it—rid of the vitreous cocoons, that is. That's what we call the deposit in the Underworld. I'd like to be rid of the legacy, rid of the pact. I want it to be over. I've wanted it to be over since 1946. I've even wanted to die . . . but that hasn't been my destiny, you see. I have a role to play, it seems, and I have no heir. Unless . . ."

"Unless I can take your place?"

"Yes. I think that might be why you've been brought here. At least, I'm prepared to hope so."

"I'm sixty-eight years old—and I have no children . . . whereas you have one."

Simon had seen James Murden go pale before, and knew what it signified. He also knew that James was expert in suppressing his surges of wrath.

"You shouldn't pay too much attention to the woman next door," he said, gruffly. "She's a liar."

"Perhaps so—but I ought to tell you that she asked me to give you a message. She says that she doesn't care about the inheritance, but that she simply wants an acknowledgement, and an apology. She feels that you've treated her badly."

The surge of rage was not renewed. James shrugged his shoulders. "Which probably means," he said, "that the only thing she really cares about is the possibility of getting her filthy hands on the estate, and the Abbey. That's not possible, under the terms of the entail, and even if it were, I wouldn't permit it. The pact can't permit that. It won't happen. Even if I were willing to let it happen, it wouldn't . . . not, at least, as long as the portal to the Underworld remains. If the neider were to take the deposit back, that might be a different matter."

"You'd be prepared to acknowledge her as your daughter then, you mean?"

"Oh, no—not in this lifetime. But the other parties involved would no longer care, then, who owned the estate, because there would no longer be any need for custodians. If she really does manage to compare her DNA and mine, and it really does demonstrate what she's always contended, and she goes to court to stake her claim to a cut of my heritage, the law might be allowed to take its course. But I won't care—I'll be dead . . . at last."

"Shall I pass on that reply?" Simon asked, with a hint of sarcasm.

"Tell her what you like. Take her side, if you like—perhaps I am the villain she makes me out to be. But it's not as simple as she thinks, and she might get a shock if and when she does get to carry out her blessed DNA test. But that's irrelevant, at least for the time being. Melusine's coming to see you this evening, I understand?"

"That's right," said Simon, keeping his voice neutral.

"I'll tell her what I've already told you, to save her the trouble of duplication. She has her own slant on the matter, which she can explain to you herself, but I don't think it will make much difference to your view of the matter. You have a mind more akin to mine, I think—we might both be insane, I suppose, but if we are, at least we're insane in much the same fashion. Melusine is . . . more typical of the Murden women."

James seemed visibly relaxed now that he had got his explanation off his chest. The reference to Megan Harwyn had upset him momentarily, but he seemed to have deliberately swept that aside. He was looking at Simon in a different way, with a certain puzzlement, and perhaps a hint of optimistic hope that was atypical of him, contrary to the normal inclination of his character. Simon had the impression that if he were to offer James a drink now, he would probably accept—but he did not want to do that. It was getting late.

James went on, however, in a more confessional vein: "Melusine's ostensible father was killed in the war too—the Great War, obviously, not the one in which I fought. All four of Rhys's sons died in France, one after another. They were the sons of Rhys's second marriage, of course. The first was a family affair, and barren. It was the same with Seymour—his first wife died young, and all his children were from the second. In those days, of course, men were supposed to keep marrying, until they sired a male heir and at least one spare.

"The wars changed all that. German machine-guns scythed down all of Rhys's male offspring, and I . . . well, let's just say that I wasn't the same man when I came back from Phase Two. Brought my medals home, but failed thereafter in my other duty. Never married . . . and never died. So far. Could have . . . married, that is, not died. I was reckoned handsome, and I was said to be a hero. But the war . . . I can't complain though. It must have been much worse for my father and uncles, in the first round. Much worse. And I had Grandmother, and Melusine . . . and Felicia too."

He paused. Simon refrained from prompting him to continue, but he continued anyway.

"If Felicia should come to see you, by the way, please be gentle with her. She's a little fragile. She's very impressed by the fact that you're a writer—she's always been a great reader, and writes herself. I couldn't prize *The Seventh Element* away from her. Cerys is impressed too. She doesn't know anything about any of this, though, and it might be best to keep it that way. If we do tell her, eventually, I'll tell her that I thought it was important for her to finish her education first. In fact, I'm hoping that she'll be able to find a decent job somewhere and leave. I don't want her ending up like . . . well, like Felicia. She's not my granddaughter . . . she's probably as closely related to you as to me, if the genealogy were analyzed, but her mother lived in the Abbey for a long time, and I was fond of her, as I am of Cerys. When you have no children of your . . . but let's not get back to that. Have I told you everything you want to know?"

"Not by any means," Simon said. "But considerably more than I can readily digest, for the time being. Do you mind if we leave it there, for now? I tend to eat early, because of the way I arrange my schedule, and I really ought to take advantage of the fresh food that was delivered this morning."

"I'll need time to have a word with Melusine," James murmured, without showing any sign of budging from the armchair. "It's the first time I've crossed the bridge in years, you know . . . I didn't intend to cut myself off, but when there was no necessity . . . Now, suddenly, there's so much to do. I need to hire some younger servants, and allow Rhodri, Edith and Margaret to retire at last. I might have a word with Mr. Gwynne and his friends . . . or even the refugees, if their English permits. But not until next week. I'd forgotten how complicated life can be, if you actually try to live it instead of just letting it go by . . ."

"I know the feeling," Simon told him.

James made an abrupt decision then, rose to his feet, and held out his hand for Simon to shake.

Simon took it, a little warily, but the contact was appropriately brief and Simon did not sense anything in the contact that he had not already sensed in James's bleak gaze and sorrow-tinged speech.

Their eyes met before James turned toward the door. "It might all be mere playing with ideas, of course," James said apologetically. "I might just be a crazy old man riding a hobby horse, with the loyal encouragement of his nearest and dearest. But I'll show you the Underworld, and you can make up your own mind as to what the vitreous cocoons might be. Yes, come over to the Abbey tomorrow, and I'll show you everything—the archives too, although they'll just be gobbledygook to you. It took me years to decipher them, and I know both Welsh and Latin. There's not a word in English dating from before Seymour's time, I fear, and even Seymour . . ."

They were already at the front door, but mention of Seymour triggered a thought in Simon's mind. "Just one more thing," he said, swiftly, as James stepped down on to the garden path. "What did you mean when you said that Shelley's death was probably accidental?"

"Just what I said," James replied, shrugging his shoulders. "If there were morgens in the lake, I'm sure they didn't drown him. They would have tried to save him, if they could, I think. There probably weren't any, but even if there were, going out in that storm was foolhardy. If he heard a siren song, it was only in his mind . . . but you already know that siren songs are all in the mind. Ask Melusine, if you like . . . she'll explain."

And with that, he opened the gate and headed for the bridge to the central Tine, moving rapidly—as if his legs, at least, were impatient to be back on more familiar ground.

XIII
Melusine

Melusine was early. She swept into the cottage as if it were perfectly familiar, and turned into the study without being ushered in that direction. She sat down in the armchair, and invited Simon to sit down too, as if he were the guest rather than her. She seemed slightly annoyed, but not necessarily with him.

"The problem with only having the one computer on the ground floor," she said to him, "is that people can read other people's emails. It was the first one I'd ever sent, and I didn't realize that the machine would keep a copy—it didn't occur to me that James could simply open it. Naïve, I suppose."

"You can protect them with a password," Simon said, mildly.

"Apparently so, but that isn't the way that James set it up. He hasn't crossed the bridge in years—I really didn't think that he'd do it today. I didn't think he'd taken what Felicia said about you seriously—he's never really believed that she and Lenore can communicate. Do you have anything to drink, by any chance?"

"Yes. I got a delivery from the supermarket today. It's a limited choice, mind: red wine or brandy."

"Red wine will be fine."

Simon went into the kitchen to open a bottle. When he came back with it, and two glasses, Melusine was on her feet again, inspecting the bookshelves, with considerably less awe than Cerys had exhibited.

She accepted a glass of wine and sat down again.

"James says that he's told you almost everything, but that he kindly left the siren songs for me, so that my visit wouldn't be a complete waste of time. Sometimes, I could almost hate him . . . but it's not possible."

"You do seem to be a very close family," Simon observed.

"That's one way of putting it. No doubt he told you at enormous length about his theories of matter, and the aether of the Underworld, and the nature of the catastrophe that supposedly overwhelmed almost all the Atlantic underworlds and what he calls their 'overflow ecosystems' a thousand years ago or thereabouts?"

"Not at enormous length, by any means," Simon told her. "Rather briefly, in fact."

"Well, it's a long story, immensely tedious in parts. Personally, I tend to focus on the most relevant aspects. James, in his patronizing fashion, says that's understandable, meaning that I don't have the intellect to understand the convolutions of his theories, because I'm a woman . . . or a morgen. He explained that?"

"He mentioned it, but I wouldn't say that what he said constituted an explanation. I certainly don't think that what he said about me being a neider constituted an explanation."

"That doesn't surprise me. You could ask Grandmother, if she's in one of her lucid moments, but you probably won't get much sense out of her either. She actually claims to have seen neider and to have slept with one . . . by slept, mind, that's all I mean. She hasn't had sex with one . . . I don't think that would actually be possible. She says that she's slept with morgens too, but only in the same way."

"As Shelley claimed to have done?"

"Apparently. Before my time—again, you'll have to ask Grandmother. She claims to have been there at the time—in the Abbey, that is, not in Morgan's Cave, where Shelley allegedly had his encounter."

"You think it was just a hallucination?"

"Probably. But that doesn't mean that the song didn't get into his head. I've never actually had physical contact with a morgen in its natural form, but I can certainly conjure the song in my head. If I slept with you, I could put it into your head . . . but that's not a proposition. If there's one piece of advice I really ought to offer you, in fact, it's: never sleep with a morgen."

"What about a neider?"

"Even more so. I've only ever caught distant glimpses of the Black Monk, Lenore isn't built for cuddling, and Felicia is too shy to ask, so you're probably safe on that score. But the advice is general—never sleep with anyone or anything that can communicate in that fashion. It can seriously mess up your mind."

Too late, Simon thought, slightly surprised that Melusine could misjudge her cousin so completely.

"And above all," Melusine added, perhaps getting to the point that she had had in mind all along, "since I have more than a suspicion that she has plans, do *not* allow yourself to be seduced into sleeping with Grandmother. That would definitely screw up your mind. Believe me, I know. Just remind yourself, if she insinuates her own siren song into your mind, that she's not only old enough to be your several-times-great-grandmother, but might actually *be* your several-times-great-grandmother, or at least great-aunt. If that doesn't do the trick, think of all the other men and things she's slept with . . . euphemistically, as well as merely literally, in some cases."

"Do you really think that's why she's asked me to visit her on Friday?"

"I don't know—she doesn't confide in me. What does James think?"

"You haven't asked him?"

"Of course I have, but for reasons too convoluted to explain, he's more likely to have confided in you than in me. He thinks you've been sent or drawn here, so he must have a theory as to why. If I had to guess, I'd say that he's hoping that you might somehow be able to persuade the morgens and the neider to take the deposit back—if they come, that is. And, obviously, he'd like you to move into the Abbey, so that you can take over as senior custodian if or when he dies."

Simon nodded. "He did hint at those desires," he said. "I must say that I found his motivation hard to fathom."

"It's not that hard. He considers the vitreous cocoons as a burden, of which he'd like to be rid, and he doesn't think he'll be allowed to surrender it unless or until a male heir can be found to take it on. He's old-fashioned in so many ways."

"But you're not?"

"Of course I am—I'm over a hundred years old. Even you're old-fashioned, and you haven't even reached seventy yet. And you have no excuse, not having had to live those seventy years in close contact with a crazy grandmother. At least your mother had the kindness to abandon you at birth, so that you had a chance of a normal life."

"I'm not sure that she did it for that reason," Simon objected, mildly.

"Probably not, whoever she was. You seem to be taking all this very calmly, by the way. Nine men out of ten, tipped into this madhouse, would be heading back to civilization, swearing never to set foot in Raven Cottage again, even if they had to sleep on the streets."

"That's not true," he said, his voice equally mild. "Nine men out of ten, in my shoes, would stick it out no matter what. They might not allow themselves to be drawn into the dance as readily as I am, but they wouldn't run away."

"And why are you so ready to join the dance, as you put it?"

"Because I'm a sucker for the unorthodox, the crazier the better. I suppose that's always been my personal siren song. Without ever committing myself to believing anything, I'm drawn like an iron filing to an electromagnet by bizarre ideas."

"And bizarre people?"

"Not so much. I've always been a little wary of people; I like them . . . I've even loved one or two . . . but I'm generally more comfortable keeping them at a respectful distance."

"Typical Murden, then. Felicia's obviously right . . . about you being related, that is. The neider business is harder to swallow, in spite of all James's allegedly ingenious decipherings of old manuscripts. I can believe that I'm part mermaid, whatever that might mean, but that you're part sea serpent . . . that's difficult."

"When you say, *typical Murden*," Simon enquired, "what exactly do you mean?"

"Isn't it obvious? I know you've only been here two days, but you've seen quite a bit of us, especially if you count the harlot next door. To judge by what I see on television, all families these days are more than a trifle screwed up, but we've had more chance to turn the screw than most. It's poor Cerys I feel sorry for. At least James is talking about hiring some new servants now, so that she won't feel obliged to go on fetching and carrying for us. I just hope we can afford it . . . we can't exactly throw the old ones out on to the street. At the very least, we'll have to let them have a cottage or two, which will eat into the income. Unless, of course, you come to live in the Abbey, in which case we can lodge the old retainers in Raven. You'd be mad to do that, though, in my opinion."

"You live there," Simon pointed out. "You must have had opportunities to leave, as Lilith did."

"It's true," Melusine agreed. "I had my choice of the traditional routes—marriage and whoredom. You're old enough to understand that there wasn't really a third alternative in my day. Cerys has a much wider range of choices, bless her. I didn't fancy either, so I settled, without really ever meaning to, for being a stay-at-home maiden aunt. So did Felicia, obviously. Sometimes, I don't know whether to feel sorrier for her or myself. Grandmother took the bravest option, I suppose, going for motherhood without bothering with the marriage, but it seems to have been possible to get away with that at the time, in a certain sector of the Bohemian upper class. It was different in the aftermath of the Great War, no matter what you might have read about bright young things and the roaring twenties—there was none of that in West Wales, believe me. But I shouldn't complain. I made my own bed, and kept men out of it. Never even tested the water the way Felicia did . . . but she has a different kind of empathy, less double-edged than the siren song. You're not interested in that, though, and it isn't why I wanted to talk to you."

"Why did you want to talk to me?" Simon asked.

"Well, I suppose I could say that I felt that it was my duty to warn you to get the hell out while you could, but it wouldn't be true. It wasn't altruism. Competition with James played a part, and simple curiosity . . . curiosity most of all. I was rather annoyed by James yesterday, to tell you the truth, and the way he went about trying to prepare the ground for the explanation, probing and teasing the way he does. I wanted him to set it out, because I was interested to see how you'd react . . . to see how an outsider, who knew nothing about us, would respond to James's claims. Later, I also became curious to know what Grandmother had said to you, and what could possibly have motivated someone who's been a career invalid for the best part of a century suddenly to get out of bed. And most of all, perhaps, I wanted to see how I might react to being in male company—other than James's obviously—for the first time in decades. I'd been on the brink of deciding to slip out a couple of days earlier, and trying to contrive a private meeting with the man Cerys was going to see at the Mermaid, but . . . well he was a clergyman, and you're a writer. I'm not making much sense, am I?"

"Perfect sense, actually," Simon opined. "And how *are* you reacting, if you don't mind my asking?"

"I don't mind you asking, but I'm not sure I can give you an accurate answer. I'm a hundred years old, and I'm not sure that I'm capable of reacting any longer. You're much younger, obviously, but have you begun to notice, yet, that your capacity to feel anything begins to diminish as you get older?"

"I'm not sure that I had as much capacity for feeling as the human average to begin with," Simon said, "and I have rather cut myself off these last seven years. Since the divorce, I've actually tried to eliminate feeling from my being, to concentrate entirely on my intellectual efforts."

"Sounds like wisdom to me," Melusine opined. "Like you, I couldn't match the human average even to begin with, it seems to me. If I had, maybe I would have gone fishing for a husband, or at least tested the water. Do you think it's because we're part unhuman?"

"I don't know," Simon said.

"Would it be a good excuse, do you think, if that were the case?"

"Do we need an excuse?" Simon countered.

"Perhaps not—but I've always felt that I did, or, at least, that it would be a relief to have one. Old maids, as you can probably imagine, have always been regarded as failures, 'left on the shelf,' as they used to put it—that was true even in the aftermath of the war, when there was such a surplus of women of my age, relative to the remaining supply of eligible men, that thousands of us were bound to stay on the shelf. It's different for men, obviously."

"Obviously," Simon agreed—but honesty prompted him to add: "On the other hand, I have to confess that I've always felt like something of a failure myself, on account of being a misfit. I've tried with all my might to be proud of it, and make it into a virtue, or a sign of superiority, but never quite managed it. If there are such things as neiders, though, and I were one of them, I wouldn't feel any relief in consequence."

"That's understandable. At least I'm part mermaid, according to Grandmother, and that has a certain cachet. If she'd told me that I'm part snake, I don't think I'd have found that idea attractive at all."

"The best-known version of the legend of your namesake suggested that she really was half snake," Simon pointed out.

"Only on Saturdays, while she was in the bath. Or at least, that was the only time it became obvious. You seem to have got away without that restriction, though, even while you were married."

"Just as well, or the marriage wouldn't have lasted as long as it did. Perhaps, though, Marilyn suspected, subconsciously if not explicitly, that I had something unhuman about me. I was never aware of the neider inside me, but I wouldn't be, would I? To me, I was just the way I was. She found it much easier to compare me with other men and find me wanting— with a void where a soul ought to be, as she once put it, when being unkind."

"To judge by what I see on TV, most women think that about most men most of the time. I keep telling myself that perhaps I've had a lucky escape, but I've never been able to convince myself. I often think I might be better off sealed away in a vitreous cocoon, sleeping while my morgen self lies dormant. Being a live carrier of the ancient legacy isn't so very uncomfortable . . . but if you look at the history of the Murdens, you can't help thinking that it's more a curse than a blessing. If they really are going to come back some day and take it all back, I wish they'd hurry. If they really do come on Friday, it certainly won't be too soon."

"But you don't think they will?"

"No. It's been two hundred years since the Shelley encounter, and even that was probably a hallucination. Outside of the vitreous cocoons, a handful of specters and a few Murdens, they're extinct."

Although Melusine had already consumed more than half the glass of wine he'd poured for her, Simon didn't think that the alcohol had gone to her head. It was nervousness that was causing her speech, and the gestures with which she accompanied it, to take on a certain exaggerated expansion and flamboyance. Like James a couple of hours previously, she was acting uncharacteristically, and not entirely deliberately. His arrival in St. Madoc really had turned everyone's world upside-down, not just his own.

"But if the vitreous cocoons really are cocoons," Simon suggested, "they might yet release live occupants."

"After sixteen hundred years—or even longer than that, if James is right about St. Madoc merely inheriting the cocoons from the bards, or Druids, or whatever? Even if you assume that things move at a more leisurely pace in the Underworld, that's a hell of a long time. Felicia says that the chrysalids are alive and dreaming, but I'm not sure that her judgments are reliable—she tends to let her imagination run away with her, poor dear. I couldn't feel anything in them, and I'm allegedly part morgen. If there really were morgens inside, and they were dreaming, I think I'd at least be able to hear their song. You can try yourself when James shows them to you."

"I've never had any kind of magical empathy."

"Not yet—maybe the proximity of the vitreous cocoons will be the trigger you've been waiting for all your life."

"But you don't believe that either."

"No—but don't take my word for it. I'm probably no more trustworthy than James or Felicia. Make up your own mind."

Simon nodded his head in acknowledgement of the advice. "More wine?" he asked, pointing at her empty glass.

She hesitated, but then said: "Better not. I was supposed to be giving you an explanation. When I sent you the email I was expecting to be able to make all sorts of revelations, and see their effect—but James has ruined all that. There's nothing else to reveal, is there. He's even going to take you down into the Underworld. I should have sneaked out last night and come to take you by surprise, so he wouldn't have had a chance of spoiling everything—but you don't care about our petty family jealousies, do you?"

"If I really do turn out to be a member of the family, it will probably be as well to be forewarned about them," Simon said. "When you're all together, though, you seem to get along very well."

"We have to. Who was it said that it isn't actually possible to love your neighbor, but that you can at least be courteous? That's us. It's impossible for us to love one another, although I think we did once, a long time ago, but if we didn't make a fetish of courtesy, we'd have murdered one another by now. If you're wise, you'll take my advice and run away. But you can't, can you?"

"Can't I?" Simon queried.

"In theory, obviously, if you wanted to—but that's the way it works, you see. You don't want to. I'm not really helping, am I? At least, if James had let me explain the situation, I could have could have had the pleasure of surprising you, but now I can't even do that."

"Actually," Simon told her, "you're not doing such a bad job. You're even filling in a few gaps in my understanding. Can you tell me a little more about the siren song, though?"

Melusine seemed mildly surprised herself. "James told me you already understood," she said. "He said you'd already intuited the essentials, in your book."

"What book?" Simon asked, momentarily lost.

"*The Bells of Ys*. He said that you already knew that the music of the Caer-Ys wasn't something that consisted of actual sounds, but of communicated feelings, which the receiving mind only translates into virtual sound in order to be able to grasp it. He says that you understand that morgen music is the same."

"Yes," Simon remembered. "I did say something like that—but he might have read a little more into that old novel than I really intended to put into it."

"Really? He said that it was crudely written but that you must have dredged up some of its ideas from the Underworld—without realizing it, obviously. He was impressed by the way you represented the sinking of Ys not simply as a matter of being covered by the waves, but actually sinking into the seabed, fusing with the strata."

"Yes," Simon remembered, "I did do that. I just wanted to vary the imagery, so that I wasn't just reiterating the familiar story. He thought it was crudely written, you say?"

"Oh, he's no judge. He says your version of the Caer-Ys was probably much more accurate than the one Peacock contrived."

"Ah," said Simon, remembering that James had referred to *The Misfortunes of Elphin* rather than *Nightmare Abbey* as the more significant echo of the tales that Peacock had heard while enjoying Seymour Murden's hospitality. He added: "He told me to ask you about what happened to Shelley, though."

"Oh, he was just teasing," Melusine replied. "Me, not you. Actually, I think it was Grandmother who first suggested that Shelley might have gone out on the lake during the storm because he heard the siren song again that he'd heard, or imagined he'd heard, in Morgan's Cave, and that it might have been a lake morgen that pulled him out of the boat. James was amused because I said that morgens were essentially benign, and that if there had been any in the lake, they wouldn't have let him drown. They might have taken him away to the underworld for a supernatural love-making session, which he wouldn't remember because he'd be in a dream state, but afterwards, they would certainly have deposited him on the shore, safe and sound. I didn't really mean it, obviously—just playing with ideas, as you put it—but I thought that I ought to defend the morgens against the slander. Felicia agreed with me, but James just laughed. He makes it a point of honor not to take me seriously. Being a male chauvinist pig, as they used to call it, back in the seventies . . . God, doesn't time fly when you get old? Forty years ago already!"

"I know the feeling," Simon assured her. "That is interesting, though. I might be able to use that in a novel some day, if you don't mind me stealing it."

"Feel free. Felicia might already have done it, though, so she might have the copyright."

"Not if she hasn't published it. Has she published anything?"

"Felicia? Not in this lifetime. She wouldn't have the nerve. She won't even let me read her stuff, although she might have given some to Cerys on an I'll-show-you-mine-if-you-show-me-yours basis. I doubt that she'll summon up the courage to show you, though, even though she's plowing her way through the books you gave Cerys. She's too frightened that you might say something unkind. She's very sensitive."

Simon winced, thinking that he might already have been unkind to Felicia, without intending to be . . . and thinking, once again, that Melusine had a completely mistaken view of what Felicia might and might not dare to do.

"Are you sure you wouldn't like a refill?" he asked, gesturing toward the empty glass that Melusine had set down on a side table.

"Better not," she repeated. "I think I'd better get back, actually. James will be waiting for a report, and Grandmother too, even though I've nothing really to tell them. They seem to be expecting that I'll have been able to gauge your reaction to what James told you better than he could—but I'm not just his pawn, damn it. I wanted to gauge your reaction to me, not to him, and he spoiled that. So stuff the pair of them. Mercifully, Felicia doesn't care. She's been locked in her room round the clock with that stack of books you gave to Cerys—hardly spares the time to come down for meals. It annoyed the hell out of James yesterday when she wouldn't let him have *The Seventh Element*. She only handed it over this morning, just as he was about to go out."

"I'm flattered," Simon said. "I hope she enjoyed it—and the others."

Melusine had gone to the door while she was speaking and had put her hand on the handle. She turned it, but before going through, she suddenly turned back to Simon and said, "Speaking purely hypothetically, if I were to ask you to sleep with me, in spite of all my warnings, would you do it?"

"Yes," said Simon, simply, although he had a strong suspicion that what she had actually wanted was to provoke some amazement, or a reaction of some kind.

"And if I meant it euphemistically," she continued, stubbornly, "do you think you might be able to do *that*?"

"I think so," Simon said, with what he hoped was perfect equanimity. "In fact, I'm sure."

She nodded her head, letting no disappointment show, if she were, in fact, disappointed. "That's interesting," she said. "I knew it, though—that you were the kind of man who's incapable of taking good advice, that is. I can tell them that, at least."

"I fear that I am that kind of man," Simon agreed. "Through and through." He followed Melusine to the door, leaned past her in order to open it for her, and said "Good night," in response to her mumbled farewell.

He watched her go through the garden gate. Almost reflexively, he looked across the road at the shadows cloaking the bushes.

At first, there was nothing there, but just as he was about to turn and go back inside, he caught a glimpse of movement from the corner of his eye. He froze, looked again, and peered intently into the gloom, while Melusine was making her way over the bridge to the Tine.

A figure emerged slowly from the shadows. It was very difficult to see, because the clouds in the sky were blocking the moon and the stars and the figure was in the darkest section of the road, a full dozen meters from the nearest street lamp. It was clad in black, so it almost vanished in the shadow, but he got the impression that it was wearing some kind of long robe, and a hood like a monk's cowl.

And it was coming toward him.

It crossed the road, opened the gate and came along the path, more distinct with every step it took, as the light behind Simon lent it shape and dimension.

"Well, don't just stand there," a voice said. "Let's get inside, for Heaven's sake."

XIV
The Fake Monk

Felicia sat down in the chair that Melusine had just vacated, and tipped back her hood.

"Why on earth are you dressed like that?" Simon demanded.

"So that anyone who saw me would mistake me for the Faceless Monk, of course," she said.

"*I* mistook you for the Faceless Monk," he retorted, a trifle resentfully. "You could have given me a heart attack."

"You won't be allowed to die," she assured him. "Not before Friday night, at any rate." She picked up Melusine's empty wine glass. "You didn't finish the bottle, I hope? Don't bother fetching a clean one—Melusine doesn't have any germs that I don't."

Simon poured wine into the glass, and then refilled his own. He sat down.

"To what do I owe the pleasure?" he asked.

"Is it a pleasure?" she countered. "I was afraid . . . well never mind. I came to apologize."

"For what?"

"For last night. I assume that Melusine's given you the warning now? Never sleep with anyone who wants to leech your dreams."

"She did say something of the sort, but I wouldn't have taken any notice."

"Even so, it was sly of me—and completely out of character. Then again, they'd made a competition of it, and they both took it for granted that I wouldn't even be in the running, and it was just so typical of them . . . it was childish, of me, I suppose. But I had no idea that it would turn out the way it did. That startled me. Maybe it shouldn't have, but it did. When I first woke up this morning, I thought it was all my fault, that I was just projecting my own gloomy feelings on to you, but after I'd thought about it, I realized that it couldn't just be that. You really do feel like that, don't you?"

Simon took a long swig of wine and paused. He had no difficulty following the implications of what she had said, but he didn't know how to react. Eventually, he said: "Given that you've looked into the inner depths of my being, I can hardly deny it, can I?"

"Don't be melodramatic. What we shared was more superficial than that. Sometimes, what you share doesn't mean anything at all—it really is just dream-stuff. But that was raw, wasn't it? It took you by surprise. Next time, you'll be better able to shield yourself . . . if you want to."

"What makes you think there'll be a next time? Or, come to that, that if there is a next time, I might want to shield myself?"

"You've got an appointment with Grandmother on Friday evening. She might not ask you to climb into bed with her, but she'll surely ask you to hold her hands—and how can you possibly refuse? As for whether you'll want to shield yourself . . . it might be wise. Didn't Melusine mention the possibility of seriously screwing up your mind, or words to that effect?"

Simon admitted that she had.

"Well, she's not wrong. There were a few minutes this morning before dawn when I thought that I might have seriously screwed up yours . . . but later, I thought that I was exaggerating, that I was just being melodramatic."

Her blue eyes drilled into his, questioningly, seeking reassurance. By comparison with Melusine, who was several inches taller and seemingly robust, Felicia seemed very frail. It was easy to see why everyone considered her to be timid, sensitive, and in need of protection. Simon already knew, though, that the appearance was deceptive—just as deceptive as her disguise as the Black Monk, but a little more convincing.

"You didn't do anything," he told her, dryly. "Mine was screwed up long ago. Not completely, until seven years ago, but since then . . . well, you saw that, didn't you? You read it all."

She nodded. "I don't know why I was so surprised. I've slept with James, and Melusine. Never with Megan Harwyn, obviously, or Cerys, but . . . well. I suspect I'd have to get a long way from St. Madoc before I found a ray of existential sunshine."

"The play is the tragedy Man," Simon recited, confident that she would recognize the quotation, "and its hero the Conqueror Worm."

"Not in Morgan's Fork, it isn't," she retorted. "Our tragedy defies that particular climax. And you're neider as well. Frankly, I'm surprised that the real Black Monk hasn't paid you a visit yet."

"As a matter of fact," Simon confessed, "I believe he has. Only once, since I've been here, but I thought I recognized him."

"Recognized him? You mean that you saw his face?"

"No, not that. It was a more general similarity—which you replicated with ease when you glided across the road and nearly stopped the circulation of the blood in my arteries. But it wasn't you two nights ago, was it?"

She took a sip of wine and then looked at him again, pensively. "No," she said, "it wasn't. And you've seen him before?"

"I think so, without thinking anything of it at the time. I'd never heard the story . . . not that there seems to be much of a story, unless you know more than I've been told."

"What have you been told?"

"At first, just that St. Madoc had two resident phantoms, Owain Glyndwr and a hooded monk. Then James told me today that he's probably the ghost of a necromancer monk of the Middle Ages, magically gifted with the ability to survive death by some kind of neider graft, just as Glyndwr later requested a similar gift, in order to await the opportunity to hound the English out of Wales, but changed his ideas after death . . ."

"James always embroiders things. There's more there than I've ever heard."

"And unlike Glyndwr's ghost, which can apparently whisper in Welsh, the Faceless Monk never speaks. That's not surprising, of course. Practically a cliché, in fact. The silent ghost with no face, who sucks the soul out of you if you let him get close enough. I've encountered half a dozen fictitious versions. This one might be a case of hallucination imitating art. It happens."

"I expect so." She seemed to have lost interest in the Black Monk, and changed the subject: "Do you think you might have been all right if your wife hadn't divorced you? That you might have been happy?"

"Happy might be putting it a little strongly," Simon replied, unperturbed by the abrupt change of tack. "Better, certainly. The marriage wasn't perfect, but it was better than nothing. It satisfied my needs, but that might only testify to the mediocrity of my needs. In a sense, I'd long ago accepted the inevitability of permanent melancholy, and the most I'd ever expected out of life was a tolerable level of misery. The divorce even cost me that. Actually, as I said this morning, it's me who ought to be apologizing to you for letting you read a mind like mine. I'd been asked to be kind to you, and that wasn't. I really ought to keep my black moods to myself . . . but I didn't know. God, what must I have done to poor Eve, if she was empathizing with me while I was holding her hand?"

"She wasn't reading your mind," Felicia told him. "She was only appreciating your kindness. Believe me, even if she glimpsed your unhappiness—and if you talked to her, she surely must have done, without the slightest supernatural aid—you did her nothing but good."

Simon wasn't at all sure that she could possibly know that, but he certainly wasn't about to challenge the assertion.

"And if your grandmother wants me to hold her hand? Will I do her nothing but good?"

"You certainly won't do her any harm—but Melusine's right to warn you that the inverse might not be the case. You're probably safe with me, though—and with her."

"Her?"

"Knowing Melusine as I do, she's perfectly capable of giving you a dire warning not to sleep with the likes of her and then asking you to do it. It's not a cynical ploy, it's just the way she is. But she's far less empathic than I am, although logic suggests that it ought to be the other way round. She's a morgen, after all . . . or so it's said."

"And I'm a neider, so it's said—but I don't have any empathy at all."

"That's not the impression I got last night. It might need refining, but . . . well, if so, Grandmother is probably the one to bring it out. And there really isn't any point in reiterating the warning, because you won't be able to refuse her. She might have lost the greater part of her looks nearly two hundred years ago, and almost all her strength since, but when she makes a request, people don't say no."

"How do you want all this to work out, Felicia?"

She seemed slightly disconcerted by the question. "I don't know," she said. "I haven't really thought about it."

"Your Grandmother seems to be hoping that Friday's storm might bring a renewal of contact with the Underworld, or its marine representatives. James seems to be hoping that the deposit made here under the terms of St. Madoc's pact might be taken back, thus liberating him from what he imagines as a burdensome obligation. Is that what you'd like to happen?"

Felicia thought about it for a few moments, and then said: "No."

"Why not?"

"Because I'm like you—which is why I thought I was looking at a mental reflection last night. To use your own terminology, I'd long ago accepted the inevitability of permanent melancholy, and had rendered it tolerable as best I could, mostly by escaping into fictions of others' manufacture and my own. I'm depressed, it's true, but that's just my normal state of being, not a mental illness. I don't particularly want to die, as poor James sometimes does, or for anything to change in my circumstances, as Melusine often dreams about—although neither of them actually does anything about it."

"But reading and writing help?"

"Writing is difficult, but reading, always. Your books aren't as good as I'd hoped, to be perfectly honest, but even mediocre books have their reward. They're better than nothing. So are you. Now you're here and I've taken the short cut to getting to know you, I wouldn't mind at all if you were to stick around, here or at the Abbey. So I suppose the answer to your question is that I don't really want this to work out at all. I don't want a denouement. Sorry if that's a disappointment."

"Well, except for the conspicuous lack of egregious flattery, no, it isn't. Perhaps it's my age, but at pushing seventy, I think I can do without a rousing climax myself. Even Storm Deirdre might be a little too much . . . but the one thing for which I do hope, quite fervently, is that no one dies. Given the ages of the various people involved, that might require a little quasi-divine intervention, but if whatever protection you've all been living under has preserved your grandmother for two hundred years, there's no reason why it can't continue, is there?"

Felicia smiled. "Perhaps not," she said. "I'm game—how about you?"

"Certainly. I'm in no hurry to die. I have work to do—and I always have at least two years planned out ahead of me. Even if nobody reads my works, and even if those who do are unkind enough to think them mediocre, their production gives me a sense of accomplishment."

"When I said *mediocre*, I was only echoing your own judgment."

"I know, but that doesn't make it sting any less. Quite the reverse, in fact. I hope Cerys isn't such a harsh critic."

"I wouldn't bet on that—but at least she might be able to maintain the illusion that you think more highly of them than you do . . . although I know full well that it was just superficial ritual self-flagellation, and that deep down, you really think quite highly of them."

"You're not actually applying balm to the wound, you know."

"No, I suppose not. Sorry—I don't want to be unkind. Quite the contrary, in fact. Grandmother would probably love *The Bells of Ys*. James has lent her the copy he stole from Cerys, but she finds reading very tiring. She quite likes to listen, though. Have any of your novels been published as audiobooks?"

"Yes, a few. I offered to download some for Eve a few years back, but her fingers weren't able to operate an MP3 player by then, and she didn't want me to read to her, although she let me ramble on about what I was writing."

"I can still cope very well with print, thanks to the spectacles," said Felicia, with a slight sigh, "and I prefer reading at my own pace. I do have an MP3 player, though—I'm not an utter barbarian. I play music on it."

"Well, the boxes in the corner are full of duplicate copies— help yourself."

Felicia didn't budge. "I can always come back," she re-marked, off-handedly.

"Any time," Simon assured her. "But preferably not be-tween five-thirty and eleven-thirty, or twelve-thirty and five-thirty. That shouldn't be an inconvenience—you'll need to wait for nightfall for the Faceless Monk disguise to work."

She nodded. "Thank you," she said. "I might have to come back quite often—you've written so many books."

"No problem. And if it starts raining torrentially during a heavy storm—which happens quite frequently in these parts, I'm told—and you need to stay overnight, that would be okay too."

The blue eyes looked at him intently. "Are you trying to seduce me, Mr. Cannick?" she said.

"Obviously. Misery loves company, they say."

"They do say that," she admitted. "Well, I'll bear that in mind too. That is egregious flattery, mind, given that I'm over a hundred."

"You don't look a day over eighty. I hate clichés, so I won't say that you're as old as you feel, and you already know how old I feel, so it would ring false anyhow. More wine?"

Felicia looked down at her empty glass, thought about it, and then said: "Better not. I really did only come to apolo-gize . . . and to make sure that I hadn't seriously messed you up. Now I can see that you're positively buoyant, by our rock-bottom standards, and I know that we might have all the time in the world before us . . . well, I might be fooling myself, but I feel that we do have an understanding of sorts. I think I'd like to savor that sensation for a while, and get a solid night's sleep. But I'll see you tomorrow afternoon, won't I, when James gives you the tour of the library and the Underworld?"

"That's right," Simon said, and went to the window to look out into the street. He was just about to say: "No one about," and go to open the door so that she could slip away surreptitiously, when a flicker of movement caught his eye and he froze. Then he sighed with relief as an owl sped along the street five or six meters above the ground, its outspread wings catching the glimmer of the street lamps as it passed them.

According to superstition, he supposed, it was probably a bad omen, but it wasn't the Faceless Monk.

For the moment, that seemed sufficient.

When he got into bed, he could hear the sea again, insistent in its presence—but its rhythm seemed to have altered subtly. He searched the steady rhythm for a message from the bells of Ys, or the section of a siren song, but did not find either. In fact, the faint splash of the waves was more reminiscent of a slow pulse-beat, tempting his own heart to slow down and fall into step with it.

It's just chamber music, he thought. *There's nothing ominous or seductive about it; it's just background. Felicia's right: there's no need for any denouement here, let alone for any kind of melodramatic climax. The best way to cope with melancholy is with routine, endless routine . . . and if you can fit a little moderate and undemanding human contact into that routine, so much the better. Not passion, certainly . . . that's far too destructive, and its compensatory rewards too evanescent . . . but something akin to the steady beat of a calm sea with slow, discreet tides.*

And with that kind of mental background music, he went to sleep easily, and his dreams—of which he retained no memory at all—were peaceful.

XV
The Library

The next day went well, by what Felicia called his "rock-bottom standards." He got up at five, showered, had breakfast, and was at the keyboard within twenty minutes. When he switched on the music player, the random selector came up with the *Eroica*, which somehow seemed more apposite as an echo of Napoleon than the previous day's doom-laden Tchaikovsky. He worked on the current translation, uninterrupted, until eleven-twenty, processing more than six thousand words without difficulty. It was raining outside, but he simply put on the hooded raincoat he kept for such circumstances and set forth.

He hesitated momentarily as to whether he ought to walk inland in the direction of Morpen for the regulation twenty minutes before turning round and coming back, but decided that too much variety too soon might be disturbing, so he turned right along the coastal path instead and followed its curve. No one ran after him or appeared unexpectedly in the distance, and the only people who were sharing the path with him when he set out were boatmen from the old fishermen's cottages walking their dogs.

After five minutes or so, however, Simon began to wonder whether he had made the right decision to employ the path rather than the road, because it was considerably muddier, even though it was reasonably well maintained. When he turned to come back the entire landscape seemed deserted. He did not see another soul while he completed his circuit, although it took him twenty-five minutes to get back to St. Madoc rather than the twenty he had planned, because he had turned at exactly the same place that he had two days before, having established that as his reference point, and the slower going meant that he did not cover the distance as easily. The loss was immaterial, given that he was not going back to work.

Fortune favored him. The rain stopped while he was having lunch and the sky actually cleared, becoming blue for once. The sun broke through. He had had to change his trousers and socks, and it was impossible to wear the trainers in which he had gone for the walk, but he had intended to wear shoes anyway, so that was not a problem.

At the grille, he rang the bell and waited. It took a full five minutes for Cerys to reach the gate and let him in. She did not run, and he got the impression that she was deliberately not running, in order to make a point.

"Come in, honored guest," she said. "They're all waiting for you, literally on the edge of their seats—except

204

Grandmother, obviously. She knows you're coming, though, and told me to ask whether you'd be kind enough to pop in to see her for a few moments before you go back—which will, it appears, be at five o'clock."

"I'll be glad to do that," Simon said, as they walked to the house.

"You're the only one getting the tour," the young woman added. "I'm over twenty-one, let along eighteen, but it seems that I'm not yet considered to be of an age when I can be allowed into the library or to see whatever is lurking beneath the chapel."

"Twenty-something seems very young to people of my age, let alone theirs," Simon told her.

"But I'm a Murden through and through, born here and firmly resident. You didn't even know the family or the Abbey existed three days ago, and already the aunts are fawning over you, James is treating you like royalty and Grandmother is getting dressed up to you for five minutes. They're talking in whispers, but not so quietly that I can't tell that they're talking about morgens, using words I've never heard before and discussing the possibility of persuading you to move into the Abbey. What the hell is going on, Mr. Cannick?"

"You called me Simon the day before yesterday," he pointed out, as they reached the front door.

Cerys had put her hand on the doorknob, but didn't turn it. "You're going to side with them, then? You're not going to tell me anything either?"

"I can't," he said. "It's not my place—but I'll suggest to James that perhaps he ought to give you the same explanation that he gave me, just in case something does happen tomorrow."

"Apart from the storm?"

"Apart from the storm."

She had no alternative but to settle for that, and she escorted him to the dining-room, where the three centenarians were waiting in the armchairs—and did, as Cerys had implied, seem to have been waiting eagerly and expectantly.

Simon felt that the pressure of expectation was oppressive, but he reflected, looking back on the manner in which his last three individual encounters had gone, that he had done nothing to lessen that expectation, and might even be thought to have gone to unnecessary lengths to augment it. He was, in consequence, partly to blame for the level of his discomfort.

That did not make it any easier to bear.

Fortunately, all three of them were thoroughly accustomed to an obsolete etiquette that was stiff and courteous, and very respectful of personal space, so he did not feel unduly crowded. Felicia and Melusine both peered through their spectacle-lenses at him with what appeared to be an evident fondness, and it only required a minute or two of formal banalities for Simon to sense that that they were actually competing for his attention, almost becoming flirtatious. James, naturally, simply adopted an imperious authority, a taken-for-granted monopoly on his attention, but he turned aside to say: "Would you go and sit with Grandmother for a while, please, Cerys?"

Simon had no difficulty reading in the young woman's expression a desire to make a sarcastic reply, or even a demand, but the habit of a young lifetime was already well set. She nodded meekly, and left.

"You can hardly blame her for being curious, and a trifle resentful," Simon observed, when she had gone. "Do you really need to keep her in the dark?"

James frowned. "She'll have to know eventually, obviously," he said, "but I'm not sure that I'd have time to explain it all to her before tomorrow evening."

"I can do it," Melusine immediately suggested.

That possibility obtained an almost reflexive reaction from James. "But I'll try to spare some time tomorrow morning," he said, still addressing Simon. "You're right, of course— we can't let her build up resentments, and she is entitled to know. Shall we go to see the library first? If you'll excuse us, my dears . . ."

"Do you have to rush off so quickly?" Felicia asked, but with a hint of innocent amusement, knowing what the answer would be.

"Time is precious, my dear," James told her.

"We could all come," Melusine suggested.

"You know that simply isn't practical, Melusine," James told her. "There simply isn't space, in the library or the crypt, for us to go in a crowd."

Although not quite as meekly as Cerys, they accepted the inevitable. "Perhaps we'll have time for a walk on the Tine before you go," said Felicia.

As they went upstairs, James looked sideways at Simon with slight puzzlement. "You seem to have made quite an impression on Melusine," he observed, "and Felicia too. She must really like your books."

Simon remembered, with a slight renewed stab of pain, what Felicia's judgment of the novels she had so far read had been, but he told himself that he ought to be grateful that she seemed so well disposed toward him regardless.

"I'm glad," he said. "My arrival could easily have been an unwelcome disturbance for all of you, but you've all been very kind and courteous. I'm grateful."

"You were warned to expect monsters, I assume?" James observed "You were unfortunate, I fear, in running into Miss Harwyn and Mr. Usher on your first evening. If we'd only had some kind of advance warning, I could have arranged a more appropriate welcome. But Evelyne evidently didn't want to say anything at all, to you or to us."

"I'm quite sure that she knew nothing about you," Simon told him, as they reached a locked door and James had difficulty fitting an old-fashioned key into the lock. "Her mother seems to have . . . protected her, much as you seem to have protected Cerys."

James got the door open, and sighed, saying: "Yes, I suppose so. I remember Lilith, obviously, but it's surprising how faint certain memories become. She hardly made any impression on me at the time, when the house was so much more populous, and at my age, such distant periods fade away almost entirely."

In spite of the fact that the room was dark, because the curtains were drawn over both the windows, it was immediately obvious to Simon why it would have been impractical for anyone else have accompanied them to the library. He knew from long experience, of course, how books tend to accumulate, even where the habit of relentlessly accumulating one's own publications wasn't applicable. He was perfectly familiar with the rule that however many new bookshelves one acquires, and however frequently one rearranges them in order to fit more in, they will immediately begin to overflow as soon as one begins to make use of them.

James Murden must have rearranged his library several times since returning from duty in the Second World War, and although he had left room enough between the bookcases lined up against the walls and the rows of wooden shelf-units to slip in between them himself, he had the advantage of his slim figure. Simon was by no means obese, but he would certainly have had difficulty maneuvering in the dark corridors that remained, even if there had not been additional piles of books on the floor. His expert eye estimated, on the basis of a single scan, that the room—which was not much larger, in terms of its floor space, than his study at Raven, although its ceiling was some two feet higher—must contain at least five thousand printed volumes.

"There are bookcases downstairs too, of course," James said, "for showpiece volumes, and I had to start accommodating the overflow in my bedroom long ago. Felicia has her own books in her room, of course, and Melusine too, although she's always been more moderate—at least until videotape was invented, and then DVDs. She has one of those big TV screens now, like a home cinema. I couldn't allow her to put it in either of the drawing rooms, so I'm not permitted to watch it, but it's no loss—I usually watch with Grandmother, and her old-fashioned set is quite adequate. Oh, don't worry about all those"—he waved a negligent hand at the rows of shelves filling all of the space to the right of the door—"all of the important stuff is here. I'll let some light in."

Here was a row of cupboards fitted to the left-hand wall of the room. They had sliding doors, in order that space would not have to be left vacant to open them, but the sliding sections were made of thin wood—not, Simon imagined, because they would have been too heavy or too brittle if they were made of glass, but because their designer had not wanted to render the contents of the cupboards visible.

James opened the curtains covering one of the windows, but not all the way, seemingly measuring the light he let in with the utmost care. There was a worktable underneath the window, with a padded stool. Simon was impressed that a scholar as old as James could work for any length of time on such a meager item of furniture, devoid of any support for his back or his elbows. He was sure that he could not have done it himself.

James slid back one of the sections of paneling. Simon's arithmetic was easily adequate to the calculation that there were thirty-six such panels, the two uppermost rows only being accessible via a mobile step-ladder. The contents were not so tightly packed as to make it difficult to observe that each cupboard was some two feet deep. The one that had been opened, in the third row from the floor, was further divided into shelves, each one containing a neat row of carefully bound manuscripts. Occasionally, two or three slender manuscripts were piled one atop another, but in most cases each individual compartment only contained a single volume.

Simon's eye immediately ran along the array of cupboards.

"Oh, no," said James, swiftly. "They don't all contain manuscripts, and not all the manuscripts are family records. A lot of the older printed volumes are here too. The family archives don't amount to much more than ten thousand pages, of which nearly half are duplicate copies and a third of the duplicated originals are as nearly illegible as hardly to be worth keeping. I don't discard anything, though, and I stopped copying by hand nearly fifty years ago, as soon as effective photocopiers came on to the market. My father used ordinary photographic apparatus in the first decade of the twentieth century, but he was never satisfied with the potential durability of the results, and rightly so."

He removed one of the bound volumes and handed it to Simon, who opened it with due care. The pages within were paper rather than parchment, and could not have been more than two hundred years old, but the text copied on to them, by an exceedingly meticulous hand, must have dated back much further. It was in Welsh—so, at least, Simon supposed.

"That is a problem," James observed "Even for me, although I learned to speak and read Welsh in childhood. That's archaic Welsh dating back to the fourteenth century, and it's markedly different from the modern tongue, the written script still being relatively young. The Latin ones are much easier to deal with—fortunately, no longer being a living language, Latin only underwent minor transmutations through the Middle Ages. Even though the monks of St. Madoc had a far better sense of priorities than many of their brethren—true scholars long before the days of Peter Abelard and the goliards—they were still monks, possessed of the vocabulary and the ideas of monks.

"My father wasn't able to make much of a contribution before the German machine guns did for him, Rhys had neglected the trove shamefully, and even Seymour was too busy living a life that was distinctly riotous by Murden standards to be conscientious in organizing the copying, let alone his own commentary. Fortunately, the more injurious aspects of the Age of Enlightenment didn't reach West Wales until the eighteenth century had ended, so the generations of that era made a very solid contribution not only to the preservation of texts but to the provision of new commentaries. If only Glyndwr had been a scholar rather than a warrior, his hauntings might have been more purposeful, but I fear that death seems to have scrambled his ideas considerably, in spite of the best efforts of the specter-forgers."

210

"The Faceless Monk wasn't a scholar either, then?" Simon queried, as he handed the first volume back to James and accepted another, of similar antiquity, but this time in Latin—equally incomprehensible to him, alas.

James did not reply to the flippant question for a full half-minute, and when he did, Simon having looked at him interrogatively, it was in deadly earnest. "Have you seen him?"

Simon's own tone became level and grave, almost involuntarily, when he said: "I believe so, yes. More than once, in fact, but I had no idea what I was seeing. The penny only dropped yesterday."

"More than once? Before you came here, that is?"

"I think so. Almost the first thing I saw, once night had fallen the day I arrived, was what I then assumed to be an actual monk, moving along the road to Morpen some distance away. When I saw him, or it, I had an immediate sense of *déjà-vu* . . . but that might have been illusory, of course, as such sensations sometimes are. Have you seen him?"

"Oh yes—but never at close range, never face to face. That's said to be . . . dangerous, although I don't know how that came to be known, if it's any more than simple anxiety."

"But you've seen Glyndwr at closer range?"

"Oh, many a time. At one time, I tried to make a serious study of him, but it was pointless. I wish it didn't sound like a joke to say that he's a mere shadow of his former self, because it's an accurate summation. I can understand why the occultists who devoted themselves to the production of specters gave it up as a bad job. Such records as they kept—such, at least, as were copied—are here."

He slid another panel back and took down another bound manuscript, bulkier than the two he had handed to Simon before. Simon opened it. Again, it was in Latin, tightly packed and utterly gnomic.

"You could actually follow the procedure yourself, with the aid of this?" Simon asked.

"Not without help. Even with access to a fragment of the Underworld and matter in the fifth state, I wouldn't be able to do it. Even if I had a morgen to help me . . . even a morgen scholar . . ."

"You'd need a neider?" Simon queried. "A neider scholar, if there's any such thing?"

"I suspect so. And even if the great catastrophe didn't obliterate the two species, I fear that it almost certainly obliterated their scientific heritage, their accumulated wisdom. I suspect that may be why we've had no contact for such a long time. Whatever portals existed on the bed of the Sargasso Sea, the Channel and Cardigan Bay, were obviously compromised, if not irredeemably sealed, but even if they became usable again, the morgens and the neider might have forgotten us, along with the pact that their ancestors made with Madoc, even though far fewer generations have elapsed in their world than ours."

James pushed two more panels aside, seemingly chosen because they were near to hand, but did not take anything out. He simply wanted to show Simon the contents—all completely incomprehensible so far as Simon was concerned.

"Alexander Usher is presumably a good Latinist," James observed, "but even he would only be able to make a difficult start on understanding a part of this heritage. How many men are alive at present, do you think, who know both Latin and Welsh well enough to get to grips with the whole of it?"

It wasn't a difficult calculation to make. "Perhaps one, or maybe two," he said.

"And how old would they be?"

"My age," Simon said, "with no younger generation coming up behind them. You started in your youth, and it's taken you all of your hundred and some years to reach the level of understanding you have now."

"Exactly," said James. "Even if Cerys were willing or able . . . how could I think of demanding that kind of life from her? In the eighteenth century, it was possible—but it wasn't even possible to demand full commitment from Seymour, or Rhys. My father was an anomaly, a throwback—and then came the Great War, and after the war . . . ."

"The Great Murden Schism," Simon murmured.

"All the other survivors cared about was the property, and living the lives that the end of the war seemed to have returned to them. I was my father's son. And just as I was beginning to make headway, it all flared up again. Six years, I was away. Six years! And it was a miracle that I wasn't killed, like my poor father. I believed in the pact's protection, then, but I knew it had limits . . . limits of which I'm all too aware today. If the heritage is kept from now on, you see, it will have to be kept in ignorance. No one will ever be able to repeat the work that I've done."

"But you have recorded it," Simon said. "Somewhere behind one of these panels is your own summary and commentary, in English."

"Not only here"—James tapped one of the higher panels, "but here." He pulled a memory stick out of his pocket. "Given another year, I can put scans of every single document on here, neatly arranged in pdf files and indexed. In theory, I could send copies to every single university library in the world. But even if the unfolding ecocatastrophe and the impending global economic collapse spare enough of our technological infrastructure to enable things like this to be read in thirty or a hundred years' time, who would ever bother to try? Who would ever understand it if they did? Who would ever believe it? And if someone ever did, what would they do with the treasure beneath the house?"

Simon nodded, to show that he understood. "You do realize, don't you," he said, "that there's absolutely nothing I can do to help? Even if I really were a neider-cum-human, and if, under the protection of the pact, I were to live to be a hundred, or two hundred, I still wouldn't be able to replace you."

"I know that," James said. "I've known since 1946 that it would end with me, that even if I'd acknowledged Gwyneth's child, and even if it really had been mine, and even if I'd tried with all my might to educate that child in the fashion that I'd been educated myself, it would still have ended with me.

In effect, it had ended in France, the day my father was shot down, if it hadn't ended a hundred years before. The scattering of what was left of the family in the twenties, and all the acrimony and pettiness, was just the froth on the wave. The rot had set in long before . . . but it's not really our fault, is it? Nor is it the morgens' fault. If they had been able to maintain contact, they surely would have done. The long aftermath of the catastrophe, like the long aftermath of our Great War, must have made it impractical.

"Even if they come back, as Ceridwen seems strangely sure that they will, it will be just like your coming to St. Madoc: they won't know anything, and they won't be in any position to learn it. Perhaps they can take back whatever is in the cocoons, and perhaps it will even be valuable to them . . . but the real legacy, the cultural legacy of the Caer-Ys, is surely already lost, and would probably take a thousand years or more to reproduce, if anyone or anything were even interested in reproducing it."

Simon looked around at the densely packed shelves containing all the modern printed books, the legacy of the last two hundred years or so of human wisdom—and of course, the infinite legacy of intellectual clutter, misinformation and disinformation. He did not imagine, even for a second, that James Murden had read all the books, or observed and understood more than a tiny fraction of what they contained. Could anyone? Could anyone even make the attempt? All but the tiniest fraction—and probably not the best—was, in effect, already lost, even though it was still sitting there, on the shelves. He knew only too well how minuscule, how misguided, how impotent and how utterly irrelevant his own meager effort had been, and how rare it was for anyone now alive even to make as much effort as that.

"Yes," he said to James Murden. "I understand your situation . . . and the situation of all this." His hand indicated the cupboard. One by one, James was closing all the sliding doors.

"Believe me," James said, gravely, "you haven't seen anything yet."

Simon did believe him, and knew that James wasn't talking about whatever the Faceless Monk might have instead of a face, if he had anything at all.

James drew the curtains again that plunged the library back into near-darkness, and gestured to Simon to precede him into what now seemed to be a brightly illuminated corridor. He locked the library door carefully, and put the key into a pocket of his black jacket, from which it brought forth a muffled clink, revealing the presence of at least one more key, and probably several.

Simon followed his host downstairs again, along further corridors and through three further doors into the chapel adjacent to the main building of the house. They did not pause to look at the family bible on its lectern, or the morgen crudely designed on a stone slab, surrounded by what Simon now knew to be a neider rather than an ouroboros—unless, of course, the symbol of the ouroboros had been a neider all along, which now seemed a perfectly plausible hypothesis.

He barely glanced at the old pews, which were free of dust, but certainly did not give the impression that they were in regular use. Obviously, the Murdens had been Christian long after the Abbey had been gifted to them, albeit in a somewhat unorthodox fashion, but they had lapsed, presumably in the days of Rhys the Engineer. He suspected that no service or ritual of any kind had been conducted in the chapel for many years.

There was a trapdoor in the corner of the chapel, secured by a padlock similar to the one on the gate of the bridge. James took another key out of his pocket, opened it and removed it from the rings that it was securing.

"Please," he said to Simon, moving aside. "It's heavy."

XVI
The Underworld

It was only with difficulty that Simon managed to lift the trapdoor. He suspected that no one currently in the house had the strength to do it without mechanical aid. When it was tipped back against the chapel wall, it gave access to a spiral stairway wrought in stone. The steps did not seem worn, but that was not because they were not old; it was because few feet had trodden them, in centuries, and probably far more than a thousand years.

Simon thought that he was in an underworld of sorts as soon as he stepped on to the stairs, clutching a powerful electric torch that James Murden had handed him. James followed him, carrying a similar device. Between them, the two beams provided an adequate light, even though the walls of the stairwell were very dark in hue, their near-blackness seemingly capable of soaking up light.

Some twenty steps down, they came to a stone floor, which stretched away in four corridors with vaulted ceilings.

"The cellars and crypts," said James dismissively, after a brief circular sweep of his flashlight beam. "We go down." He knelt down beside another trapdoor, unlocking another padlock with another key.

"Would you do the honors again?" he requested.

Simon lifted the heavy wooden panel with no less difficulty than the one up above, and tilted it back. There was another spiral staircase, similarly cut into the rock, with astonishing neatness: the stairway to the Underworld.

Simon neglected to count the stairs, but he was astonished by their quantity. He soon lost all sense of lateral direction as the stairway wound around, and he also had the strange sensation that he was losing track of time as well as he seemed to be repeating the same circular movement over and over again, within the same few seconds, rather than actually descending.

He was descending, however; there was no doubt about

that—and descending a long way. He was soon sure that he must be below sea level, and far beyond the level of the entrances to the two caves that he had seen from the coastal path.

Alexander Usher had been wasting his time trying to get access to Nyder's Cave from the shore, he realized, at least insofar as gaining access thereby to the most intimate secrets of the Abbey was concerned. There could not possibly be any tunnel or vent connecting that entrance to the stairway, or it would be flooded, and whatever was at the bottom would have been drowned beneath several fathoms of sea water.

Simon played the beam of his torch over the walls.

"Is this granite or basalt?" he asked, simply to break a silence that was becoming oppressive.

"Neither," James told him. "Solids are denatured over time by an alliance with the fifth state of matter. What surrounds us now is something akin to an aetheric colloid, in which the rock of the seabed has become a mineral distinct in its crystalline structure from basalt, although it might have started out as that. Even the air is different—can't you sense that?"

Simon realized, as soon as it was pointed out to him, that he could. He was drawing it into his lungs without difficulty, and deriving oxygen from it with less effort than he surely would have done had it merely been atmospheric air that had fallen into a deep shaft, unrenewed by any vegetation and polluted by damp and various chemical residues.

"I see what you mean," he said. "And the seal is obviously hermetic. There's no seepage at all."

"We're below the seabed now," James told him. "You might feel a little extra pressure on your eardrums, but don't worry about the possibility of the bends. Even if we came up rapidly, our bodies will be saturated by the time we return. You won't feel anything physically, of course . . . but can the fraction of our make-up that's already constituted by the seventh element enable you to feel anything yet? I'd be interested to have a description, if so."

"I do feel slightly queasy," Simon admitted, "but I think that's just the effect of going round and round. Is there much further to go?"

"In terms of distance, no," was the reply. "Eighty more steps give or take a few. In conceptual terms, though, that constitutes a big stride. This is already the Underworld, but . . . well, you'll see. Not much, but you will see. More to the point, you'll feel . . . probably more than me. Don't be afraid though. You can't come to any harm."

It occurred to Simon that James could not possibly know that, but he let it pass. Now, he did begin to count the steps, but he stopped when he got to forty, because there was no point in continuing. As James had said, they were already in the Underworld. Although arithmetic still worked, the information it delivered seemed to have become irrelevant. The same seemed to be true of geometry. That, at least, was what Simon felt—and the import of what James had said about feeling became suddenly clearer to him. His senses were becoming less useful to him as channels of information, and his intellect less useful as a means of calculation and ratiocination.

He became aware that, within the near-silence, he could hear the sea . . . except that it could not possibly be the sea in any literal sense. What he had the illusion of hearing was a deep of a different, and less fathomable kind, and his mind could only grasp it by constructing it, not as a kind of whispered speech, but as if it were a kind of music.

The bells of Ys, he thought. *This can't be where the last Caer-Ys sank into the bed of Cardigan Bay, but it has a similar pulse-beat, a similar rhythm — not so much a siren song as the impression that an embryo must have of the maternal pulse-beat, and the placental tide.*

Did the shaft close in around him? Simon wasn't sure that that was an apt or adequate description of what happened, and there was certainly no sensation of the solid walls and the air they enclosed being replaced by another fluid. He still had his material body, and it was still capable of movement in what was presumably, in terms of the conventional three states of earthly matter, solid-free and air-filled space. He could still feel the hand-grip of the flashlight in the fingers of his right hand, but he could no longer see its beam. And yet, there was light, or something that substituted for light with regard to his consciousness.

It was blue: not quite the same blue as Felicia's eyes, even at their most intense, but similarly cerulean, similarly celestial. He could see why a sincere monk descending into this environment, might leap to the assumption that he had reached the threshold of paradise.

He reached the last step, and his feet, through his socks and shoes, could feel a level floor, but he could not see the floor in question. All he could see, for the moment, was the blue.

"Don't be alarmed," said James Murden's voice, still audible in a very ordinary fashion and coming from above. "Your brain will adapt, just as it would to the information transmitted by your retinas if you had stepped from a dark room into the light. Take two steps forward, please, to make room for me to join you, and be patient. You might well see more than I can, when the cocoons become visible."

Simon took two hesitant steps forward, instinctively putting out his left arm, ahead of the flashlight that he was holding in his right, to make sure that there was nothing solid in front of him.

His hand did not collide with anything, but he was no longer sure that he could interpret that to mean that there was nothing solid there. He suspected that there might be, but that it had been rendered intangible by its quasi-colloidal alliance with the seventh element. Like Alice down the rabbit hole, he was now in Wonderland; the normal rules no longer applied.

But James was right. His eyes adapted to the blue, and he saw the vitreous cocoons emerging from the uniformity, taking on appearance. Whether or not they took on the form that the appearance implied, he was not entirely sure, but the appearance told him readily enough why James or one of his predecessors had appropriated the word "vitreous" to describe them. In terms of their perceptible texture, they resembled glass: blue glass naturally, but translucent, if not actually transparent. The surfaces of the individual units or cells were concave, and their shape was vaguely cylindrical, thus providing some license for thinking of them as cocoons.

But were they cocoons?

Certainly, they seemed to contain something, something possessed of form, and the forms that they contained, in thousands if not tens of thousands, certainly seemed to be larval, akin to worms or grubs . . . but worms or grubs that had already embarked upon a process of metamorphosis, which implied that they might ultimately become something not very wormlike at all.

The chambers—Simon decided to call them that in order not to assume too much—were stacked in a fashion that he could not help likening to a honeycomb, although it had no hexagons. It had no angles at all, in fact, and he had the curious impression that what he was looking at was actually a four-dimensional structure, although the sight of his mind's eye was not adapted to perceive more than three of them.

He was able to turn his head and his body to see that they surrounded him, and that he and James Murden appeared to be standing in a circular space approximately four meters in diameter, with the stairway—seeming now to consist of steps suspended in space—in its center.

The floor beneath his feet now seemed to be made of royal blue glass, but the ceiling above his head, if it really was a ceiling, was a much paler shade. The stacks of cocoons were not much more than a dozen units high, and when he tried to track them around the circular space as if they were a wall they seemed to be not much more than twenty in a line, but the total was far greater than the multiplication of twelve times twenty implied.

Perhaps, Simon thought, they were stacked ten or twelve deep, but he was somehow able to see, or to sense by some other means, the extra-dimensionality of that array, and form the greater estimate that way.

Are they really cocoons? he wondered. *Are they really larval morgens, neider and Heaven only knows how many other species native to the Underworld overflow ecosystem? Or are they something else? Do morgens and neider really have larvae? What sort of life-cycle might they have? Might they be the same species at different points in that cycle, rather than different species? If they're capable of metamorphosis, what meaning can even be attached to the label of "species?" And whatever they are, what could their contemporary kin do with them if they were to take them back? How could they take them back, in fact, and where would they take them? What has become of the spaces of the ancient Underworld—if "spaces" is even an appropriate term—since the great catastrophe, the aetherquake, or whatever it was? I'm out of my conceptual depth here.*

That was only too true, he realized—but he realized, too, that it was more complicated than that. It wasn't just his sight, or pseudo-sight, that was gradually adapting to the new material environment in which he found himself. Another form of sensation was adapting too, which was more emotional than sensory, more intimate than any normal form of passion.

He had never believed himself to be capable of any form of empathy. Even when he had been lying beside Felicia, supposedly sharing some kind of dream with her, he had not experienced it as a form of communication or commonality. It had simply seemed to him that he was following a train of thought, which he had had no other option but to think of as his own.

Now, though, he really did feel that what he was feeling was coming from without. It did not feel as if something inside him were awakening, as if he were somehow developing a new form of extrasensory perception; it simply felt, to begin with, as if he were being invaded, or flooded, by something insistent, massive and overwhelming.

Had he been religious, he thought, he might have been able to think of what was happening as a kind of revelation, a contact with the divine; had he been an optimist as well, he might even have been able to construe it as a wave of divine love.

But he was not religious and he was not an optimist—quite the contrary. He did not construe the feeling that welled up within him as divine, and certainly not as any kind of love. On the other hand, nor was he so prone to fear and dread that it seemed to him to be a form of demonic possession, essentially diabolical: a kind of damnation. It was intrusive, to be sure, but it did not seem infernal; it did not even seem to pose any threat to his sanity. He was able, without mustering any kind of valor or heroism, to experience it simply as something new, something peculiar, to which his terms of good and evil, or even pleasant and unpleasant, simply did not apply.

In much the same way that, from the limited viewpoint of the three traditional phases of matter, the seventh element appeared to be "unreal," so the inherent sensation that invaded him seemed, however paradoxical the assertion might seem, to be "unfeeling," and certainly "amoral." To extrapolate the seeming paradox even further, however, it did not seem impersonal and it did not seem irrelevant. It seemed, somehow, *interested*. It did not seem simply to be something washing over him. It seemed inquisitive . . . perhaps even puzzled.

But as he became accustomed to the seeming invasion, he ceased to experience it as an intrusion of something alien. He began, instead, to experience it as a kind of becoming, as a kind of coming to, after a long period of quasi-unconsciousness, of being trapped in a kind of dream state.

He no longer felt small. He no longer felt lost.

Gradually, he began to feel powerful. He began to feel capable. He began to feel that he could not only summon spirits from the strangest of deeps, but that they would come when he called. But he also felt that the faculty in question was a trivial matter, something that he could simply take for granted. The more important faculty, he thought, was to be able to look inside himself, to know himself.

He felt godlike, self-enclosed, self-sufficient, in control of his own becoming, of his own evolution.

For a moment, he felt an immense pride . . . but then his intelligence caught up with the surge of his new-found passion, and he realized that his perception was inverted, that it was not himself that he was feeling at all, but that what was actually happening was that another self was feeling *him*. He was caught in empathic communication with . . . what?

Something strange, and alien, but also tentative. As his sensation became even further refined, he had the sensation that he was not even a whole being, but merely a fragment, something more than a mere cell, but less than a true individual. He felt that he was an instrument: an instrument with a degree of independence, to be sure, an instrument with a mind of his own, but an instrument nevertheless.

And while he tried to construe the surge of emotion in those terms, the music swelled, becoming far greater than the orchestral equipment of his imagination could reproduce. The bells of Ys became deafening, pounding his mind, driving away thought and feeling alike, becoming nothing but noise: lacerating, shattering noise.

He felt no pain; the nerves of his body were not tormented; he felt no impulse to scream, writhe or collapse; it was pure illusion, and he knew it—but he knew, too, that it was a kind of illusion that could kill a mere human, or condemn him to catatonia and a vegetal existence, if it had the desire to do so, or even became careless.

It did not. He had the impression that as soon as whatever had contacted him had perceived his distress, it withdrew. It left him. Except that it did not feel like something draining away, or letting him go. It felt that he was unbecoming. Whatever he had been momentarily—for the entire experience surely could not have lasted for more than a few seconds— he no longer was. Instead, he was his old self again, or very nearly . . . so very nearly that it would have been extremely difficult for him to specify the difference.

But there was a difference. He had not been reconfigured or rewritten, but there had been a shift in his attitude.

And he had the feeling, too, that whatever he had begun

was, indeed, only a beginning. He had the feeling that the real exploration, the real ordeal, was yet to come.

"Well?" said James Murden sharply.

Simon knew that his cicerone wanted a description of his reaction. He did not believe for an instant that he was capable of synthesizing an account that his host would find acceptable as an answer to his brutal inquiry. He had no recourse but ludicrous understatement. Of that he was capable.

"One would have to have a limited imagination to mistake it for the mind of God," he said, "but it's surely a mind, albeit very alien."

"Did you get any sense of what the vitreous cocoons actually are?" James demanded.

"No."

"Did you get any sense of what's about to happen?"

"No, except . . ."

"Except what?"

"Something is. You're right: I was impelled here. My presence changes things—perhaps very slightly, but significantly. Something is coming, from the deep."

"Tomorrow?"

"Soon. Very soon. A storm . . . but not necessarily Storm Deidre . . . not, at least, the Met Office version of it. But we already knew that. Lenore knew it on Monday. The Storm was always coming."

"Is that all?" James sounded disappointed.

"What did you expect?"

"I don't know. Something specific."

"That's not the way it works, James. You've been here before, perhaps many times. Have you ever obtained anything specific?"

Simon tried to make out the expression on James's face, but it was impossible. Everything was blue; he knew where James was, and could hear him clearly, but seeing him was a different matter, for the moment.

"No, I haven't but . . . never mind. It's not your fault. I couldn't help hoping, although I ought to know better by now. Was it worthwhile, though? Do you understand any more now than you did before?"

"Yes, I think so—I understand, at least, how little I understand, in proportion to what there is to be understood. It's certainly very different from anything I could ever have expected. I would never have imagined that a portal to an alien universe could be crossed simply by going down a spiral staircase, and I would never have imagined that a place could exist where it was so easy to breathe, where there must not only be air but some kind of air-conditioning, and a place to stand, from which to stare, without its topography or its materiality making any evident sense. I can see why you call your mysterious legacy 'vitreous cocoons,' for the sake of calling them something, but I don't really have any conceptual category in which to place them. As for feeling . . . I honestly have no idea *what* I'm feeling now, although I have no doubt at all that I that I just felt something beyond the ordinary reach of human sensation."

"And that's all?" James still seemed disappointed, as if he were desperate to hang on to some shred of the hope that he had dared to entertain in bringing Simon into the Underworld.

"I fear so. Except that I can't help feeling, although I don't know why or how, that you were right to bring me down here—that my being here *matters*. Something *is* changing, as a result of my being here. Not that it was really you that brought me, of course. I came of my own accord . . . whatever that can actually mean."

"You were brought," said James, confidently.

Simon wanted to resist the notion, to insist, in spite of everything that he had just experienced, that he was a free agent, in control of his own destiny. But he knew that James was right. He had been brought to St. Madoc, and to the Underworld. He had no idea what had brought him, or why, but something was certainly going on within him of which he was not the master.

"Are you afraid?" James asked.

"No," Simon replied. "Oddly enough, I'm not. But I think perhaps I ought to be. How about you?"

"When one gets to my age," James said, "the capacity for feeling diminishes to the point where it's difficult even to feel fear. No, I'm not afraid—but I know what you mean when you say that perhaps we ought to be."

"As flies to wanton boys are we to the gods . . . ," Simon quoted, pensively. "But no—that's entirely wrong. The morgen and the neider aren't gods, they're not wanton, they don't regard us as flies, and they have no intention of killing us for their sport. But still, a storm is coming, and if they come, they will come in the storm, or in its echo within the Underworld . . . because here, as opposed to the liquid surface of the planet, the gulf stream isn't just a thread of slightly warmer water in an ocean. In this vasty deep, it's something far more potent."

"Are you certain of that?" James demanded.

"Certain of it? Of course not. But if I'm to make any sense at all of what I felt just now, that's the only sense I can make. Something is coming, and we need to be here to meet it."

"If we can," he said, curtly.

XVII
The Contest

Melusine and Felicia were waiting in the chapel, sitting side by side in the front row of the remaining pews. Simon felt slightly dazed and rather disorientated, but when James had asked him to lower the trapdoor again he had not had any difficulty doing it. James had watched him carefully, but seemed to be satisfied with what he saw, and knelt down to lock it. The two old ladies came to stand to either side of him.

Now that Simon could see James clearly, he saw that he was very pale—not the kind of pallor that overtook him in his fits of anger, but something more enduring, and perhaps more ominous. His face was drawn, his expression haggard, but he seemed to be trying hard not to let anything show, to maintain his self-discipline.

He had been into the Underworld before, Simon knew, and perhaps many times, but he was evidently still vulnerable to its effects. He had already asked his guide, on the staircase, whether he was all right, and had received an affirmative answer that he suspected to be false, so he knew that there was no point asking again. In any case, he was not given the opportunity.

"It's our turn now," said Melusine. "We're going for a walk on the Tine—but you'll have to lend us an arm each, and walk quite slowly. We're very old."

Simon recalled having watched both of them walk away from Raven Cottage with a perfectly confident stride, at a reasonably good pace, but he thought that they might be putting on an act for James's benefit—or, perhaps, lending him their arms in case he needed their support. He did not. Although he felt somewhat spaced-out mentally, in physical terms he was perfectly steady.

"Is that all right with you, James?" Felicia asked, as she took the flashlight out of Simon's right hand before taking possession of that arm.

"Of course, dear," James replied, tautly. "He's all yours. I have to go and see Grandmother now."

Melusine took Simon's left arm, and the two of them led him away gently—not toward the door to the house but to the one opposite, that led outside. It wasn't locked, and it swung easily on its hinges when Melusine opened it. Outside, the sun was shining brightly, and the day seemed entirely spring-like, although the grass of the headland was only just beginning to show signs of fresh growth. The sea was placid, and, although more gray than blue, pleasant to behold.

"It's beautiful," said Felicia.

"The calm before the storm," Melusine reminded her. "This time tomorrow it will be blowing a gale."

"Don't mind her," Felicia said to Simon. "She's never been very good at living in the moment."

"Says the woman who's never been very good even at living in the real world," remarked Melusine, but without any evident hostility.

"We're not doing that any more, remember," was Felicia's only reply.

"I haven't forgotten," Melusine assured her. To Simon, she said: "We've agreed not to fight. Not that we usually do, of course, but that might be because we don't usually have anything for which to compete."

"Not that we see you as something for which to compete," Felicia assured him, swiftly. "It would be very silly to allow any jealousy to infect our relationship, because it could only spoil things, so we've decided to eliminate the possibility."

Judging by the way that both of them were clinging on to his arms, unnecessarily, it did not seem to Simon that the possibility had been eliminated, but he decided that it would be a bad idea to encourage any such competition, no matter how flattering it might be, at his age, to have two women— even eccentric centenarians—fighting over his attention . . . attention that he was still trying to refocus, not entirely sure that he had fully readapted mentally to the vulgar world above the surface.

"I'm delighted to hear it," he contrived to tell them. "I'd hate to be a bone of contention within the family."

"That ship has sailed, alas," said Melusine. "But you mustn't feel bad about it—it's not your fault. James is annoyed with both of us, and Cerys is annoyed with absolutely everybody. It's her age, you see. She's trying to build up sufficient resentment to be able to leave us without feeling guilty."

"As if we'd hold it against her," Felicia put in. "James has been moving heaven and earth trying to find her a good position on the mainland, but the distant cousins are no help at all. They seem to make it a point of principle to oppose him on everything he tries to do with regard to the estate, but it's really very unfair to turn their hostility on poor Cerys."

"Let's not start on the distant cousins," said Melusine. "I want to hear what Simon thought of the Underworld. Are you feeling all right yet, Simon? Have you come back up to earth?"

Both of them turned to look at him expectantly.

"It's . . . unexpected," he said, after a long pause. "You've both been down there, obviously?"

"Obviously," agreed Melusine. "It was a long time ago, though. It's certainly not something we do regularly. Once was enough for me, although Felicia actually wanted to sleep down there at one time."

"I did," Felicia confirmed. "And it wasn't pointless, no matter what you think. You felt it, didn't you, Simon—the neider?"

"I certainly felt something," Simon affirmed. "I'm just not sure what it was. It's left me feeling a little disorientated—but I'll be all right in a minute or two."

"It's not anything we can describe," Felicia told him. "We don't have the words. It's even worse for you, because you're neider, like me, and they don't even have words of their own. But it *is* real, isn't it?"

"Yes," said Simon, slowly. "It's definitely real. Until I went down there, I admit, I still thought that all of this might be a tissue of delusions, but not any more. There's no more room for even a shadow of doubt. But you're absolutely right: we don't have the words to describe it, and in spite of all James' heroic efforts of scholarship—and yours too—understanding remains frustratingly out of reach. I still have no idea what might happen tomorrow, if anything does, and I can't see any possibility of a denouement to all this."

"You say that as if it were a bad thing," murmured Felicia.

"Of course he does," Melusine put in, before Simon could reply. "He's a writer. He wants every story to have an ending, as neat as a bow on fancy gift-wrapping."

"He not that kind of writer," Felicia said, again before Simon could open his mouth, "as you'd know if you'd bothered to read his work. His books aren't the sort that just end tokenistically, with a marriage and an inheritance. He likes to play with the ideas, and let them lead his imagination where they will. He doesn't care about neat endings."

Simon was glad to observe that Felicia no longer seemed disposed to insist on the mediocrity of his literary abilities, and he suppressed the urge to tell her that, although she was absolutely right about his liking to follow his ideas wherever their hypothetical logic led him, he did still care about trying to establish some kind of terminus into which his trains of thought could pull, and that it was a responsibility that he sometimes weighed heavily upon him. If and when she had read more of his fiction, he knew she would observe that he was certainly not above paying lip service to the orgastic theory of fiction, although he rarely featured literal wedding bells and convenient testaments.

In fact, he didn't have to say anything, because Melusine was quick to say: "I've started *A Midwinter's Night's Dream*. I'm really enjoying it so far. That's one of your more recent ones, I believe, Simon? Look out for the hole."

"True," admitted Simon, finally getting a word in, if only edgewise, while looking down in slight alarm. The hole to which his attention was being drawn, however, was still some distance away, and both of his hangers-on were already steering to the right in order to give it a wide berth.

"James really ought to put a guard-rail around them," opined Felicia. "Someone's going to fall into one of them, one of these days, and they'd be bound to break a leg, if nothing worse."

"Good," said Melusine. "Nobody's going to fall into it except a trespasser, and it would serve them right."

"Is it a well?" Simon asked, curiously.

"No," Melusine explained. "It's the shaft that leads down to Nyder's Cave. There's another one about thirty paces that way, behind the mound. That one leads down to Morgan's Cave, and has stone steps. I think there used to be a sort of glorified dumb waiter in this one, back in the days when

Seymour was the kingpin of the West Wales smugglers, but it's long gone. It's said that he wept bitter tears the day after Waterloo, because he was hoping that Napoleon would regain power and reinstate the trade sanctions. The family was prosperous in those days."

"It was still prosperous for some time afterwards," said Felicia.

"Not really," said Melusine. "Rhys was a great engineer but a lousy accountant, James says. He was famous, but he left the family far poorer when he died than it had been when he took control. Poor Matthew never had a chance of restoring its fortunes, even if he hadn't been gunned down in France."

"Is that why your grandmother says that Rhys has a lot to answer for?" asked Simon, vaguely remembering his conversation with the old lady.

"Probably," Melusine confirmed.

"Actually," said Felicia, in frank defiance of their supposed agreement, "it's more likely because of the cesspits."

"The cesspits?" Simon queried.

"Yes," said Felicia. "The newspapers of the day hailed the system as a major contribution to public hygiene, and there are history books that give him credit for being a significant precursor of urban sewer systems, but Grandmother thinks that diverting all the natural fertilizer away from the bays altered their ecology, making them less hospitable to the morgens."

"That sounds more like the kind of idea that James would come up with than Grandmother," Melusine opined. "She must have got it from him. She takes him far too seriously."

"And you don't?" challenged Felicia.

"It really is beautiful out here," Simon said, trying to pull himself together and focusing his attention outwards, wanting to absorb some of the reality of the view by looking out over the tip of the Tine, which they were now approaching, at the sea. He also hoped that it might defuse the simmering dispute.

"We have the channel in Bristol, of course," he went on, still trying to reinsert himself into normality, "and the Avon gorge, but nothing like this." He peered ostentatiously to the left and the right, at the other tines of Morgan's Fork, as if to draw a comparison between their equal charm and those of the two white-haired heads over which he was peering—with difficulty, in Melusine's case.

"It gets distinctly tedious after the first hundred years," Melusine opined, regretfully. "Even though there are only twenty days a year as pleasant as this one—and they're calms before storms."

"Actually, Simon," said Felicia, "it's nearer a hundred days than twenty. It's even nicer in summer—quite glorious in July."

Simon became aware that the grip on each of his arms had tightened noticeably, and that a subtle but definite pressure was being exerted in opposite directions. He sought for something else to say that might help to restore harmony, but his mental creativity had not yet recovered sufficiently. Mercifully, he was saved the trouble.

"Excuse me," said a voice from behind them, "but I've been sent to fetch Mr. Cannick. Grandmother wants to see him."

Both his arms were released as their holders spun around to face Cerys.

"What, now?" snapped Melusine. "She said she just wanted him to pop in for a moment before he left at five. It's isn't even half past three yet."

"She's changed her mind," said Cerys, not sounding particularly regretful. "She wants to see him right away."

"Why?" asked Felicia.

"She doesn't give me reasons," said Cerys, in a martyred tone, "just orders."

Simon got the distinct impression that both cousins would have liked to seize his respective arms again and declare that they would let him go when they were good and ready—but neither of them dared.

"Well, if it's an order," said Melusine, petulantly. "You'd better go, Simon. I'm sorry. She can be so inconsiderate, sometimes."

"That's true," Felicia agreed, acknowledging that harmony had, indeed, been restored at a stroke, in the face of a common adversary with the authority to out-compete them both.

Simon set off behind Cerys, having to use the full length of his stride to keep up with her, and glad to do so, because the solidity of his tread seemed to be reasserting his own solidity and stability.

"I'm sorry too," she said. "You seemed to be having such a good time."

"I was," said Simon, only a trifle hypocritically. "Your aunts are quite charming. I like them."

"Don't let it go to your head," said Cerys. "They're only competing for your attention on a point of principle, and because of the novelty of having some attention to compete for."

"That thought had occurred to me," Simon told her. "Don't be too hard on them. They don't have your advantages any more, when it comes to claiming attention, and they miss it. They must have been as beautiful as you are when they were your age, and you must be a constant reminder of what they once were."

All she said in reply to that was: "Mind the hole."

Once again, the hole at which she waved her arm vaguely was a good ten yards to the right of their course.

"That's the one that leads down to Morgan's Cave?" Simon queried, glancing to his left, in the direction in which its counterpart lay.

"That's right. Can't take you down there now, though— not that there's anything to see, especially while the tide's in. Grandmother was insistent—and don't ask me why. Nobody ever tells me anything."

"Actually," Simon said. "I suspect that James is going to tell you everything, or at least make a start, tomorrow morning."

Cerys turned to look at him sharply. "You said something?"

"In passing—but I can't claim any credit. I'm fairly sure that he'd already made the decision."

"God, you really have stirred things up, haven't you?"

"Again, I can't claim any credit," Simon insisted. "My only intention was to find a quiet place to get on with my work in total isolation. If I'd had any idea that my arrival would stir up so much excitement, I'd . . ." He stopped.

"You'd have avoided the place like the plague?" Cerys suggested.

Simon laughed, although the laughter made him feel somewhat light-headed again. "Hell, no," he said. "But I'd have been able to savor every minute of the experience properly, instead of spending so much time dazed by astonishment . . . and worse."

The young woman laughed with him. "Well, I'm glad we're such a rich source of amusement," she said. "The family treasure didn't disappoint, then?"

"Absolutely not," he told her. "Seeing it, and feeling it, almost makes the last sixty-eight years of misery and humiliation worthwhile."

She evidently did not think for an instant that he might be serious. "I'll look forward to it, then," she said dryly, before adding: "Feeling it?" inquisitively.

"I can't say any more," he told her, as they entered the house by the back door. "I'm a writer—I hate spoilers."

She shook her head in mock exasperation, and preceded him up the stairs. As before, she opened the door of her ancestor's room for him, but didn't close it behind him. She left that task for James, who was sitting beside his ancestor's bed, although he got up as Simon approached.

"I'll come back," he said to the old lady. "We need to settle this." He sounded uncommonly grave, even for him.

"Don't be so melodramatic, James," she instructed him, sternly, "and do as you're told."

James barely glanced at Simon as he left, closing the door behind him.

Ceridwen Murden was sitting up in bed, wearing a night-dress, but her hair was neatly combed and she had put on a subtle trace of lipstick. Her back was solidly supported by a heap of pillows, but she did not seem unduly weak, and her gaze was alert and intelligent. She glanced at the clock on the wall opposite the bed as she waved a diaphanous left hand to invite him to sit down in the chair that James had vacated. As soon as he was seated, she offered the same hand to be held, and left it resting in his as if she had no intention whatsoever of withdrawing it until he stood up again to leave the room.

"How do you feel?" she asked.

"I don't honestly know," he confessed. "Odd . . . not quite myself. But then, I'm not quite myself, am I? I never have been, really . . . but now I know."

"Now you know," she confirmed. "But you don't know what it is that you know. We've all been there, but we mor-gens seem to fit our other selves a little better than Felicia. And you know the results of all James's careful study, too. Not everything, obviously, but . . . well I won't even say 'enough'. At any rate . . . you believe me now?"

"I didn't disbelieve you before," he said

"Yes, you were very courteous, and I was grateful for that. But there's no doubt left?"

"Lots—but none regarding the reality of the situation. Why did you want to see me so urgently?"

"Did I annoy Felicia and Melusine? Too bad. You shouldn't be playing them off against one anther, though—it's not kind."

"I'm not playing them off against one another. I'm just trying to be as kind as possible to both of them."

"Too successfully, perhaps. Melusine came back yesterday almost licking her lips, and I assume that Felicia paid you a visit afterwards, since the black mood she'd been in all day had dissipated when she came in to wish me a belated good night. I suppose you'd even volunteer to get into bed with me, if I were to ask. You need to be careful about raising expecta-tions that you might not be able to meet . . . but that's not what I needed to talk to you about, and that won't wait. Age has its privileges, including making peremptory demands . . . although I have been making use of that prerogative for more than a hundred years, and James, at least, thinks that my demands have become excessive. How was I to know, though, that I'd last this long? I've been expecting Death to come calling any day since 1860. I really do feel, though, that if the grim reaper was going to hold off for so long, he could at least have granted me a little more strength and vitality. It's not exactly fun being an invalid for a hundred and fifty years . . . but get to the point, Ceridwen . . . that's my name, you know."

"I know," Simon affirmed.

"The Celtic goddess of inspiration, rebirth and transformation, some say. If only! Others say she was just a second-rate enchantress with a hideous son, which might be nearer the mark. I had more than one hideous son, alas, but it was my own fault. Enough of that, though. I saw Owain Glyndwr last night."

"I've heard that you're on good terms," Simon said, in a carefully neutral voice.

"We are now. I've tamed him somewhat, and tried to soothe his woes. Not easy . . . but at least I've taught him to speak good English, so he'll be able to hold a decent conversation with you, if he isn't too resentful of my asking him to pay you a visit. It's the ideal time, because the effects of your excursion to the underworld won't wear off for at least twenty-four hours. You'll have no difficulty seeing him."

"You've asked Owain Glyndwr's ghost to pay me a visit?"

"Yes. There are things that even James can't tell you . . . quite a lot, actually. Owain can fill in a few of the blanks, if he's willing. I can't promise anything, but I've done my best."

"You couldn't tell me yourself?"

"Some things are better coming straight from the phantom's mouth, especially now that your neider self has been agitated. You had to see the Underworld for yourself, too, obviously. And if you ever get to meet a morgen, it will only take an instant for you to realize that nothing a frail little old lady on her death-bed could have told you could have substituted for a split second of staring into her face. Trust me—I've been there."

"And you've slept with the neider too, so rumor has it."

Her bright eyes looked at him a trifle sharply. "Yes I have," she said. "But you know enough now to take that literally rather than lewdly, don't you?"

"Yes," he admitted.

"Mind you, I'd rather have been fucked by the neider than some of the men I have been fucked by, if the neider were actually capable of fucking as well as wrapping itself around you and leeching your dreams. Oh, don't look so shocked. They even say fuck on television these days, and they do it on-screen too." She glanced briefly at the old-fashioned set on a wheeled stand, pushed discreetly back into the alcove of the bay window. "Melusine has a huge plasma TV, you know? She says it's marvelous. I should get one, she says: it's a high-definition screen. 'What good is a high-definition screen to someone without high-definition eyes?' I asked her. I'd quite like to see the high-definition fucking, though. It was all very low-definition in my day, believe me. But that's by the by. I thought I'd better warn you about Owain. Not that I thought you'd be frightened, mind, but it's better to have advance warning, isn't it? About some things, anyway."

Simon agreed, in spite of his dislike of spoilers—but he was astonished to see tears suddenly forming in the corners of the old woman's eyes. "What's wrong?" he asked.

"Nothing," she said. "I just let my tongue run away with me for a moment, dragging my thoughts with it. I'm a foolish old woman. I'd ask you to forgive me, but I've been saying it for more than a hundred years, and it's no excuse. Still, I don't have to put on an act with you, do I?"

"No," said Simon.

"I wish I'd read some of your books. I wish I still had time. Cerys say they're wonderful."

"She's very kind. Felicia thinks they're mediocre."

"Did she say that? The cow. That's not like her, mind—she's usually far too timid to criticize."

"I've forgiven her," Simon said. "I even tried to be grateful for her honesty, but couldn't quite manage it, even though I tell myself they're mediocre all the time. When I say it, it passes for modesty, but from other people, it hurts."

"I know the feeling," the old lady murmured, and lifted her free hand swiftly to wipe away a furtive tear.

"Something *is* wrong," Simon judged. "Would you like me to fetch James?"

"Good God no. He'll only scold me again—but he'll do as he's told. He knows that he doesn't have any alternative. Just keep doing what you're doing."

"I'm not doing anything—just holding your hand."

"That too." She fell silent, and closed her eyes, but he could tell that she was only collecting herself, and that she would open them again when she could. He had seen Eve do the same thing, and knew that the important thing was to keep holding her hand, communicating a little of his strength to her.

Eventually, the eyes opened, their gaze as bright as before. "I'm sorry," she said. "I am a little shaken up, I confess. I had a bad dream last night, and although I've been telling myself ever since I woke up that that's all it was, I keep getting nasty flashbacks. Silly. Losing my mind as well as my strength now, it seems. I saw the Black Monk."

"The Faceless Monk?"

"That's the one. You've heard the story?"

"Yes. It's a cliché: anyone who sees what's inside the hood dies. The stuff of B-movies."

"Yes. Did you know that he was seen in St. Madoc the night you arrived? The Syrians were quite alarmed, apparently."

"Yes. In fact, I think I saw him myself—but he was headed in the opposite direction, toward Morpen."

The old lady uttered a slight sound that might have been a strangled cough. "Did you?"

"I didn't realize it at the time, but yes. I've seen him before, but only at a distance."

"Really? That comes of being neider, I suppose. I haven't. You should remember that, though, Simon. The Black Monk was seen in St. Madoc and in Morpen that night. He passed through both hamlets, but nobody died. Remember that, Simon. *Nobody died.* His reputation is exaggerated."

"Of course," said Simon. "Reputations always are. I'm no more afraid of the Black Monk that I am of Owain Glyndwr. And I already know what's inside the hood."

Her eyes suddenly took on a hint of alarm. "Do you?" she said.

"Of course. Nothing. He really is faceless. He doesn't wear the hood to hide something monstrous, but to hide the fact that there's nothing there. Trust me—I'm a writer. Ghost stories tend to follow the same melodramatic ruts."

"You're right," she said, in a whisper.

"Dreams tend to follow esthetic ruts too," Simon told her. "The unconscious mind is wayward, but fundamentally respectful of the Muse. Just like me." He was thinking about what Felicia had said about his insouciance in regard to endings. He paused, and then said: "I saw Alexander Usher again, after the last time I saw you. I tried to probe a little. I don't think there's anything to worry about; he really doesn't have a hidden agenda, and as long as he's kept out of the library, he's not likely to acquire one."

"Good," she said, dully, as if it were no longer a matter of any importance.

"He did say one thing that worried me slightly, though."

Her eyes narrowed slightly. "What was that?" she asked.

"He said that he believes that we're all divided beings, and the there's an active force of evil within us, constantly doing battle with the force of good. He refused to characterize the former as Satan, even though he's quite content to personalize the latter as Jesus, but it wouldn't take a great deal for me to begin to wonder whether the neider really has our best interests at heart."

"Of course it doesn't," she said, in a voice not much about a whisper. "I've never been under that delusion. It wouldn't care a fig about us if we didn't have some small utility. But that doesn't make it evil, and it certainly doesn't make us good. Our moral criteria don't apply—but it isn't cruel, and has no interest in punishing us. Tempting us, yes . . . but it isn't devoid of a certain courtesy, perhaps even mercy. It isn't our friend, but it isn't a villain either."

Simon nodded. "That's the impression I got, in the Underworld. But that wasn't the neider, was it?"

"Yes and no," she said. "There's a sense in which everything down there is the neider—life in the Underworld is a good deal more coherent than it is here, but nevertheless dispersed. The vitreous cocoons are only a detached fraction of the neider, much as the morgens are—or you and me—but they're in closer contact with the master-mind. I can't be sure obviously, but you might yet get to sleep with it. If you do, try to get more out of it than I did. You should—you're a mature man, and a writer. I was only a wayward girl, uneducated and criminally stupid. If Cerys ever has the chance . . . but that's a long way off yet. You will be kind to Cerys, won't you?"

"Of course," said Simon. He thought of adding something, but decided against it.

"I'm very glad I had a chance to meet you, Simon," the old lady said, after a pause, during which her eyes did not close. "I liked Lilith. I'm sorry that I never got a chance to meet Evelyne. So many of them went away in those days—and there was so much acrimony! There was nothing I could do. It was the war, you know. The soldiers declared an armistice in order to have a rest and rearm, but the war didn't end. It never ended. It had sowed too much misery, and too much hatred, everywhere. Sometimes, I don't know whether to feel sorry for the ones who fell into whoredom, like poor Lilith, or the ones who didn't, like poor Melusine . . . or stupid me, who tried to have it both ways and certainly didn't get the best of both worlds . . . but I shouldn't complain, should I? Not many people get to live to be two hundred, and have their hand held by their long-lost seven-times-great-grandnephew, do they? This makes up for a lot." She lifted her hand slightly, in order to put slight pressure on the one that was holding it.

"I'm glad it helps," he said, sincerely. "It means a lot to me too." The addendum was far less sincere, but he thought that it would probably become true, given time to sink in.

"You'll remember what I said, won't you?" she said

"About the Black Monk?"

"That as well—but what I said just now . . . and before . . . about being kind to Cerys and Felicia."

"Of course," he repeated.

"And there really is no need to be afraid. If the morgens do come, go to meet them bravely. You won't have any option, obviously, if you hear the song, but go bravely, and hold your breath. And whatever happens, remember that it's happened to me too, and I didn't die. I slept with the neider, and I didn't die. Quite the contrary, in fact. It might not happen, but if it does . . . well, I certainly can't promise you that it will all work out for the best, but it *will* work out. One way or another, it will work out. I really wish that I knew what to hope for—whether or not to hope that the morgens come, and what to hope for, if they do. But you understand that now, don't you? You've seen the vitreous cocoons, and felt the pressure of their dream, and you have an inkling of how important the pact has been, for seventeen hundred years? You understand why we've all had to sacrifice our lives, willingly or not, one way or another? You can imagine, now, what I've been through . . . what we've all been through . . . and why . . ."

"I believe I can," he told her, thinking that if the statement of belief was nowhere near honest yet, it might become honest, given time—and that in the meantime, the important thing was to humor her.

"Good," she said, her eyes glancing sideways at the clock on the wall. "I suppose I'd better see James again, to make absolutely sure that he sorts everything out in time. Will you kiss me on the forehead again, like a loving grandson?"

"Of course," he said, and stood up in order to lean over and do it.

She let go of his hand then.

"Thank you," she said. She didn't make any formal gesture of dismissal, but he knew that he had been dismissed — reluctantly, it seemed to him, although he wasn't sure he could trust his judgment entirely, while he still didn't feel quite himself.

"I'll see you tomorrow, Grandmother," he said, as he stepped back.

She didn't say a word. She just looked at him, but he read in her expression that she didn't think she would see him tomorrow. He knew that she had just had another flash of dream-imagery, another glimpse inside the hood of the Black Monk.

It's just a dream, he wanted to say. *It doesn't mean anything. There's no need to be afraid. You mustn't be afraid. He passed through St. Madoc and Morpen only the other day, and nobody died.*

But he didn't say it. He had been dismissed, and he went, quietly.

XVIII
Owain Glyndwr and the Faceless Monk

Simon's stride was steady again as he walked to the gate with Cerys. "Are you all right?" she asked him, as she opened the padlock.

"Of course," he said.

"You seem a little . . . different."

"No, I'm the same. You shouldn't leave your Grandmother alone tonight, though. She's trying her hardest not to let on, but I think she's a little distressed."

"James is with her. He's annoyed — I think she upset him before you arrived, and then his little excursion with you shook him up more than he anticipated. But it's not the first time Grandmother has upset him, by any means. It always gets sorted, though. I'll check on her when James comes back down, and ask Felicia to sit with her while I help with dinner. It's all the excitement—but things will calm down. See you tomorrow, I expect? I'll unlock the gate after lunch and leave it unlocked, so I don't have to come out in the rain. I'll give you a spare key if you go back to Raven afterwards, so that you can lock up. That's all right, isn't it?"

"Certainly," Simon said.

Dusk was falling as he arrived back at the cottage, and the street lamps came on as he inserted his key into the lock, but no lights were on yet in Sanderling or the Mermaid. He sat down at the computer and switched it on, but only to check his email. As usual, there was nothing but junk—nothing from any of his publishers.

He switched the machine off again, but remained seated for a couple of minutes, gathering his mental resources yet again, as they seemed to be slipping away again. While he had been in the company of others, their presence and their conversation had provided his consciousness with an anchorage and a point of focus, but now he was alone his sense of disorientation seemed to increase quite markedly.

There was an illusory sound reverberating in his consciousness, but it was neither the bells of Ys nor the song of a siren. It was just the orchestral pulse-beat of the deep, the background music of the supernatural. It would fade, as he readapted more fully to the natural.

He switched on the television and watched the end of a quiz show before the six o'clock news, trying to answer the questions, and trying to summon up enough engagement to be annoyed with himself when he failed to find the answers.

The news, as usual, was all Donald Trump, Brexit and the woeful state of care for the elderly in the face of rocketing demand. The most exciting part by far was the weather forecast, which followed the current fashion for meteorological melodrama. The presenter evidently loved the opportunity to issue warnings about high winds and the possibility of flooding; the days of false reassurances about the impossibility of hurricanes were long gone.

He got up to switch off the set and turned round, intending to go into the kitchen and make himself an evening meal, even though he did not feel particularly hungry.

There was a ghost standing in front of the study door, watching him. It gave the impression of having been there for some time.

Simon nearly jumped out of his skin, but settled himself almost instantly. He was in no doubt at all that what he was looking at as a specter, because it seemed to be both there and not there, manifesting a casual paradoxicality in a manner that seemed almost insulting. He could see it quite distinctly, even though he could also see the door through it. It was all too obviously mere appearance, but the appearance in question was so assertive as to be almost aggressive—an impression enhanced by the fact that it was clad in leather armor and had a sheathed dagger attached to a broad belt. It had no helmet, though. Its hair was dark, but streaked with silver, and its gray-brown eyes gleamed as they reflected the light of the bulb in the center of the ceiling.

"You're early," said Simon, hoarsely. "Midnight is hours away. Don't you find the electric light a trifle harsh?"

Owain Glyndwr did not appear to be impressed by his attempt at humor.

"I used to hate the English," he said, with a fluency in the hated language that paid a considerable compliment to Ceridwen Murden's educative efforts, although he was speaking in the same manner as Lenore, without actually making the air vibrate. "When I begged the sorcerer to preserve my intelligence, so that I could continue the rebellion beyond death that had faltered in life, I expected to be able to continue that hatred eternally. But it was too much of the flesh—your kind of flesh."

"You do appear to be a trifle short of that," Simon agreed. "And yet, you must have some ordinary matter about you, else I surely wouldn't be able to see you, in spite of my heightened neider sensibility. You're not entirely a figment of my imagination, are you?"

"No," the ghost admitted. "I can borrow the molecules of the air. Opacity is an effort, but without opacity, I couldn't see you. Invisibility entails blindness. Your heightened senses are useful, but you'll have difficulty holding on to the effect. To become a true seer requires time and effort. Summoning requires even more time, and more effort. And please don't quote Shakespeare at me—I never said any such thing in my lifetime, and his representation of my character was mere caricature. By the time I heard about it, though, he was on his way out. I haunted him as best I could, and he certainly saw me, but he thought I was just a figment of delirium. It's a common error."

"Would you like to sit down?" Simon asked, painfully aware of the incongruity of his politeness.

"No," said Glyndwr. "I have no such need, and the stance is inconvenient."

Simon, by contrast, did feel the need. Without asking permission—he was in his own home, after all—he sat down in the chair at his desk, after swiveling it to face his visitor.

"Ceridwen Murden asked you to appear to me?" he said, interrogatively.

"She made the suggestion," Glyndwr conceded. "She wanted me to make a point, or to emphasize one. And . . ." He stopped.

"And what?" Simon asked.

"She imagined that she was being kind . . . to me, as well as you. She fancies herself a saint . . . or a mother superior, at least."

"Why would she think it kind to you to send you to haunt me?" Two or three hypotheses sprang readily to Simon's mind, but none seemed particularly plausible—unsurprisingly, since the situation seemed to reek of absurdity.

"She thinks specters must feel lonely. Many people have glimpsed me, but only a few have been able to hear me, and the willingness to converse is rare . . . but she was sure of you."

"But you don't feel lonely?" Simon queried.

"No. The issue doesn't arise."

"Because you have other specters with which to converse."

"No," said Glyndwr, briefly. "Because the issue doesn't arise."

"You don't hobnob with the Black Monk, then?" said Simon, encouraged once again toward ludicrousness. He reminded himself that although the ghost was undoubtedly real, and even material, it was also drawing upon his own creative imagination.

"I've seen him," Glyndwr said, "but only in the distance."

"Snap," said Simon, pensively. "So, if your mission to expel the English from Wales no longer gets you excited, what has replaced it? What motivates you now?"

"Nothing. I've discovered the true pointlessness of existence. Unfortunately, I don't seem to be ready, or even able, to give it up. Some can, apparently . . . but I haven't quite learned the trick, even after five hundred years. The old lady says that she sympathizes, but she has no idea. It isn't hell, by any means, but it isn't paradise either. The other way obviously has its defects, but it's probably better."

"The other way?"

"Not bothering to die."

"Do I have that option?"

"How should I know? The old lady puts her longevity down to sleeping with the neider, but the younger generation haven't had that option. Sleeping with Felicia doesn't count . . . or perhaps it does. How would I know?"

"Five hundred years of afterlife must have given you the opportunity to learn quite a lot. You can't have spent all your time perfecting your English."

"I was never a scholar. Those who tried immediately before or after me were—but none of them seemed to have lasted as long, and a taste for learning probably goes the same way as hatred. I've learned things along the way, but not by design. Even the English . . . that wasn't my idea. The old lady wanted to be kind. I didn't like to disappoint her."

Simon had no idea what rules of tact and discretion ought to govern intercourse with ghosts, so he took the risk of saying: "You've slept with her, haven't you?"

The ghost did not seem shocked or offended, but it let a few seconds go by before saying: "Ghosts don't sleep. But yes: she wanted to share dreams, if possible. I didn't want to disappoint her. Nor will you, when she asks. You didn't even want to disappoint Felicia."

And there's another point of information gained, Simon thought. *Even Ceridwen didn't seem to know about that—but Owain Glyndwr does. I hope he wasn't watching from the shadows . . . but Felicia would surely have been aware of his presence, even if she couldn't see him.*

There were, however, more important issues to address. "You're not so very different from Ceridwen," he said, pensively. "She's still alive because of the pact. The entities in the cocoons needed her, or at least wanted to keep her in hand just in case. And they're holding on to you for similar reasons."

"How would I know?" retorted the ghost, again.

"You wouldn't," Simon hypothesized. "Even though you're morgen, and not neider, and thus have the capacity to think about it with the aid of language, you'd actually have to learn the language first. Do you even hear the song?"

"It's not a literal song," Owain Glydwr told him. "That's just a metaphor—although some people do translate the summons in their mind into something akin to music. Yes, obviously I'm vulnerable to the summons, else the old lady wouldn't be able to summon me. Necromancy is a dying art, though, and there's no one else left with her gift, so far as I know . . . unless I'm simply not on their list. No one is immune, though, whether they're morgen, neider or merely human. If the morgens do return with the storm, and they call you, you'll go to take the plunge like anyone else and you'll have to hope that they bring you back to shore alive when they're done. You might be right, though: perhaps it's a kind of summons that maintains me in existence, and impels me in spite of knowing the pointlessness of it all. Perhaps that's true of all of us, even the ephemerae . . . but I doubt it. Many are called but few are chosen, and none can tell which are the fortunate. How do you feel?"

"Odd," Simon repeated. "Disorientated. Not quite myself. But you know that, don't you?"

"I don't know anything," Owain Glyndwr told him, stubbornly, although it was plainly untrue. He wasn't simply lying, though, Simon thought. It was an expression of regret. The ghost knew a great deal, but he didn't understand—not completely, and not enough to satisfy himself.

I know the feeling, Simon thought. *I surely do.* "Thank you," he said to the ghost. "You've been very helpful. If I understand correctly, it's something of an effort for you to maintain yourself in a condition in which you can communicate, and the electric light surely can't help. Feel free to fade away, if that's what you want."

"I don't want anything," said the ghost of the ancient warrior—but he faded away regardless, and was gone in less than a minute.

I'm going mad, Simon thought. *Completely round the twist.* But he couldn't convince himself of that, and knew that it wouldn't be any consolation even if he could.

The conversation with Owain Glyndwr had, at least, given him the ghost of an appetite. He made himself a meal with a certain amount of enthusiasm, and ate it with a modicum of pleasure. Afterwards, he thought about trying to work, and then about trying to read, but decided that he didn't feel sufficiently himself to concentrate. In the end he just watched television. The set in Raven Cottage didn't have as many channels as the one in his old flat in Bristol, which had been hooked up to a satellite dish, but it still had a couple of hundred. Naturally, there was nothing he actually wanted to watch, but there were repeats of shows that he had enjoyed the first time around, many years ago, the detail of which he had completely forgotten, and watching them again, although accompanied by a constant sense of *déjà-vu*, was novel enough to be amusing.

He was, in any case, quite drowsy, and by the time ten o'clock came around, he felt entirely ready for bed.

In the morning, he thought, *I'll have slept it off. I'll be myself again. I'll be up at five, as usual, and I'll be able to get down to work. I'll be able to put everything out of my mind and absorb myself entirely in the translation, living inside the mind of a long-dead writer for a while, playing the role of his ghost. Everything will be normal again. Everything will be manageable again. Everything . . .*

That train of thought had carried him up the stairs and into the bedroom, but he was paralyzed by dread when a voice from the dark spoke to him, in the echo-chamber of his consciousness, and said: "Don't turn the light on."

He had never heard the voice before in his life. Indeed, he suspected that nobody presently alive had ever heard the voice before, and perhaps for several generations before those now alive; but he recognized it anyway. And even though the room was dark, with the curtains closed, he had sight enough—or something that could substitute for sight—to see the Black Monk sitting on his bed, much as Felicia Murden had sat there two nights before, waiting for him.

Obedient to earlier instructions, Simon carefully remembered that the Faceless Monk had passed through St. Madoc and Morpen on the night of his arrival, and that nobody had died. He had also been advised to be brave. He was slightly surprised to find that he didn't need to be. The paralysis wore off, taking the dread with it. He knew that he was dreaming. He was not asleep, but he was dreaming. Unlike the ghost of Owain Glyndwr, the Black Monk needed darkness. As apparitions went, he belonged to a more liminal species, lurking on the edge of imagination.

"It's still not midnight," he managed to say, in a steady voice, as he sat down in the chair.

"It's always midnight somewhere on Earth," the Monk retorted. "It will arrive here soon enough."

The Monk's hood hid the place where his face would have been completely, but Simon knew perfectly well what wasn't there, and he wasn't about to be intimidated by mysteries of that puerile sort.

"You can't see me," he said. "Invisibility entails blindness."

"I can feel you," the specter told him.

"You don't mean me any harm," Simon stated, confidently.

"Of course not," said the Monk. "I don't mean anyone any harm—you especially."

"You're here for the same reason as Glyndwr—to tell me something, to inch me a little closer to understanding. But who sent you?"

"No one. Unless your hypothesis regarding the chrysalids in the cocoons is true and we're all just pawns in their game. That might be true—but even if it is, we still have to make choices and take action."

"Who are you? Who *were* you, should I say?"

"I am who I am. The person I was wore a name in the monastery that wasn't his, and he wasn't really a monk. To be honest, I'd rather be known as the Great Bard, but everybody judges by the hood."

"Are you trying to imply that you were Myrddin Wyllt?"

"If only. When I say *great* bard I'm flattering myself. I went unrecorded by history—even the Murden archives. I'm no one now. I always was, truth be told. At least, I was until I began to make choices and take action . . . a trifle belatedly, I admit."

"You're a walking cliché—or would be, if you could walk. Is this the moment when you tell me that you're my father?"

"Of course not. Your father was a worthless piece of human scum, whose seduction of your poor mother was effectively a rape—but his sperm was healthy enough, and essentially innocent. I was, however, present at your conception, and able to make a contribution of sorts at the critical moment. So, if what you're really asking is whether you owe the seventh element of your make-up to me, yes, in a way, although it was already innate and only needed a slight stimulating nudge."

So much for James Murden's estimation of the bounds of plausibility, Simon thought. But what he said aloud was: "Why?"

"Good question. Why did the scum want to stick his filthy prick into your mother's virgin vagina? Why anything, rather than nothing? Your mother didn't want to abandon you, by the way. She wasn't given a choice. It was Evelyne who took the decision out of her hands. Did Evelyne have a choice? Strictly speaking, yes, but she didn't feel that she did. That wasn't my doing, though. She tried never to give you another thought, but didn't succeed. She didn't have the faintest idea who you were, though, when you met again. She hadn't been watching over you. She didn't begin to get an inkling until you told her about being a foundling, and she compared dates—but even then, she didn't want to believe it. She tried as hard as she could to remain in denial, even though it didn't ease the guilt. Strange how the living mind works, isn't it?"

"But you always knew where I was and what I was doing?"

"It's easier for someone . . . in my condition. Yes, I did, and I brought the two of you together again, subtly. I helped to bring you here: to this place, and this moment."

"Again, why?"

"Again, why anything? Because it's where you belong? Because the neider made me do it? Your guess is probably as good as mine by now. You still have a choice, obviously—but I've been around long enough to know how those kinds of choices work out. So has the old lady."

"The morgens really are coming back, then?"

"Oh yes. More to the point, the neider is coming back, at least momentarily. The present situation can't endure. It needs a patch. Don't expect an ending, though—not to their part of the story, at any rate. As for yours, that probably depends on what you can contrive."

"And yours?"

"If I'd been able to contrive an end to mine, I'd have done it long ago. You know how the esthetic logic goes—I'll be here until the end of time . . . or not. Either way, it doesn't depend on me."

"But your reputation is exaggerated. You're not actually a personification of Death?"

"I wish. I'm just an anonymous lay brother who got caught up in an experiment in . . . well, let's call it *applied necromancy*. Unlike Glyndwr, I didn't even volunteer. Believe me, if I were personified Death, I could do a much better job than the Grim Reaper. I wouldn't be that kind of Death at all. I'd be a seductive Death, a *femme fatale*—inevitable and inexorable but nevertheless capable of providing an unparalleled thrill, that would make dying seem more worthwhile than living ever was. But I never had the option.

"I try not to get too close to people, you know, because I'm all too well aware of the effect their fear can have. When I saw you coming out the other night I headed in the other direction, the way I always had before. Tonight, though, I knew you wouldn't be afraid. Tonight, I knew that I could look you in the face, if necessary, without your being terrified by the fact that I don't have one. Not that I've ever understood why it's so terrifying that I don't . . . I try to remember how I might have felt when I was alive, but I can't. It was a long time ago."

"Why make yourself manifest, then? Why not remain totally invisible?"

"Mostly, I do. But when the summons comes . . . wherever it comes from . . . I answer. I do have a choice, and it's an effort to answer, even to produce the pathetic excuse for an apparition that I am, devoid of flesh and crude in costume, but I do answer."

"And were you summoned here tonight?"

"And how."

"By whom?"

"I rather assumed that it was you—unconsciously, of course, but nevertheless you. I made the same assumption the other night, although it seemed so very obvious that you had no idea what you were doing that I limited you to a glimpse, as usual. But I might be wrong. It might be someone else, human, unhuman or spectral. Who can ever tell? Maybe it was a combination of factors. Maybe such things need a combination of factors. Unlike Glyndwr, though, I *am* glad to have the opportunity, at last. As you can imagine, I don't get to have very many conversations. I don't need them any more than he does, but . . . well, let's just say I'm glad and, leave it at that. I shouldn't be, really. I ought to hate being a bird of ill-omen, and I do . . . but in a way, I don't. Confused and conflicted . . . but isn't that the human condition, alive or dead?"

"You're a bird of ill-omen?" Simon queried.

"Metaphorically speaking. A harbinger of disaster, if you prefer. I'm not Death personified, but I do seem to be dogged by misfortune. You have nothing to fear, though—as I say, I made certain of that . . . as certain as I could be, anyhow. And nobody died the other night, did they, even though I was glimpsed all the way to Morpen and beyond. Maybe the curse is wearing off."

"Your English is good," Simon observed, "for someone who hasn't had many conversations, and can hardly have spoken it while you were alive."

"I'm borrowing yours, more adeptly than Lenore— although she has the disadvantage of having a bird's brain, and can't be blamed for her reliance on reiterated phrases," the Faceless Monk told him. "And you can do a lot of listening over the centuries. I've listened to the best. Peacock, Shelley, Southey . . . not that Southey was really the best, mind. Shelley was the only one of the three who caught a glimpse of me, but he was tougher than he looked, even though he panicked when the morgen took him. Most do. If it happens to you, hold your nerve . . . and your breath. She won't mean you any harm—quite the contrary. If the old lady could manage it, so can you."

"Shelley's drowning really was an accident, then?"

"Of course. Mind you, there was a certain amount of contributory negligence in going out hunting morgens in a lake they'd abandoned three generations ago. But there again: the human condition, confusion and conflict. It won't get any better, I fear, even if you live to be two hundred."

"Do you think I might—live to be two hundred, that is."

"Probably not, but who knows?"

"If James and I were to resume his ancestors' experiments, though, I might get the chance to be a specter, continuing my career as the Faceless Writer until the end of time."

"The experiments mostly went awry . . . and neither Glyndwr nor I really qualifies as a shining example . . . we're more in the horrible warning category, most people might think. It isn't Hell, though. If the chance ever comes along, I wouldn't blame you for giving it serious consideration. You might make a better fist of it than I have . . . and if I get to pass on the family legacy, we might yet make a dynasty."

"I'm not sure that I can qualify as a shining example either," Simon told the Faceless Monk. "Most people might put me in the horrible warning category, too."

"Maybe—but for what it's worth, you haven't been that much of a disappointment to me."

And after damning him with that faint praise, the Black Monk's faintly discernible hood and robe faded away into the shadows of the obscure bedroom.

Simon, confused and conflicted, had no idea whether to be glad or not that the encounter had been a pure hallucination, born of a kind of dream-state, or to be pleased or disappointed by what it had revealed about the quality and character of his imagination.

In the bathroom, he took a long, hard look at himself in the mirror, but all he felt was dismay at seeing himself so old and so haggard.

He hoped, as he went to bed, considerably later than usual, that he would still be able to get up at five, in order to make yet another attempt to recover his sacred routine. But the sea seemed strangely loud, and full of songs, and he knew that his adaptation process still had a long way to go.

XIX
Storm Deirdre

In fact, Simon did wake up at five, feeling much more himself. The effects of his excursion to the underworld seemed to have worn off completely, and the utter absurdity of his encounters with Owain Glyndwr and the Black Monk now seemed positively comical.

There must be something in the water, he thought. *Perhaps I'd be safer sticking to wine and cider.*

When the sun rose he had been at the keyboard for more than an hour, and he was solidly ensconced in translation mode, listening to Edward Elgar. He barely took time out to remind himself that the sunshine would not last, and that the wind that brought the clouds would also bring Storm Deirdre—but not until after he had stubbornly finished a full day's work.

When the doorbell rang at eight o'clock, cutting through the *New World*, he was inevitably annoyed, and considered the possibility momentarily of ignoring it, but he knew that if he did that, it would only ring again. He took off the headphones and went to answer it, therefore, determined to send away whoever it was with the minimum possible delay.

It was Cerys. She simply pushed past him and turned into the study while he closed the door resignedly. When he appeared in the doorway, she turned round to look at him. He had not uttered a word of protest, because he already knew from the expression on her face that catastrophe had struck, although he was not yet aware of what form it had taken.

"Grandmother died in the night," she said, flatly. "An ambulance came to take her body away—you might have seen it. James has gone after it in a taxi. He's in a terrible state. He told me to come and tell you at eight. So here I am."

Simon was dumbstruck. The word *condolences* shot

through his mind, but for the moment, he could not attach a meaning to it.

"There'll be difficulties with the formalities," Cerys went on. "She had no birth certificate, no passport, no driving license, no bank account, and no national insurance number. She's recorded in census returns and the electoral register, but apart from that she has no official existence. The doctor from the hospital signed the death certificate, because she was undoubtedly dead, and he was perfectly satisfied in attributing the death to natural causes, but she had no G.P. and never saw a doctor while she was alive. He wasn't happy at all. People are supposed to be in the system, and they're supposed to be in the system with plausible birthdates, not 1789. James says they'll just settle for ignoring everything that doesn't fit their preconceptions, though, and washing their hands of it. He'll arrange for the cremation and that'll be the end of it, he says. There's no will to prove because she didn't own anything. It's just the end. The end."

She dissolved in tears.

Simon sat her down, and then sat down himself. The young woman had summed up the situation perfectly. It was the end. He cursed himself for not having foreseen it—not because she had dreamed about the Faceless Monk and kept getting flashbacks, but because she had insisted on seeing him in order to say goodbye even though she was obviously in the middle of some sort of argument with James. She had known. She had known that it was the end. She could not have made it more obvious without hoisting a flag and then running it down to half mast. And he hadn't realized. He was an idiot.

"Damn," he said softly. "I didn't realize. She was saying goodbye, and I didn't realize."

"None of us did," Cerys said, through the tears. "She saw us all, and none of us realized. It's hit James very hard, because he was arguing with her. He just thought she was being . . . the way she always was. She's been like that all his life. He thought she couldn't die. He's shattered—but he's soldiering on regardless."

"What were they arguing about?" Simon asked.

"I don't know. If I had to guess . . ." She nodded her head toward the left. It took Simon a few seconds to realize that she was indicating the direction of Sanderling Cottage. "Megan?" he said surprised.

"I suspect so. Grandmother's asked him before to acknowledge that she's his daughter. Why she cares, after all this time, I don't know. But James has always said: 'Never in this life.' He doesn't believe it, you see. Even if she were to get her famous DNA test, and it were to prove him wrong, he'd just say that she'd faked it. He's given in to Grandmother over everything else, over the years, but not that."

Simon shook his head, to signify that he couldn't explain it either. "No will, you said. She didn't own anything at all?"

"No—not the Abbey, obviously, or any of the dependencies. There are conditions attached to the inheritance, apparently—it has to go to the male heir. There are other conditions, though. Grandmother had a right of permanent residence. I can't imagine it was a problem, though. James would never have wanted to throw her out—or anyone else, come to that. The problem has always been persuading people to stay. Just because she didn't own the house in a legal sense, though, it didn't mean that she didn't think that she was in charge. There's always been a contest of sorts between them—and James always got the worst if it, except on that one issue. Now, I suppose, he can have his own way . . . but he certainly isn't feeling good about that at present. It's as well that he has things to sort out in town—at least he'll be busy all day. Felicia and Melusine don't even have that."

"Will there be a funeral service?"

"Don't ask me. That's up to James—unless Grandmother has given him instructions, yesterday or in the past. He might arrange some sort of family gathering in the chapel. He was trying to arrange a meeting anyway, to discuss the estate, but nobody wanted to come. Whether they'd come for Grandmother's memorial, I don't know. Probably."

Simon carefully refrained from making any remark about two birds and one stone. Instead, he said: "I'm truly sorry.

I can't imagine how distressing it is for all of you. If there's anything I can do . . ."

"No, there isn't. Not yet, anyway. If there is . . . I'll let you know. I need to nip over to the Mermaid now, to let Dai know. Can I ask you one favor, though?"

"Of course."

Again, she nodded her head in the direction of Sanderling.

"Of course," Simon said, again. And while Cerys ran to the other side of the road before turning toward the Mermaid, he slipped along to the next cottage.

Megan Harwyn had the door open before his finger reached the bell push. "I saw the ambulance and the taxi," she said, ushering him inside. "Who is it and how serious is it?"

"As serious as it gets," Simon answered.

"Dead?"

"Yes."

"The old lady?"

"Yes."

Megan exhaled, forcefully. "Damn! I really thought she'd live forever. I never met her, of course, but I know she claimed to be my umpteen-times-great-aunt. Yours too I guess, although you didn't know her either."

"Actually," said Simon, "I rather thought I did know her. I only saw her twice but . . . well, I feel that I knew her. She was so pleased to meet me . . . so very kind, and charming."

"Lucky you," said Megan, bitterly. "I've been here for most of my life, and she never took the trouble to be kind to me."

"Actually," Simon corrected her, "I think she tried. I believe that she tried several times to persuade James to acknowledge you. They had a row yesterday, which might have been about that."

That startled her. "Are you serious?"

"It's not something I'd joke about, especially at a time like this. If James had come clean, I think she'd have summoned you just as she summoned me, for exactly the same reason."

"Oh. Thanks for telling me. That puts a slightly different complexion on things. The bastard's got away with it, though, hasn't he? Now she's dead . . . ."

"Unless he changes his mind in order to grant her last wish," Simon suggested.

"James? Never in this life!" She studied him carefully. "You really are shaken up, aren't you?" she said. "In fact, you don't look too good at all. Rough night?"

"Unusual," Simon admitted. "Strange dreams."

"It's the electricity in the air—the prelude to the storm. The sort of time that people start seeing the Black Monk." She looked him speculatively.

"I heard that he passed through the first night I was here," he said, in a carefully neutral tone. "Actually, I saw him as I was on my way to the pub. He was running away from me. I think I scared him off—and nobody died that night."

There seemed to be a further remark hovering on the tip of her tongue, but she decided against letting it out. "Sit down," she said. "I'll make a cup of tea. You look as if you could do with one."

Simon thought hard about saying that he had to get back to work, but he knew that his ability to concentrate had been torpedoed, for the morning at least, if not all day.

Megan misread his hesitation. "Unless you're so well in with them now that you think it would be supping with the Devil?" she suggested, ironically. "Cerys sent you round here, didn't she—in order to avoid coming herself? So they can't send you to Coventry for being here, can they?" There was actually a note of supplication in her voice.

Simon did not want to be caught in the middle between the Murdens and Megan Harwyn, any more than he wanted to serve as the rope in a strange tug-of-war between Felicia and Melusine, but he was not at all sure that he could avoid either eventuality.

"All right," he said, finally.

"Brave boy," she said, sarcastically. "It's not as if I'm trying to seduce you, you know."

He suppressed the temptation to retort: *Aren't you?* He sat down in the armchair, and tried to figure out exactly how he felt about Ceridwen Murden's death, while his next-door neighbor made the tea.

She's right, he thought. *I only met her twice. I didn't even know she existed four days ago. How can I be grief-stricken?*

But he was. He felt that a hole had been ripped in his life. She had been so pleased to meet him. So kind. So charming. And now she was gone. But not before he had been let into the family secrets, bound into the pact. And Ceridwen, he reminded himself, had wanted Megan to be brought into the family too, or at least to have her membership admitted. He didn't just have Cerys's word for that. She had mentioned it herself during their first meeting. He was not betraying Ceridwen by drinking a cup of tea in Sanderling. Quite the reverse.

"I'm sorry," said Megan, as she handed him the cup and saucer, and then poured tea from the pot. "I was a bit insensitive there. I'm in danger of turning into the neighbor from hell, aren't I?"

She was practically begging to be contradicted, so Simon obliged. "Not at all," he said. "If you hadn't helped bring me up to speed that first evening in the pub, I'd never have coped with everything that's happened since. I didn't know your situation then, but I appreciate the honesty with which you explained it to me the next day."

She exhaled again, more discreetly this time. "Good," she said. "Will there be a funeral, do you know?"

"Cerys won't know anything until James gets back from town. He's sorting out the formalities."

"That might be awkward, if he's telling them that she was two hundred and some years old. Or has he put his hand on a decently recent birth certificate?"

"I don't know," Simon said. "I can't imagine that anyone is going to kick up a fuss, though."

Megan took a sip of tea, smiled, and muttered: "Shit!"

"What?"

"I could have kicked up a bit of a fuss," she said. "Except, that now you've told me that the old lady was on my side, I'd feel bad about it."

"Better to let it go," Simon opined. "It really wouldn't do anyone any good to drag your quarrel with James into the public arena on the coat-tails of Ceridwen's death."

"You're probably right. I'm probably too old to care anyway, and any publicity I attracted would be bound to turn into a game of let's-kick-the-old-whore. Not everyone's as tolerant as you."

"You really don't have to stay here, you know," Simon pointed out. "Like me, you could run your business from anywhere . . . anywhere that no one knows anything at all about your past, and needn't find out anything about your present."

Again, something hovered on her lips—presumably a sarcastic reply—but in the end she settled for saying: "Don't think I haven't thought about it. Maybe I should never have moved in here. The cousin who left Sanderling to me did it to stick two fingers up at James, not because he liked me, even though he must have fancied me, or he wouldn't have paid me so often. It seemed like a good idea to move in, at the time. Now, I'm beginning to think that I made a mistake. Perhaps I should have let it go years ago, just got on with my life and let my dear father get on with his. It's a shock to hit seventy, to look back at your life, and suddenly get the feeling you might have wasted it."

"I know," said Simon.

"You? Don't tell me that. I've looked you up, remember. All those books! You must sweat and piss self-satisfaction."

"Not exactly," Simon said. "In fact, just no."

"Bollocks. It's much better to have that to look back on than having been a waste bin for men to jack off inside. You can't deny it."

"You did what you had to do," Simon said. "And that's only a fraction of the story. You taught yourself to operate on the web. That's a real accomplishment, and a rare one.

It's something to be proud of . . . at least as much as my writing. To publish one book that nobody wanted to read might be regarded as a misfortune, to publish ten as a triumph of hope over experience—but three hundred is just ludicrous insanity."

She laughed at that. "I've ordered a couple of your books from amazon," she said, "so there's some demand."

"You didn't have to do that. Cerys and Felicia just took a pile of spares. You could have done the same."

"Yes," she said, "but then I'd have had to let you fuck me to return the favor." Immediately, her face turned brick red. "Damn," she said. "I really need to have my tongue surgically removed. Forget I said that, please. Oh shit! Why don't I just hang myself and get it over with?"

Simon attempted a forced laugh. "It wasn't that serious," he said. "In fact, it wasn't serious at all—just the sort of joking banter in which friends indulge all the time. I've had far worse things said to me in my time, and said more than a few myself. Nobody gets to our age without having put their foot in their mouth a hundred times over."

"I bet the old woman got to two hundred without," Megan muttered.

It didn't seem to be an appropriate time to contradict her on that matter, so Simon let it pass. He set down his empty teacup. "Thanks for the tea," he said. He refrained from inviting her to drop in some time to rummage through the spare copies of his novels, in case she took it the wrong way.

She was still too embarrassed to make any attempt to try and retain him.

In the distance, he saw Cerys hurrying back to the Abbey. He noticed that she had left the grille wide open.

He sat down at the computer again, because he had nothing better to do. Eventually, he resumed the translation, again because he had nothing better to do. His mind wasn't really on the work, but he was sufficiently fluent by now to be able to keep the translation going even with only partial concentration. He was glad when twenty past eleven arrived, though, and he went out for his daily constitutional.

He turned south along the coastal path. He passed half a dozen other walkers, in ones and twos, many of them walking dogs, and all of them casting anxious glances at the sky and turning up their collars against the increasing wind. The rain started when he was only halfway home on the return journey, but it was relatively light to start with. A glance at the south-western horizon testified all too clearly to the fact that it would not be light for long. Storm Deirdre was on the way, and would be unleashing her initial fury within a couple of hours, building up to a crescendo thereafter.

He had a quick snack, and then returned to the computer. He resumed work, and this time contrived to absorb himself more fully. The darkening sky outside and the squalls of wind hitting his windows helped. He was settled in for the afternoon, with Ravel's *Bolero* ringing in his ears when the doorbell interrupted it with a very different ring.

He assumed that it would be someone with updated news, but was surprised to see Felicia in her hooded cape. He ushered her inside hastily, and took the soaking wet garment from her.

"You really shouldn't be out in this weather," he said. "Even I could get blown away in this wind—and it's only going to get worse.

"I know," she said, "but I simply had to get out of the house. Stupid, I know—I've been cooped up there for God only knows how long, rarely going any further than the gate, and all of a sudden, it's become unbearable. It's not as if she ever left her room . . . but everything seems to have changed. I had to get out . . . and I had nowhere else to go. I'm truly sorry. But I also wanted to apologize about yesterday."

"For what?"

"For the business with Melusine. She was just so smug after she'd seen you, as if she'd somehow made a conquest with the aid of her siren charms, as if you were now her private property. I could hardly tell her that I'd staked my claim first, could I? But I couldn't just let her strut round, either. So it seemed then, anyway. It all seems ridiculously petty now. I feel stupid because I didn't realize about Grandmother either. Looking back it seems obvious that she was saying goodbye, but at the time, I just never gave it a thought. And I'm supposed to be the sensitive one! James was upset with her, and Melusine only saw her briefly to say goodnight, but I was with her for the best part of two hours, chatting about this and that, and I never realized."

"Neither did I," Simon put in, helpfully.

"Is there any wine left in that bottle?" Felicia asked, although the bottle was standing on the side table, and it was perfectly obvious that there was at least a glassful in it.

"Yes, but I forgot to cork it and it'll be undrinkable now," said Simon. "I'll open another—then we can both have one."

"It's not too early?" she said, anxiously.

"Not in view of the circumstances," Simon assured her. "Medicinally necessary, in fact."

He uncorked the bottle and brought two clean glasses.

"Things are going to be different, now," said Felicia, after swallowing a mouthful. "James phoned from town to say that he was calling a resident's meeting for seven, immediately after dinner. A *residents' meeting!* He's going to lay down the law. Grandmother's kept him on the leash all his life, and now he's off it, I suppose he's going to make us all see who's boss. I know he's got plans to bring in new servants, but he surely can't sack the old ones on the day of Grandmother's death! They're just as cut up as we are. It's too cruel!"

"It's more likely that he wants to start a process of collective mourning," Simon guessed, really having no idea what James' intentions might be.

"I don't know. He's my brother, and I love him, but sometimes . . . he only calls me the sensitive one because he's so very insensitive. I honestly don't know. I have no idea what he and Grandmother were arguing about yesterday, but it obviously wasn't settled when we went to bed last night. It can't have done her any good, can it?"

"I don't think it can have made any difference," Simon said. "She seemed quite serene when I saw her. She'd just been talking to James, so he can't have upset her seriously. It's hardly the first argument they've had, I gather?"

"Oh, by no means. Yes, she's always taken all that in her stride—and she seemed quite calm when I sat with her as well. She told me how glad she was to have met you, by the way. I didn't realize when she said it that she meant *before the end* but I see now that she did. I think she was proud to find that she had a writer for a seven-times-great grandnephew. I never really knew Lilith, of course, but Grandmother liked her, and she was glad as well as sorry to have news of Evelyne and . . . was it Angela?"

"I believe so," said Simon.

"And you, of course—but to have abandoned you as a tiny baby! That Angela must have been a nasty piece of work!"

"Actually," Simon told her, "I don't think it was her fault. She was very young, and that was back in the late forties, when it was a serious matter for a girl to get into trouble. I suspect that it was Eve who persuaded her—or forced her— to . . . well, she probably thought of it as giving me away for adoption, in the hope that I might have a better life than Angela could give me. I didn't know that Eve was my grandmother when I met her, any more than she knew that I was her grandson, but I liked her, and I know that she wasn't a bad person. I don't bear her any grudge, I assure you. She left me Raven Cottage, after all. It's thanks to her that I met your Grandmother . . . and you. I know you don't approve of neat denouements, but in a way, that was pure soap opera. And I was at least as glad to meet Ceridwen, before the end, as she could have been to meet me."

He became aware that she was looking at him with a puzzled expression. "But the other night," she said, "you seemed so sad and bitter? Unless it really was me, projecting."

"No, that wasn't your fault," Simon assured her. "But all my failures have been self-made. I don't blame Eve and Angela for them at all. My adoptive parents were all that a foundling could have wished for . . . it was only after I left home that I began to screw everything up. And you mustn't take my misery too seriously . . . I wallow in it far too much. I wish I'd been able to offer you a better shared dream, to provide you with a soupcon of delight. That must have been what you were looking for."

"Quite honestly," she said, "I have no idea what I was looking for. I was being daring, throwing caution to the winds, for once. I thought that it might be my last chance . . . I would have sworn that I'd be the one to die, not Grandmother, if anyone was going to. I really had accustomed myself to thinking that she was never going to die. Why now, of all times? She really thought that the morgens might come back tonight, and she's been waiting and hoping for that all her life. They won't come now, will they? Not if she's not here?"

"I don't know," Simon said.

"Well, it'll be sad if they do—to have missed them by twenty-four hours after two hundred years. Too sad."

"Unfortunate," Simon agreed.

After a pause, she said: "Who'll be next, I wonder? We know, now, that we're not really immortal."

"On form," Simon suggested, "it might be another hundred years before any of you dies. If your Grandmother has established a reference point, it seems to me that it ought to be one from which you can take heart."

"It might," said Felicia, bleakly, "if I could actually make up my mind whether living another hundred years would be better or worse than dying tonight."

"That's just grief talking," said Simon, and reached out to take her hand.

Much to his surprise, she started, and drew it away. For an instant he thought that the reaction was to his gesture, but then he heard the sound of a car accelerating in the road outside, speeding in the direction of Morpen. It had to be the taxi that had brought James back, now fleeing St. Madoc in a hurry.

"I have to go," she said. But she didn't get up. Instead, she sat back in the chair, as if she needed to gather herself for the effort of returning to the house. Simon leaned forward, concerned, but she shook her head. "Don't be kind to me, for the moment," she said. "I feel that it would make me dissolve. Be stern with me, if you can, and I'll try to grow a little backbone." She paused, and then fixed him with her gimlet stare. "You promised to sleep with Melusine, didn't you? That's why she was so smug."

"She asked me, hypothetically, if I'd be willing to," he admitted. "I said that I would. It didn't occur to me that you might think that our . . . previous arrangement ought to be exclusive. I'm sorry."

"There's absolutely no need," she replied, positively, stiffening her spine and raising her head. "You're right, of course. What else could you say? What else could you have done, if she'd been as bold as I was? And what possible grounds for complaint would I have? Of course you must sleep with her, if that's what she wants. You'll probably find the dream more pleasant."

"It's not a competition," Simon said, softly. "And I'm certainly no prize."

"You're not seventy yet," Felicia observed, as she rose to her feet decisively, "and we're both past a hundred. You're a writer. And you're kind. Believe me, you're a prize. It shouldn't be a competition . . . but somehow, it is . . . which means that we'll probably both lose. But I shouldn't be talking about it today, of all days. I shouldn't even be here. I should be there, side by side with Melusine, waiting for James to summon us all and lay down the law. The servants must be frightened. They must have been frightened for some time. I wish I had the backbone to stand up for them, or to help them stand up for themselves. Perhaps I have, and will. In any case, I have to get back, before the wind gets any worse. Luckily, there are no trees on the island to blow down . . . probably because they all blew down long ago. Will you be all right?"

"Yes, of course—but you must let me walk you back. I'll just see you to the door and then come home. Don't protest, I beg you. I can't possibly let you walk back alone."

"But what if Melusine sees us together? Or James, if he's home."

"What if they do? Why should it matter if anyone sees us? We haven't done anything wrong. We're just providing one another with a little moral support, being kind to one another. And even if we'd been making mad passionate love all afternoon, we still wouldn't have been doing anything wrong, and we'd have no reason at all to be afraid of being seen together, by anyone."

He placed her cape over her shoulders, and put on his own coat while she pulled up the hood.

"You're right," she said. "You could even put your arm around me, to shield me from the worst of the wind and rain, and make sure I don't get blown over. And if anyone were to comment—even James—I can simply say: 'Well, so what?'"

"Exactly," Simon agreed.

"Well then," she said, "let's go, before it gets *really* dark."

And they set forth. Simon put his arm around her, as promised, even though her tread was firm, and shielded her as best he could from the pouring rain. Although it wasn't yet six o'clock, the sun had already set, and the sky was full of black clouds, so there would be no real twilight. The lights of the Abbey were an unmistakable guide, though, and their course was unerring, albeit exceedingly damp.

As they approached the bridge they saw a huge plume of spray rise up to the left as two waves, compressed by the bays and squeezed into the narrow gorge between the Tine and the shore, collided and rose up explosively.

Simon stopped dead, suddenly fearful on Felicia's behalf.

"Oh it always does that," said Felicia. "That's nothing— the spray from the really big crashes reaches all the way to Raven and drenches everything in between. The trick is to cross the bridge between waves—there's always time. We'll go after the next one."

She was right, of course. She had been living there for a hundred years; it was all familiar to her, even though she hadn't crossed the bridge for years until the last few days. They crossed without difficulty after the next splash.

The huge grille was still wedged wide open. James had not bothered to come out to close it after the taxi had gone—very sensibly, Simon thought, as he felt the water seeping into his clothing in spite of the raincoat. He hurried Felicia along. They reached the door without incident, and found momentary shelter beneath the porch, protected from the wind by the body of the house.

"Thank you," said Felicia. "That was exceedingly gallant of you. You're going to get fearfully wet on the way back."

"No problem," he said. "I'll have a quick shower and change, and I won't budge from the cottage again until the storm is just a distant memory. Please send Cerys over tomorrow morning to bring me news, though. You've whetted my curiosity with regard to your residents' meeting, and I'd like to know the outcome, if it isn't secret."

"Not from you," she said. "You're party to all the family secrets now. However you sign your books, you're a Murden. I might bring the news myself. Don't forget to recork the bottle."

She opened the door, and slipped inside, without inviting him to come in—presumably, he thought, because she knew that he would be obliged to refuse.

He started back along the driveway, with the wind behind his back. Lightning flashed between clouds out to sea, and then lashed out toward the ground somewhere to the south, perhaps over St. David's Head, and the two rolls of thunder fused into an extended cannonade only a few seconds afterwards. The thunder echoed in his consciousness like percussion music, ominous and melodramatic, but his mind immediately retaliated with a song of its own: a martial music full of aggression and triumph.

The sirens are angry tonight, he thought—but corrected himself almost immediately: No, it wasn't anger. There was defiance and determination in the opposition to the thunder, but no wrath.

Lightning, Simon knew, was a much more complex phenomenon than had been imagined in the days of Jove's thunderbolts. The downward stroke, he had read somewhere, was only a leader; most of the energy of an earth/air discharge actually streamed upwards, from the ground . . . perhaps all the way from the Underworld, if the geology of the four terrestrial states of matter permitted it.

Just before he got to the bridge, there was another explosive collision of opposed waves, sending a waterspout high into the air—to the right of the bridge now that he was facing in the opposite direction—which disintegrated into a plume of spray and a great cascade. Simon stopped for a second, and turned his head to look back at the house over his left shoulder.

He was immediately blinded by a lightning-flash that seemed simultaneous with a crash of thunder that had no music in it at all, but was pure noise. He couldn't see anything, but he *felt* the discharge, and knew that the lightning-conductor on top of the Abbey had been hit yet again. He turned round completely, but his eyes were still blinded. Because of that, he didn't see the huge gate composed of iron spikes tear free from the wedge that had been holding it in place and swing toward him, smashing into him head-on and catapulting him off the driveway and on to the bridge, where he fell heavily, the impact only slightly cushioned by the inch or two seawater with which the falling spray had filled the concrete span.

Although the bars if the gate had hit him in the face, his body had folded slightly as he fell, and the base of his spine took the brunt of the impact, jarring him horribly.

He lay there, supine, and as his retinas began to recover from the shock of the flash, his vision seemed to be filled by floating corpuscles of vivid light, like falling stars.

XX
The Morgen and the Neider

The impact of the iron mass had been forceful and painful, but Simon's head had been tilted slightly backwards because he had automatically looked upwards, even though he was blind, in the direction of the lightning-conductor. The iron bars had missed his nose and only made a glancing impact with the two sides of his face, while his torso absorbed most of the force of that initial impact. The collision did not fracture his skull, or even cause him to lose consciousness. For a moment or two he was overwhelmed by shock and pain, but as he had landed face upwards in the temporary flood with which the cascading spray had filled the bridge, he had still been able to formulate the thought that he had to gather his strength sufficiently to scramble off the bridge before the next big wave was impelled into the narrow gap.

By pushing down on the concrete with his uninjured elbows he found it easy enough to raise his head above the surface of the turbulent water, but the second part of the plan was not so easy. The shock delivered to his spine of crashing down on to the concrete, even cushioned by the water, had reverberated through the nerves of his lower body, and the response of his legs to the commands issued by his brain was sluggish. He knew that he was not paralyzed, but that only made it all the more frustrating that his stupid legs would not do as he wished and allow him to sit up, or to turn over in order that he might crawl.

He cursed, and pushed down with his arms, as if he were trying to substitute with the strength of his still-obedient upper body for the recalcitrance of his lower half. He managed to lift his head up, but not very far.

Then there was a mad flutter of wings, and something else tossed by the storm wind crashed into him from behind, this time impacting his skull.

"Lenore!" he cried, in frank amazement.

The raven made no reply in his imagination, but he felt her claws seizing his hair, and the mass of the bird immediately settled over his scalp, her wings enveloping his head.

Instantly, he felt the body of the bird change texture and shape, becoming soft and fluid, stretching and warping, and he felt the blackness that had been a raven become something else: something strange and serpentine, wrapping itself around his head like a living turban.

Then he did manage to sit up—not because his legs had recovered their natural force but because he was *lifted* up, twisting as he rose, so that his gaze turned to the right just as the next explosion of spray surged over the parapet like a tidal wave, far greater than any of its predecessors.

And riding the wave was the morgen.

Simon had less than a second to take account of the creature, but he had time to gauge the power in her lower body, which was indeed more seal-like than piscine, albeit far more flexible and elegant than a seal's hind-quarters. His gaze must have been traveling upwards, because he caught sight of her breasts and her arms, and the claw-like hands at the ends of her arms, before his line of sight reached her terrible, beautiful and youthful face, and her black, snaky tresses.

Terrible, beautiful and youthful as her face was, and medusal as the tresses of her hair were, he had no difficulty in recognizing her. It was Melusine.

Then the full force of the wave hit him, with even more brutality than the iron gate, and the clawed hands grabbed him, snatched him up and carried him over the parapet, and into the precipice between the Tine and the mainland.

He remembered the advice he had been given, took one last gulp of air, and held his breath.

For several seconds, the water was pure turbulence, utterly chaotic. He could have been smashed against the walls of the gully beneath the bridge and broken irredeemably, but he was held too firmly and too forcefully by a creature who was in her element, who knew exactly how to glide through that turbulence without suffering any collision with brutal solidity.

The morgen sped through the gully and out into the bay on the north-eastern side of the Central Tine of Morgan's Fork. And as soon as she was in open water she dived. In less than a second, it seemed, she had cut through the turbulence at the surface of the sea, where the wind and water were in conflict, and she was in calm water: still, heavy water, which was presumably pitch dark, although Simon's eyes were now tightly closed, and he couldn't make any such judgment.

Simon was still holding his breath, but he was conscious that he couldn't hold it for much longer. Had he filled up his lungs with greater care, he knew, and exerted all his will-power, he ought to have been able to hold his breath for at least a minute, perhaps two, but he knew that he hadn't taken in sufficient oxygen for that, and that all the will-power he possessed wouldn't be adequate to sustain his life even for thirty seconds.

I'm drowning, he thought—but not, oddly enough, in panic. It was merely a fact that he was registering, ready for storage in his memory, even though there did not seem to be any possibility that it would ever be recovered therefrom.

But the morgen—the morgen Melusine—was still diving, plunging into the depths of the bay, which were becoming increasingly massive, increasingly oppressive.

Boldness be my friend, he thought. *Screw your courage to the sticking-place.*

Except, he realized, that he would never have formulated his own thoughts in that manner, unaided—and the references, once again, were mixed, from *Cymbeline* and *Macbeth*. It could only be Lenore. A bird no longer—any more than Melusine was still human—she was still alive, still active, still capable of rooting around in his memories of all the texts he had once had to strive with all his might to drill into the minds to ingrate adolescents, and reiterating phrases therefrom.

Melusine's thoughts were untranslatable, in spite of the fact that she had her arms wrapped tightly round his body, clutching him to her bosom. He could feel the warmth of her breasts, and sense the ardent beating of her heart, but her dreams were inaccessible.

He did as he was told, and screwed his courage to the sticking-place, but he knew that it couldn't last. The morgen was still diving, still plunging, unimaginably deep.

And that, he realized, was the point. They were still under water, but it was no longer the water of Cardigan Bay. Once again, he was in the Underworld. But he didn't open his eyes, knowing that this time there would be no blue.

But I still can't breathe, he thought—not in Lenorian Shakespeare-talk, this time, but on his own account. He could not resist adding, however: *When we have shuffled off this mortal coil . . .*

He had a pang of regret that he hadn't been able to begin the quote earlier, and that he wasn't able continue at least as far as the whips and scorns of time, but he could already feel the bubbles leaking from his lips, and knew that he would never have got even that far, let alone the undiscovered country from whose bourn . . .

Then the neider seized him, and he realized that the morgen had not been trying to drown him at all, but merely to deliver him, and he scolded himself for ever having been able to think otherwise, even for a moment. Melusine, drown him? How absurd! He was one of the family now.

The neider coiled around him, starting with his legs but slithering with astonishing rapidity over his loins and hips, his abdomen and his torso, before swallowing his head, Lenore and all. In a trice, he was wrapped up like a mummy—or a worm in a silken cocoon.

His lungs did not fill up with air—indeed, they seemed paralyzed, though not collapsed—but his blood filled up with oxyhemoglobin, and he sensed that there was no blue left in his veins. He was all red now, red through and through . . . and not merely red but read, in feeling if not in thought.

The neider—the vast, integral neider—had no language of its own, but Simon knew full well that it could have borrowed his, plucking elements from his own consciousness and memory, as Lenore and the Black Monk had. It could have given him the illusion of a conversation, had it made the effort. Unlike Lenore and the Black Monk, however—or, for that matter, himself—the neider of the Underworld was not at a loose end, exiled far from home, lost in a mental twilight of ennui, going through the motions of some arbitrary obsession in order to maintain an illusion of life, while waiting for a summons that might never come. The neider was in its element, occupied in real concerns and real endeavors. The neider had a task to fulfill, a work of art to produce.

That endeavor was, essentially, a work of translation, but Simon knew better than anyone that translation really was true artwork, and not just paint-by-numbers. The palette of matter was vast, and flexible, and required great care in its deployment, if the optimum of elegance were to be attained.

The neider was busy multitasking; it had too much to do to devote more than a tiny fraction of its attention to Simon, and even that was purely to attend to its own objectives. It had not summoned him into the Underworld in order to have a conversation, or in order to inform him—but while it was fulfilling its own mysterious purposes, in reading him, he had an opportunity to eavesdrop on its mentality, and to make what he could of any snatches of insight that he managed to pick up.

Because that was the nature of their brief congress, the neider did not actually *tell* Simon anything. It did not give him any instructions or orders, let alone impart any explanations or negotiate a pact. But it was wrapped round him, bandaging him body and soul, and although it had no verbalized trains of thought that he could detect, it had a kind of emotional intelligence such as no mere human had ever imagined, or ever could. Those perceptible emotions, Simon knew, lost an enormous amount in translation, but he was able to absorb at least a modicum of their conception of the world, and grasp at least a few threads of their meaning.

At least, he thought so.

The extensions of the neider into the overflow ecosystem that had once colonized the Sargasso Sea and various outposts of the gulf stream, Simon realized, had indeed resembled sea-serpents, especially when detached from the nucleus of the entity, but viewed from within—*felt* from within—the neider was more like a gigantic ameboid tree, or a gargantuan hydra, with detachable serpentine branches. The fragmentary neider of the overflow ecosystem had, inevitably, made far more versatile use of the three familiar phases of surface matter than the neider of the Underworld, but the neider of the Underworld was a fundamentally fluid creature. The fluid making up the portion of its form that was aetheric, however, was not water but molten metal and molten rock. The neider's native habitat was not the Earth's crust, or even its mantle, but its core, and its normal body temperature was thousands of degrees centigrade.

Colonization of the crust, let alone the surface, of the Earth was, Simon realized, not an easy project. In a sense, it was impossible, conditions there being simply too alien, but the neider was, or were, ingenious—he understood now that the word neider was both singular *and* plural. The neider had ways and means of using surrogates, of engineering organisms capable of operating within the crustal and surface environments. The neider's detachable serpentine branches were capable of complex metamorphoses, of forming independent organisms, and hybrid organisms, including self-replicating organisms. The ocean had been the most logical starting point, and the morgens the most effective artwork of that kind. The morgens were tough—extremely tough, by comparison with many of the neider's subcreative endeavors. They had even survived the catastrophe that had laid waste to the enormous work of art constituted by the vegetation of the Sargasso Sea and its most complex and delicate fruits, the Caer-Ys. The price of that survival had, however, involved the employment of their residual metamorphic capacities to take on forms mimicking land-dwelling human beings.

The treasure buried beneath St. Madoc's Abbey was not an Ark intended one day to regenerate the Sargasso Sea ecosystem, Simon realized. The continents had once been intended to supply that refuge . . . but the metamorphosed morgens, or a majority of them, had gone native. In becoming human, many of them had become fully human, and little or nothing more. Some had become Murdens, and doubtless others had become strange, maladroit families with other surnames.

But that was not a matter of overwhelming importance to the neider. The reconstitution of an oceanic ecosystem similar to that once generated in the Sargasso Sea was a project, to be sure, and a challenge, but it was only one project among many, and not the one the neider felt to be the most important. It was coming along, slowly, but it was being managed, to the extent that it was being managed at all, patiently and without any great urgency, effectively sidelined for the time being . . . a *time being* measured in millennia.

The focus of the neider's principal attention, at least for the moment, was not the renewal of its attempt to colonize the ocean and, ultimately, the land, but its attempt to reach the stars. The neider was far less interested in establishing elaborate communication with human beings, or even with those of its own offspring that had adopted human form and human intellect, than it was in establishing and extending communication with the life-forms of the sun, whose physical forms made far more use than any kind of planetary life of the fourth state of matter: plasma.

Because Simon had felt compelled to integrate plasma into the hypothetical elementary schema he had designed in *The Seventh Element*, even though it had no role to play in his plot, simply because it was known to exist, it had become the fifth element, while the two he had added had been his version of the aether—the new hypothetical state of matter—and the new agent of transition analogous to heat: the agent employed by the neider and its detached fragments in their metamorphoses, in a fashion vaguely analogous to the ways in which humans had harnessed fire in countless technological devices.

In making that move in his novel, Simon had been deliberately parsimonious, employing an esthetic variant of Occam's razor. Seven elements were sufficient for his fictitious purposes, so he had settled for seven. More would have been superfluous.

Had the neider been a novelist, however, it would not have been so economical. It was already familiar with "elements" analogous to his seven, and more. Human physicists knew about the existence of plasma because of their theoretical calculations and deduction. It had been a discovery of ingenuity and intelligence: a triumphant advertisement for the power and elegance of human intellect and method. The neider knew about plasma because it *felt* it. It felt it in the sun around which its own native planet orbited, and it felt it in all the other suns in the galaxy. It felt it because it was not only sensitive to a single additional agent of transition, analogous to the one that Simon had built into his hypothetical schema to supplement fire—or electromagnetic energy, in more modern parlance—but to at least two.

That process of imagination, not unsurprisingly, defied any kind of translation that Simon could apply. Any analogies he drew could only be extremely distant—but he remembered one that had been stimulated by Lenore. When she had warned him that the storm was coming, she had also referred, with a little help from Oberon, to certain stars shooting madly from their spheres, to which he had added, by way of momentum "to hear the sea-maid's music."

He had "seen" such shooting stars as his retinas had recovered from the effects of the lightning flash, and that had been an ironic gesture of fate, the symbolism of chance. The starlets that the stars "shot" in response to the siren song of the neider were not visible to ordinary human sight any more than radio messages and television signals riding their electromagnetic carrier waves. Nevertheless, they were real, and they constituted a storm of their own, which fused and collaborated with electric storms at the surface of the earth in order to carry their communication into the Underworld.

Melusine, Simon assumed, had heard the song that she had long had in her head, summoning her back to the sea— but egotistical human beings had it wrong, as usual. The primary purpose of the morgens' music was not to beguile human beings, in order that they might be drowned. That was a mere unintended side effect, and rare. The "ears" for which their siren song was intended were a great deal further away than that, intended to attract the attention of stars . . . or certain star-like entities, at least. Clearly, other agents of transition between unusual forms of matter were not bound by the velocity of light, which limited the reach of "fire."

It was in the context of that project that the structure that the Murdens had called the vitreous cocoons had been constructed, and which the Murdens had been invited to guard and protect from human investigation and interference. Was it some kind of living interstellar transmitter, or a cosmic beacon equipped with strange mentality? Simon could not obtain a feeling precise enough to make that discrimination. What he could feel, however, while the neider worked patiently upon his painless vivisection, was that what was happening to him at the moment, the role that he had been called upon to play in the drama being enacted by the spirits of the vasty deep, was a very tiny one.

What the neider was doing was an odd job, a trivial repair, something way down on its list of priorities. For himself, obviously—for all the Murdens—it was a matter of life and death, but for the neider it was more akin to sewing a button on a shirt, or putting a drop of oil on a squeaky hinge. In order to do it, the neider had worked what seemed to Simon to be miracles, but from the neider's point of view, they were comparable to threading a needle or unscrewing the cap from the nozzle of an oil-can, and almost absent-minded.

The operation was, however, painless. Brutal at first, not to mention cold and wet, it was now proceeding quite comfortably. Whatever was being done to Simon's vulgar flesh was being done with the aid of an anesthetic. The more important aspect of the operation, however, concerned the aetheric aspect of his being—what Simon could not help regarding as his neider fraction, although it was not really a fraction, detachable from him in the same sense that fragments of the neider's vast serpentine extensions were detachable. He was all neider as well as all human, just as Lenore had been all neider as well as all bird, and Melusine all morgen as well as all woman. It was difficult to imagine what was being done to that aspect of his being, because that aspect of his being was difficult to imagine in itself, and he was not perceiving much in the way of relevant backwash from the neider's own feelings. Nor was he certain that he could apply his own logic to the situation.

Even so, he tried.

Obviously, when the operation was over, he would be returned to the surface. There would be no point in what was happening otherwise. He would surely be returned with the same outward appearance that he had had when he was snatched away, in order that he could step back into his life seamlessly. He would not be evidently metamorphosed or spectacularly rejuvenated . . . but that did not necessarily mean that he would not be equipped to live much longer than the human norm—at least as long as James Murden, if not as long as Ceridwen. That would be necessary, if he were to play a significant role in maintaining the pact made between the Underworld and St. Madoc: the obligation to maintain the treasure and keep it secret from potentially troublesome investigation. Evidently, James and his associates were no longer adequate to that task. The family needed new blood, both literally and figuratively. He was being adapted to that task, emotionally and intellectually as well as physically.

But he had been told, by more than one informant, that he would still have choices. He was not being turned into an automaton, or even a slave. He would still be able to do as he wished . . . except that what he wished might itself be redesigned.

But why not? Was that not what he needed more than anything else, and what he had needed for a long time—perhaps all his life? Had he not weighed up his life within the last few days, with the aid of Felicia's oneiric magic, and found it utterly wanting? Had he not determined, with fatal accuracy, that he had always wanted the wrong things, and had never been able to achieve anything truly worthwhile? Had he not decided that his life had hardly been worth living? What had he to lose, then? And if he gained anything, no matter what it turned out to be, would it not be an improvement?

Even if he never managed to figure out exactly what the "vitreous cocoons" where actually *for*, even if their nature and function remained permanently beyond his imaginative scope, would he not be better off as one of their guardians than as a recluse pecking out texts that hardly anybody read on a plastic keyboard and a glowing screen, just to give himself something to do? Even if he were simply to be James's apprentice, another servant to add to his staff, to support him in his scholarship and his vanity, would that not be a desirable destiny, especially if his mind had been deliberately adjusted to make it desirable?

At least he would no longer be alone.

He knew that if he attempted to speak to the neider, the neider would not hear him—or, if it did, that it would not pay the slightest heed to him. The neider could not possibly care what he thought. There was no need to signal his acquiescence, and no point in trying.

Nevertheless, he thought it worth telling himself that he was all right with what was happening, that he approved, that he was even grateful. He was grateful to Eve, to Angela, to the Faceless Monk, to Lenore, to Cerys, to Ceridwen, to Felicia, to James and to Melusine, for the parts that each had played in the drama, in bringing him, link by link, to the terminus of the chain of his destiny. They had begun to make of him what he had never been able to make of himself, and now, at last—hopefully not too belatedly—he was becoming real, instead of merely the stuff of which dreams were made. He was becoming a qualified agent of the Underworld, a functional neider rather than a dormant one, ignorant of his own true self.

It had required a storm to disrupt his sterile existence, but he would come safely through that storm, which was blowing itself out high above his head. He would come through it triumphantly, tempered and seasoned and ready for whatever was required of him . . . even if it were merely the trivial equivalent of sewing a button on a shirt or intruding a drop of oil into a rusty hinge. Even the smallest role made a measurable dramatic contribution to the great play that was the universe, and the neider was, when all was said and done, reaching for the stars.

Or was it?

All of that, Simon realized, was his translation of the dream that he was sharing, very peripherally, with the neider, and he was putting into verbalized thoughts something that had no words of its own, or even visual images. How much error was there in the interpretation? More importantly, how much was he importing into the interpretation, in order to help it make sense to him? It was not—how could it be?—*pure* fantasy; he really was sleeping with the neider, obtaining information from the neider's mind while the neider was obtaining information from his—but in translating what he was able to experience in the neider's mind, in making it comprehensible in human terms, some pollution was inevitable.

Did that work the other way as well? he wondered. In all probability, yes. The neider had the same problem of translating, not merely from an alien language, but an alien mode of experience. There, too, there had to be scope for mistakes and for the superimposition of its own way of seeing. But to the neider, that was probably a minor issue, a matter of small concern.

Perhaps it was not of very great concern to him, either, if his interpretation of the neider's nature and motives were mistaken to some degree. Perhaps it was more important for him to have a story that had some kind of esthetic shape, and made some kind of sense, rather than for the story to be correct in every detail.

But he understood, now, not only why the story that Ceridwen had derived from sleeping with the neider was different from his but why she had been so uncertain herself about the import of her own deductions . . .

And it was at that point in his reflections that the neider presumably released him—but of what happened after that, Simon retained no memory, merely a vague notion that a considerable interval of time passed while he was still in the underworld, with no intuition of when, how, or whether he would be returned to his own element.

The last thing he could remember thinking, however, was a reiteration of the conviction that the whole exercise would have been utterly pointless if he were not returned safely to the shore of his own world, at least as safe and sound as he had been before, if not safer and sounder.

XXI
The Denouement

Simon remembered that thought when he became conscious again of being in his own world. In theory, he felt sure, the argument had been perfectly sound. In practice, it was not so simple. When he regained consciousness, in fact, he found himself in pain. It seemed that he ached all over. Furthermore, his clothing was completely sodden, and he was chilled to the bone.

He was lying on shingle, with his bare head on a pillow of damp, reeking wrack. The sky was clear and blue—Storm Deirdre had obviously blown over—but it was still the end of February. The wind was brisk and chilly.

It required a considerable effort even to sit up. When he did so, he found the shore deserted. There was not a single dog-walker visible on the coastal path—but he judged by the height of the sun that it was less than an hour after dawn, and he assumed that it was Saturday morning. It only took him a minute to get his bearings. He was some two hundred meters away from the bridge over the more northerly of the two gullies running to either side of St. Madoc. He turned his head to the right, to look at the Tine and the Abbey.

Everything seemed normal, for a split second, as his gaze ran over the façade of the house. Then he saw the fire appliance and the ambulance parked on the driveway, and realized that there were people all over the headland, moving purposefully, as if they were searching for something.

For me? he wondered. *Are they searching for me?*

He was tempted to wave his arms, to signal his distant presence. As he hauled himself to his feet, in fact, that was the intention he had in mind.

But why was the fire engine there? he thought, scanning the Abbey more carefully, unable to see any evidence of a fire. Something was missing, however: the lightning conductor was no longer pointing at the sky, but was hanging down over the roof, twisted into a serpentine shape. He remembered, then, that lightning struck twice in these parts—and not only twice, it seemed, but three times. In fact, he remembered being blinded by the flash and deafened by the crash of thunder, before time had slipped completely out of joint. The conductor must have done its job, however, because there was no sign of damage to the roof of the house, and no evidence of any conflagration.

Slowly, Simon climbed up to the coastal path. Painstakingly, he began walking along it.

Eventually, he reached the bridge over the gully, and paused, leaning on the parapet. There was no one at the nearer end of the bridge to the Central Tine. In the distance, he could recognize some of the people walking along the edge of the cliff. He saw Alun Gwynne, Megan Harwyn, and Dai from the Mermaid, but most of the people milling around were strangers to him.

He knew that they could not be searching for him. No one would have had any reason to suppose that he had been on the Tine. He knew—he felt, at least—that they were searching for Melusine. And he knew—he felt, very strongly—that they would not find her. He felt that there was something to do with Melusine that he had forgotten. He assumed, however, that she was the one who had brought him back from the Underworld and deposited him on the shore.

I need to get cleaned up, he thought, *and put on some dry clothes. Then I'll go to the Abbey.*

He turned left and headed for Raven Cottage. The door was unlocked. He staggered inside, hauled himself upstairs, took off his brine-soaked clothes—all ruined—and switched on the shower. As soon as it was running hot, he stepped inside and sat down, letting the hot water cascade over him. After four or five minutes, he no longer felt chilled to the bone, but he still ached all over.

He had only just managed to stand and step out of the shower when the doorbell rang. He put on a dressing gown and staggered downstairs.

It was Cerys.

"Thank God you're all right," she said. "When you didn't come to join the search, I thought something might have happened to you too . . ." She paused. "But it has, hasn't it? You look as if you've been smashed in the face—beaten up, in fact. What the hell happened?"

Simon stepped away from the door to let her in, and went to collapse in the armchair in the study. She followed him.

"Well?" she said.

"I went out in the storm. Stupid. I fell in the sea. Fortunately, I didn't drown. Nothing broken—just bruises."

She shook her head. She had no bruises, but she looked distraught nevertheless. "Melusine's missing," she said. "They're searching, but they aren't going to find anything else. They found her clothes on the steps of Morgan's Cave. She must have gone into the water there, some time last evening. There's no way of knowing what happened, but she must be dead. So is James."

"What!"

"He died in the house yesterday evening. The Abbey was struck by lightning—not the first time. The other times, we all escaped without a scratch, thanks to the lightning conductor. Not this time. There seems to have been some kind of power surge—a side effect. I was safely isolated, and so was Felicia, but James was at the telephone, making a call—to you, in fact, although he got no answer. I don't think it can have been a very powerful shock, although it fried the phone, but he collapsed. His heart had stopped. I tried CPR, but I couldn't start it again. He was dead long before the ambulance arrived. Thinking back, Melusine must have disappeared even before the lightning bolt hit, so I don't think that was what caused her to go outside, but I didn't even notice that she wasn't there until I'd given up trying to revive James. Felicia hadn't noticed either, but she was panicking, on the verge of hysteria. The paramedics had to give her a sedative. She's in bed now—asleep, I hope. I'm sorry I didn't think about you sooner, but . . . how on earth did you fall into the sea?"

"Just carelessness, as I said." He thought it diplomatic not to say anything about the timing of the accident.

"But you managed to climb out again? Was it the rocks that did that to your face?"

"I must have managed to scramble out. I was very dazed. I lost consciousness for a while, but when I woke up, I managed to haul myself back here. There was no one about—everyone was on the Tine, I expect, joining the search."

"I'm not surprised you were dazed. You must have been frozen. You're lucky you weren't carried away by the tide."

"I suppose so—all the more so as I can't swim. Never mind me, though—you must be in shock yourself. First Ceridwen, now James and Melusine. That's terrible."

"I've been running around in panic too much for it to have sunk in. I'll have to pull myself together, though. There's no James to take care of the formalities this time, and they're bound to be a lot more complicated. Felicia isn't going to be much help, I fear. It's all on me."

"I'll help if I can," said Simon.

"You look as if you ought to be in hospital yourself. But thanks—there's probably not that much I can do over the weekend, but come Monday . . . I might need you then, if you can actually stand up. Dai will help too, and I might even have to call on Miss Harwyn. God, this is such a mess. I'd better get back—the leader of the fire crew organized the search, but I need to be there. I'm sorry."

"That's okay—go. I'll be fine."

She went. Half an hour went by without Simon summoning up the energy to get up from the chair. At the end of that time, Megan Harwyn swept into the room without having bothered to ring the doorbell. She stopped dead at the sight of him.

"Damn," she said. "Cerys said that you'd taken a battering. She wasn't kidding, was she? You've really been lying unconscious on the rocks? For how long?"

"I don't know," said Simon, trying to sit up straight.

"I told you not to go out in the storm, didn't I? Falling into the sea in dirty weather is almost a qualification for a Darwin Award. As if two people dead isn't enough . . . unless Melusine's lying on the shore somewhere too, washed up by the tide. But she's a hundred years old . . . this is all completely crazy."

"Completely," Simon agreed.

"Don't move—I'll make you a strong cup of coffee. Have you got any brandy?"

"Yes, in the cupboard above the microwave. You don't have to . . . you have just lost your father, after all."

"We weren't that close," she retorted, dryly. She came back five minutes later, and handed him a mug of black coffee, sugared as well as enriched with brandy. "Not that I'm about to say good riddance, you understand," she added, as if there had been no substantial gap since her previous remark.

"I do," Simon told her.

"And not because I didn't get my acknowledgement either. He was a bastard, but I didn't wish him dead. I can't imagine what poor Felicia must be going through. The old lady, her brother and her cousin, within thirty-six hours. I just hope the trauma doesn't kill her as well."

"I hope so," said Simon, pensively. The doctored coffee seemed to be having an energizing effect.

"Open that dressing gown," Megan Harwyn ordered him. "I want to have a look at your injuries." Simon made no move to comply. "Oh, don't be stupid," she said. "I've seen naked men before." She took hold of the lapels of the gown and pulled them apart. Then she lifted the hem in order to examine his legs.

"You're practically black and blue from top to toe," she said. "If nothing's broken, it'll be a miracle."

"Nothing's broken," Simon assured her. "Not so much as a rib. I'll take a couple of paracetamol to dull the aches, and I'll be fine. As you say, I've been very stupid, but I seem to have got away with it. I need to get dressed and go over to the Abbey. Cerys might need me, at least to keep Felicia company."

"You'd be a lot better off going to bed yourself. There's an ambulance still at the house, waiting on the end of the search. I'll go back and ask the paramedics to come and check you over. They can drive you to town for a proper check. You need X-rays, at the very least."

"Nonsense," said Simon. "Thanks for your concern, but I really am fine."

He got to his feet in order to prove his point, and went into the kitchen to find the paracetamol. Having swallowed two, he then set about persuading Megan to go home. Eventually, he succeeded. Then he got dressed, and headed for the Abbey.

The crowd was slowly dispersing. Dai met his gaze and shook his head significantly. He knew, as they all did, that Melusine was gone for good.

"I have to go to the morgue," Cerys told him, "to sort out . . . well, James's death certificate, I suppose, and God only knows what else . . . God and the family solicitor that is. I've left an urgent message in his voicemail, and sent him an SOS text—even though it's Saturday, I'm sure he'll see me and get things moving right away. Edith's with Felicia now, but if you wouldn't mind relieving her, that will help. She won't mind finding you there if she wakes up—she seems to think of you as one of the family."

"I'll be glad to," Simon assured her.

He did as he was asked, and replaced the cook by Felicia's bedside. She was asleep, under the influence of the sedative she had been given, but she seemed restless, stirring in her sleep. Her left arm was outside the bedclothes, moving. Simon sat down, and took the hand in his, holding it gently but firmly. Felicia didn't wake up, but the contact seemed to soothe her, and he maintained it.

Simon tried to stay awake, but he soon became drowsy, and fell asleep himself. He didn't wake up until Felicia pulled her hand away, when he opened his eyes with a start and found her blue eyes peering at him anxiously. She reached out to the bedside table to recover her spectacles, and put them on, presumably bringing him into clearer focus.

"Damn," he said. "I'm sorry. I was supposed to be watching over you."

"That's all right," she said. "I feel a lot better now. When James collapsed, I panicked—I thought I was going to die too, but I'm calm now, and I feel a lot stronger than before. Do you know what's happening?"

"No—what time is it?" He glanced at the window, but the curtains were drawn. It still seemed to be light outside, though. He looked at his watch. It was half past three. "Damn, he said, again. "I'm truly sorry."

"There's no need. What happened to you?" asked Felicia, staring at his face.

"I got hit in the face by the gate when I turned round as the lightning struck while I was going home, and then I got swept off the bridge by a big wave. Stupid. I'm all right, though. Just bruises. It looks far worse than it is."

"Well," she said, faintly. "That's one small mercy, at least. They haven't found Melusine, though . . . Cerys would have come to tell us if they had."

"Cerys went to town . . . but no, they can't have found Melusine, and they won't. She's gone. So has Lenore. I'm sorry."

"Lenore?"

"I'm afraid so—I'm truly sorry."

Felicia merely nodded, perhaps still feeling the after-effects of the sedative. "I don't understand," she said. "About James, yes . . . but Melusine? How could she do that?"

"I don't know," Simon answered, not entirely insincerely.

The door opened then, and Cerys came in. She stood there for a moment or two, staring at them both, her expression quite unreadable. It was almost as if she thought that they were both strangers, or even alien beings.

And she might not be wrong, at least in my case, Simon thought.

"Good, you're still here," Cerys said eventually, addressing Simon. "I need to talk to you, urgently. Do you mind if I do it here, Felicia?—this concerns you as well. Do you feel up to it?"

"It must be serious," said Felicia, evidently judging by the grave expression on the young woman's face. "I'm fine, now. Simon's been looking after me. Go ahead."

"It's extremely serious," said Cerys. "I've seen the solici-tor. It appears that James made several alterations to his will, yesterday. I think I know now why he called that meeting of the household last night, and why he was trying to phone Simon when the lightning struck." She sat down on the edge of the bed.

"Go on," said Simon, already having a suspicion of what she was about to say.

"He'd presented the solicitor with all the evidence that Megan Harwyn had so kindly dug up regarding the prob-ability of your parentage, Simon. The solicitor had advised him that it was all speculation, at least until the results of the DNA test came in, but James rode roughshod over his objections. He's appointed you as his heir, with the condi-tion that you live in the Abbey. Obviously, he didn't expect to die the same day, so he would have had time to alter it again if the DNA test had come in negative, but it seems that Grandmother was absolutely certain that it wouldn't, and she'd given James very strict instructions."

"And that's what they were arguing about?" Simon

guessed. "It had nothing to do with Megan Harwyn?"

"Actually, it did," Cerys said. "The amended will also contain a formal acknowledgement of the fact that Megan is James's daughter, and grants her a right of residency in the Abbey similar to the one that Grandmother had. The same right is granted to you, Felicia, and to me."

"Are you saying that Simon now owns the Abbey?" Felicia said, incredulously.

"If the will is proved, yes. There might well be challenges, though—you know what the relatives are like. The matter could be tied up in the courts for years, and the fight could get ugly, even if that DNA test does indicate a familial match."

"I wouldn't have thought that the relatives would be falling over themselves to get their hands on the Abbey," said Felicia. "It's not exactly worth a fortune, and what remains of the estate on the mainland is caught up in a terrible tangle."

"Oh, they'll be queuing up to contest the will once they hear the rest of it," Cerys assured her. "I wouldn't count any chickens just yet, Mr. Cannick—but the solicitor says that if a DNA test really does demonstrate that Angela Richardson is your mother, and that she's a direct descendant of Rhys Murden, it's unlikely that anyone will be able to prove a closer relationship to James."

"What do you mean by *the rest of it*?" Simon asked.

"Well, as I told you, the inheritance had always had certain conditions attached to it, as corollaries of the entail. One is that the heir is required to take out a particular kind of life insurance policy on the acquisition of the Abbey, and to maintain the payments. James inherited the estate in 1918 when his father died, so the policy has been running for ninety-nine years, during which time the fund has been invested in the stock market, with dividends automatically reinvested. Although the monthly payments seemed trivial enough, the solicitor estimates that it will pay out at least seven million pounds, perhaps more. That's not such a vast amount nowadays, I suppose—people get as much in annual salary, and now that the Bank of England has abolished interest it probably won't produce much income—but even so, if the will is proved, Mr. Cannick, you certainly won't be poor any more."

"If," repeated Simon, although there was not the slightest doubt in his own mind that the will would hold up. It was, after all, the will of destiny.

"If I were you, Mr. Cannick," Cerys said, with a slight sigh, "I'd move in straight away. Possession might not be nine points of the law, but it's always useful in these cases. You might also invite Miss Harwyn to take immediate advantage of her right of residency. If what I've heard about her computer skills is true, we might find those a useful asset too."

"We?" Simon queried. "Does that mean you intend to take advantage of your right of residency—and that you'll side with me if it does come to a legal battle?"

"I'm certainly not going anywhere in a hurry," she said. "In the longer term—well, that depends on all sorts of unforeseeable contingencies. But while I'm here, yes, I'll side with you. It's what Grandmother wanted—and nobody likes the distant relatives. You'll be with us too, won't you, Aunt?"

Felicia still seemed to be mulling something over, but she echoed: "It's what Grandmother wanted."

"I'd better go and bring Edith and the others up to date," Cerys said. "Can I leave it to you to inform Miss Harwyn of the situation, Mr. Cannick?"

"Of course," said Simon. "And please stop calling me Mr. Cannick."

Cerys nodded, and left the room.

Simon looked at Felicia. "Well," he said, "that's a bit of a bombshell."

Her eyes narrowed slightly, as she looked at him speculatively, still following her own train of thought. "No, it isn't," she said. "You expected it, didn't you? You knew."

"*Knew* would be putting it too strongly," Simon said, "but I had a suspicion."

"You know something I don't?"

"Again *know* is putting it too strongly, but I have a number of suspicions that you probably don't."

"Such as?"

"Melusine isn't dead. She's just . . . changed."

"Into a morgen? Yes, I would have suspected that, if I'd dared. Did she pull you out of the water?"

"Probably. She certainly pulled me in."

"Ah." Felicia paused before adding: "And you've slept with the neider, as Grandmother once did?"

"Yes."

"And how long did that take?"

"I've no idea. I lost track of time."

"And how long was it before Melusine dumped you back on the shore?"

Again, all Simon could say was: "I honestly have no idea."

"And you don't remember having any . . . dreams?"

"No."

Felicia shook her head, slowly. "Will we see her again, do you think?" she asked.

"I don't know. Possibly."

Felicia's lip twitched, as if she was not sure whether she ought to be pleased or annoyed by that possibility. *Confused and conflicted*, Simon thought: *the human condition, alive or dead.*

"Does this mean you'll live to be two hundred, like Grandmother?" Felicia asked, after a further pause.

"I have no idea," Simon confessed. "Possibly."

"But the neider has guaranteed that the will can stand up to any legal challenge?"

Simon laughed, briefly and humorlessly. "I don't think it has the power to do that—not directly, anyhow. But I'm confident, provided that the DNA testing proves that I am Lilith's great-grandson. The law will probably take our side. If not, we probably have a few secret weapons."

"Miss Harwyn's computer skills?"

"I was thinking of stranger allies than that—the Faceless Monk, for example."

For the first time, the centenarian seemed incredulous. "You can't be serious."

"Three days ago, I'd have said the same. Today, perhaps for the first time in my life, I think perhaps I can be serious. And if I can, I intend to be."

She looked at him speculatively, and seemed to decide that perhaps he could, and would. "Are you going to marry Megan Harwyn?" she asked, suddenly.

"Good God, no. Why on earth would I want to do that? Come to that, why would she?"

"You've just inherited seven million pounds," Felicia pointed out, "and I've had a glimpse of your inner being. I know how easily persuaded you are, in such matters."

"I think my inner being might have undergone a considerable metamorphosis," Simon told her. "And you know full well that I can't possible marry anyone."

"Why not?" she asked.

"Because I'm not that kind of writer, as you so shrewdly observed. I can't help the present story culminating with an inheritance, it seems, but a marriage as well would be far too conventional. Certainly not to Megan Harwyn, given that she's the girl next door."

Felicia managed a faint smile. "Well," she said, "I suppose Miss Harwyn wouldn't be able to supply the estate with an heir. For seven million pounds, though, you could probably get a pretty gold-digger with healthy ovaries."

"No thanks. I shall invest my hopes in Cerys, and hope that she can find a young man worthy of her, in order to supply a healthy sperm."

"Better hope that she's not like me, then," said Felicia. "We Murden women are far from fecund . . . and far from passionate, in that sense. I used to think that was a good thing, a merciful release . . . but I'm not so sure now. But you'll be kind to me, won't you? It's what Grandmother wanted, after all."

Simon picked up the hand that he had been holding, apparently for hours, while they both slept, she under the influence of a sedative and he under the influence of enormous fatigue. He couldn't remember dreaming, but he knew that that didn't mean that he hadn't dreamed. He squeezed her slender hand gently. "Absolutely," he said. "And I hope I can rely on your support in all the impending conflicts."

"Possible challenges to the will, you mean? I thought you were confident about that."

"I was thinking more of resentments among the rightful residents. Megan Harwyn might not approve of my plans for the estate."

"You have plans for the estate? Already?"

"Vaguely. I think it might be a happier place if it were to become a real village, with permanent residents, facilities and a primary school. It could be done, I think, now that computers facilitate distance working. I've always been something of a utopian, and I'll need to do something with my seven million pounds, if I eventually get it. I'm too old to take up riotous living. Whatever I do, though, I'm going to need support, from you and from Cerys—Megan too, if possible. I'll need you to take your Grandmother's place and I'll need Cerys to do the bulk of the legwork for the estate management, and Megan to supply the IT wizardry. I'll make it worth their while financially, obviously."

"You're going to let them both in on the family secret?"

"Obviously. James was planning to do as much for Cerys yesterday, before his attention was deflected."

"And Megan too?"

"Certainly, if she decides to take advantage of her right of residency."

"And if she wants to continue running her . . . business from the Abbey?"

"I certainly won't interfere. Do you think I should, even if I could?"

Felicia thought about it for a moment, and then said: "Grandmother wouldn't have. I always suspected that she had a sneaking admiration for Miss Harwyn, even in the days when she used to parade around the village in summer half-naked, offering herself to the holiday crowds. To tell the truth, I sometimes felt the same way . . . except that she never really seemed to enjoy her work. Sometimes, I suspected that she only did it to needle James. If so, it certainly worked. Poor James! He really didn't seduce that Gwyneth girl, you know—it was the other way round. He was a soft target, just back from the war . . . and it really soured his love life, for ever after. I tried to help, but there was nothing I could do. And now he's gone! And Melusine too, so soon after Grandmother. And even Lenore! Things are going to be very, very different. I'm not sure I can cope."

Simon squeezed her hand again. "I'm sure you can," he said. "It's what destiny intends—and no matter how little you care about denouements, sometimes, you just have to go with the esthetic flow."

She bit her lip. "It was the neider, wasn't it?" she said. "It killed Grandmother and James, and took the others away?"

"It certainly had a hand in what happened," Simon admitted, "but I don't think it killed anyone. It doesn't kill, any more than it grants wishes . . . but sometimes, it establishes circumstances in such a way that desires can be met."

She took the inference readily enough. "You have no idea how close I came to wanting to die too," she said. "But in the end . . . if I hadn't . . . if we hadn't . . . but in the end, I didn't."

"I'd far rather no one had died," Simon told her, "but sometimes, you have to face up to the inevitable, and hope that things will work out anyway . . . or, if they don't work out, that at least they go on. They will go on, after a fashion .. . the neider wants that, and esthetic propriety demands it."

He leaned forward and kissed Felicia on the forehead.

"What you and I will have, of course," he said, "isn't a marriage."

"What we'll have? Even though you said . . . I thought you were just being kind . . . I thought, after the other night, that